PAMELA SERIES 13

Volume 3

The Melding of Time and Space

By

Patricia Lee Strunk

AB FILM PUBLISHING

New York, NY

ISBN: 978-0-9971715-5-6

Cover Design by Thomas Romano, USA

Published by AB Film Publishing
290 West 12 Street, Suite A
New York, New York 10014
(212) 741-1441
2021

Dedication

For my children, Trevor and Vinciane

And

In Loving Memory of my nephew, John D. Strunk

(1979 – 2019)

ACKNOWLEDGEMENTS

My heartfelt gratitude goes to all my friends and family members who have, in their own ways at various moments in my life, encouraged me to pursue my dream of writing and publishing science fiction.

I feel strongly indebted and thankful to my children, Trevor and Vinciane, my ultimate source of happiness, for their inspiration, encouragement, and critical review.

I want to extend my most profound appreciation to Cornelius for his meticulous reading of "The Melding of Time and Space," providing me with necessary corrections and precious suggestions that turned the draft version of Volume 3 into a publishable work, and to Christine, for her insightful comments and in-depth reflections on the nature and substance of Volume 3.

My heartfelt thanks go to Frank Romano whose meticulous reading and editing of my volume 3 turned my manuscript into a publishable work.

A very special thanks to Céline for adding her comment on the back cover and to all my friends, like Christine, Gwenaëlle, Marie-Christine and Gwenaëlle who have been active in the promotion of Pamela Series 13.

I would like to commend Thom for his brilliant and magnificent actualization of a cover design that was conceived and drafted by my daughter.

And, finally, I want to extend my most sincere and humble thanks to my publisher, Alan Baxter, of AB Film Productions, for the confidence he has placed in me by giving me this extraordinary opportunity to present Pamela Series 13, Volume 3, "The Melding of Time and Space," to the public.

AUTHOR'S NOTE

The arrival of Volume 3, The Merging of Time and Space, is perhaps the right moment for me to remind my Readers of my vision of a future world.

Pamela Series 13 introduces the Reader to a post-holocaust planet Earth, home to former and hybridized life forms in both the plant and animal kingdoms. The Reader is confronted, as the Series progresses, with a world populated with life forms of varying physical appearances, capacities, and capabilities in the form of programmed humans, intelligent androids with human appearances, possessing diminished and fragmented emotional intelligence, primitive robots, hybridized humans, genetically modified humans and, eventually, the ultimate, or Trans-humans, possessing the potential for augmented physical and intellectual capabilities.

Even though the characters portrayed and the future advances in science and technology remain fictitious, products of my own over-active imagination, the story raises many ethical questions like: At what point can the beneficial effects of technology on humankind suddenly topple, endangering the Planet Earth and its inhabitants?

Should limits be set on genetic research, genetic engineering, and eugenics? Does genetically engineering different species, like reptilian-humans, defy the laws of nature or is it a novel way to create more physically powerful humans, necessary for the survival of the human race? Will the existence of naturally hybridized creatures like WD (walrus-dolphin), be the norm, rather than the exception, in the future?

Maintaining harmonious interaction of humans living and working together in this New World Society raises plaguing questions like: What is human nature? Are humans visual creatures incapable of interacting with someone who does not meet their criteria of perfection? Are delusive methods the only solution? Can humans only live in harmony together if they are programmed to see the world in 'rosy colors', or more precisely, a world in concordance with their personal perception of beauty, intelligence and physical perfection? How does human emotional intelligence weigh in on relationships with others in all aspects of human lives, including sexual attraction? Must the emotional intelligence of humans be suppressed in order to create an unnatural, yet harmonious environment?

The organization of human society begins to play an important role in volume 2. Are the new generation humans in Pamela Series 13 different from past generations of humans? Do humans need leadership? If so, is the struggle for power a natural consequence of the human condition? Are humans easily manipulated? Are they more hypocritical than sincere in their objectives and feelings? Is it natural for humans to plot and scheme, or is it a learned behavior, rather than a primitive desire to vaunt physical and intellectual force? How far will a human, or a group of humans, go in a struggle for power?

The treatment of other life forms, animals and plants, is of paramount importance, and emphasis is placed on respect for the environment and ecological balancing. Propagandizing humans to respect different species by using films portraying beautiful plants and animals in their natural environments centuries before the holocaust is one of the technics recommended by the Group of 5. The eventual contrast between what was, what could have been and what exists is also meant to sensitize the Reader and inspire ecological practices.

Is the symbiotic relationship between Dr. Reinhart and her biological Daughter, Pamela, within the realm of possibilities? In the context of Pamela Series 13, the answer is yes. Dr. Reinhart, whose origins will be revealed in the final volume, is the ultimate of a trans-human. She is comfortable with her symbiotic relationship with her biological daughter, Pamela. The fact that Pamela was a Concert Pianist and not a Scientist provides Reinhart with a natural comfort zone in which her personality can develop to its fullest and her own mind can expand outward, recuperating her fathomless knowledge, restoring her intellectual capacities and recuperating, while reinforcing, her Trans-human physical force. From time to time, she is obliged to undergo phases of metamorphoses, leaving Pamela alone to fend for herself, as she reconnects with her former incorporeal or ethereal self in order to more efficiently and rapidly augment her physical and intellectual capacities.

Admittedly, Reinhart is cautious about the information she shares with her colleagues and downloads into Pamela's mind. Fearless, lucid and self-confident, she laughs at danger, loves a challenge, and is respected as the self-proclaimed leader by all categories of humans and androids, including the burgeoning group of Trans-humans. Because she has programmed the most sophisticated class of Androids, or the Group of 5, the android opposites of her former human scientific team, to act in her behalf, she turns to them in moments of incertitude.

Amassing all the information necessary to give a degree of coherency and charm to the Story of Pamela Series 13 has preoccupied me. Throwing out scientific or technological projects, without elaborating a bit on the reason or importance of these projects, inviting the reader into new, unknown territory without describing the visual aspects and signaling the dangers that might be lurking, inviting the Reader to participate, as a spectator, in the decision-making and military tactics without at least insinuating some of the risks, and so forth, does not correspond to my notion or definition of Science Fiction. The Reader should be able to comment on the choices the characters make and even imagine a better strategy, in some cases. Science Fiction should stimulate the Reader's imagination and ultimately raise primordial questions: What kind of World do we want to leave to other generations? Even though advances in technology might bring beneficial effects, could these advances reposition the role of humans in the future? And finally, should the human race, as we know it, survive or be replaced...and if so...by... What?

In conclusion, as a very dear friend reminded me recently, the pace of a science fiction novel is, by its nature, always very different from the laconic spare descriptions found in a detective novel or spy thriller. And, in keeping with the imaginative future worlds portrayed by acclaimed and brilliant science fiction authors, like Jules Verne, whom I wish I could emulate, there can be no defined limit to the amount of scientific information, descriptions, and characters taken on board in a science fiction novel and series. And yet, this does not mean that the Author should not take a step back from time to time, as I have done, to remind the Reader of the major themes that appear and reappear in a science fiction series, and, of course, add a character list when the number of players has expanded considerably.

To the future...whatever it has in store for us!

Patricia
December 2020

CHARACTER LIST

Dr. Elisabeth Reinhart: A beautiful, sensual, commanding Woman, admired and respected by everyone... human, hybridized, Android. The ultimate Trans-human, in every aspect...intellectually, physically and emotionally, presently in a symbiotic relationship with her biological child, Pamela 13. As to why Dr. Reinhart opted for a symbiotic relationship in the beginning will be revealed in Volume 3. And her origins will eventually unravel, to the Reader's surprise and satisfaction.

MAJOR CHARACTERS:

1. **Pamela Series 13** is a Concert Pianist, the biological daughter of Dr. Elisabeth Reinhart, who is gradually transferring her scientific and technological knowledge to Pamela, reinforcing her physical and emotional structures with the intention of making her Trans-human, in all aspects of the term. Pamela has two children, Frederic, fathered by Peter, and Rhea, fathered by Randolph.

2. **Dr. A. Murdoc** is Reinhart's most trusted friend, her confidant and ally, and also her closest intellectual equal, in all fields of science, technology, and other natural processes, including the humanities. This physically and emotionally strong, adept, and persuasive figure is presumed dead.

3. **Dr. Stuart Rever**, a very tall, well-built and handsome Aeronautical Engineer and Expert in Martial Arts, with a mysterious, aloof and seductive nature. The biological son of Dr. Reinhart. Stuart and Diana have a son, Aaron.

4. **Dr. Randolph Murdoc**, a Nuclear Physicist, adept in most scientific and technological fields, the biological son of the infamous Dr. Murdoc and Pamela's closet friend, ally and lover. They have a daughter, Rhea.

5. **Dr. John Gunther**, an expert in Telecommunications and a Computer Engineer, was the leader of the outside Community and the organizer and leader of the Revolution. In Reinhart's absence, he is in charge of all activities in the Main Center,

supervising the various exploration teams and the personnel at the Marine and Air and Space Centers. Reinhart rejuvenated him at the end of Volume 2. He is the father of Samuel and Rebecca.

6. **Dr. Sarah Brown** and **Dr. Ruth Fielding**, Geneticists living in a polygamous relationship with Dr. Gunther since their escape to the outside cavern, almost 10 years earlier. Dr. Gunther is the father of Ruth's daughter, Rebecca, and Sarah's son, Samuel.

7. **Dr. Mathieu Le Clerc** is a Mining and Civil Engineer, also interested in Space travel.

8. **Dr. Isabel Radcliff**, an Engineer specialized in Military Defense systems and Weaponry, shares Dr. Le Clerc's interest in Space Travel. She and Mathieu have a son, Gaetan.

9. **Dr. Mathilda Vernon**, a beautiful and seductive woman. She is a Psychiatrist, who played an important role in helping her friends adjust to living outside the Main Center. She is the Mother of Randolph's first born child, a daughter, Samantha.

10. **Dr. Diana Ming** is a tall, sensual and seductive woman, skilled in all fields of martial arts. She played a vital role during the Revolution, killing one the Group of 5's trans-human combat warriors. Also an Engineer, specialized in the design and construction of Air, Land and Ocean transporters. She is the Mother of Aaron.

11. **Dr. Peter Feragan** is an Engineer specialized in bio-chemistry and bio-physics, with sub-specializations in human surgical procedures and Astro-physics. He and Pamela met in the outside community where their love and intimacy gave them courage and hope for the future. The father of Frederic, the first born child of Pamela.

12. **Dr. Benjamin Davis** and **Dr. Stanislas Borsky** are Bio-chemical and Bio-technical Engineers, who have a long standing affective relationship. To reproduce without recourse to the Group of 5's former method, they solicited the assistance of two of their closest female friends. Dr. Davis has a son, Vivien, conceived with and carried to term by Sarah. Dr. Borsky has a daughter, Helen, conceived with and carried to term by Eunice.

THE GROUP OF 5: The Group of 5, the *crème de la crème* of Androids, worked in complicity to assure a future Symbiotic relationship between Pamela and Dr. Reinhart. In the Context of that objective they assumed the following roles;

Dr. Victoria Gordon played the role of psychologist, encouraging Pamela to open up and express her concerns. She used various forms of manipulation, such as films portraying humans as wretched, insensitive, cruel creatures, to gain influence over her. Dr. Gordon even entered into a romantic relationship with Pamela, hoping this would help her activate and control Pamela's burgeoning emotional configuration. She also pursued a sexual relationship with Randolph, both for fun and to make Pamela jealous.

1. **Dr. Edward Flanders**, the Android in charge of the Birthing Center, opened Pamela's eyes to how she was created. He explained that all humans were conceived by in vitro fertilization and the fecundated ovum was transferred to an artificial uterus, where the baby developed until term. He also explained how she and others were educated and the method the androids used to prevent the development of emotions. She both liked and detested Dr. Flanders at the same time.

2. **Dr. Rudolph Crawford** played the role of the villain. His personality fluctuated from hot to cold. He eventually threatened to have her and others exterminated. These constant mind games with Dr. Crawford eventually brought about the right result, or Pamela's development of a complete emotional configuration. His role as a trusted friend and advisor for Dr. Elisabeth Reinhart becomes very evident in Volume 2.

3. **Dr. Agnes Miller** played the role of the kind and helpful Librarian. When Pamela met her, Dr. Miller's beautiful face was connected to a primitive robotic exterior. She pretended to care about Pamela and to give her what she contended was classified information. Pamela eventually saw through Miller's game and realized she could not trust her. When Dr. Reinhart returned as Pamela's symbiote, she reconstructed Miller's android body, making her taller and more physically seductive than before.

4. **Dr. Eugene Venderkof** played the role of the Governor of the Main Center before the revolution. He pretended that he was acting in the interests of the humans and that he was taking risks by making concessions. He put pressure on the members of the outside community to treat Pamela as an enemy and ostracize her in the beginning, with the aim of forcing her personality to develop more rapidly. He ceded his position to John Gunther on Reinhart's Return.

The Group of 5 now works in complicity and harmony with all those showing allegiance to Dr. Reinhart.

OTHER INFLUENTIAL MEMBERS OF THE HUMAN SOCIETY:

1. **Jonathan Craig**, former flat mate of Pamela during their programmed years, when Pamela was a Concert Pianist. A versatile musician who plays many different wind and string instruments. After the Revolution he was appointed as the Conductor of a small group of musicians. He and **Imogene,** a human of no real distinction, entered into a relationship together and have a daughter, Iphigenia.

2. **Ferdinand Hakim** is an Historian and Philosopher. Since the Revolution, he presides over regular meetings held by the humans. All humans respect him for his knowledge, diplomatic skills, poignant truthfulness and advice. He was rejuvenated by Dr. Reinhart in volume 2.

3. **Ralph**, an Agronomist, whom Ferdinand saved from an end of life termination by the Group of 5, is head of the Agricultural Unit at the Main Center. He was rejuvenated by Dr. Reinhart.

4. **Tirence,** a human of no distinction, responded badly to his deprogramming, which took place weeks after the Revolution. He was restrained and imprisoned. Dr. Reinhart, finding him to be physically and intellectually promising, gave him the opportunity to integrate with her elite members. He works as an assistant to Randolph. A close friend of Joseph, he is in love with Rebecca, daughter of John and Ruth.

5. **Francis** is an Agricultural Engineer who works closely with Ralph.

6. **Drager,** an experienced Android pilot, residing at the Air

and Space Center, accompanies Reinhart on explorations on Earth and in Outer Space. His fidelity to Reinhart and Murdoc during the Doomsday Explosion qualifies him as a valuable friend.

7. **James,** a deprogrammed human with Trans-human force and intelligence, has become an important member of Reinhart's exploration team.

8. **Jason** broke through his cryogenic capsule long after the Holocaust, managing to escape from the Main Center He became an explorer. He befriended Pamela when she was on the outside. Participates in explorations on the Planet Earth. Was recently rejuvenated by Dr. Reinhart in volume 2.

THE REPTILIAN HUMANS AND WD

The Reptilian Humans were an experiment in genetic mutation and modification effectuated by the Group of 5. The Reptilian Humans accompany Dr. Reinhart and her team in exploring the Deep Sea, in Volume 2.

1. **Joseph** is the largest and the most physically powerful of the 4 male Black Marine Iguanas with Human DNA. Opposed to genetic engineering, eugenics, and to the genetic modification of species, Reinhart is nonetheless fascinated with the Reptilian Humans. She has confidence in Joseph.

2. **Adam** is a Black Marine Iguana with more human DNA, making him more physically and physiologically closer to a human male than to a Reptile. He is nonetheless capable of extraordinary underwater feats. He and Eunice, a human, are very much in love with each other.

3. **Daniel, Leonard, Jill and Karen** are smaller than Joseph and Adam, but still surpass humans in strength and endurance.

4. **Clarence and Linda** are a genetic blend of a Bearded Lizard with Human DNA. They have the physical traits of the bearded lizard and have formed a couple. They have a daughter, Ophelia.

5. **WD (Walrus-Dolphin)** is a naturally hybridized creature. His ancestors, dolphins, survived the holocaust and then mated with walruses. He is the only active, non-programed

Walrus-Dolphins. His Wife and a few others are the last of these species. At the outset, he was a dangerous, clever, manipulative creature, but is now a vital member of Reinhart's exploration team and a devoted member of the human society. He has a son, Weldon.

MINOR CHARACTERS:

1. **Dr. James Fleming** and **Dr. Kevin Jarod**, Androids in charge of the Air and Space Center.

2. **Ludovic,** the last survivor of the people of many colors, genetically fabricated by Dr. Fleming and Dr. Jarod.

3. **Stella and Adam** are, physically, genetic misfits that Reinhart eventually reconstructed to look human.

4. **Andrew** is the architect of the Floral Garden and the cavern where John and the other humans lived before the revolution.

5. **Basil, Birch and Iris** are deprogrammed, renegade humans who were assigned to work in the agricultural unit and participate in explorations.

6. **Eunice and Imogene** were deprogrammed humans. Through their affective relationships they managed to integrate the upper echelon of the Human society

THE CREW OF THE SPACESHIP *BENEVOLENCE*

1. **Colonel Shannon and Lieutenants Ranier and Trend.**

2. **Valerie Reynolds (alias Jennifer Marshall) and Captain Robert Cray (Alias Major Richard Wilberly)**

A Reminder: As the Pamela Series 13 progresses, some individuals become less important and are mentioned only in passing, while other, new individuals appear and will take on the important roles. Despite making concerted efforts to reintroduce a character that has been absent for a while, and to describe new characters as they appear in the Story, I do believe that at this point adding a Character List is a Good Idea!

MALWARIAN ANDOIDS

Dorothy Lansley   Graham Christenger
Jeremy Milhouse   Meredith Weber
Elena Yung   Charles Deringer

1. during the Doomsday Explosion qualifies him as a valuable friend.

2. **James**, a deprogrammed human with Trans-human force and intelligence, has become an important member of Reinhart's exploration team.

3. **Jason** broke through his cryogenic capsule long after the Holocaust, managing to escape from the Main Center He became an explorer. He befriended Pamela when she was on the outside. Participates in explorations on the Planet Earth. Was recently rejuvenated by Dr. Reinhart in volume 2.

PAMELA SERIES 13

Volume 3

The Melding of Time and Space

Chapter 1: The Dawning of a New Time

"Certainly," I said in a soft voice, "I would have preferred to have been in the protective confines of a cocoon, savoring existence in an ephemeral state. "

"What would have been my last thoughts, before this long sleep and what would they have been on awakening?" There seemed no answer. My heart throbbed in synchrony with my gasping breaths. My throat muscles tightened over my dry mouth as I began to tremble. I felt nauseous.

This went beyond a mere forecast of the future with stimulated pangs of anguish turning into a nightmare. For my anguish turned into anger when I realized I had overlooked something important during hasty preparations that I had recklessly defined as inconsequential. But what would be the consequences?

I leaped out of bed. Imagining an enemy, I confronted it, but lost my balance and fell backwards, deflating my bellicose intentions. With my eyes fixed on the pale ceiling above, I sighed. Resigned, I stretched my arms above my head and for a second time leaped out of bed. "I have to face today." I muttered, as I hustled to get ready for the early morning meeting.

I dashed through the empty corridors of the inner circle exiting through a side wall close to the rejuvenation machine. The Group of 5 was waiting for me.

"Pamela, we were hoping that we chose the right exit and, even more, that you would invite us to attend the meeting this morning,"

Crawford said, as his cold, android hand curled firmly around my wrist. "We believe that you are going to need us, if not today, in the near future and that our collaboration now would be very useful."

Still hampered by my awakening thoughts, my eyes drifted slowly from one expressionless face to another. "You might be right." My words fell solemnly.

"We have always been your faithful servants," Flanders quickly joined in, putting pressure, "you must begin to trust us, confide in us and let us help you, Elisabeth."

Reinhart was still meditating deep inside of me and did not awaken to his plea, so I answered him. "The meeting this morning is for us humans. I shall tell them of your offer and, as a group, we shall decide if, when and how your collaboration, as you put it, might become necessary."

Crawford gradually released his grip, but not before he noticed my mouth twitch as I struggled to repress a smile, pointing to his mouth and then to mine...smiling.

I walked slowly, pensively in the direction of the conference room. It was years now that my biological Mother, Dr. Elisabeth Reinhart, the most brilliant of all human scientists before the Dooms Day explosion destroyed the Planet Earth, chose me as her symbiote. Her DNA, coveted by the Group of 5, who were programmed by Reinhart, before her death, to bring her back, spent years recreating physically identical versions of her, hoping she would accept to merge with one of their human creations, all of which were highly intelligent scientists, but she refused. She finally found her symbiote in me, a concert pianist.

For years now Reinhart has been sharing my mind and body. One might ask how someone can share another's mind in a rational, non-schizophrenic way. She knew how. As she told me once, humans never use all their cerebral potential, their brain power and capabilities, like Reinhart's generation of humans did. She was kind to me, caring, and protective with me. She passed information to me, educating me. But she did not change my basically kind, emotional, caring personality, keeping her cold, rational, logical side for herself.

She protected all of us humans, surging inside me when danger loomed and her protection was imperative. Fearless, she boldly faced challenges, conflicts, threats and danger, confident she could and would prevail. Her laughter was raucous, ear-splitting, almost primitive, especially after a long, arduous victory. We joined willingly in her folly, as we laughed, danced, even stomped our feet...in time with hers.

The other members of our human society recognized our different personalities, even our demeanor. I walked with a natural grace, my arms swinging casually by my side. I liked to smile, letting my lips spread nonchalantly and pleasingly, my green eyes sparkling my inner warmth. Reinhart walked in a very erect military style, with a straight back and squared off shoulders. Her former human accent, something the Group of 5 was unable to transmit to my generation of humans, with her special inflection, tone, and choice of words was easy for all of us humans to recognize. No one ever questioned which one of us was addressing them.

She passed through short and long stages of metamorphosis over the years in which we shared the same body. I missed her presence and felt lost and vulnerable in her absence. When she returned she was more brilliant and powerful and certainly more dangerous for those who sought to up-seat her. I came to love, trust, admire and like my Mother and knew I would feel the same as she continued to evolve in the future.

She had a positive impact on all of us and we came to rely upon her to protect and defend us. We even adopted her choice of terms, like "android opposite," when referring to the Group of 5 and other androids crafted physically in the image of the human they replaced; or, human-opposite, when addressing the contrary.

When Reinhart's personality rose inside of me, suffusing me, I stepped aside, letting her take command. She never effaced me, just put me in a position of observation, so I could watch and learn. If she worked at night, she let my mind sleep, restoring my body to a vigorous condition before I awakened.

Interestingly, she even worked in the daytime hours, while I was alert and interacting with others, keeping her projects and thoughts to herself. She was without a doubt a workaholic, unable to take time off.

I feared the day she might leave me on my own. She knew this and consoled me regularly. "You are my child and I shall always covet and protect you."

I stepped into the conference room today with my Mother's energy stirring inside of me.

* * *

The conference room was alive with laughter when I entered and I was immediately drawn into their high-spirited mood, tapping shoulders and giving quick hugs and kisses as I shifted to the far end of the table, taking the empty seat between Randolph and Diana. Then reality hit me. Joseph, Adam, Clarence, and Jason had taken the places normally reserved for Peter, Stuart, Mathieu, and Isabel, who had left the day before on special missions in outer space. Fortunately, these feelings of remorse and abandon that clouded my thoughts dissipated rapidly under the pounding of Ferdinand's gavel, leaving me with a happier thought: 'They will return unharmed.'

Before opening the meeting for general discussion, Ferdinand delivered a short, charismatic speech, honoring our talented astronauts on their way to accomplish major scientific studies and discoveries and encouraging the rest of us to work together to accomplish the exploration of the northern hemisphere.

Ferdinand's final words were from his heart. "We have come a long way over the last few years, most specifically learning how to live and to work together for the benefit of all of us, without seeking only personal gain. Our future depends upon making the right choices. But we must stay alert to avoid worst-case scenarios." He paused for an instance, our attention assured. "Onwards together to a glorious future!" His voice trembled, as if he were choking back tears of impending joy or...sorrow, as he raised his youthful, yet spindly, arms high above his head. We stood up and vigorously applauded him.

Stanislas broke the ensuing silence. "We are curious about why you, Pamela, did not go with Peter, Stuart and Frederic."

"Yes, I do believe that you are all entitled to an explanation," I replied softly. "It is because I am pregnant." I was not ready to share more information with them.

"Congratulations, Pamela!" Mathilda laughed excitedly. "We were all wondering when you would finally conceive for a second time." She tapped her fingers expectantly on the table top.

"Anything else you would like to know?" I glared with disapproval.

"How many months along are you?" Ruth posed the next logical question, turning my attention away from Mathilda.

"I am in the very early stage...around three weeks." I gazed at the others, anticipating the next question. "Peter and I both agreed that my using the cryogenic cocoon would be too risky for the baby."

"I agree with them." John replied. "I could not care less why Pamela is still here with us. I am just pleased that she is. We are going to need her, and Reinhart's advice, on the exploration of the northern hemisphere." He cracked his knuckles. "Do you have a crew in mind, Pamela?"

"Some of you," I looked at Joseph and Randolph, "already discussed the exploration of the northern hemisphere with me, voicing your interest in exploring a particular region, just before Peter, Stuart and Frederic left. But, enthusiasm is not enough to ensure the success of the exploration of the western and eastern regions of the northern hemisphere. We must take the time to learn more about these regions—how they were in the past, and what we might encounter today, and then decide on the final composition of the exploration teams."

"I mentioned that I wanted to go to the western region, spotted with lakes, rivers and wide, sandy beaches splashed with warm to temperate water." Joseph interrupted me.

"Yes, I know and I understand the attraction of this region for you and perhaps other members of our community, who have not yet had the opportunity to express their preferred interest."

The Group's rush of enthusiasm to leave now for unknown turf made me uneasy reflecting on their utter lack of understanding of the inherent dangers, they would confront. There were other things that were bothering me. Granted, some members had received basic training in sports like skiing and mountain climbing and were ready to test their skills. But was that enough? Even though some members of our Group felt ready to explore an area today, they might change their mind, choose another region. Others were undecided. It was important to retrace our steps.

Fighting to stay calm and avoid conflict, I froze my lips shut and looked straight ahead.

"Who, at this meeting is not interested in exploring the northern hemisphere?" I asked, going straight to the point, a better way to approach the issue. John, Sarah, Ruth, Mathilda, Stanislas, Benjamin, Jonathan, Imogen and Ferdinand raised their hands. Ralph and other members of the agricultural unit were not present at this meeting, so I would meet with them later

Ruth added: "Pamela, I want you to know that Rebecca and Samuel would like to participate. And, of course, Jason, Tirence, Leonard, Daniel, Karen, Linda, Jill, Adam, Eunice and Francis mentioned to me that they would like to be part of the exploratory mission."-

"That is excellent news," I replied, realizing that if Francis participated other members of the agricultural unit might also be interested. "Of course, Rebecca and Samuel are the right age." I finally replied, closing my eyes. "They are both in their late teens, slightly older than Frederic."

"Surprisingly, Ludovic, the person of many colors, is now more interested in agronomy than exploring the planet alongside Jason." Ruth commented.

"I am sorry that Ludovic will not be with us, but respect his decision," I added.

"Pamela," Diana nudged me with her elbow. "Did you know that Tirence and Rebecca are a couple now?"

"No, I didn't." The information didn't really interest me much, unless, of course, they were thinking about having a child. Tirence was not one of the original members or a descendant of Reinhart's scientific team. But did that matter? And, her irrelevant comment annoyed Reinhart, who mentally nudged me back to the original subject. "I would like to include Drager, Gordon, Flanders, Miller and Crawford. Does anyone have any objection?"

"Did you already speak to them, Pamela?" Ferdinand asked in an impersonal, administrative tone.

"Actually, no." I replied after a long silence.

"Why do you want them?" Randolph asked, a hint of annoyance in his voice.

"I think that Sarah, Benjamin and Stanislas should also participate." I said. Looking away. "Take some time to think about it."

"Wait a minute, I want to know why you want those androids with us." Randolph turned his head toward me.

"Reinhart wants them, Randolph." I answered. "She just sent me that message. She must have her reasons, which she will reveal to all of us later."

"I don't like it, but then perhaps it is better if they are under our surveillance and not plotting against us here at the Center." He muttered under his breath.

"How do you envisage the exploration of the northern hemisphere, Pamela?" John asked.

"I believe that we should make a group decision." All heads nodded. "This supercontinent, the southern hemisphere of which we have already explored in some detail, is not in a transitional phase. Neither John nor I detected any volcanic activity or tetanic tension visible on any of the satellite imagery." John nodded to me.

I waited a second before continuing. "I want to give you a brief description of the two main areas to help you make your choice," I began. "There appears to be a dichotomy in topography between the eastern and western regions of the Northern hemisphere, which are divided by a very high mountain range. In brief, the western region has open ranges, comprised of prairies and deserts, and a seacoast, with moderate to hot weather and seasonal showers. There is a large pool of water, certainly a lake, and a long, wide river, dividing the region."

There were no comments so I continued. "Whereas, the northeastern half is covered with large, thick, coniferous forests comprised of evergreens, and the south-eastern section is home to deciduous forests and perennial trees. There are also high rocky areas, with deep caverns, clustered together in the northeastern section. The temperatures are moderate to cold."

7

"So, our choice will be principally based upon climate." Joseph commented. "I can officially confirm my choice, I want to go to the western region and hope that my other reptilian human friends will follow me. Nonetheless, I would be happy to have other members of our community join in with us."

I let the others mull over Joseph's suggestion, which was exactly what I considered to be an excellent team composition for the western region, before picking up the discussion. "I shall display the latest satellite images of the northern hemisphere that John and I have captured on the big screen in the inner circle tomorrow. I shall also ask Ralph, who is not with us this morning, to give you information about what kinds of animal life and vegetation we might encounter based upon the climate and topography in the eastern and western regions." Their heads nodding led me to believe they understood the need for better preparation.

Even though I wanted the reptilian humans, along with Jason, Tirence, Francis, Ralph, Eunice, Samuel and Rebecca, to explore the western region, I knew how important it was to give everyone the right to choose.

So instead of putting pressure on anyone, I expressed my preference, knowing that Randolph and Diana would accompany me. "I am interested in exploring the eastern region."

"I think you are the only one that knows how to fly a plane." John changed the subject.

"That is not a problem, John. We shall use android pilots." I hesitated to say more, but decided that the moment was right to continue. "In fact, we are going to need androids to accompany us. As we shall be entering unknown territory, I believe that we should use androids as scouts. They should also be programmed to rescue and/or defend us, if need be. I know that Reinhart has been considering this for some time now and has various programs in mind."

"So, we are not only going to invite 4 members of the Group of 5 to join us, but we are going to bring an android army and technical team with us," Randolph said, as he pushed his chair back.

"I think we should give thought to what Pamela has suggested." Ferdinand's voice full of spirit and vigor, broke some of the tension in the room. "We can discuss this again after we see the different satellite images." He said, bringing the meeting to an abrupt end.

The atmosphere in the room was no longer convivial, so none of us lingered around. We just jumped up and headed in different directions.

I didn't realize that Randolph was following me until he came up behind me and grabbed me, turning me brusquely in his direction. His normally playful, sparkling eyes were dark and menacing.

"What are you up to, Pamela?" He asked in a deep, guttural tone.

I whispered in his ear. "I need to talk to you but not here." He released his grip. "You are the only one I can trust 100 percent. I need you to help me."

"Ok, when can we talk?"

"I suggest you and I leave for the Air and Space center in a couple days. We can talk in the air. It will be safe."

"What are you going to tell the others?"

"I am simply going to mention that Reinhart wants to recuperate other gear at the Air and Space center and select a number of android pilots to accompany us, and that this trip will give you the opportunity to test your piloting skills."

"What?"

"You need to practice." I answered. "I shall need you to take over because the flight up north is going to take more than 5 hours and I won't be able to handle it on my own. So, this will be a very valid excuse for you to leave with me." I raised my eyebrows teasingly. "If I were you, I would spend some time today on the flight simulator."

"I like it." He replied. "And..."

"Don't say any more for the moment." I interrupted him.

He dashed off to work on the simulator.

Chapter 2: A Mind Set

I knocked lightly on the office door and walked in. The Group of 5, huddled together, dispersed, on viewing me. I went straight to the point. "I met with the others this morning. Even though they have not yet given me their approval, I want four of you to participate in the exploration of the northern hemisphere. Dr. Miller and Dr. Flanders, you will accompany me to the East coast, and, Dr. Gordon and Dr. Crawford, you will accompany the team exploring the West coast."

"But..."

"There is no 'but', Dr. Gordon, because Dr. Reinhart decided." Gordon and the other four bowed their heads. "There are other important matters that need to be resolved," I continued. "Do you have the names of all the human scientists that had android opposites, or an android, with their identical physical appearance and intellectual capacity, on board the spaceship *Benevolence*?"

"We shall have to retrieve that information." Crawford answered, in a grating android voice. "And, Pamela, you made a very big mistake. You forgot these androids, unlike us, also possess the emotional intelligence of their human opposites."

"That is a potential problem," I felt my throat tighten. "Well, get me this information as soon as possible."

"Can I be so bold as to ask why, Pamela?" Flanders weighed in. "The scientists on board that flight were handpicked by Dr. Reinhart. She should remember them well."

"Yes, she selected them," Crawford intervened, this time with a smooth, refined human voice, "but they were not the elite members of her scientific team." He stared at me while talking. "Actually, I don't think she expected that spaceship to arrive at its destination, even though she did not sabotage it, like she did the one with the non-intellectuals on board." He stopped to observe me.

"Remember, Pamela," he picked up, "to prevent, rather postpone as history proves, outright war between the intellectuals and the non-intellectuals, she constructed an imposing spaceship that could carry thousands of humans to another planet. She easily recruited a vast number of non-intellectuals by offering them a better world on another, presumably, human friendly planet. They came willingly and, one might say, with hope for a better life. The ship was programmed to explode in deep space years after its launch," he snapped his fingers. "Mission accomplished."

"I want the names, the qualifications and, if this is not beyond your intellectual capabilities, I would like a description of the personalities of the scientists who had android opposites on board the *Benevolence*," I ordered, ignoring his commentary.

"Oh, I would be very happy to give you a detailed report on their emotional structures," Gordon replied, in a lively, euphonious chime. "This project really interests me!"

"I want something very detailed." I paused while scanning the room, to capture their full attention. "I want to know how loyal they were to each other." I could feel their eyes searching mine. "I want to know the probability of rivalries among members and the probable winners and losers in a battle for power." I swallowed slowly. "And, I want to know whether it would have been possible for the android opposites to have themselves activated, other than in the prescribed manner, or with the voice of their human opposite."

"What do you mean?" Crawford asked.

"If you remember," my eyes slowly fixing on everyone, one set at a time; "the android commander was programmed to deactivate the cryogenic sleep tubes of the human scientists and run the awakening program that would assure proper organ functioning when these humans entered the final awakening phase. The android opposites of these scientists were programmed to reactivate, but only when this command was given by their human opposite. And, for reasons of security, only the voice of their human opposite was registered in their systems."

I felt Reinhart stirring inside of me, but continued. "I want to know if they could have bypassed this programming before or during the voyage and, if so, how? Could they have taken control before their human opposites were awakened, or did they need to revolt just after their human opposites activated them? And assuming that they took control, would they have enslaved or killed their human opposites? And, finally, which android opposites would have become the ruling class?"

"We are honored to carry out this kind of study for you, Pamela. It will be very challenging." The former Governor replied.

"But, I haven't finished yet." They moved closer to me. "The spaceship did not arrive at its original destination, but rather close to another planet light years closer to the planet Earth, not considered habitable by humans. So the only members of the *Benevolence* living on this planet are the android opposites of the six high ranking members of Reinhart's scientific team."

"Really?" Miller finally entered the conversation. "Perhaps the spaceship was forced off course, the reason why they are not in what was referred to in the past, as a 'habitable zone'?"

"That is possible. But Reinhart is not convinced. So, let me make this clear. If the android opposites are in power, then the lives of Peter, Stuart and Frederic, who will disembark on the *Benevolence,* are in danger."

There was a long silence. "We shall give Dr. Reinhart a very thorough report," Crawford finally said. "Off hand, I can confirm that, in the beginning, we androids were capable of manipulating our programming, which is why Dr. Reinhart sabotaged us with that inhibiting virus. The android opposites on board that vessel were not only capable of independent thinking but were, as mentioned, privy to the emotional structures or intelligence of their human opposites. I believe that our study must start first with the emotional intelligence of their human opposites, because their android opposite's quest for power would be inherently linked to a human emotional structure."

"I agree, Dr. Crawford," Gordon replied. "But, it is also possible that the androids worked closely with their human opposites and simply replaced them, one by one, as their human opposites' lives terminated. They may not have planned a *"Coup d'Etat."*

"I feel differently, Victoria," Reinhart, surging inside of me, replied in an unusually calm, yet, authoritative voice, bringing the Group of 5 to attention. "If that were the case, then the human scientists would have had the mind set to reprogram their android opposites, like I did with you. They were not the most brilliant of my overall scientific team, but they were still geniuses for their time." I felt my eyes piercing those of the Group of 5 as Reinhart studied their reaction. "I count on you to give me a very thorough study." She then disappeared.

"Dr. Reinhart," Flanders' voice full of energy.

"She has disappeared." I interrupted him.

"Actually I wanted to talk to you, Pamela," Flanders continued. "All of us were ill-at-ease with the two astronauts, Captain Jennifer Marshall and Captain Robert Cray, who spent time here in the center. They were not programmed in the same way that we programmed you humans, but there was something very unnatural about the way they interacted with all of us. And they were uninformed about their own lives and existence. I believe that this information void was responsible for their underdeveloped communication skills." He presented a new problem.

"How do you know that—I mean what they communicated?" I queried. "Were you spying? Are you still spying?"

They stood to attention. Miller finally answered for them. "Yes, we followed them closely and did increase our hearing volume at its optimum, whenever we were close to them." She wobbled back and forth. "And, yes—to protect you, Pamela—we did install more advanced audio equipment in various rooms. Actually, we were surprised you were not more suspicious of them."

"Well, I want you to show Randolph and me where you installed the audio equipment so we can remove them!" I screamed. "I don't like you spying on them or us, which I am not convinced was for our protection!"

"Yes, we shall accompany you straight away." She continued. "But, we can let you listen to the strange conversations that took place between them."

I cleared my throat. "Yes, I will listen to those recordings but later, much later." I fired back. "But I want you to know that you do not have the right to take any initiatives, not just those that are in contradiction with my policy, without getting approval. Remember that we Humans are in command." They glanced down, subdued.

"Reinhart might want to listen to those tapes before we leave for the northern hemisphere, or over the next 10 to 14 days." They nodded. "And, as I already mentioned, I want four of you to accompany us on this exploration," I continued. "I am considering the following: Gordon and Crawford, you will go to the western region and Miller and Flanders, you will come with me to the eastern region. The former governor will stay here and assist John. But, Reinhart may decide otherwise."

There was no response, so I continued. "I want to activate 25 intermediary class, series 3, androids, and reprogram them to scout for our groups and to defend us. I'll need you to come with me, Dr. Gordon, to select the androids."

"Pamela," Flanders addressed me, "we are very pleased to be invited to work more closely with you and members of your team. This is the opportunity that we have been hoping for and what we were alluding to when we met you this morning. You will not be disappointed." Surprisingly, his voice rang truth.

I leaned forward in my chair, preparing to stand, when Flanders dashed over to me, gently placing is hands over mine.

"We believe that it is time for you, Pamela, to learn leadership skills and, in particular, the art of manipulation." I coughed nervously. He pretended not to notice and continued. "'Much to our surprise, Elisabeth convinced the non-intellectuals to board that spaceship programmed to explode in space. But, later, she faltered. Guilt ridden, she refused to address the subject to anyone, most specifically the non-intellectuals, who interpreted her silence as a blatant disregard for them. They never imagined she could actually feel the pain and suffering of the non-intellectuals. For that reason, she not only lost control of the non-intellectuals, but eventually, the intellectuals, as well." He shrugged. "That despicable Dr. Murdoc excelled in manipulating the masses."

"Ferdinand is in charge of informing all of us as to what is happening. He has also resumed his audio courses...recounting the history of the human race, including religion, wars, treachery and so forth. I do not see any reason why I should be asked to manipulate anyone." My words sounded rather naive, even to my own ears.

Flanders made a hoarse, grinding sound, "Pamela, your community is growing. Among the members are the original members of Reinhart's scientific team, like John, Ruth, Sarah, Mathilda, the children of the originals, like you, Randolph, Stuart, and others, as well as your children, or Frederic, Samantha, Rebecca, not to forget our human creations, or Tirence, Ludovic and James, to mention a few, as well as the reptilian humans, like Joseph and Adam. WD, or the Walrus-Dolphin, and his son are mutants."

He stopped to collect his thoughts, before adding. "All these people, as members of your society, seek recognition and satisfaction in their lives. Their needs may be different. For example, the young generation might have their ideas, relating to life style, which differ considerably from your own." He glanced at his colleagues. "We have found films that would be very interesting for you to see."

"Like, 'The End,' you forced me watch years ago, just after I deprogrammed?" I interrupted with laughter.

"No!" He protested.

"Pamela," Gordon jumped in, "for the moment, you govern as a group, even though other very important members of your community do not participate regularly in the meetings. This is certainly because Reinhart is the leader and decides who should be present and heard." Her lips tightened. "You should probably put certain matters up for vote...let those who are not present at the board meetings participate."

"So, you are in favor of a democratic government?" I asked.

"We are only in favor of the semblance of a government, democratic or otherwise." The former Governor threw his arms up in the air.

"The semblance—I don't understand."

"You must always pretend that everyone counts, Pamela." Gordon replied. "Humans like to think that their opinion matters, so you have to give them the idea that their opinion does matter, when in effect it doesn't."

"And you must be very careful to avoid being manipulated by others, even close friends," Miller added.

"I hope the five of you don't imagine I am that naïve?" I shook my head disapprovingly. "And, even if I were, you don't honestly believe that Reinhart would not surface and intervene to protect me. She is certainly not someone who is unfamiliar with manipulation. And, she is probably not opposed to reverting to it on occasion."

"Agreed." Miller acquiesced. "But, you cannot continue to rely upon Reinhart to protect you. You might find yourself alone one day. Your symbiotic relationship with Dr. Reinhart may not endure forever. You will need to be prepared to rely upon yourself."

"Maybe," I sighed.

"In the past, humans were incited by charismatic figures, sometimes very cruel political leaders, demagogues, like Adolph Hitler, who caused severe divisions in society based upon race, religion, sex, natural origins and more. He even went so far as to convince his constituents that certain classes of individuals should and must be annihilated." Miller began.

"These films will only take a few hours of your time, Pamela. A few hours that will bring you years of inner peace," Flanders weighed in.

"Stop," I put up my hand. "I shall keep your offer in mind, but, for the moment, I have more important matters to take care of," I insisted. "And, quite frankly, manipulating friends, colleagues and other members of society does not appeal to me." I pulled my shoulders back, mimicking Reinhart's authoritative stance before adding I would watch her slide show focusing on pre-existing life forms.

"Ok, Pamela, I shall leave now for the Library and do some research for you and Ralph," Miller changed the subject. "I can't promise much, because a lot of this information was lost during the Doomsday explosion, and/or destroyed by the non-intellectuals who ravaged the main center, during the revolution. And the research that Ralph is involved in today is in no way related to former studies of fauna and flora." She hesitated. "And yet, he is surprisingly adept at comparative study of existing species." She threw her hands in the air, as if Ralph's prodigiousness was inexplicable, as he was not one of the original members of Reinhart's scientific team.

She is right, I thought to myself. His knowledge is not limited to just the plants in the agricultural unit, but extends to those we discovered in the Floral Garden, in the oceans, and in the botanical garden at the recreational center. He is adept in bio-engineering, creating new, more resistant plants. I turned back to Agnes. "Thank you, Agnes, I really appreciate your offer to participate in this slide show. And, I, like you, am pleased with Ralph's research." I stopped to take a long, deep breath. "We shall come by this afternoon."

"I shall go now to prepare a slide show for you. I suggest we meet tomorrow afternoon in the Library." I nodded.

Chapter 3: Revelations

I turned the corner to take the monorail in the direction of the agricultural unit. This monorail existed for a long time. When I escaped from the Main Center to join the outside community, Mathieu led me through the monorail's underground tunnel. I have used the monorail for years to get from one part of the Main Center to the other. But I changed my mind at the last minute, deciding that a 20 minute jog to the Agricultural Center was what I needed to calm my nerves. When I arrived, I saw the members of Ralph's agricultural team working in the fields and they waved to me, as I passed by them.

Ralph was in the lab, classifying new forms of algae that the Marine Center had recently sent to him. Apparently the Captain was very conscientious, supervising the harvesting of crops and the collection of new specimens for study.

"Hi, Pamela, what brings you to this far away part of the world?" he asked, as he rushed towards me to give me a friendly hug.

"You were not at the meeting this morning."

"I am not that interested in participating in those sessions." His lips turned downwards. "I don't like participating in board meetings." His remark reminded me of how wrong the Group of 5 might be about the need to manipulate the masses.

"Actually, I want you to give a presentation tomorrow to all members of our community in the large conference room in the inner circle, tomorrow morning." I didn't give him chance to reply. "I have organized everything. Dr. Miller is doing the research for us. Later this afternoon we shall go together to the Library and review the slide show she has compiled for us."

"Wait!" He exclaimed. "Start from the beginning, I am completely lost and confused."

"You are right," I said as I pulled myself up onto one of the lab stools. "You know that we are organizing a trip to the northern hemisphere." He nodded. "The northern hemisphere is divided into two topographically distinct regions by an imposingly high mountain range. Based on the satellite images we have collected, the eastern half is home to coniferous trees and underbrush, which translates into temperate to cold, sometimes very cold, weather. There are large mountainous zones, deep caverns and long, wide rivers. The western region has large prairies and deserts, indicating a warm to hot climate. Its north-western section is replete with streams and lakes." I repeated what I had said earlier. "We need to be prepared for the different climates, but also for the potential plant, animal and insect life that we might come in contact with in these areas. Dr. Miller's slide show should give us an idea of what life forms we might encounter."

"So why are you asking me to present this?"

"Simply because the presentation for all members of our community will be taking place in the inner circle and, as you know, Dr. Miller cannot enter the inner circle, because of the bio-readers, or the integrated programming in the wall that reads the bio-physiological nature of the party seeking passage. The walls will only allow entry into the inner circle if the party is human, or has a dominant human bio-physiological nature like the reptilian-humans. Dr. Miller is a machine." He chuckled.

"Even though Reinhart could adjust Miller's system to give her a human bio-physiological reading, she is opposed to that," he nodded. "And, Ralph, you are an expert in agriculture and will be able to answer any questions about the different kinds of vegetation. You may also have knowledge of insect life?"

"I am well informed about flora and fauna in general. My strong background in agronomy is also very useful in imagining and describing new vegetation." His eyes seemed to sink as he was thinking. "Insects played a vital role in the food chain and in other meaningful ways, like pollination. Sadly, the floral garden is pollinated by those android drones, as there is no insect life in our immediate area." He took a deep, seemingly painful breath.

"The bees, he picked up, "had an effective defense system, able to plant what was referred to as a stinger or dart which was part of their body into an animal or human when they were under attack. Anyway, they were nature's pollinators."

He continued his disjointed monologue. "True, sometimes their defense system was on, let's say, hyper sensitivity. So, they stung, even when they were not being threatened." His eyes met mine. "Actually, Pamela, I am not exaggerating when I say that they played a very vital role in pollination. Perhaps other insect life was equally important for maintaining a healthy ecological environment."

"Perhaps insects are prevalent in the northern hemisphere." I squirmed as Reinhart reminded me of her loathing of these creatures. I silently wished that he had not brought up this subject. "The southern hemisphere," he continued, "is rather limited in terms of habitation, as the central to southern region is covered with thick layers of ice. So, hopefully, insect life has not been completely eradicated and exists in the northern hemisphere."

I had nothing to add, so I waited for him to pick up his monologue.

"Let's hope life forms are prevalent in the northern hemisphere." He rolled his tongue along his teeth. "And, effectively, we might even find insect life that can survive freezing weather later, when we explore the cold, southern polar region."

"Perhaps." I said. "Would you like to go to lunch and then to the Library?" I asked, changing the subject. He nodded.

We decided a walk down the lane would be nicer than taking the land rovers. As we got close to Francis and his friends, he called out to them. "Francis, Birch, Basil and Iris, we are on our way to have lunch. Do you want to join us?"

"We'll catch up with you in the dining room. We only need another 20 minutes or so to finish what we are doing." Francis replied.

"So, you chose names for the three other workers?"

"I had to. At first, I called them 2, 3, and 4, and then one day it came to me. I should name them after plants or flowers. So what do you think?"

"I really like your choices." It was evident that he had given a lot of thought to his very clever choices because the names captured the very essence of these young agronomists.

I stood my place, watching and studying them for a long moment.

Iris had a tall, slender body, with soft, thin, long fly-away hair that gave her a rather sexy, disheveled look. And, her eyes were a deep blue violet. Birch, with his very white skin, ash blond, shoulder length hair, and medium-sized, sturdy body, with long arms that dangled by his sides, like long droopy twigs, was the human version of a White Birch tree. Basil had mahogany brown hair, an athletic body and a charismatic voice. His sublime sweet, spicy odor, riding on the air was that of the Basil plant.

I felt Ralph tugging on my hand, breaking through my thoughts, and I moved rapidly with him to the monorail. We arrived the same time as the others for lunch.

A thick, suffocating silence reigned and we found ourselves playing with our food. Ralph finally broke the tension by bringing up the meeting, scheduled for the following morning. "Pamela stopped by to spark my interest in the different species of animals, plants and insects that we might find in the northern hemisphere," he said.

He received no response, so he continued. "As you probably already know, Pamela and I shall be meeting with Dr. Miller this afternoon to get the information and watch the slide show she has prepared for the group meeting. All this is so exciting. She shall present the slide show to you tomorrow morning."

"Wait, just a minute. Do you really need Dr. Miller?" John asked. I could feel everyone's eyes on me.

"Of course, we need her." Ralph commented, getting everyone's attention. "She has access to whatever information is still available regarding the Earth before that Doomsday explosion." He took a deep breath. "Yes, we don't know how much data she will be able to retrieve, but it will certainly give us a bit more information about the various life forms that previously existed on Earth."

"Well, then it sounds like a good idea for you and Pamela to see and approve the slide show and educational tapes this afternoon. We shall wait until tomorrow morning." John said as he clapped his hands together. "And, as you said, she will be able to properly prepare your different groups for the different life forms they might encounter. You could always run into mutants, but at least we will have some idea what kinds of creatures and plants from the past might be living and roaming about."

The mood changed abruptly and the others joined in the discussion. "So we shall see the slides tomorrow at the meeting?" Sarah addressed me.

"Yes. Remember though, that as Ralph and John just mentioned, some of these animals may be extinct or mutated. And, there may be species of plants, animals and insects that inhabit this planet that are not in any of the existing records." I sighed deeply. "What is most important at this point is to be prepared for predators, poisonous reptiles, amphibians, plants and insects. We shall have to be very cautious."

"That reminds me, Pamela." Diana weighed in. "The Captain has continued the exploration of the ocean. His crews are very meticulous and enlarge the circumference and the ocean to land distance with each new exploratory venture. He has been sending me dead, but well preserved specimens of new life forms. He just informed me that his crew encountered very dangerous, and what he called hideous creatures, living in the very deep ocean. As a number of android divers were virtually ripped apart by these enormous sea monsters, the divers opted for enclosed dive tanks," she commented.

"Incredible news." I wondered why Diana had not mentioned the Captain's discoveries before now. But then she was not the only one keeping secrets because I only discovered today that Ralph was receiving aquatic plant specimens from the Captain for a long time. I observed the stunned, startled expressions on the faces of the others. So, I was not the only one in the dark.

"You were so busy, Pamela, preparing yourself and the others for the exploratory mission that I did not want to bother you with more work." As if reading my mind, Diana gave me the answer.

"This information is very important and potentially useful for all of us," my strained voice grated the words. "Those of you who are interested in learning more about these ocean creatures should contact Diana." Heads nodded.

"Perhaps we should ask the Captain to send a ship, carrying smaller boats to facilitate exploration of inland waterways in the western region of the northern hemisphere," I suggested.

"And on the eastern seaboard?" John asked.

"No, for the moment the eastern region is inaccessible. There is no natural water crossing. We may have to build another marine center on the east coast so that we can house ships and boats. In the meantime, we shall have to use inflatable rafts to explore the rivers in the eastern region."

"You mentioned that you wanted to explore the eastern region of the northern hemisphere." Randolph commented.

"Yes, but Reinhart has made that choice for me," I replied. "I hope that after tomorrow morning's meeting, all of you will have a marked preference for exploring the eastern or western region of the northern hemisphere." Heads nodded.

They attentively watched me as if trying to divine what I was to say next. After all, Diana and Ralph had kept their projects secret for a much longer period of time. "I met with the Group of 5 after our meeting this morning and asked Dr. Gordon, Dr. Miller, Dr. Flanders and Dr. Crawford to participate in the exploration.

No one said anything, so I continued. "Dr. Miller will go to the eastern region. I chose Dr. Miller for the eastern region because her limbs are long and more resistant than those of her colleagues. As you know, Reinhart gave her the most sophisticated technology when she reconstructed her. The eastern region, with its mountainous terrain and deep caverns will be more difficult to explore, so Miller seemed the logical choice."

"Anything else, Pamela?" John asked.

"Yes." I took a deep breath. "I invited Dr. Gordon to accompany me over the next few days to activate 25 of the intermediary class androids. I shall pick up Drager when Randolph and I visit the Air and Space Center the day after tomorrow. Drager will help Reinhart to program them."

"Sorry, Pamela, that is a lot of information at one time. Remember, we never approved your offer this morning of android assistance. In fact, Randolph," Benjamin staring into Randolph's eyes, "was opposed to working with the Group of 5 or other androids. We split up because the tension between the two of you made us uneasy." He stopped abruptly. "So, Randolph, where do you stand on that and when did you decide to accompany Pamela to the Air and Space Center?"

"You are right, Benjamin, I put everyone ill-at-ease this morning. I over reacted, I guess." Randolph replied. "She has since convinced me that Reinhart had confidence in Flanders, Crawford, Gordon and Miller, to be good team players. They did offer assistance and advice when we were exploring parts of the southern hemisphere and we used androids in the past to pilot aircraft and navigate ocean vessels." He rubbed his chin slowly. "Also it's more rational to send android scouts rather than human scouts to explore deep ocean monsters. Humans would not have survived."

"Any objections?" Benjamin asked with no response. "Ok, then we can turn to the next issue. Why are you and Pamela going to the Air and Space Center?"

I jumped into the discussion "Reinhart wants me to pick up other equipment that we will need to explore the northern hemisphere." I closed my eyes, visualizing the equipment. "There are exoskeleton robotic suits for humans at the Air and Space Center."

"What are exoskeleton robotic suits?" Mathilda entered the conversation.

"We shall be using exoskeleton suits created by Dr. Reinhart," I began. "They are sleek, form-fitting robotic power suits that will adjust automatically to the wearer's size and shape. The bio-readers in the exoskeleton suit receive brain signals which determine the wearer's desired movements and how much force the wearer needs to exert. The bio-readers are integrated into the suit, like the bio-readers in the wall for the inner circle. They read and reinforce the wearer's skeletal-muscular system, assure proper organ functioning and power-up, producing the right amount of force when an individual is under attack or in life-threatening situations." I stopped to let that sink in.

"For example," I continued, "the exoskeleton can help the wearer lift several hundred pounds, move with rapid agility and accomplish dangerous tasks, like leaping from high levels or climbing treacherous terrain without risk. They also provide protection. These exoskeleton suits are laser resistant and will form an impenetrable shield when under attack by a predatory animal." Reinhart was sending me so much information that I had to stop. "Reinhart also designed exoskeleton robotic suits with more complicated sensors, actuators and controllers incorporated into their systems for astronauts."

"Are there enough for everyone?" Sarah queried.

"I don't think so, but some of us like you, Joseph, are naturally more resistant and agile than us humans, so these exoskeletons would only be an encumbrance." I continued…"Sorry, she has just informed me that there are enough suits for everyone."

"So why did you choose Randolph to go with you?" John asked, changing the subject.

"John, you mentioned this morning that I was the only human pilot at the Center. When Randolph and I met, I realized that he had trained on the flight simulators and that this would be an opportunity for him to test his piloting skills. Besides, I didn't want to travel alone." Heads nodded.

"I have also worked on simulators, Pamela." Diana spoke up.

"True. Perhaps you can try your skills with me another time. Is there anyone else who would like to make a test run with me another time?"

Francis surprised me when he mentioned that he and Basil had worked on the simulators, without offering to participate in real flights.

Chapter 4: Glimpsing the Past

Dr. Miller was waiting for both of us at the Library when we arrived.

She led us down the hallway and opened the door to a room with several rows of chairs placed in front of a large wall screen. Memories of another time when Dr. Miller, with her heavy, primitive robotic casing, wiry arms, but so beautifully crafted very human-like android head and face, appeased my quest for knowledge about human history, by bringing me interesting learning tapes, stirred inside of me. 'I shall never forget her kindness to me at that time,' I thought.

Today, instead of sitting on an uncomfortable metal chair in front of an antiquated computer screen, I was sitting on a soft, cushioned arm chair next to Ralph, observing the tall, sleek, sexy Dr. Miller begin her presentation about pre-existing plant, animal, reptilian and insect life on the planet Earth. "How time can change everything."

Ralph and I sat for hours watching her exquisitely crafted slide show, featuring various animal and plant life native to the northern hemisphere thousands of years ago. She honored me by incorporating musical compositions of some of my favorite composers like Chopin, Liszt, Dvorak, Pachelbel, Bach, and Beethoven as mesmerizing background music, hoping, perhaps, that this would spark a binding between our community and other terrestrial life forms, her ultimate objective being, respect and admiration for nature.

One could only praise her excellent cinematic skills, capturing the beauty of even the most aggressive carnivores, like the Siberian tiger, and inspiring a deep, emotional connection between us and various species of predatory and herbivorous animals, birds, reptiles and even insects, living in the Boreal and Deciduous forests on the eastern seaboard, as well as, those living in the deserts, prairies and plains in the western region.

She captured the beauty of fields filled with vibrant colors of wild flowers and the forests with diverse varieties of trees and underbrush, highlighting the exquisiteness of seasonal changes specific to certain forms of vegetation in the eastern region. As backup to her slide shows, we spent a few hours, at precise intervals, receiving more, excessively, detailed information about animals and plants, from learning disks she inserted into our individual headsets.

The slide shows were mesmerizing and would have stood out as a major achievement for Dr. Miller if Reinhart had not detected the subliminal messaging embedded therein.

"Interesting...Subliminal learning techniques," Reinhart's firm, non-emotional voice in direct contrast to my soft, musical one, caught Miller's attention immediately.

"Yes, Dr. Reinhart, I used subliminal learning techniques to transfer the names of various life forms appearing on the slides." She lifted her arms in annoyance. "And to inspire humans to respect other life forms; yes, to respect nature."

"Oh, Dr. Miller, I am not opposed to inspiring respect for nature, but did stay alert. Fortunately, you did not digress from the subject and try to gain control over the human brain for a future, let's say, *"Coup d'Etat."'* Reinhart took a deep breath.

"I would never do that, Dr. Reinhart," she protested.

"And, even though sometimes excessive, your warnings about new species which might be more aggressive and the danger of finding oneself alone with a renowned predator, like a lion or a wolf, were necessary." She stopped to observe Miller.

"I have your permission to use the same cassettes for the rest of the humans and reptilian humans?" she asked, after a long silence.

"Yes, I have taken the necessary steps to prevent you from adding to or deleting anything from the slide shows and commentaries." Reinhart replied, before she disappeared inside of me.

"Thank you, Dr. Miller, for these informative and inspiring slide shows and learning cassettes," I said in a soft voice, as I got up to leave.

"Thank you, Pamela," she replied.

"Well," Ralph began when we were alone, "the slides were very entertaining, sometimes so captivatingly beautiful that I now yearn to visit the different areas and reach out—caress—the different life forms." I nodded.

I noticed he was rubbing his fingers, like someone suffering from arthritis. I took his hand in mine, to reassure myself he was ok.

After a long silence, I went straight to the point. "What are you worried about, Ralph?"

"I don't know." He said so softly that I barely heard his words.

"She warned us that her entire project –slide shows and educational tapes-could be of no importance." I began. "Respecting nature and recognizing danger when confronted by a potentially aggressive carnivore means one has to stay alert. It is only natural that she insist upon potential inaccuracy in the nature and content of her cassettes, reminding us that there could be dangerous creatures, even hybridized species, lurking in the forests. She wanted to put us on guard, while inspiring an environmental and ecological consciousness."

"True." He said, as he scratched his head. "That's it." His lips parted slightly. "I understand. She doesn't want us to imagine that danger looms behind every tree or under every rock, but we must always be on alert."

"Yes. Reinhart just confirmed to me that Miller wants to inspire us to explore these areas, but is covering herself with constant warnings of potential danger, in case something happens to one of us. She wants us to be inquisitive, respectful, but careful. Yes, that's it. She does not want us to let ourselves be so mesmerized or seduced by the beauty of these environments- if they are as she described them- that we relax our guard." I replied.

"You are right." Ralph replied, in a restrained, nervous voice. "It was nice spending time with you, Pamela. You should come and visit me more often."

"I would like that, but I have so much to do," I sighed. "I won't be with you tomorrow morning. I count on you to pay close attention to the slides and learning tapes and do what you mentioned earlier, remain vigilant, and critical." I said.

"Right. You can count on me." He patted me lightly on my shoulder and we parted company.

I decided to head in the direction of the zoo. Even though WD and his son were free to circulate in the Center, they spent most of their time relaxing in the polar bear enclosure.

As I walked slowly past the cages, the stale odor of stuffed animals impregnated the air, making me feel dizzy, but I stood my ground, letting my eyes wander from one enclosure to another. I was finally struck by the aura of power emanating from territory occupied by the large predatory cats. I held their gaze for a long moment before meandering onwards to admire other species of mammals, reptiles, amphibians, and birds on display in this zoo, observing and imagining them roaming freely in their natural environments.

They were no longer just stuffed animals, vestiges of a very distant past, but rather magnificent life forms that we might encounter in the near future when exploring the northern hemisphere. "So, I was right." I spoke to all of them. "Dr. Miller's slide shows did work magic, at least on me, by bringing you back, if only for a brief instance...to life!"

'Why does Reinhart and the Group of 5 believe we are so uncivilized that we would take pleasure in annihilating other life forms?' I thought. "We demonstrated our respect for different life forms when we explored the southern region, especially the ocean."

"I won't laugh at your naïve belief that humans are basically good, because I was also very naïve when I was young." Reinhart surfaced inside of me, dialoguing on a cerebral level. "But," she began in a strong, firm tone, "humans are by nature the most adept and ruthless of all predators, something that is authorized and reinforced by a common belief that humans are superior to other life forms and can, therefore, decide the ultimate fate of other species."

"We are not ruthless. We respect life forms!" I replied, my voice rising an octave in our defense.

"Today, you are eating life forms—fish, shellfish, sea mammals. Tomorrow you will be hunting terrestrial life forms for their meat, their fur and other body parts," Reinhart retorted.

"If history repeats itself," she continued, "eventually you will begin to hunt for pleasure or for sport, but not for survival. And you will long to live and relive that adrenaline spurred energy that accompanies the chase and the primitive, savage pleasure of a kill. And what will you do with that dead animal that represents your victory? You will hang its head on the wall, wear its claws around your neck, or throw its fur, like a carpet, on the floor. No matter what, the animal you killed will be nothing more to you than a trophy....that one day you will throw away."

Not finding a proper defense, I tried to make her feel guilty. "So you let Dr. Miller send us those elaborate, subliminal messages, even after she outright lied to Ralph and me about their limited scope."

"Her subliminal messages are not dangerous," she contended. "But, you are absolutely right, she lied, but, not intentionally. There is a problem with her programming, and that of the others, which I shall look into later this afternoon."

She paused for a long moment. "I did not object to her attempts to make humans more responsible and caring individuals, because I found her efforts very touching. If her subliminal learning has a positive impact on you and the group, I shall be very pleased. But, I am not convinced of the success of her efforts and am more prone to believe that human nature will prevail."

"We shall see, Dr. Reinhart."

"Yes, we shall see, Pamela." Reinhart replied in turn.

Reinhart disappeared and I continued my tour of the zoo, wondering if she was right, humans killed for sport. I grimaced at the thought, as I hastened my pace, looking forward now to a chat with WD.

WD's living quarters, the polar bear enclosure, was finally in sight. I approached his quarters so discretely, hoping to eavesdrop on a conversation between father and son that would reveal WD's objectives. Instead, I found them sleeping next to each other, close to the large pool. I cleared my throat loudly enough to awaken a very deep sleeper and their eyes popped open instantly.

"Pamela!" WD screamed in his delightfully refined British accent, as he approached the glass. "How nice it is to see you." He pulled his heavy body up into a half sitting position. "What can I-or we-do for you?"

"I have not yet had the honor of meeting your son." I replied.

"Oh, yes, an excellent idea!" He motioned to his son with his front flipper to join him and proceeded with introductions. "Pamela, I am happy to introduce you to my son, Weldon."

"I am very happy to meet you, Weldon."

"Out of curiosity, how did you know that I was the one approaching your enclosure and not Dr. Reinhart?"

"Oh, that was easy. Reinhart holds your body in that straight, commanding, almost intimidating, military style, and you walk with the elegance of a dancer as your arms swing gracefully by your sides." He replied and I nodded.

"My father," Weldon broke in, "has told me so many wonderful things about you, Pamela." He said mimicking the refined, practiced British accent of his father.

"Weldon and I took a short leave of absence." WD's dolphin mouth moved into a tight smile. "Just spending time together in our little paradise." He slumped into a more comfortable position.

I studied both of them for a few minutes. I felt my eyes naturally withdraw into a stone cold mode, as they met theirs. I felt ill-at-ease and wondered if there was something unnatural about their behavior that triggered my suspicion. 'Why did they want me to believe that they were just on vacation? Were they hiding something from me?' I decided against pursuing those angles, saying instead, "I want you to join us in the exploration of the northern hemisphere."

"Uh..." WD stuttered, "...in what respect?"

"I want the Captain to bring one of the big, sea-faring vessels up the west coast and meet the group that will be exploring the western deserts, prairies and plains when they arrive on the western seaboard."

"Interesting." He replied, turning his eyes in the direction of his son, a smaller, but exact replica, of himself.

"I also want you to fly down to the Marine Center and prepare to accompany the Captain and his crew on this mission."

"But, Pamela, my son is not ready for this kind of mission." He retorted, as he pulled himself into a towering, upright posture, commanding obedience.

"Relax, the mission is not dangerous," I replied. "I will not be putting either one of you in a dangerous situation." I took pleasure in seeing his tusks droop loosely from the corners of his mouth. "I thought this would give your son an opportunity to develop his walrus-dolphin skills—diving, swimming, foraging...fighting."

"Perhaps... but, I would like to discuss this with him. I shall let you know what our decision is."

"I don't think you understood. You have been given an order, WD, not an offer." His eyes opened very wide when he heard Reinhart's firm voice.

"Of course, Dr. Reinhart. But, there are dangerous predators in the deep oceans, even along the coastline, and, well...the safety of my son could be compromised in the interest of scientific discovery." He stopped abruptly. "And, he is not ready to accompany me on this mission."

"Do you think that Weldon would be happier staying here at the center during your absence?" Reinhart asked as she continued to replace me.

"After all these years of fidelity, you still don't trust me, Dr. Reinhart?"

"I need you, WD." She said, putting him off guard by ignoring his question. "And you need your son by your side." She replied, this time her voice, soft and gentle, sounded so soothing even to my ears.

WD tilted his head slightly, a gleam in his eyes. "You need us, Dr. Reinhart?" She nodded. I heard a long, painful sigh flow from between his slightly parted dolphin lips. "Then, Dr. Reinhart, I am ready to show you today, like in the past, I am your faithful servant. But," he stopped to move close to the glass wall that separated us, "I will be the one who decides on which diving missions my son will accompany me."

"Agreed." Reinhart said in a firm voice before leaving me to say goodbye to WD and Weldon. "Hope to see you for dinner tonight." I heard a long-winded "yes" as I dashed out of the zoo and rushed to catch the next monorail.

"There are too many things on my agenda." I shouted in frustration, before getting off the monorail and jogging in the direction of the office of the Group of 5. I opened the door brusquely to find them seated behind their desk waiting for me.

"Dr. Miller told us that you were pleased with her slide show and learning disks." The former Governor opened the discussion.

"That is true. But, she must have told you by now that Dr. Reinhart wants to take a very close look at your programming."

"What are you talking about, Pamela?" Crawford asked. "Our programming is functioning very well."

"Apparently, too well then." Reinhart spoke in a haughty tone, getting their immediate attention.

"It is always a pleasure to speak to you, Dr. Reinhart." Flanders entered the conversation.

"Did you tell them of my intentions, Dr. Miller?" Reinhart queried.

"Yes, I mentioned that you wanted to verify our programming. We are, of course, ready to cooperate." Miller replied.

"Before going further, I would like to inform you that we have the list of the scientists and their android opposites that were on board the spaceship *Benevolence*." Flanders commented, hoping that this information might distract Reinhart.

"This is wonderful news, but I would like to verify your programming first."

"Dr. Reinhart, we shall certainly cooperate with you on this programming issue which, as you surmised, we have already discussed in great detail." The former Governor replied as he turned to Crawford.

"Discussed in great detail?" Reinhart taunted. "I left Dr. Miller less than an hour ago..."

"I know." The Governor interrupted. "But, we have been aware of changes in our behavior for more than a month now."

"What?" painful burning of Reinhart's anger seared.

"Please, let us explain," Flanders said, leaning on his spread-fingered hands placed on the table in front of him, like this action would reduce the tension building up in the room.

"Ok, but get on with it. I have a very busy schedule."

"You know that we each have, in varying degrees, the remnants of an emotional structure," Flanders dwelling on the obvious from Reinhart's point of view.

She sat down on the soft cushioned arm chair and listened

intently to their concerns. They insisted they no longer had the ability to remain cold and detached, at least where humans were concerned. They characterized their behavior as too altruistic, suggesting that they might even sacrifice themselves to save not just the humans but also the reptilian humans. They said in unison that they had become too nice. Their cold, logical side was effervescing, and they didn't understand why.

"You are going to need us." Crawford said boldly. "And it is better that we are logical and cold."

"Yes, I know that I have to upgrade your systems. Some of your altruistic sensations may possibly be caused by the malfunctioning of your original programming. I was planning to do this anyway," she replied in a serious tone of voice.

"But in order to interface with the android opposites of the original human crew on board the *Benevolence*, who we believe are now in command of that vessel, we will need to understand how emotions are perceived and later expressed by androids," Crawford turned to his colleagues who nodded in approval.

"Interesting!" Reinhart repeated the word several times, as she rubbed my hands together methodically.

"We know you are worried about activating the emotional configurations of our defunct human opposites, but you can maintain ultimate control over us, like you did with your android opposite, adding your voice controlled self-destruct program, forcing us to explode or shutdown, should we try to overthrow you or initiate a revolt." Crawford commented.

"It is a two-step procedure," Flanders weighed in. "You add a self-destruct program to assure our loyalty and you remove the virus you put in our systems so our human opposite's emotional intelligence will resurface."

I felt my hands move into a steeple position, as my eyelids closed in front of an array of intricate mathematical equations that passed rapidly in front of them. "Yes, I can easily accomplish what you have requested. I have just developed the program. But,

I must discuss this with the others first," Reinhart finally said.

"Dr. Reinhart, please forgive me for being so direct, but that would be a mistake. You must make the decision. It does not have to be today, or even tomorrow, but it should be in the very near future." Dr. Gordon entered the discussion. "It is too early to confide in other humans."

"Perhaps, you are right. Let me think about it," she stood up and huddled close to the 5 androids. "You believe I made a mistake sending Peter, Stuart and Frederic to the *Benevolence*?" My heart began to beat rapidly.

"We have no reason to believe that humans are not in command of the spaceship *Benevolence*," the former Governor replied.

"Nonetheless, it is better for you to go forward with adjusting our emotions." Flanders spoke in a low, paternal voice, hoping to strike a chord with me and gain, at least, my confidence. "You can always reverse the program later on. But if the worst scenario plays out, we will not have been in touch with our emotions long enough to properly interface with other very intelligent androids operating for years with emotional intelligence. We might not be able to control them."

"Here is my study of the psychological profiles of the six brilliant scientists on board the *Benevolence*. If they are now replaced with their android opposites, you can anticipate better how they might react. Please let me know what you think." Gordon interrupted, handing the file to Reinhart.

"I shall adjust your programming accordingly, to retrieve and accelerate the development of the emotional configurations, or emotional intelligence, of your human opposites. But pay heed to my warning! If you try on your own, or as a group, to augment or otherwise interfere with these new emotional capabilities, and/or decide to join with adversaries to challenge my authority, you will regret it, for I shall always remain your Master."

She swallowed slowly like she was savoring the taste of power she would continue to hold over them. "I shall definitely add a more efficient security system than the one I used for my android opposite so that I will be able to activate it from a distance, if necessary." Her eyes slowly moved over the faces of the Group of 5. "I shall not hesitate to order all or any one of you to shut down, something that you will be incapable of resisting." She sighed. "And, should that happen, I shall never reactivate you again. Is that clear?"

"We trust you, Dr. Reinhart." The former Governor finally broke the silence. "And, we are ready to accept the brutal consequences of even inadvertent negative actions or reactions to protect you and the others who have become, "family to us."

She laughed softly, finding humor in the Governor's final words. They stood obediently with their heads bowed, as she passed in front of them. "Your risk is greater than mine!" She slowly articulated her words in her strong, commanding tone.

"We can assume that Pamela will certainly bring this up with Randolph." Crawford could not resist.

"You can assume whatever you want, Dr. Crawford." She said. "Don't forget our meeting tomorrow, Dr. Gordon, to select and program the androids that will accompany us for the exploration of the northern hemisphere." She called out as she left the room with Dr. Gordon's computer disk tightly under my arm.

Chapter 5: Hypothesizing

Reinhart disappeared inside of me and I rushed back into the inner circle to put Dr. Gordon's file in the safe. I knew that the Group of 5 was right. Whatever Reinhart's concerns were about a possible change of power, from humans to androids, on board the *Benevolence*, there was no information to support this, and yet... Flanders' concerns should not be taken lightly. I knew that Reinhart intended to read this report tonight and I too was curious about what Gordon recommended.

The meeting made me late for dinner and I felt weak and hungry. When I arrived, most of the group had finished eating and were picking Ralph's brain about the slides and learning tapes they would be watching and absorbing tomorrow. My guess was that they didn't have time to do this over lunch.

"I told them that there was a change of plans. We would meet in the library and use the same comfortable theater we used today." Ralph commented.

"Ralph really enjoyed the slides and learned a lot," John commented, hoping I would reveal a bit more.

"Did WD and Weldon stop by for dinner?" I asked, changing the subject.

"No, but they are arriving now." Francis said, pointing to the door.

"We made it, Pamela or...Dr. Reinhart," WD said, in a voice drained of energy, as he and Weldon positioned themselves on top of the large, inflated airtight sacks that the android kitchen crew quickly moved in place.

I ate while the others chatted with our walrus-dolphin friends. "Are you going to the slide show tomorrow?" I heard John ask WD.

I put my fork down and picked up the conversation. "Yes, you and Weldon should go to the slide show."

"You did not mention this earlier, Pamela." WD raised his body high enough to look me straight in the eyes.

"You are right, WD. But now that John has brought up this subject, it might be interesting for you to watch the slides. But I am not certain that you will be able to absorb the information on the learning tapes."

Reinhart's energy suffused me, as she entered the conversation. "Pamela was right to question this, but, let me assure you, WD, you and Weldon will be able to download the information from the learning tapes. You have the same ability to retain everything you see and learn, just like the other members of our society here at the Center. I shall ask Dr. Miller to bring two more, large sized helmets, like the size reserved for our reptilian humans. As you have not used one of these sophisticated, download programs before, it might take you a few tries for your subconscious mind to accept the information in rapid sequence."

She hesitated for a minute. "I already asked Dr. Miller to prepare a program focused on pre-existing ocean life, some of which you have already encountered. I believe this might be even more interesting and relevant for you."

"Ok. We will give it a try." WD replied, slapping his right front flipper down on the side of the table. "Where do we meet?

"I'll come and get you just after breakfast." Ralph suggested.

"And, you, what are you up to tomorrow, Pamela?" Diana asked.

"I shall stop by at the end of Miller's slide show and take a look at the film that the Captain sent to you, Diana." She nodded. "You said it was a short film, with just pictures of various former species, some of which showed physical signs of mutation."

"Yes. I have it in my possession." She hesitated. "Actually I could get my computer and we could all skim the pictures now?"

"Excellent idea." I nodded and she rushed off.

"You didn't answer Diana's question. What are you up to tomorrow?" Benjamin pressured.

I swallowed a big gulp of water, before answering. "Gordon is going to help me reactivate some of the androids from among the more sophisticated series and upgrade their programming so that they are alert and prepared to intervene to protect us. I also want to make certain that they will follow our orders." I scooped up what was left on my plate and chewed it slowly.

"We will also need these androids, as I mentioned before, to scout for us and to clear out underbrush." I noticed that all heads were nodding. "And, having them ready to protect us will reduce the overall risk for all of us."

"And, you and Randolph," Mathilda's voice was sullen and hardly audible, "are leaving for the Air and Space center the day after tomorrow?" We nodded and her gaze narrowed into a tense squint.

Diana arrived with the film. In a short ten minutes, she showed us pictures of various horrifying species of fish, living in the darkness of the ocean depths, producing their own bioluminescence when hunting. They shared many of the same characteristics, long snouts, razor sharp outward pointing teeth, and long, slender, often times leathery, eel shaped bodies, resembling in some cases the Dakosaurus and Nothosaurus of the prehistorical period.

"I only received one dead specimen of the Fang Tooth fish for dissection, if anyone would like to assist me." Heads turned away from her and the film. She definitely got the message.

"Well, I am going to get some sleep so that I am alert for tomorrow." John said, as he moved to stand up. The others did the same, while WD slid off the air sack, Weldon by his side.

Only Randolph stayed behind. He pulled me close to him and whispered in my ear. "Is there anything new that I should know about, Pamela?"

Overcome by the ripples of desire that the simple touch of his warm, moist mouth against my skin evoked, I was unable to answer, so Reinhart pushed me aside and replied in her native accent. "No, everything is fine, Randolph. We shall see you tomorrow for dinner."

"Ok," he said, as he brusquely pulled away. "I need some sleep if I am going to be able to concentrate on the slide shows and learning tapes."

I waited a few minutes before leaving the dining room to be certain that no one would be lingering in the pathways of the inner circle. I was ready to enter the inner circle, when I remembered that I had to inform Miller that WD and Weldon would be present for the slide shows and remind her to bring two extra large size helmets. I quickly passed by to see the members of the Group of 5, who were involved in conversation. Miller handed me her report for Reinhart to study.

I could feel those sparks of energy that Reinhart sent me when she was ready to tackle a complicated problem. "I don't understand, Dr. Reinhart," I asked, as I leaped into the inner circle, "why you need Gordon's profiling of your former scientific team?"

Seated in her private office, ready to open the file, she answered my haunting question, informing me that she did not recall any rebellious or disloyal behavior on the part of these scientists, but that she did not carry out the psychological studies.

"Dr. Granger, a renowned psychiatrist for whom I had ultimate respect and confidence, interviewed each member of this scientific team and approved their intellectual competence and undivided loyalty to me and to the success of the mission."

After a brief pause, she continued. "Actually, I found them all rather mediocre intellectually, but capable as a team of building a community on another planet. Their perseverance and meticulous attention to details convinced me that they would accomplish their mission and build an equitable, unbiased social order based upon a democratic government that would endure and flourish." She leaned our body back in the chair.

"I was completely unaware of Dr. Milhouse's, can I say, excessive precautions---that is if Flanders' fragmented memory of this can be taken seriously." I could feel my stomach drop. "And yet, Pamela," I had a tendency to trust others, at least in the beginning. Then, even as I grew indifferent, ruthless and cruel, I was still naïve in some situations and misread certain personalities. That is the weakness of humans! And I was then stuck in a very human mode!" Her voice rose an octave.

"My metamorphosis has given me new insight and, hopefully, will prevent me from succumbing to any aspects of human fragility." She sighed. "So, let's see what mistakes, if any, I made in the past!"

Report (Dr. Victoria Gordon)

She opened the file. Gordon did not mention the physical characteristics of these scientists, concentrating exclusively on the psychological profile of the subjects, drawn from Granger's report and from her own observation of them, in comparison to the other members of the Group of 5:

"Interesting," Reinhart commented. "It would appear that the members of the Group of 5 were involved in espionage activities, independently and together, even at that time. They will certainly say they were merely protecting me but, well, let's be honest, they are diabolical!"

Jeremy Milhouse was at the top of the list. He was considered to be underhanded, power hungry and jealous of Reinhart. His wife, Ann, a weak-minded person, was prone to bouts of hysteria which Gordon suggested were based upon jealousy.

Gordon mentioned that she overheard Milhouse on several occasions bragging about his acumen and leadership ability, and recorded the following comment for posterity.

"I believe that we will have to rely upon ourselves only. Dr. Reinhart will no longer be our mentor or our protector. She is sending us like guinea pigs into space, to another planet of her choice. If we survive, she will send others. If we disappear, she will forget us, write us off as failures, and choose new scientific teams. You must always remember that we are no more than an experiment for her, so we shall have to be strong together, if and when we arrive on the suitable planet. Be assured that I shall be there to guide us and secure our futures."

Graham and Zena Christenger were highly regarded biologists and genetic engineers. They specialized in flora and fauna, focusing their research on fortifying, ameliorating, and improving upon the quality and resistance of plants and animals as food sources. Their interaction with others was usually conflictual. Graham, more than Zena, wanted to work closer with the Group of 5 and, in particular, with you, Dr. Reinhart.

Walter and Elena Yung were robotic engineers. They participated in the creation of humanoid machines and were closely involved in the construction of their android opposites.

"But, Dr. Reinhart, I want to remind you that the programming of all the android opposites of these various scientists was to be exclusively your domain." Gordon's comment in quotations.

Her report called Reinhart's attention to Elena, who did not follow procedure, gained access to Reinhart's files and was charged with espionage. My records show that you, Dr. Reinhart, altered the programming, and intellectual capacity of her android opposite, as punishment. In a private conversation between Elena and Walter they addressed their total hatred for you. Elena swore she would redeem herself and punish you and your descendants. Nonetheless, you authorized her departure on the interstellar mission to colonize another planet.

Virgil and Dorothy Lansley were involved in cryogenics. Their contributions were exemplary and you, Dr. Reinhart, did commemorate them on several occasions during dinners or receptions, reserved for the scientific community. Virgil had a very dominant personality, in contrast to the submissive personality of Dorothy. Their difference in age, Virgil being 15 years older, played to his advantage.

Yannick and Meredith Weber were specialized in planetary studies, most particularly, environment, geology, oceanography and climatology. Their knowledge of the radical environmental and ecological changes that the Earth suffered through wars and human negligence, coupled with their research in improving living conditions on Earth, made them an excellent choice for this mission. You even gave them an active role in the selection of the most human friendly planet for colonization.

Charles and Margaret Deringer were assigned projects related to the field of biochemical engineering. They were the only couple who got along well with the other 10 members of the scientific team. Nonetheless, they were not the Pierre and Marie Curie of their generation, as there was neither love nor respect that molded them into an invincible team.

There were 8 remaining members with android opposites: Admiral Baron Davis, Major Richard Wilberly, Captain Valerie Reynolds, Communications Officer Tiffany Brown, Medical Officers Dr. Angela Dower and Dr. Shawn Underwood, Chief Engineer Douglas Henderson, and Lieutenant Beverly English.

In other cryogenic tubes, there were 100 military officers and soldiers, trained for combat, as well as 220 civilians ranging from

15 to 30 years old who were selected for their intellectual ability, craftsmanship, manual skills, courage and more, all of whom would be capable of building viable settlements on a new planet. In addition, from among the 300 androids of different series on board the Spaceship *Benevolence,* only 50 androids were activated to assure the safety of the voyage.

The spaceship *Benevolence* was equipped with aircraft, large vessels to carry out asteroid mining, land vehicles, military aircraft, small boats—the list is long.

I added the last few paragraphs to the first part of my report as a reminder of the size, capacity and numbers of occupants that were on board this spaceship even though I know, Dr. Reinhart, that you are well aware of how the *Benevolence* was designed, equipped and staffed.

"Yes, Pamela, Dr. Gordon is rather insightful for an android without emotional intelligence" she commented before disappearing for a long moment, giving me the opportunity to consider Dr. Gordon's report from my point of view.

I was certain Dr. Reinhart knew these scientists were not her loyal friends, but believed they might be capable of carrying out their mission, reaching another planet and inhabiting it. The real question was why the android opposites of these scientists were given emotional intelligence. Reinhart knew the danger of doing this. Reinhart's android opposite, imbued with Reinhart's emotional intelligence, tried to kill her. Maybe Reinhart wanted to study how androids with emotional intelligence would interact with their human opposites in another context, like on board the *Benevolence?* If so, why?"

My thoughts stopped when Reinhart surfaced and returned to the cassette.

"I have given a lot of thought to what may have happened on board the *Benevolence,*" Gordon began.

Firstly, there is every possibility that there was no foul play and that the spaceship went off course, or was driven off course, by no fault or miscalculation on your part, Dr. Reinhart, but because the universe is in constant motion and the wormholes you mapped out did not carry the ship in the right direction, but into another constellation.

This change of course might have occurred at the very moment that the revolution and ensuring Doomsday explosion took place on the planet Earth. When the android crew did not receive any replies or instructions from Earth, they awakened the high ranking officers to navigate the vessel and identify a planet that might be life friendly.

If these officers could not reenter a cryogenic state after being awakened, they would have eventually activated their android opposites to work with them. The remaining members, scientists, military and civilian, were awakened from their cryogenic states and began to carry out exploratory missions, mining operations and so forth. The original members must have died, so the crew on board the ship today are descendants of the original civilian and military humans. If this is the case then all the android opposites of the original scientific team and high ranking officers are now in command of the *Benevolence.*

Secondly, there is the possibility that the *Benevolence* was damaged in deep space, by space debris, hostile aliens, or simply because its systems malfunctioned. Many of the cryogenic units could have been damaged, causing loss of life, prompting the android command team to open all the cryogenic units in an effort to save the lives of the remaining humans. The damaged ship may have run off course, entering into another constellation, before the humans had the opportunity to gain control. So today, the *Benevolence* is home to the descendants of those who survived this tragic interstellar catastrophe. And, the android opposites of the original high ranking officers and scientific team are at the head of the government.

The third and last scenario draws its credibility from the information that Dr. Flanders communicated to you earlier, or the use of a primitive robot in which the voices of all the scientists were registered. In order to have absolute control over the mission, Milhouse might have programmed the primitive robot to activate Milhouse's android opposite at a given moment during the voyage. Milhouse's android opposite would have then ordered the primitive robot, carrying vocal registrations, to activate the android opposites of Milhouses's closest friends and colleagues. These android opposites would eventually have taken command of the vessel.

I believe the following androids took command and are still in command: Milhouse or Graham, because they didn't like you; Elena, because she was gorgeous and defied you; Dorothy, because she was brilliant and submissive; Meredith, because she had no enemies and was a good team player; and, Charles because of his specialization. It is possible that Ann, the partner of Milhouse, and Walter, who was easy going and did not take sides, was also activated. I am certain, though, that the android opposite of Milhouse would not have activated Virgil, Yannick, Zena or Margaret, for reasons of loyalty and emotional instability

If this happened, the android opposites of these scientists could and might have rerouted the spaceship. An android does not need a life friendly environment to survive, so they probably selected a planet that was strategically situated in a constellation that you would not venture into.

Did they open the cryogenic tubes of their human opposites when they arrived at their determined destination? I don't know. From a logical standpoint, No. We the Group of 5 do not have emotional intelligence. We reproduced humans and brought you back, because we were programmed to do so.

I hypothesize that certain humans, like members of the original flight crew, as well as others that the androids did not consider to be dangerous, were revived from their cryogenic state. That would explain their descendants.

After reading this it is our hope that you better understand the importance of giving us our emotional intelligence. Only an android can understand the cognitive emotional processing of another android. Most specifically, will a given android favor personal gain or the protection of humans? You, Dr. Reinhart, are cold and calculating, but you are still human. We can be your saviors, but only if you give us our emotional intelligence!'

I sighed, as Reinhart disappeared inside of me, leaving me alone and very awake to ponder the situation on my own. This last scenario was very disturbing, but needed to be proven. For the moment, we were working very well with Colonel Shannon and her crew.

The members of our team on the inflatable space station were sending us images of our planet and learning how to manipulate materials in an environment with artificial gravity. They roamed outside the inflatable center, learning how to successfully maneuver in a weightless environment. They were wasting no time learning how to survive in outer space and were in contact with and receiving guidance and instruction from the crew of the *Benevolence.*

I remained suspicious of Gordon. Her report, especially the last chapter, was more than a subtle ploy on her part to have emotional intelligence reactivated in the Group of 5. Were they looking to overthrow us and join forces with the android opposites of those former scientists?

Other thoughts ran through my mind. Perhaps those android opposites did not leave their human opposites in a prolonged, endless cryogenic sleep. Perhaps they stayed very loyal to their human opposites, awakened them, and worked closely with them. Additionally, I was certain that Reinhart would not have forgotten to add a backup system to activate an android opposite, should one of the human scientists die during the voyage.

And why and when did the High Commissioners of the spaceship, *Benevolence,* send astronauts back to the planet Earth? Certainly they came to Earth in friendship for hundreds, maybe thousands of years, looking forward to working closely with us. Unfortunately, the Group of 5 systematically ordered their extermination.

"No," I said out loud, "we cannot be certain these android opposites, if they activated, sought to gain power." I felt more positive. Gordon's report was too neat and simple. It was calculated to motivate Reinhart to take immediate action to reinstate their emotional configurations.

I put the report back in the safe and wandered off to my room, collapsing on the bed. The baby was moving inside of me, a reminder of her existence. I slowly caressed my stomach, sending her a message of maternal love, as thoughts of Peter, Frederic and Stuart joined together, filling me with positive, happy feelings. "Tomorrow is another day." I said in a soft voice, as I closed my eyes and fell into a deep sleep.

Chapter 6: Outthinking

"Wake up, Pamela! Quick, there are several important things that I must take care of, before going with Dr. Gordon to activate android scouts." Her high decibel voice jolted me from my sleep. I leaped out of bed.

Her high pitched voice continued: "I want to consult my records. We must hurry."

I showered quickly, wondering the whole time how I managed to stay sane, sharing my cerebral consciousness with Reinhart. Her symbiotic presence was so reassuring at difficult moments, but there were times when her compulsiveness for a cerebral high resulted in long hours of uninterrupted work that would have drained me mentally and physically, if she had kept me awake at night.

But, she was considerate. She let my mind rest and boosted my physical side. 'She was definitely tireless in her cerebral dedication to challenging projects but was she, when she was in her own body, also physically indefatigable?' I wondered.

I walked slowly down the main corridor in the inner circle, passing in front of familiar places, bedrooms, cozy corners, endless numbers of labs, the medical unit, eventually reaching the back wall, which was for me, nothing more than a dead end. I knew from experience that this wall had no bio-readers and that I could not pass through it into the main center.

Reinhart knew differently, she moved rapidly to the far right corner of the wall and pressed down on a slight indentation, invisible to the naked eye, something curiously reminiscent of her action years ago in the Air and Space center. A narrow passage appeared and we rapidly entered into a small chamber, before the wall closed behind us.

It was a library, the shelves filled with paper files, books and outdated computer disks and recordings. The perfumed odor of this enclosed space was both pleasant in its sanctity and suffocating in its agedness.

I grabbed a book from the shelf and so slowly, so delicately, opened it, turning the pages, running my fingers over the words, imagining I could absorb the content through physical contact. She gave me a few minutes to explore the area before explaining why we were in this library she had designed and concealed for her use only.

"I collected these books. Like you right now, I enjoy holding bound copies of literary and scientific works, turning the pages and running my fingers along the lines. When I hold a paper-bound copy of an author's work, I feel a certain intimacy with that author and that text, that I don't find when I use virtual versions."

"I was impressed," she continued, "with Gordon's description of the members of the scientific team on board the spaceship, the *Benevolence*. Fortunately, I kept a paper- bound copy of Dr. Granger's report for my future use, because his diagnostic skills were irreproachable," she said, as she reached for the file. "Gordon had no access to this report."

"Be patient, I want to verify a few points." She said, as she turned the pages in rapid sequence in front of me, preventing me from reading anything.

She flipped through the long report in a matter of minutes, reminding me of how rapidity she can read, absorb, reason, understand and draw rational conclusions.

"So, did Dr. Granger's report add new elements that might change your strategy?" I asked.

"Oh, his style and method of psychological analysis always impressed me, but there was nothing of real value in this report, unless of course we wanted to take on case-studies of members of our team," she chuckled.

"So, it was a waste of time?"

"No. I wouldn't say that. It gave me more insight into personality disorders. Learning is never a waste of time." She stopped to collect her thoughts. "I do believe, though, I have a better idea which android opposite might be in command and how to interact with that android and the others who might also show erratic behavior."

"Are you worried about giving the Group of 5 their emotional intelligence?" She sat back down.

"Cognitive emotional processing," she repeated the words several times.

"I don't understand."

"Without belaboring the subject, intelligence encompasses cognition, the method by which humans assimilate and integrate knowledge. Cognitive emotional processing is evaluating right and wrong using emotions which are innately programmed in a human brain's subcortical circuits. These emotions do influence reasoning, memory and attention. Emotions like anger, fear, disgust, happiness, sadness, surprise, contempt play a role in decision-making."

She got up and paced back and forth before directing her attention to me. "So, the question is how cognitive emotional processing will impact on a given android's decision making?"

"That is what Gordon suggested as the reason why you should make them, "whole," I interrupted.

"You know that I ordered my android opposite to self-destruct." She picked up. "In the beginning, I was fascinated by how she integrated my emotional experiences into her decision-making. Her cognitive emotional processing of me was both reckless and cruel. Certainly, I should have ordered her to self-destruct much sooner than I did, but I bowed to my scientific curiosity, until I ran out of patience with her quest for power and her desire to dispose of me, and I ordered her to self-destruct."

"I worked very well with the human opposites of the Group of 5. None of them had any personality disorders, like the human opposites of the six High Commissioners in command of the crew on board the Benevolence," she added.

"So, why then are you so worried about giving the Group of 5 their emotional intelligence?" I repeated my question.

"Because they have conspired together for a long time and in their logical mind set, absent any emotional intelligence, they decided that my death at their hands would be kinder than a death at the hands of the non-intellectuals. So they killed me." She grimaced. "Admittedly, their decision turned out to be the right one. They offered me a rapid, less painful death."

49

"Today, surging remnants of a pre-existing emotional configuration may be weighing in on their decision-making, the reason why they developed a certain outlook vis-à-vis life forms like us. Remember Humans were fabricated and disposed of over a long period of time." She said, grimacing slightly.

"As logical beings," she continued, "they are working well with us and appear to be more considerate and amenable only because of me, my presence is indispensable to achieving their objective. They want their emotional configurations, something that they believe was unjustly denied to them."

"You know, Pamela, emotions could render them kind and tolerant. Or only the negative personality traits of their human opposite might surface, making them competitive and more diabolical. Emotions could even render them less efficient," she sighed.

"What I hope is that their cognitive emotional processing will reflect that of their human opposites. And that the Group of 5 will be able to properly interpret and control the negative, emotional side of the android opposites on board the *Benevolence,* if we discover that these android opposites want to conquer and destroy us."

"So why not wait until we are certain that Peter, Frederic and Stuart are in danger?"

"It is simple, but I could not reveal this, in all its complexity to the Group of 5. As their emotional configurations are beginning to surface, in a fragmented manner, there is a problem with their programming. They need to be upgraded, for want of a better term. So I have no choice but to intervene now because they play a vital role in our community. We need them." She replied with conviction.

"And," she continued, "I am willing to take the risk of reactivating the emotional configurations of their human opposites, because I have developed a new stabilizing element, or different kind of virus, with a very efficient self-destruct program. It will give me ultimate control over them if they get out of hand."

"They won't be able to detect, read or delete this new program on their own," she asserted, "so there is no danger they will be able to deactivate, or in any manner, circumvent the virus."

"When did you develop this new virus?"

"Like most of my research, I did it when you were asleep. The body we share needs to rest, and your cerebral consciousness needs time out. My cerebral consciousness is working 24 hours a day." She sighed. "And, I restore your bio-physiological system so when you awaken you feel rested and full of energy."

"One last question. Did you set up a voice-activating backup system?"

"Yes, of course. Admiral Davis and his android opposite had the voice registrations. And, in the event they perished, there was a voice activator in the main computer system on the ship. Several different officers were given the code to activate this part of the system," she replied. "But, we shall not mention this to Gordon. Let her think that I can make mistakes. It will make them all the more reckless in the future if they decide to try to take command." She said under heavy laughter that left my sides aching for hours afterwards.

"Thank you. Things are starting to make sense to me." I said. She disappeared inside of me as I turned, opened the door, re-entered the corridor, and retraced my steps until I arrived at the right exit point in a wall, close to the office of the Group of 5.

When I opened the door Dr. Miller almost knocked me over, as she dashed past me to be on time for the slide show.

I stood for a moment studying the remaining four, wondering how they would act once their emotional configurations were activated. Dr. Reinhart was convinced that their human opposites never had any serious relationships with other humans. But I had some doubts about Gordon, a depraved, sexual predator, ipso facto, an authentic version of her human opposite, who was perhaps equally frustrated by a desire to be loved. I shook my head in denial. Just being in the presence of these Androids aroused a delirium of doubts and bizarre thoughts.

"Pamela," Gordon's harsh voice, dragging me brusquely into the present, "I am ready to accompany Dr. Reinhart to activate the androids in the storage unit."

We left and I walked in silence.

"You are very quiet, Pamela. Is something bothering you?" She asked in a dry, clinical tone.

"Just thinking—yes, just thinking." I answered.

"Interesting." She replied, as she dragged out the syllables, inferring that I was not someone who resorted to cerebration on a regular basis. My brows unwittingly corrugated and she in turn took longer, more rapid strides, forcing me to jog to keep up with her.

As always, I found the android storage unit overwhelming in both its size and its seemingly infinite number of columns of androids, representative of a stupendous era of human scientific achievement. Gordon let me stand in awe for a few minutes before attending to business.

"Dr. Reinhart, are you ready to get started?"

"Yes." She replied, taking over my body and imposing her consciousness, as she moved to the series that interested her.

"How can I help?" Gordon asked.

"Just activate 25 of the androids in series 3 and I shall readjust the programming accordingly."

From my post of cerebral observation, I noticed they worked well as a team, Gordon activating an android and Reinhart downloading the new programming. Each of the 25 newly programmed androids were tested for intellectual capacity, skillfulness, physical endurance, combat, observation skills, reasoning, perceptibility and more, all of which were vital for the proper protection and defense of us humans exploring the northern hemisphere.

After completing this long and tedious task, Gordon took initiative by recommending that Reinhart consider activating at least 10 of the series 4 androids, who were already programmed and trained in survival and military tactics, a proposition that I sensed, by the waves of enthusiasm that Reinhart sent through my body, pleased her. Reinhart actually asked Gordon to activate 15 of that series and then upgraded their programming accordingly. The 40 newly activated series 3 and 4 androids were placed in a small room in the storage unit where they would remain in a deep sleep, until our departure in a few days

I accompanied Gordon to the office of the Group of 5. Definitely curious about why I wanted to meet with them again, she tried to engage me in conversation.

"So you have nothing to say, Pamela?" She taunted me. "You are thinking again?" Her voice vibrating, as she feigned laughter. I pretended not to hear her and she left me in peace.

When we entered the office, I thanked Gordon for her help and then asked to see Flanders in private. He followed me to the birthing center, going straight to his former office.

"What can I do for you, Pamela?" He asked, his voice a sweet, low paternal tone.

"I am how many months pregnant?"

"You are in the middle of your fourth month." I stepped back to get a closer look at him. He told me only weeks ago that my pregnancy was in its very early stage.

"I know, you are going to tell me I lied to you a few weeks ago." He shuffled his feet in front of him. "I prefer to say that I avoided the truth on purpose so that you would be worried about transferring the baby to the artificial uterus too soon. I did not think that it was a good idea for you to leave with Peter, Frederic and Stuart." He confessed.

"So you really are worried about the safety of my team?" He nodded. "And you were looking for a way to keep me from going with them?"

"Yes."

"Thank you for caring," I finally said, before adding, "But, you should have told me the truth, even though it does not matter today."

"So why did you ask about your pregnancy?

"Because I want to move the baby to the artificial uterus before I leave to explore the northern hemisphere."

"You are certain?" I nodded. "I find this to be an excellent decision for the survival of your child."

"So we can do it today?"

"Today!" Like an optic illusion, his eyes seemed to protrude outwards from their casing. "I have to do a lot of tests-the amniotic fluid in the amniotic sac, which, at this point in your pregnancy must be preserved or reproduced and there are the blood tests, scanners, and so forth, not to mention reactivating and programming the artificial uterus to receive a four, maybe four-and-a half month, old fetus." He rambled.

"You can do it. I know that you can."

"Yes, probably." He replied. "But, I will have to do a cesarean section. The baby can only be removed this way. It would be dangerous to induce contractions." He backed away from me. "And, you're leaving with Randolph tomorrow and then on your return, you will be reprogramming us." His eyes met mine. "You will be tired and may even be suffering."

"I shall be just fine. Reinhart will be able to rapidly repair my— or our-- body."

"Yes...yes, that is true. She is capable now of doing that." He sat down heavily. "I would like someone to assist me. Do you think Ruth would be able to help?"

"I shall talk to her about that as soon as I leave you."

He gently took my hand in his. "I must examine you now. It won't take very long, so, let's get on with it."

He led me into the birthing center and quickly took all the samples, using efficient, painless, high tech equipment. He rapidly scanned the results before commenting. "I might be able to transfer the fetus inside its amniotic sac into the artificial uterus. But just in case the amniotic sac perforates before the fetus is in the artificial uterus, I shall have to be ready to transfer the fetus into an identical amniotic fluidic environment, to prevent damage to the fetus. Remember we did his for Mathilda, but we had everything ready and in place, awaiting the right moment." His voice screeched slightly, reminding me that he, like his colleagues, was receiving erratic emotional vibes. "I shall start to work on that now."

"Will the uterus be ready in a few hours?"

"Yes." He grabbed my hands tightly in his. "I shall covet this child as if she were my own."

"Thank you, Edward." I said, as I gave him a quick kiss on the side of his cold, android face.

I left him to his work and ran off to find Ruth. I caught a quick glimpse of her work, before she had time to turn off the computer, and was surprised to discover that her work was in genetic engineering.

"What are you doing, Ruth?"

"Well, I did not go to the slide show, because I plan to stay here in the Center."

"And?"

She realized it would be better for her to disclose her research.

"Eunice and Adam came to see me the other day. They want to have a child."

"Really?"

"I know, Pamela, or Dr. Reinhart, whichever one is upset with me, but I wanted to study the probabilities of their producing a baby in a physically perfect human body, while retaining the reptilian physiological aspects."

"You should have asked me." Reinhart's voice made her jump. "I would have told you that it is impossible for you to accomplish that."

"Could I at least ameliorate the physical aspects?"

"Either you remove all the reptilian features and engineer a perfect human baby, or you can accept that the physiological aspects of the reptilian side of Adam are dependent upon certain physical traits and let human nature choose the right combination."

"You are serious, Dr. Reinhart? Or, you just don't want to do anything for them?" She raised her voice in protest.

"I don't have time to study the problem, and I am sorry to say this, Ruth, but this kind of genetic engineering is outside of your competence." Ruth's eyes took on a red glare. "I am just being honest. It is best to let nature determine the right combination—at least for the moment." Reinhart paused. "I shall talk to them because their project can wait until after the exploration of the northern hemisphere. By that time, I might be able to help you. At least, I shall give this problem some thought, in my spare time."

Ruth took a deep sigh. "I was not feeling comfortable with this, so to a certain extent, Dr. Reinhart, I am glad that you have put an end to my research."

"I need you to help me with something urgent." I finally spoke up.

"What do you need, Pamela?" Ruth asked, recognizing my voice.

I explained the situation to her and she agreed to accompany me and assist Flanders. "I promise to follow the progress of your child during your absence, Pamela." Her voice was charged with energy, indicating that any hard feelings she may have had with Reinhart, regarding her genetic engineering project, were forgotten.

"One last thing, Ruth." Her eyes met mine. "I have not mentioned this to anyone else, so I hope that I can count on you to defend me over dinner."

She tilted her head slightly, as if she were studying my behavior. And then, with a glimmer of a smile on her slightly parted lips she asked. "When do you want me to be at the birth center?"

"Actually, I am going to return now, if you want to accompany me." She nodded.

'Reinhart will be able to observe and participate, if necessary, and I have nothing else urgent to attend to,' passed through my mind.

"It will take me 10 minutes to put everything away."

I was absent for less than an hour, but Flanders had everything set up and was waiting for me when I arrived. Reinhart pushed me aside and looked over the artificial uteruses. Flanders had activated two: one for the baby in its amniotic sac and the other with a comparable amniotic fluid inside of it. It looked like a no-risk situation, and that is exactly what it was.

I knew that Reinhart would diminish, if not efface the pain of a caesarian, so at the last minute, I told Flanders that I wanted to stay awake. He agreed.

Flanders, with Ruth's assistance, carried out the caesarian without any difficulties and moved the fetus still in its amniotic sac into the artificial uterus, programmed to function at the proper temperature. Flanders then pierced the amniotic sac letting the fluid seep into the artificial uterus, filling it with this natural cushioning solution, before he connected the umbilical cord to the artificial placenta, integrated into the wall of the artificial uterus, which would provide the proper nutrients, while recuperating waste.

Flanders and Ruth carried out different tests to verify that the baby was properly connected to the artificial uterus and was in perfect health. At the same time, Reinhart quickly repaired and remodeled my body, returning it to a non-pregnant state.

'She no longer needs the rejuvenation machine, something I knew, but still impressed me. She is able, when she knows a person's genetic code, to rejuvenate that person and give him or her back a youthful, strong body. Yes, it is wonderful to have a Mother who can repair damaged tissue, sagging muscles, serious injuries, and more by using her mind.'

I stood admiring this healthy 4 and half old fetus, imagining how her perfect little body would develop into an exquisite baby girl, before slowly running my hands over the sides of the artificial uterus, reassuring my child of my presence, and my love.

"Do you have a name for her, Pamela?" Flanders asked, as he leaned over the artificial uterus.

"Yes, actually I do." My voice in a whisper. "I shall call her...Rhea."

"Rhea." He repeated slowly as his eyes turned to mine in silent complicity.

"I like it." Ruth released all the emotional stress that had built up inside of her with laughter. And, I joined in with loud, enthusiastic laughter that Flanders' attempt to duplicate only produced jarring, sporadic sounds.

"Thank you, Edward. Thank you, Ruth." I said as I hugged and kissed them.

I grabbed Ruth's hand. "I won't be able to spend much time with her, but I know that you will take good care of her in my absence."

"I shall be back after dinner, Edward." He nodded and I left. I held onto Ruth's hand.

As I approached, voices from the dining room grew louder and louder.

"Where have you been?" John asked, his fork falling on his plate when he saw my flat stomach, imagining I lost the baby. "Oh, Pamela," He got up and rushed towards me, "I am so sorry. What can I do to help you over your loss?"

"Come sit down," he said, as I took my place next to Randolph.

"Everything is fine. Flanders and Ruth moved my baby into the artificial uterus an hour ago." My eyes scanned the Group. "I did not tell anyone that I was going to move the baby to the artificial uterus," I confessed.

"I understood," I continued, "that the safety of my child must be my priority. I could not climb mountains, chase wild animals, explore forests, and otherwise engage in the rugged exploration of the northern hemisphere while pregnant. Thus the only way to assure her safety was to transfer her into an artificial uterus."

The silence in the room seemed heavy with surprise, maybe even opposition.

And then, as promised, Ruth spoke up in my defense. "I think

Pamela made a difficult, but good decision. I was worried about how the baby would survive the rigors of a grueling trip to the northern hemisphere."

This prompted the others to join in with similar supportive statements.

"Is the baby doing well?" Mathilda asked, switching to her maternal side._

"Yes, Rhea, is in perfect health. She is actually older than I realized." I spoke rapidly. "I was in the middle of my fourth month of pregnancy."

"I shall take good care of Rhea!" Mathilda replied enthusiastically.

I gulped down my food, ignoring the others, discussing the benefits of wearing exoskeleton suits. When I finished I told everyone I wanted to check on Rhea. Heads nodded.

"I would like to see Rhea, if you don't mind," Randolph said. I grabbed his hand.

"She is taking after her Mother." His voice mellow, as he leaned over the artificial uterus and studied Rhea. "There is no doubt. She is going to have your beauty, charm, and, of course, your energy and intelligence, Pamela." He said, as he planted a tender kiss on my forehead.

I would have stayed longer if Flanders had not interrupted this special moment, mentioning that Gordon wanted me to see another video in her office, this time about manipulation. Randolph offered to go with me. Gordon, Crawford, Miller, and the former Governor were waiting for us when we arrived.

Her film was short and to the point, focusing on human society in the very distant past. Much about what the Group of 5 had already mentioned, like subliminal messages, dichotomization, shaping public opinion by the media and public relations industries, working together to control the thinking and interests of the public, and doublespeak, or lies and ambiguities used by governments and media to shape public opinion took up the greater part of the film. I recognized the names of certain renowned authors, like George Orwell, Noam Chomsky, and Ray Bradbury who addressed the dangers of propaganda used principally by totalitarian governments to control the masses.

Moreover, unsophisticated android machines and elementary algorithms of a distant generation of humans were used to collect data about individuals via social networks, so that they could use psychographics to send the right messages to the users, manipulating them. Governments encouraged the use of soft forms of propaganda by the media, public relations and artistic industries to indoctrinate people at all socio-economic levels. Apparently, individuals were unaware of the use of duplicity, deceit and other forms of trickery by governments and industries.

"So that is how doubletalk, doublespeak, doublethink can be used to manipulate the masses,' I sighed before being struck with another more pertinent thought, 'Were the manipulators also being manipulated?'

I was ready to get up and leave, when Gordon opened up a new subject, Dr. Murdoc. "He lived among the non-intellectuals for years, arguing their cause and fighting for better rights and living conditions for these people. He risked his own health, apparently, living with them, breathing in the polluted air, when he could have lived in a healthy environment inside the domed city of the intellectuals. And yet, he turned against them." She sighed.

"He convinced the intellectuals, who presumably distrusted him and frowned on his efforts to help the non-intellectuals, to let him lead the revolution. He up-seated Reinhart in a few minutes with his charismatic speech that had the intellectuals on their feet, applauding and bowing to him, while Reinhart faded into the background. And he did this knowing that the intellectuals would never be able to win."

"I want to play his final message to Dr. Reinhart when she was addressing the intellectuals, just before the revolution broke out."

Randolph and I listened attentively to what he told Elisabeth, before pushing her aside and taking command. "I don't understand you, Elisabeth," he said in a low, mellow voice. "Have you forgone leadership for indifference? You know them, Elisabeth, you know them inside out. You have an exact profile of each of them and can put pressure on them to follow you. As you refuse to use your talents, to take command, to give orders, like you did in the past, you leave me no other choice but to use mine."

The film ended. I turned to Randolph, whose glaring, wild-eyed expression made my insides jump. "Are you alright, Randolph?" My voice shaky.

"I am him?" He stuttered. "That was Dr. Murdoc?"

"Yes. He is your biological father." I said, in a low voice, hoping to calm him.

He looked at me, his expression changed. His eyes grew large and bright as he burst into hearty laughter. I joined in, without knowing why.

"I like the man!" He shouted. "I really like him. He had guts! He had power! I understand why she loved him."

"Do you have any questions?" Dr. Gordon asked, putting an end to Randolph's vaunting.

"Was he an astute manipulator or was he just lucky, the last time they were together? Was Reinhart capable of manipulating others?" I asked.

"There is no doubt that Dr. Reinhart was and still is the epitome of a strong-willed person, Pamela." Gordon began. "Reinhart had great power over others in the past. Her power was predicated on her extraordinary intelligence, scientific acumen, disregard of trivialities like ordinary conversation, and logical approach to problem solving. She loved challenges, and her cold, unemotional way of resolving differences and making decisions discouraged opposition. She never used trickery or manipulation to get other's support or approval. But she did resort to cruelty to secure her objectives."

Gordon continued, stepping back from Pamela, as she sensed Reinhart's presence mounting. "No, she did not manipulate. She ordered, and she was obeyed because some feared her and others admired her. Her last appearance was alarming. Instead of declaring war against the non-intellectuals, she put the issue up for discussion. That made her vulnerable. And Murdoc recognized her vulnerability."

There was a long minute of silence before she picked up the discussion. "I believe that Murdoc tried to provoke her. He must have hoped she would order the use of force to calm the revolution, but she didn't. Perhaps she felt guilty about how she had treated the non-intellectuals, something that her android opposite had cruelly brought to her attention. Her android opposite argued that she would make a better leader than Reinhart." Air passed through Gordon's system like a human sigh. "Only Dr. Reinhart can answer that question."

"But, yes, Murdoc was a highly intelligent and very persuasive man. He interacted well with the non-intellectuals as well as with the intellectuals." Gordon continued. "Dr. Reinhart understood that and probably appreciated his way of bringing about good results. People did not hate or fear him, they admired and trusted him, because he was very adept at what I consider persuasion mixed with an honest empathy for those in difficult situations. Everyone felt that he was on their side. So they trusted him."

She lifted her hands spasmodically in the air to make her point. "We androids believed differently and therefore avoided him. We were certain he would order us to shut down, the reason why we organized our escape to this center, hoping to outsmart him, but we didn't fool him."

"So you prefer Reinhart's method of governance?" Randolph asked.

"Yes, because it is android...logical!" Her lips curled upwards. "And you, Randolph, prefer Murdoc's method because it is human... emotional." She said, slowly pronouncing the word.

"Reinhart gave orders and Murdoc listened to people's problems," she continued. "He tried to find solutions, and eventually persuaded people to follow what he honestly believed was the best solution. He loved Elisabeth and, for that reason alone, wanted to protect her. And, as you must interact with other humans, we are hoping that both you and Pamela will recognize and resist the manipulation of others, and will preserve and always put the interests and well-being of human society first." She then smoothed out her robe and invited us to leave.

Once outside her office, Randolph again expressed his admiration for his biological father. This time, Reinhart answered. "I want you to understand that when Dr. Murdoc addressed the intellectuals, he recognized the need to calm the crowd and he did so very effectively," she replied.

"But, I thought that you and Murdoc were lovers. Where would you have gone?" I asked.

"We both went to our deaths!" she screamed. "We lost and the world came to an end!" I could feel a gripping pain in my stomach, as my body quivered, and her voice resounded in my head.

When she finally regained control over my quivering body, she continued. "Of course, Murdoc and I were lovers. And, I was definitely deeply affected and profoundly touched by the depth of his love for me when I listened to the recordings he downloaded into Drager's memory. He saved our lives when the Captain tried to kill us. His confessions of love gave me courage then, like they did in the past." She stopped abruptly.

"I miss him and shall always miss him," she said slowly, "and even though it is not consistent with my basic thinking that is supposed to be void of human weaknesses, I wish that he too had survived."

She hesitated. "But appeasing the masses was his field of expertise and mine was, like Dr. Gordon mentioned, making rational decisions that others would obediently carry out. When the revolution broke out, my only interest was to seize my destiny which was more important to me than rescuing a lover, or saving that deplorable group of intellectuals."

"And what was that destiny?" Randolph asked, a touch of authority in his voice.

Her energy disappeared. I was on my own. "You are with me, now, Randolph. She is meditating," I answered.

"Ok. Understood." He said. "I need to get some sleep, if I am going to fly a plane tomorrow morning." He replied.

We dashed down the corridor and plunged through the wall, toppling on the floor under the force of our entry, our bodies facing each other. He leaned over me, his lips moving so slightly over mine, as his hand caressed the back of my neck, drawing me up closer to him. He rubbed his cheeks so tenderly along the contours of my face, confessions of love pouring from his warm, moist mouth, spawning tingles of desire overcame me and I reached out, caressing his face.

He seemed more determined than ever to be the seducer rather than just a superficial playmate like before. Even his odor was not the same, for he no longer smelled of those intoxicating, ambrosial fragrances that the Group of 5 mixed in male cologne. His special blend of bold, intoxicating sexual pheromones filled the air, making my heart flutter.

I knew from the sparkles in his eyes that he was aware of my change of heart and that he understood that our relationship was reaching a new level. He pulled me close against him as he moved his hands slowly up over my body, lightly caressing me."

"Randolph," I pushed him gently, and he moved off of me.

"Tired, or not interested in me, Pamela?" he asked.

"Tired," I whispered. "It has been a long day." He forced a smile.

"I love you, Randolph." I said, as I grabbed his hand and led him to my room.

He was smiling, as we cuddled up next to each other.

I must have slept well, because when I awakened I felt refreshed and energetic. On my side, with his arms wrapped tightly around me, I listened to his slow, deep breathing, savoring the strength and comfort of his presence. Eventually, I got up to take a shower.

From behind the veil of warm water flowing slowly over my face, I saw him enter the room. But before we had chance to savor a moment of love, I felt Reinhart's dynamic energy rush through me, pushing me aside.

"We have a lot of things to do today. I suggest you both finish your shower rapidly." She ordered.

"Of course, Dr. Reinhart," he said in a lively, but obsequious tone, while mumbling something inaudible under his breath.

Chapter 7: Ground Plan

We were the first to arrive for breakfast and the first to leave. The Group of 5 was waiting for us when we entered the transport unit, the large military helicopter that could carry android pilots and crew members, exoskeleton suits, weapons, and anything else that Reinhart would consider necessary for our exploration of the northern hemisphere, was ready for boarding.

The Group of 5 stood, at a respectful distance, while we boarded the helicopter. I closed the door and activated the propellers.

"So, who is flying?" Randolph asked, his eyes focusing straight ahead.

"You!" I replied in a firm, commanding voice.

"But, the lift off....perhaps you should handle that." His voice quivered slightly.

"No. I want to see what you can do."

He turned in my direction. His eyes had lost their normal luster and a wistful smile crossed his face. "If I miss, it's your fault, Pamela," he replied tersely. I just laughed.

"Ready to lift off!" He announced over the radio and the androids moved out of the way.

The plane moved smoothly upwards. He glanced quickly in my direction, looking for a compliment, but I said nothing.

"Well, now that we are up in the air, I shall move aside and let Reinhart disclose, let's say, top secret information," I replied, as Reinhart surged inside of me.

"Randolph," Reinhart's native accent visible, "I have decided to install and activate the emotional configurations of the human opposites of each member of the Group of 5."

"What do you mean by emotional configurations, Dr. Reinhart? "He asked.

"Emotional configurations—ah, yes, that is my preferred term, but it may not be clear to you, so I shall explain," she began.

"Emotional configuration could be defined as the personality of an individual, their preferences, how they interact with others, and so forth. And yet, it is more complex because it also refers to the emotional intelligence that is inherent and specific to each individual." Randolph cocked his head slightly toward Reinhart.

"Emotional intelligence," she continued, "presumes a capacity of intelligence, knowledge by way of emotions and a capacity to take into account the emotional component inherent to the assessment of a knowable situation, or a prescribed set of facts." She lectured. "This is referred to as cognitive emotional processing."

"And you are going to let the Group of 5 acquire the personalities, with the emotional knowledge embedded therein, of their human opposites?" He asked abruptly.

"There is nothing to worry about, Randolph. Even though I can easily order any member of the Group of 5, other androids and robots to shut down with voice command, the situation will change slightly when I give the Group of 5 emotional intelligence. So I developed, let's call it, a super virus that I can activate if any of them begin to vie for power or otherwise threaten human dominance. And, they understand that once I activate the virus, their android existence will be terminated forever."

"Why do we need them?" He asked, his voice subdued.

"I believe that I acted too rapidly—perhaps trusted Colonel Shannon too much." She sighed. "I have no excuse for my actions."

"You may have no reason to be worried," his voice remained calm.

"I hope that you are right, but I have to prepare for the worst," she said and then informed him of her discussions with the Group of 5. She revealed the personalities of her colleagues who left with their android opposites, the protocol for activating the android opposites when the *Benevolence* arrived at its destination or encountered difficulties during the voyage and the android composition of the flight crew.

"Am I following the right route?" he asked, changing the subject to buy himself some time to think about what she just said.

"Yes. Everything is fine." Reinhart replied.

He stuttered a bit, searching for the right words, "But, Dr.

Reinhart, some members of the Group of 5 will be accompanying us on the exploration of the northern hemisphere. Gordon and Crawford won't be with us, at least not with you and me, because you assigned them to the western region. How are you going to prevent them from gaining control when you are not there to oversee them?"

"It is not a problem. The programming I am going to use will protect us, because I shall be apprised instantly of their behavior," she replied. "I would like to concentrate now, on the Group of 5's role later on. I have taken steps to bring the Group of 5 into my confidence, asking them to analyze and then help me to control, rather than destroy, the android opposites of my former scientific team."

"You are certain that the Group of 5 can be trusted?"

"Yes, I am certain that the Group of 5 is our best weapon, should my worst fears be realized. Let's just hope that Peter, Frederic and Stuart will not be walking into a deadly trap."

A cold, chilling sensation passed through me, before Reinhart continued. "I know that I worried about these android opposites taking me hostage—the reason why I chose not to go on this mission. But, as I needed a valid excuse for staying behind, I informed them that Pamela, my symbiote, was pregnant, thus thwarting the High Commission's logical game plan."

"It was a good move for another reason," she continued. "I needed to find out whether androids or ambitious, ruthless humans were in control. Because the High Commissioners did not reply immediately and when they did their message lacked human sensitivity and concern, my suspicion that the High Commissioners are androids was confirmed."

"I read defiance in the messages that they sent me, lacking amicable, polite terms. They certainly recognized their lack of human subtlety, even politeness in the use of language. For that reason they decided to send their messages to me through Colonel Shannon, who they believed would use the right ethical and polite words. But, oddly enough, she simply repeated what they had sent to her."

"Huh!" Randolph exhaled.

"And," Reinhart continued, "I am inclined to believe that, as the Group of 5 mentioned, there is a small group in charge—not all the android opposites of the original crew are active. And I even adhere to the Group of 5's conviction that the 5 to 7 androids—the exact number still uncertain—that comprise the High Commissioners, are imbued with the psychotic personalities of their human opposites."

"What does that mean?"

"It means that certain members of that scientific team were psychologically unstable."

Reinhart went on to reveal the manipulative and power hungry side of the members that Gordon identified as the most dangerous.

"Does not sound good," Randolph

"A machine with human emotions is less predictable, even for someone like myself, prone to emasculating and dominating emotional behavior. I fear that it will be difficult for me to outwit and control them, and to identify the fragmented from the intact, let me say, emotional intelligence of their human opposites." She confessed.

"Ok, makes sense," Randolph said pensively.

"That is why I believe that the Group of 5 will be able to un-derstand how the emotional structure of their human opposites af-fects their android logic. And, more importantly, they will be able to anticipate and defend us against these androids in their quest for power, use of cruelty and so forth. Their cognitive emotional processing will be the fabrication of a robotic, not a human, mind."

She stopped and I felt vibrant waves of energy rushing through my brain, sparking under her high cerebral charge. "In anticipation of your next question, programming my android opposite with hu-man emotions was a disaster. I had no choice but to order my an-droid opposite to self-destruct. I now know where I went wrong in her programming and how to ensure a better balance between android logic and human emotional behavior, which is why I am ready and capable of installing emotional intelligence in the Group of 5."

Randolph just listened as she revealed the information the Group of 5 gave her regarding the various members of the scien-tific team on board the *Benevolence,* incorporating, where neces-sary, Dr. Granger's psychological profiles of these scientists. She also revealed the report from Gordon, regarding the transfers of command, and Milhouse's use of a robot to carry the voice registrations necessary to activate the android opposites of each member of the scientific team, making it possible to override the prescribed procedure."

"But why?" Randolph asked.

"I believe he was not creating a back-up system in the event one or more of the scientists died during the voyage, making it impossible for the android opposite to be activated, but was preparing to take command at some point during the voyage." She sighed.

"And, if one of the scientists died..."

"I had already provided back-up systems." She interrupted him. "What he did was a major breach of procedure, motivated by personal gain."

Randolph sat silent for a few minutes, milling all this information round in his mind, before replying. "But, you are assuming, Dr. Reinhart, that the Group of 5 will not join forces with these other androids."

"There is a risk, but it is a calculated risk. One can never be absolutely certain of anything. But the human opposites of the Group of 5 were the "*crème de la crème*" of my scientific team. They did not regard the other scientists as their equals. So it is highly unlikely that the Group of 5 will take orders from the android opposites of former, less prestigious scientists. But, if I am wrong, I do have my safety valve--my ability to dispose of any and all of the members of the Group of 5 by activating the virus. Knowing that their future is in my hands, they will have no choice but to remain faithful to me."

"I hope you are right." His voice barely audible.

"I am confident that I am." She replied adamantly.

"So, I guess that we better enjoy exploring the northern hemisphere. It will be a vacation compared to what we will be facing later." His voice crackled under a weak laugh.

"There is something else that I want to share with you and Pamela." He nodded and I acknowledged her on a cerebral level.

"I could not care less about exploring the eastern region and collecting animal and plant life. I am exploring it for another reason." She said. "There is a high mountain at the outskirts of the Boreal forest region. My satellites—the ones that only I can track, as I have not given the access codes to all my camouflaged satellites and other interstellar objects to John or others."

She stopped for a second to let that sink in, before adding, "I have detected a vibrant source of energy, perhaps nuclear, in the interior of that mountain. When we get to that region I shall ask you, Drager, Miller, Diana and Flanders to accompany me, no one else." I felt her disappear inside of me.

"Do you know what she thinks is there...Pamela?"

"No—I have absolutely no idea what she expects to find."

"Can you take over? I need to rest a few minutes."

"Ok. I like flying." A quick glance confirmed that he was already leaning back in his seat, his eyes half closed. "Are you ok?" I asked.

"I am worried now. Worried about us, here on Earth, and very worried about Peter, Frederic and Stuart. I hope that all of our enthusiasm about meeting and working with the crew and scientists on board the *Benevolence* is not going to turn into the worst nightmare of our lives!" His voice bursting forth.

"Don't be so dramatic, Randolph," I said, while keeping my attention on flying the plane. "Elisabeth has analyzed the problem from all possible angles and is ready to confront the worst scenarios. The only thing that will be a surprise for her is that there are no problems at all, with the humans or the android opposites, and that we can work together in peace and harmony."

Chapter 8: Passing Over

Drager and the Commander rushed towards us, welcoming us with friendly handshakes, before escorting us through the arrival terminal. I felt Reinhart's energy mount as she replaced me, marching forward holding my head high and my body straight, as she glanced from time to time out of the corner of my right eye at the rank and file android pilots, acknowledging us with ceremonial bows, as we passed in front of them.

When we reached the entrance to the Center, Drager pointed to the various containers that housed the 30 exoskeleton suits that Reinhart had requested.

"There are other things at this center, besides what you ordered, that might be useful for your expedition." Drager commented.

"For instance?" Reinhart queried.

"Parachutes, gliders, surveillance and combat UAV's, drones, and..."

"Add whatever you think is necessary." Reinhart interrupted him. "But as some of the drone series are heavy and rather bulky to transport, give priority to the smaller ones, like the surveillance and reconnaissance UVA series, rather than the combat series." She hesitated. "I created a special series that could track and rescue injured humans. They were very efficient."

"Yes, I know which series you are referring to and will provide at least 6 of these drones for each of the two different regions."

"Perfect" she replied. "Randolph and I are going to leave you now and will meet you later in the lounge."'

When we were out of the androids' hearing range, Randolph spoke. "They seem to be very cooperative—something that always makes me a bit nervous."

"I think that everything is fine," I replied in my soft, musical voice.

"I am glad that you are back, Pamela," He grabbed my hand in his. "Where are we going?"

"I don't know." I giggled nervously. "She is leading." I said, making it clear that I was only watching and learning like him.

We jumped into a motorized cart and sped off, traveling miles, past spacecraft and equipment. As I had no idea where we were going, I thought that perhaps she wanted to inspect, for the umpteenth time, those small space vehicles launched from the *Benevolence*, but when we got close to that unit, she veered off sharply to the right, stopping in front of a small alcove and instantly disappearing inside me. I jumped out of the cart and rushed to the back wall. With Randolph by my side, we leaned against it and passed through, arriving in a pitch black inner circle.

"What is this place?" Randolph's voice echoed in the hollow.

"I don't know. Be patient. She will be back. She must be searching her memory for more details." I clutched at Randolph's hand.

"Ok, I am back," Reinhart surged, taking charge. "Stand still and watch." She reassured us, before she gave a simple command, her voice tone, coming through loud and clear. "All Systems Activate."

Bright lights danced off the circular walls reflecting this vast space. I felt minute, next to a monstrous metallic structure, rising high above the cloud cover.

We advanced slowly, until we were close enough to touch the control panel, when Reinhart shouted, above the noise. "It survived the explosion! Now, everything will be fine!"

"What is it?" Randolph's voice trailed off.

"It is the largest spacecraft ever built." She breathed deeply. "It is larger than our Center. It is amazing that it is still intact." Her voice returned to its normal calm. "As you can see, only the launch pad is part of the Center's foundation. The vessel itself is encircled with high, protective panels that will lower automatically when the vessel is launched," she continued without taking a breath, "It was built to resist any form of space debris like asteroids or meteorites, temperature and speed variations, wormholes, and more, while maintaining a healthy living environment for humans, when traveling light years away at accelerated warp speed."

"So, it is bigger than the *Benevolence*?" Randolph's voice rose to a high pitch.

"Yes, much bigger, more powerful and more technologically

advanced. It was constructed hundreds of years after the *Benevolence* was launched." I was drowning in all the information that she was transmitting to me. "But there are improvements and vital changes that must be made before it can be launched." There was a long silence. "I need the right help to accomplish this."

"Us humans and the Group of 5 are not enough?" Randolph lashed out at her.

"Unfortunately, No!" She burst out in a loud chuckle. "But we must leave now," she said calmly.

The systems deactivated under her command and we struggled to find our way back to the wall. I found myself in the driver's seat of that the motorized cart. I was not as practiced as she, so it took longer for us to return to the meeting place.

"You were gone for a long time. We were concerned," Drager said, as he rushed towards us. "Come and relax."

"We put everything on board the aircraft," the Commander commented. "We placed the same number of exoskeletons, drones and other equipment, for camping, protection, and so forth for use in the eastern and western regions. And to make it easier for final cargo transfer onto the aircrafts leaving for the eastern and western areas, we loaded the various cargo in equal numbers, on the left and right hand side of your cargo plane." He hesitated. "But, with all the extra equipment, we did not have any space for the androids you requested, Dr. Reinhart."

"That is not a problem, Drager can have them put on his aircraft," she commented. "Your efficiency is very much appreciated."

"If there is anything else that you need, let us know." Drager hesitated. "I didn't know that I was part of the exploration team."

"Your presence for the exploration of the Eastern region is mandatory."

"But..."

"The Commander is perfectly capable of managing this Center in your absence. And I want you to be part of my team."

He nodded obediently.

"When do you want me to arrive at the Center?" Drager queried.

"I want you and 10 planes equipped with sleeping compartments large enough for the reptilian humans, along with the requisite number of android pilots, crew and explorers to arrive late tomorrow." She replied as we boarded the aircraft.

"You are the pilot for the return, Randolph."

"Ok, Pamela, that is fine for me. I too like flying!" We both burst out laughing, not because what he said was funny but because laughing with Randolph was the best way to unwind.

The members of the Group of 5, standing at attention, were waiting for us when we arrived. I detected no marked changes in their behavior, at least not physically, as they were standing very straight, with squared off shoulders.

Reinhart left the Group of 5 to supervise the moving of cargo onto the planes leaving for the western and eastern regions. She told them to meet her afterwards for the downloading of their emotional intelligence.

Reinhart then left me on my own, while she entered into her private section of my brain to make a final check on the emotional intelligence of each member of the Group of 5. And, astonishing as it always was, I was not in any way adversely affected, I could continue to be myself, interact naturally and solve problems, because she knew how to occupy another space in my cerebrum.

"I am back." Reinhart returned rapidly. "I have verified everything. I shall take you one at a time to Edward's office and install the program." She informed the Group of 5, standing at attention, like statutes.

For unemotional androids, they gave me the impression that they were more worried than pleased with the changes that Reinhart would make. Admittedly, I felt a wave of self-satisfaction perfuse me, as they finally revealed the kind of behavioral change that I was searching for earlier.

"I have a question." Flanders broke the silence. "How will these various emotions present themselves?" He made a gurgling sound like he was clearing his throat. "I mean, could we shut down because the surge of emotions will break down our existing system?"

"Are you afraid?" Asked Reinhart, a touch of levity in her voice.

"Of course not!" He protested. "I don't know what being afraid is. But, we," he looked at his colleagues, "are, let me say, curious, about how the emotional configurations will evolve."

Elisabeth, controlling my body, turned my eyes on the Group. "Your logical android system will filter, if you like, the emotions, keeping your logical side in control."

"So, we will not become human?" They replied in unison.

"Of course not. You are machines!" She replied in an agitated tone. "But having the emotional configuration of your human opposites will make it possible for you to better understand humans—interact more naturally with them—and help us to defend ourselves against the android opposites of my scientific team that were on board the *Benevolence*, should that be necessary." She drew a deep breath. "I do not know how long it will take for your cognitive emotional processing to develop, so I shall keep you all under close observation."

She took a deep breath "This, of course, is an experiment. If it does not work out, I shall shut you down. The shutdown could be permanent, so if anyone of you would prefer to stay as you are, let me know now."

They formed a tight huddle, as if discussing a secret game plan, their voices barely audible.

"I hope that they decide not to go through with this!" Randolph's voice sounded the alarm and Reinhart scoffed.

"Who do you want to go first, Dr. Reinhart?" The former governor asked, as they all moved back into a straight line.

"I shall start with you," she said. Randolph followed us into Flanders' old office.

She carried out the same procedure for each of them. Before downloading the program, she showed respect, asking the android to shut down. In each instance, she corrected the android's programming errors, the cause of certain erratic behavior in each individual android system. She upgraded their performance and verified the accuracy of the emotional program specific to a given android before uploading it. She double-checked everything, paying close attention to proper installation of the emotional program, before ordering the android to reactive.

"I don't notice any change in their behavior." Randolph's brows furrowed.

"It will take time for their different personalities to develop. But you have already been privy to certain differentiating behavior because of their fragmented emotional configurations. So you will not be surprised—yes, that is the word, surprised—by their behavior. But you will hopefully be happy to see that their behavioral differences are more refined and that they will be more enthusiastic about working with you, with all of us, for that matter."

"I hope that you are right, Dr. Reinhart."

"You are a skeptic, like your biological father. I find that rather amusing."

"You know, Dr. Reinhart, you did not tell the others that you were giving the Group of 5," he paused, "their emotional intelligence."

"I know. I shall tell them over dinner."

"This was a breach of protocol. They will be upset."

"Interesting," she replied, in a hollow, distant tone. "Perhaps I bring the Murdoc out in you." She turned and left the room, Randolph following close behind.

The Group of 5 stood behind their table awaiting our arrival.

"We have noticed no change." Crawford spoke for the group.

"That is normal. The changes will come with time, catalyzed by different situations, problems and whatever." She stood observing them for an instance.

"We are leaving now," she motioned to the Group of 5, "so be vigilant. Keep me informed of any problems that you find in your system or the system of one of your colleagues." They nodded.

"Reinhart wants to tell you all something very important. Please do not interrupt her before she has finished."

I backed aside and let Reinhart give them the story, the same story that she had recounted to Randolph.

"I am ok with this, Dr. Reinhart." John began. "Actually I have never been comfortable with the messages that we received from the *Benevolence*, but I could not put my finger on the reason why. Now, what you said about that possible change of command from humans to android opposites makes sense to me. And, quite frankly, we have been working well with the Group of 5. Having the loyalty of their human opposites inside of them will take a lot of pressure off of me; but, of course, that is if the human opposites' personalities and emotional intelligence will dominate."

75

"You probably should have mentioned this to us first—protocol." Ferdinand's voice quivered slightly. "But I can understand that it was a decision that only you, Dr. Reinhart, were competent to make."

"And what if they enter into a stage of, what you called 'irrational madness'? How are we going to control them?" Mathilda asked, in a dull, clinical voice.

"You just notify me and I shall either erase the programming or shut them down."

Reinhart's energy effaced as she retreated and I found myself alone, patiently awaiting other questions, but no one said anything. I fidgeted and took deep breaths, signaling all of them that Reinhart had disappeared inside of me.

"Perhaps you need time to think about this. We can discuss your concerns tomorrow, if you like. We will be meeting early, I believe," I looked at Ferdinand, who nodded, "to finalize our individual preference for exploring the eastern or western region, before practicing with the exoskeleton suits."

"Actually, you told us that you would be taking Miller and Flanders with you to the Eastern region." Stanislas mentioned. "That means that only the former Governor will be with us here at the Center."

"Yes, that is right." Reinhart sent me more information concerning the composition of the different android exploratory teams so I could continue. "Crawford and Gordon will be accompanying the team leaving for the western region. The human Crawford and Gordon worked very well together, no animosity between them, like we have witnessed with their android opposites. And the former Governor will be at the service of those of you remaining at the Center. His human opposite was an excellent team player and a very brilliant scientist so," I continued, "she believes his presence will be very useful to all of you," I added.

We sat in silence for a good 15 minutes, before one by one we split up and left for the inner circle.

"Well done, Dr. Reinhart!" Randolph said, as he applauded her performance.

"She is resting, Randolph," I replied.

"Of course, she is avoiding conflict. She does that regularly." He said, knowing that this would provoke her.

She surged inside of me, replying in a playful, yet soft, seductive tone. "Randolph, based on my personal experiences, the truth is often times the best form of manipulation. You can agree or disagree, but at least think about it."

We walked slowly down the corridor until we reached the wall and entered into the inner circle. Randolph turned me abruptly in his direction, his eyes piercing mine.

"What is the matter with you, Randolph?" I stuttered.

"I am worried, Pamela. I told you that earlier. Things are going too fast. I didn't have time to react. She took control of you and me. We just let her do what she wanted. Even the others did not contest her decisions. Well...Ferdinand made a weak attempt."

"Perhaps because everyone, except you, believes that she is making the right decisions."

"Maybe. But maybe not." He ventured.

"What is really bothering you, Randolph?"

"I don't know. I want to think that it is the Group of 5, but I am not certain that I am worried any more about them. We have gotten much stronger and she could always deactivate them." He paced in front of me. "I think it is her references to Murdoc." He stopped and turned his boldly glaring eyes in my direction. "She constantly compares me to him."

"From what she has disclosed in conversations over the years, I do believe that she misses him. Perhaps she wants to believe that she can find whatever compelling force Murdoc had over her, in you."

"That is as good an explanation as any, Pamela." He ran his fingers through his disheveled, long hair. "I need to get some sleep. Perhaps everything will be clearer tomorrow." He gave me a quick kiss on my forehead and headed to his room. Mathilda was certainly waiting for him.

I turned in the direction of my bedroom. Images of Peter and Frederic passed through my mind. I shivered as I thought about the danger that Reinhart imagined was awaiting them.

I dashed out of the bedroom, passed through the wall, and sprinted at high speed to the control room. Crawford and the former Governor were there.

"Are you ok...Pamela?" Crawford asked, his voice replete with a soft, melodic ring of kindness and concern.

"I don't know." I rushed to the controls. "But I need to know."

"No, Pamela, do not contact the *Benevolence*!" The former Governor exclaimed.

"They have already passed over," I thought to myself, as I stepped back.

"Come with me." Crawford said, as he gently took my hand in his. "Your family—Peter, Frederic and Stuart—are still in a cryogenic state. It will be months before they arrive." And then, as if he were reading my mind, he added, "You will have time to rescue them and we shall be by your side."

Neither his words, nor the tears that were gushing from my eyes, turned my fear into calm. It was only when I felt Crawford's arms move around me that my trembling body found solace. I laid my head on his shoulder, cuddling up against him as he pulled me with him into a large, comfortable chair, where I closed my eyes and fell into a deep sleep.

Chapter 9: Ingenuity

"Pamela." I felt someone lightly stroking my arm. I responded by slowly opening my eyes. "I believe that it is time for you to enter your inner circle, before your colleagues awaken." Crawford spoke.

"I want to apologize…"

"There is nothing to apologize for. We are, as we have always told you, your faithful servants." His eyes reflected a worrisome sparkle.

An air of self-satisfaction enveloped me when I entered the dining room, alive with vibrant conversation and impromptu laughter.

"I ran into the former Governor today," Benjamin commented, as I took the seat across from him. "You know he was walking with his arms swinging naturally from his side, whistling a rather upbeat tune." His eyes met mine. "Don't ask me if I recognized the name of the song or the composer. That is outside my field of competence." He snickered.

"Interesting," Ruth jumped in. "I had an unusual experience as well this morning. I passed by Miller who was swinging her arms and hips, in girlish fashion. I actually stopped and rubbed my eyes. She noticed my reaction and waved to me."

"They've passed over into our world." I said, as I slowly turned my spoon in my cereal bowl.

"So, their human opposites were nice and friendly scientists?" Eunice asked.

"No!" Reinhart, surging inside of me, protested. "I don't think that this kind of conduct will continue, because their human opposites were very much like me." Heads slumped involuntarily. "Well, perhaps a bit more cordial and friendly than you think that I am," she added sweetly, without sarcasm.

"I guess that it is time for us to leave for the meeting." Ferdinand stood up.

I looked at my half-eaten bowl of cereal and put my spoon down.

"I shall be with you all in a few minutes, I just want to stop by and see Rhea."

"I'll go with you, Pamela," Randolph offered and I nodded.

"No problem." Ferdinand called out. "We shall wait until you both arrive to have any serious discussions."

"So, what do you think, Pamela?" he asked.

"About what?" I raised my voice an octave.

"About the Group of 5?"

"Their emotional configurations are only just settling in. It is rather nice, though, to see a bit of genuine warmth in their personalities."

"Yes, but that is not what we need." He scoffed in frustration. "We need them to save us, not entertain or patronize us!" He said, in a loud, bellowing voice.

"I understand your frustration, Randolph." I poked his side. It didn't make him laugh. "Reinhart just sent me a cerebral message. Their systems are in an emotionally confused phase and within the next few hours the real personalities and emotional behavior of their human opposites will appear."

"If not..."

"She will erase the programming and begin again." I interrupted him.

"So, what we are witnessing now is diametrically opposed to their real personalities?" He pushed for answers.

"I don't know. But, if she liked and trusted them, they must be very much like her." I stopped to collect my thoughts. "She even admitted that to the Group a few minutes ago."

"Yes and No."

"I think she only said that because she believes that no other human could be as logical and cold as she is. And she might be right." I pushed open the door and rushed to the artificial uterus.

"She is growing rapidly, Pamela," Randolph commented.

"Yes, you are right." I replied calmly, hoping to communicate only calm, warm feelings to my child. In only a few weeks, she was the size of a 5 month old fetus.

"Pamela, is she your child or Reinhart's?" His question slipped out so innocently that he quickly raised his hands in denial.

Satisfied that both of us were under Rhea's spell, Reinhart suffused me and she spoke. "Pamela is her Mother."

He took my hand in his and we walked slowly down the corridors to the conference room, where the others were seated.

Ferdinand opened the meeting reminding everyone that the departure date was rapidly approaching and that it was important we agreed on the composition of the exploratory teams for the two regions in the northern hemisphere.

"Everyone present today came to me over the last few days and gave me his or her regional choice. On the basis of your reasoned preferences, I compiled a list of team members for the eastern and western regions." He sat silent for a few minutes, letting our curiosity mount, before projecting the regional lists on the back wall, for us to study. "If anyone has any objection, now is the time for you to react."

His remark was met with smiling faces, for everyone agreed to the individual choices of others, which fortunately resumed in accordance with my preconceived preference. Clarence, Linda, Daniel, Jill, Leonard, Karen, Adam, Eunice, and Francis, along with Gordon and Crawford, under the leadership of Joseph, would explore the western region and Jason, Ludovic, Tirence, Rebecca, Diana, Randolph, Birch and Basil, along with Drager, Miller and Flanders, would explore the eastern region, under the combined leadership of Reinhart and myself.

WD and his son Weldon would fly to the Marine Center and join forces with the Captain and his crew. The ship would move meticulously up the coastal waters, stopping regularly for WD, Weldon and android divers to explore and collect ocean fauna and flora, arriving on schedule for a pre-determined rendezvous with Joseph's group.

"Is there anything else that anyone has to say?" Ferdinand asked.

"Yes, I would like to add something," I replied. "It is very important that all of us recognize that the slide shows and the educational tapes that Miller compiled and presented were her vision of what might be close to accurate versions of the northern hemisphere today. And, the appearances of life forms might match up to those that we either saw on the slides or later discovered in the educational tapes." I noticed that no one was smiling. "Naturally, we should all stay enthusiastic, but Cautious!"

"That is good advice," Joseph said. "We, reptilian-humans, are genetically modified creatures like WD. The difference between us and WD is that we have strong human sides and we received the same education as all humans. WD was educated to believe that humans, an inferior species, are nothing more than a rare delicacy!" His remark was met with uneasy laughter, fraught with diverse memories.

"And yet," he continued, "we had to learn how to accept, control and exploit our reptilian capabilities. The creatures that we will be encountering will be life forms that might or might not have any human DNA, and, like WD, could be mutants, carrying the genetic codes of different animal species." He stopped and stared at his reptilian hands and protruding claws. "They might be complacent, friendly, and curious, and they might be more ruthless and aggressive than their ancestors. And their cunning, combined with a desire to survive, could make them very dangerous predators."

"We shall keep in constant touch," I continued. "Detailed reports from both groups should be delivered to John every day." I looked at John. "You will provide the teams with the various updates and vital information. And I have assigned Jarrod and Fleming to our Center to help you."

"You know my son, Samuel, has been working very closely with me." He sighed. "Even though tempted to volunteer for one of the exploratory teams, he decided to stay here and continue to work with me. I think it is a good choice, for the moment." He announced, his eyes turning to Sarah, the mother of Samuel.

Without comment, I then turned back to the others, giving instructions. "You must make films, take photos and remember to collect samples of various forms of vegetation. Your objective is to carry out the same thorough, conscientious search of a given area, like we did when we were exploring the outskirts of our main center, the interiors of the other centers and, of course, the ocean environment. The androids will bring the samples back to the center for analysis." I hesitated an instance. "You should capture rather than kill animals, whenever possible."

"Ok, that is understood," Diana commented. "We should only kill an animal when there is no other alternative." She sighed. "Are you also inferring, Pamela, that we should not succumb to our carnivorous tendency?"

"Yes, that would be my preference," I replied, knowing not everyone was opposed to eating meat. "But taking into account different dietary preferences, I recommend that you flesh eaters try to control your carnivorous side, at least until you have confirmation from the scientists here in the center that the meat is safe to eat."

"One last point," I shouted over loud voices, "we must use the android scouts. They will clear out the zones and inform us of any visible or hidden dangers. They will also be our guides." Heads nodded.

"And the androids will program the drones, if we need them. So do not hesitate to use the drones. The androids will also set up camp and make certain that food and water are available." I let out a wisp of a sigh, before adding, "They are programmed to protect us."

"And for those of you going to the western region, Crawford and Gordon will make certain that the androids carry out their assignments. So you have nothing to worry about." I continued, under loud ruckus.

"I believe that it is time for you to test the exoskeleton suits?" Ferdinand looked at me and I nodded.

After the meeting, everyone rushed to the exit, pushing and shoving, as if the threshold of the conference room was a starting block for a race and an ensuing order of priority for testing the exoskeleton suits, which were distributed 15 minutes after our arrival.

I explained in detail how these ingenious suits functioned, so the 15 minute wait was a welcomed delay. "The exoskeleton suits have bio-readers in them and will adapt to your bodies. We can put on our tight, fitting body suits, like a second skin, before trying on the exoskeleton suits. Or we can put the suit over our naked body, which, admittedly, is my preference." I raised my eyebrows, expecting a response, but no one replied.

"These suits are going to reinforce and fortify your existing muscular system, while reducing stress on your skeletal system. They will also protect your organs and regulate their physiological performance."

"You will not feel," I continued, "any atypical stress on your heart, lungs, kidneys, and other organs, when you exert your muscles, because the suit will, for example, automatically maintain proper, slow and regular heartbeat and breathing, while adjusting other organ functions accordingly."

I had their attention. "In addition, you will be able to lift, climb, pull, drag, and leap, without feeling any strain on your body. Your physical force will be greater than usual and your durability will be preternatural. The suit will also react to protect your bones, in the case of a fall, converting into a durable, but flexible, safety cushion encasing your body."

"The helmet is not bulky. It will, like the suit, adjust to your head size. It will cushion and protect your skull in a fall and adjust sounds, preventing inner ear problems, as well as regulating your equilibrium. It will also protect the neck region, preventing disk or bone damage."

"The visor on the helmet will adapt to different forms of light, like white and infrared, and levels of luminosity, automatically making it possible for you to see in very dark or very bright zones, preventing damage to the optic nerve and the retina."

"The gloves and boots that go with the outfit should be worn at all times. They will protect your hands and feet from injury while augmenting their performance."

I heard the androids arrive and turned towards them. I asked them to open the containers and distribute the suits. "The suits will be distributed according to your height and weight. It is important that you use the same suit each time, because the suit will be programmed for your system. To simplify procedure, when you give the suit back to the androids, the androids will register the suit in your name."

"Wait!" Joseph shouted in a deep voice, bringing everyone to a quick stop. "What about us?"

"There are enough extra-large suits for all the reptilian humans, but I am not certain that you really need them." I lowered my eyes to avoid their stares. "Your reptilian skin, or scaly carapace, and overall skeletal-muscular systems provide you with greater force and protection than purely human anatomical and physiological systems."

"I have a tingling sensation in my body." Joseph replied. "I believe we will have to wait until we are on the outside to put these suits to the ultimate tests.

We spent hours in the sports center, testing our skills before leaving for a late lunch. In spite of the fact that the suits increased our performance, protected us from erratic physiological behavior and prevented injury, it did not suppress, rather stimulated our hunger. Famished, we stacked layers of food on our plates and, without savoring a single bite, devoured the contents.

I felt someone coming up behind me and turned rapidly. The Group of 5 had entered from the back door. "We would like to see you, Dr. Reinhart, for a few minutes."

"Let's return to your office," she said with a slight smile, dissimulating my staccato thumping heart.

Once inside the office, Flanders opened the conversation. "We are back in control, Dr. Reinhart."

"What does that mean?"

"The emotional configurations of our human opposites are now under control."

"And what does that mean?"

"It means, Dr. Reinhart," Gordon weighed in, "that our purely logical sides are predominant."

"I see," she replied, in a mocking tone.

"It is true, Dr. Reinhart." The former Governor protested. "We were very much aware of the emotional intelligence of our human opposites, which in the first 12 hours, was so intoxicating that it was definitely controlling our every move, emasculating our normal logical reasoning. But we were eventually able to disassociate our rational intelligence from the emotional intelligence."

"How did you do that?"

"Actually we didn't do it on our own." He replied ardently. "You did it for us, Dr. Reinhart. Your programming is perfect. We are not slaves to any emotional intelligence or personality traits of our human opposites, rather we have the ability to judge the lucidity of integrating and processing our human opposite's emotional intelligence."

"But simply judging the lucidity of integrating emotional intelligence could be an emotional rather than a logical decision."

"Yes, Dr. Reinhart, there will always be the risk that a final decision might be the integration of all or some aspects of the emotional intelligence of our human opposites, but with your program, we will at least recognize that." Flanders picked up the discussion.

"The android opposites of the human scientists on board *the Benevolence* have a less refined programming incapable of delineating and excluding purely emotional aspects of a decision," Flanders continued. "They are probably acting more like humans than androids, by unknowingly mixing emotions with pure logic. It is a common, irritating problem that we have come to refer to as "human irrationality.""

He scratched the top of his head brusquely. "It is rather difficult to articulate this emotional/logical reasoning, so I shall try again," he commented. "The emotional intelligence is a reservoir of experiences that instinctively produce a given physical or mental reaction. Emotional intelligence could be referred to as subliminal reasoning as humans are neither aware of its existence nor its impact upon their decisions."

"And," he raised his index finger to keep Reinhart's attention, "just to reassure you, even if one of us could digress, bypass your programming and thereby act with human irrationality, the rest of us would recognize that there was a system breakdown and contact you directly."

"So you believe that my programming is effective enough to prevent you from—how did you say that— acting with human irrationality?" she asked mockingly.

"Dr. Flanders was not referring to you, Dr. Reinhart, when he mentioned 'human irrationality.'" Miller replied.

"Have you had any news from Colonel Shannon?" She disappeared and my eyes settled on the former Governor, as my face muscles twitched in nervous anticipation.

"No." He replied in a soft voice. "Don't worry. Everything is going to be fine."

I raised my eyebrows unwittingly. "I'll try not to worry, but it won't be easy," I finally replied, before I left.

I wandered aimlessly through the corridors, before going back to the birth center to spend a few minutes with my daughter.

I stood observing her beautifully formed body and the contours of her face, imagining the sublime eyes of a brilliant scientist and the full lips of a seductress, when I was again hit with the size and maturity of my child. Visibly, she was in her sixth month of gestation, something that was impossible even with the Center's time warp, the distortion occurring in the flow of time, at this center, moving events from one time period to another. I thought.

"Yes, this time-space displacement was the result of the Dooms Day Explosion," I spoke out loud.

I looked at the monitor and read her weight at almost 2 pounds and her length at 12 inches. I noticed that her wrinkled skin was taking on a reddish color and her veins were visible through her translucent skin. I could even see her finger and toe prints and noticed her eyelids trembling, as she struggled to open her eyes. I stepped away from the artificial uterus, emotionally separating myself from my child, who, for a moment, frightened and confused me.

"Why didn't I notice all of this when Randolph was with me?" the thought passed through my mind at the same instance that I felt Elisabeth's energy rising inside of me.

"Listen to what I am going to tell you and try to control your emotions. You will need time to think...rationally." She said in a soft voice.

Just hearing her words sent my heart racing. "I shall try."

"The Group of 5 removed the birth control from your food, months before my metamorphosis terminated." She began, as strong emotions swelled inside.

"They knew that you and Randolph were having, let's say, casual sex." She hesitated. "A passive observer, I know that it is only recently that you have come to realize that you feel more than just friendship for him." Her cerebral message stopped, giving me the time to calm myself and sit down.

"Today, my child, you know that your feelings for Randolph bind you to him, but you are also emotionally and physically bound to Peter."

I jumped off my stool, toppling it, and stumbling as I tried to gain my equilibrium. "It is your fault!" I protested. "You loved his father, and it is you who wants him for yourself, through me, because he is the closest you can get to Murdoc." I continued, as I struggled to hold back my tears.

"You are right, Pamela, that my affection for Murdoc is probably very close to what humans define as love. But you are wrong about a hidden desire inside of my consciousness to reproduce with him, through Randolph. I am not like you or any other human, for that matter. I have no natural desire to reproduce, and was not destined to do so. My origins and my existence are different from yours."

She paused, allowing me to absorb that, then proceeded: "The Group of 5 was searching for ways to bring me back and they finally decided that if you became pregnant I would have to return to protect you and the baby." I felt a strange breeze pass through me, like a long-winded sigh. "I could not interfere with your organs, prevent a pregnancy, because my metamorphosis was imperative and imposing."

"The only thing that I could do was prevent you from realizing that you were pregnant by focusing your thoughts on me and on scientific projects." She continued.

"When I returned, I waited for the right moment to signal your pregnancy to you by introducing an early sign of pregnancy, or morning sickness. But you were already at the end of your third month." She paused again, then continued.

"Much as I was against the decision of the Group of 5 on the issue of procreation, it served us, because it became a valid reason why you could not accompany Peter. Neither Peter nor anyone else, especially those on board the *Benevolence* could contest the lucidity of your decision to remain on the planet Earth."

"What you do now is up to you. You can tell Randolph that he is the father or you can keep the secret. I will surrender to your will because this issue of pregnancy and paternity does not really interest me," she scoffed. "Nonetheless, you might want to confront the Group of 5 on this issue. This will remind them that you are not a puppet and it will give me the opportunity to study their use of emotional intelligence."

I sat for a long moment, stunned by the absurdity of my situation. Reinhart answered the question that was bothering me:

Could I love 2 men with the same intensity? I conceded to the truth. Whether my child was fathered by Peter or Randolph really made no difference, because I honestly believed that I loved them both with the same intensity. But did I have the right to keep this my secret?

I smiled at my little girl, before leaving to confront the Group of 5.

When I entered their office they were relaxing, with their feet on the table top and their arms folded behind their heads. I cleared my throat and Crawford signaled me, with a slight gesture of his hand, to join them.

I grabbed a chair and sat down, my hands placed visibly on the table top. They quickly took the same position, their eyes focused on mine.

"How is everything going?"

"Nothing new since we met earlier, Pamela." Gordon replied. "We were, as you noticed, relaxing. We have had a lot of work lately and needed time out." Her eyes scanned her colleagues. "We have no immediate assignments and are waiting for you to give us the departure date."

"Who is the father of Rhea?" I asked, going straight to the point.

"Peter, of course." Flanders replied.

"Strange that you feel comfortable avoiding the truth so easily." I said, briefly looking away.

"Ok, you want the truth." Miller said, her voice rather scratchy, showing her irritation.

"We wanted Dr. Reinhart to return, not just for your safety, Pamela, but for the well-being of the Center." I nodded. "Yes removing the birth control from your diet was rather vicious. But, it was a rather logical and effective way to send a message to Dr. Reinhart."

Her eyes met mine, with harsh, android brightness forcing me to lower mine. "We believed that this would be the least radical method of assuring her return, but it did not work, the reason why we eventually resorted to another way of reaching her."

"You knew I was pregnant?" I asked the Group.

"I didn't know it before you came to see me." Flanders admitted. The others raised their hands as if it was something they didn't care much about. "I did not notice anything different about you physically—but then your physical appearance was, and still is, of no interest to me."

I turned to Gordon. "And, you—you did not recognize any change in me?" I asked, knowing that she could not deny having a physical interest in me.

"I probably should have." She answered, revealing her human opposite's smooth sense of diplomacy. "But our objective was not you, or your physical changes, if any, but rather the return of Dr. Reinhart."

"Dr. Flanders, why didn't you mention the exact age of the fetus when you removed my baby?"

"I wanted to avoid an issue," he replied. "And, Pamela, Dr. Reinhart knew. If she did not send you that information, it was logical that we should also keep it a secret."

"And if this had happened today, would you have told me?"

"I am speaking for all of us," the former Governor began, "we are members of Dr. Reinhart's team. We have sometimes disagreed on methods or projects, but we have always followed her decisions and leadership. So the answer is quite easy. No, we would not have told you. We might, though, have discussed it with her."

He leaned back in his chair, his eyes meeting mine, and added. "And, Pamela, you have to admit that our foolishness in precipitating your pregnancy was not based on nastiness but rather the well-being of everyone here at the Center. John had to be removed from office. And even if by inadvertence or stupidity, whichever you prefer, this pregnancy has saved you and Dr. Reinhart, and given you the time you need to implement an effective strategy to save humanity."

"Well, thank you for this insightful discussion," I replied, recognizing that the members of the Group of 5, even with access to emotional intelligence were still operating on a strictly logical level. "I hope that you will take good care of Rhea during my absence?"

"Are you going to tell Randolph that he is the father?" Miller asked, a glimmer of enthusiasm in her voice.

I hesitated an instance, questioning the reasonableness of revealing my own insecurity and inner concern. But they seemed different, less diabolical, perhaps because they were all using the natural voice tones of their human opposites, which, seemed pleasant.

"I don't know what to do. Dr. Reinhart has thrown that problem onto me." I hung my head.

"He has the right to know, Pamela." Flanders said.

"Oh, he will react like Murdoc." The former Governor replied.

"Meaning?" I asked.

"He loved Elisabeth. He would do whatever she wanted. If she asked him to keep the secret until the end of time, he would have done that."

"And you think that Randolph loves me, as if you know anything about love."

"I don't have to know what love is to recognize that he loves you," a light-hearted laugh spilling from Gordon's lips.

"I see that you are acting in human ways with sweet laughter and real or feigned concern," I commented.

"We believe that Dr. Reinhart will not be opposed to our using our human opposites' voice tones when engaging in conversation or even reflecting human emotional sounds by simulating, for example, pleasant forms of laughter."

Flanders then remarked, "Who parented which new member of our community is not the most paramount problem for the moment."

"Did you change the subject on purpose, Flanders?" I asked.

"No. These young children are our responsibility and it is so important to protect their futures." He fidgeted. "We must find competent people to replace us when we leave for the *Benevolence*." His eyes met mine. "We have to select androids to assist the humans here on Earth. We shall be absent for a long time," his voice quivering. "There is no time to waste. We have a lot of work to do."

"Yes, absolutely." Reinhart surged, replacing me. "I want you all to look for replacements." She hesitated. "This is a point I completely ignored. We absolutely need to ensure the security of this planet, so find the right people!" She ordered.

"We shall need to download our information into other androids. Just the information along with your original program to inhibit emotional development." He added. "What do you think, Dr. Reinhart?"

"Yes, that is an excellent idea. Now find the androids that we can program," she ordered.

"We shall let you know before you leave which ones we have chosen." Crawford called out to me, as I turned and left the room.

I only went a few feet before I ran into Randolph. "Where have you been, we have all finished dinner?" He asked. "If you want I can go back to the dining room with you—keep you company, so to speak."

"Yes, I am a bit hungry and could use some good company." I said, as I tapped him lightly on his cheek, realizing that I would have to make my own decision regarding Rhea.

Incredibly hungry, I concentrated more on my plate than on his interminable chattering about exploring the planet.

When I finished my plate, I broke into his conversation, informing him of what we had come to realize—the need to provide replacements for the Group of 5. His body stiffened. "How could we have overlooked this?"

I had no answer.

"The Group of 5 is right." He broke a long silence. "We must trust them, I guess. Actually we have no choice." He rambled. "They would never select androids that could or would replace them entirely, which is an excellent point. And Dr. Reinhart won't give the androids more information, scientific or otherwise, than they will need to work effectively and efficiently with our diversified community."

"There is one problem that I can foresee. Perhaps these androids should not be given any historical information regarding the programming of humans—well, everything that happened before the revolution. They will not be governing the Center but working as assistants for John and his team."

"Excellent!" My enthusiasm returned.

"Do you think that this can be done?"

"Do we have some time to arrange for all of this over the next 24 hours?"

"Yes, I believe that Reinhart will return soon with solutions—the type of programming to download, along with the safety values, in the form of viruses or blockers, to ensure the safety of our community here on Earth and assist us throughout our voyage in space."

"Let me know when this happens so that I can be present as well, Pamela." He proposed and I nodded.

"Anything else I should know, Pamela?" He asked, more out of politeness than inquiry.

"Yes." The word just slipped out, like someone was prompting me to speak.

"So?"

"I am not comfortable telling you this, Randolph." He sat back in his chair with his brows furrowed, his mouth in a smug half-smile, and his eyes focused, unwaveringly on me. I could feel my blood rush as anger and humiliation invaded me.

He waited until the silence annoyed him. "Are you going to tell me or not?"

"It is about Rhea."

"She is ok?" His voice shaking with concern.

"Oh, she is just fine." I lowered my eyes. "I have a story to tell you," I said, as I revealed the truth.

When I finished, his burst of hearty laughter was not what I was expecting. I covered my face to hide my tears. He moved rapidly to my side and took me in his arms.

"I am so sorry, Pamela. I was not laughing at the serious side of the situation, but rather the humorous, stupid efforts on the part of the Group of 5 to bring back Reinhart. It is amazing how unscrupulous they were in the past." He said, as his warm kisses and tender caresses calmed me. "There is nothing to worry about. I love you, Pamela. I loved you from the moment that I set my eyes on you. I promise to be there to cherish and protect you and my daughter, Rhea."

"But Peter?"

"What about Peter?"

"He thinks he is the father. How can I tell him? He is already slightly jealous of you and our relationship—which I have always defined as platonic." I stuttered.

He released me, his hands moving elsewhere, now, lightly scratching his chin. "Do you want me to keep the secret?"

"It might be the better solution." I murmured, as I turned my head to avoid his eyes.

He drew me back into his arms and whispered in my ear, "Then I shall keep our secret." His warm breath sent chills through my body, building waves of desire. That plaguing question: Could I love two men with the same intensity at the same time? The thought disappeared in his warmth as I clung desperately to him, seeking his strength and reassurance. "I love you, too, Randolph. Yes, I love you, Randolph, and believe that I always have."

"I know, Pamela. But, it is so nice to hear you say it!" His lips spread into a wide, glowing smile, for my expression of love freed him, raising him above the status of a friend and lover.

"Come, Pamela." He said, taking my hand in his. "I think that it is time for us to leave the dining room—before the clean-up crew arrives—and we do need to get some sleep?"

Chapter 10: Duplicity and Manipulation

I woke up early, with Randolph's arms firmly around me, holding me in place. I pushed and shoved until he finally stirred. "It is time to get up, Randolph, we have so much to do before we leave tomorrow."

"I am tired!" he groaned.

"I have to see WD off and meet with the Group of 5." I kissed him lightly on his lips and rushed off to take a shower.

I arrived just in time to say goodbye to WD and Weldon. WD promised me that he would keep a close eye on the Captain to make certain that his systems did not malfunction and would carry out his mission of exploring the coastal waters.

"You know, Pamela," he began, forcing his British accent, "I am going to surprise you with all my discoveries," he stopped abruptly, adding with a glimmer of concern in his voice, "and, I shall also protect my son."

His eyes rested unwavering on his son as he watched him enter into a medium-sized aquarium before moving towards his own. He stopped short and turned to me, his massive walrus-dolphin body in full view, towering high above me. "I was wondering if I could negotiate a small recompense for this mission."

"What might that be?" WD recognized Reinhart's accent and direct manner.

"Oh, Dr. Reinhart, I am so happy you are present to wish me success," he replied, moving into a less imposing sitting position. "Actually," he cleared his throat, like the word was blocking his vocal chords, "I," he stuttered, "was wondering whether you reviewed my request to have my female partner inseminated. My sperm was frozen by the Group of 5 for future use." His eyes drifted about in their socks.

"I do believe," he picked up, "that it is a reasonable request in view of the danger that I shall be facing on this new mission. And

I think that I have shown you that I can be very civilized and that I am a good father to my son." He hesitated before adding, "It would be sad if my species disappeared."

"Agreed," Reinhart replied in a dignified way, suppressing her laughter that I could feel building up inside of me.

'Yes', I thought, Reinhart laughs easily, at her successes, at danger, at what she considers to be human stupidities, yes, she laughs at life's many challenges. And, she does not cry or fret or worry like our generation of humans, because she knows she will find the right solution. She has told me on many occasions that she does not know fear. She can get angry with shortcomings, which she refers to as stupidities, but loves challenges. When she laughs, she laughs heartily, with loud, earth shakings screams. She even laughs at her achievements.' My eyes turned back to WD, who was awaiting her response.

"You will have another child ready to join you here at this center shortly after your return," she continued. "And I expect you and Weldon to return to the center, so please do not disappoint me." She didn't need to say more, because he knew that she would find him, if he tried to escape or hide, and even resuscitate him if he were being drawn into the arms of death.

"Well, we are off on a real adventure, Weldon!" He called out, his voice drifting on different frequencies, reminding me of the sonorous tones of the deep sea. "And we shall see you soon, Pamela." He recognized my gracious, delicate manner, as I waved goodbye.

He entered his aquarium. I watched as the androids lifted him and his son on board the plane. I then turned to the androids and asked them to make a final check of the aircraft and verify that the planes were properly loaded and ready to take off early the following day, before rushing off to catch up with Randolph, who was certainly on his way to meet with the Group of 5.

We entered together. I was pleasantly surprised by the breakfast that awaited us. Neither one of us had time to eat so this touch of human attention was very much appreciated by both of us. We ate as the former Governor informed us they had five androids from the elite series ready to be programmed.

"Randolph mentioned to me," I said between bites, "that perhaps we should avoid downloading any of the past history of human programming, revolutions, and so forth into these androids."

"Absolutely, they should only receive scientific information, along with all the inhibitory viruses that Reinhart prepared for downloading." Randolph replied. "The element of curiosity must be controlled, so it is imperative that all members of the community—human, genetically modified humans and mutants—rely upon these replacements of the Group of 5 for scientific assistance and nothing else. In other words, they should not confide in these androids."

"Agreed," Reinhart surfaced, entering the conversation. "But curiosity is a human trait, linked in great part to a competitiveness, embedded in emotional intelligence rather than logical, scientific reasoning. Normally this Group of 5 should not run astray in their scientific research. But be assured that my program will wipe out all residual personality traits or emotions that might interfere with their pure android logic today."

"Yes, that is what I am referring to, the fragmented personality traits that rendered us less efficient." Crawford replied, expelling a whiff of cold air.

"You do not have to worry. I am not arranging for permanent replacements for the 5 of you!" Reinhart replied, underlining the word replacements. "They will resemble Drager, Fleming and Jarrod in their manner of working and participating in projects, taking orders from their human supervisors. And in the future, they will be your support group."

"Are you ready to transfer our knowledge into these machines?" Flanders asked, going straight to the next point.

"I want to first download all the inhibitory viruses, and other, let's call them, system blockers, before downloading your intelligence."

"There is a slight problem, though, Dr. Reinhart." Gordon spoke up. "How will the community know which machine represents the different members of our Group."

"I understand your concern, because these androids will not have your physical characteristics, or, more precisely, those of your human opposite." Reinhart replied. "I did order android identification chains with the first initial of your names as a medallion. They were delivered to you this morning. Is there another option you prefer?"

"Oh, we did not open the box," Miller replied. "We thought that it was for you."

They quickly opened the box and examined the contents and unanimously opted for tattooing the first letter of each member's name in the neckline region, claiming the necklace could be removed by their replacements.

"But they will know which one of you they represent," Reinhart replied. "And personally I don't see why they would pretend to be someone else. Oh, if you prefer tattooing their identity then that is what you should do."

"Will they be wearing clothing, like us?" Gordon asked.

"As you know, they are the elite series that has very smooth skin with a soft human touch, a much better quality than the other series. And for future security reasons, I have not given them either your facial or physical features. They are machines! You are, and will remain, the android opposites of my human team!" Reinhart protested. "But if you want to put a robe on your replacement, feel free to do so." Reinhart would discover later that they all chose to put a robe on their replacement.

"Have you mentioned our replacements to the others?" the former Governor queried, pointing out a breach of protocol. Reinhart just scoffed.

"Where are they?" Reinhart asked and the Group of 5 led her to Flanders' old office.

"Ok, I want to register the scientific knowledge of each of you. You do not need to shut down for this. I have to first install the different programming I just mentioned into these machines. I shall call you one at a time for the installation of the scientific knowledge."

She flashed the programming through my mind for me to register for the future, while Randolph watched, stopping her from time to time, asking her to divulge the algorithms for future study, complaining that the sweeping visual formulae were too complicated for him to follow and understand. "Ok, but not now. I shall let you study the procedure later on—when we return form the exploratory mission."

"And the encrypted viruses?" He put pressure.

"Just try to follow what I am doing and stop looking for an easier way out. Use your brain!" she protested.

Randolph sat silently observing her and watching the machines begin to activate. "I shall be right back, Randolph," I said.

"Oh, it is you, Pamela, what a relief." He huffed, recognizing her voice. "She has no patience!" I nodded. "And I only understood 40% of what she was doing. And you?"

"She downloads the information into my mind and rapidly explains the procedures." I sighed. "It took time for me to assimilate and understand what she was rapidly downloading, but, after all these years as her symbiote, I catch on. I shall explain it to you another time."

I rushed back to the office of the Group of 5. "I'll be the first one," Gordon said, moving to the front.

We were back in Flanders' old office. Reinhart took over, hooking Gordon up to an intermediary computer terminal of sorts that looked incredibly complex, and even Gordon jumped back, balking at its design. "I am still active, Dr. Reinhart."

"Of course! I told you that you would not need to shut down!" She stated as she transferred scientific information so rapidly preventing Gordon from downloading any part of Reinhart's complex transfer of knowledge program.

"Finished. You can leave with your replacement, Dr. G.," Reinhart said.

"Are you sure that you transferred my scientific knowledge?" she asked, as she stayed glued to her seat. "My systems did not detect any form of interference."

"I know," Reinhart replied. "Please just leave now and ask the next member of the Group of 5 to come quickly."

"Oh, Dr. Reinhart, we have ordered one of the working class androids to bring us the products that we will need to tattoo our initials on our replacements." She added.

The 4 remaining members experienced the same rapid transfer of their knowledge banks and then returned one by one to the office they shared.

When Reinhart arrived, they were seated with their android replacements next to them. "I want you to take the rest of the day to verify the efficiency of the transfer." They nodded. "I know that you don't need me to engrave the tattoos." They nodded again. "I need to meet with the other humans—it is lunch time—and explain to them what I have done."

I stood up and started to leave when Gordon grabbed me. "I am a bit worried."

"That is your emotional intelligence speaking," I replied. "Sit back and get control of yourself. You want to make certain there is no programming error or malfunctioning in your replacement." Gordon hung her head.

"Think of it this way, Dr. Gordon." I spoke in a mellow tone. ""She is a reassurance of your continued existence because all your knowledge is now preserved, in safe keeping, inside of her. If anything happens to you, Reinhart can easily create an identical physical version of you, reintroduce your knowledge, history and emotional intelligence."

"You are right, Pamela," The Group of 5 said in unison. "We are eternal."

"Well done, Pamela," Randolph said, when we were in the corridor.

"You were very quiet, practically invisible during all this time." I poked him lightly in his side.

"She broke my spirit, early on." He sighed. "I thought that remaining discrete was a good approach."

"Pamela," Diana called out to me, as I was piling layers of vegetables on my plate.

"Pamela, I have a question." She persisted.

I sat down next to her, quickly observing, out of the corner of my eye, the faces of my colleagues observing me. "Ok, what is bothering you, Diana?"

"Are the exoskeleton suits insulated?"

"Oh, sorry that is a good question. I should have mentioned this earlier. When you are wearing them they will also adapt your body temperature to resist heat and/or freezing weather."

"That is what we thought," Joseph replied.

"Actually, I have something that I should have spoken to all of you about yesterday, but it was only late last evening that the Group of 5 brought this problem to my—rather Reinhart's—attention." Their eyes grew wide.

"Is it bad news?" Jason asked.

"No. It was an oversight." I drew in a deep breath of air to calm myself and clear my mind. "You know that 4 of the members of the Group of 5 are accompanying us on the outside." Heads nodded. "John, Sarah, Ruth, Samuel, Mathilda, Jonathan, Imogen, Ralph, Benjamin, Stanislas, Ferdinand, and other members remaining in the center will discover quickly that the absence of these members will cause certain organizational and research problems. Their knowledge and experience in running the center is something that we have taken for granted, because we unconsciously rely upon it."

"True," John replied in a low, pensive tone.

"So Reinhart had the Group of 5 select 5 androids from the elite series. She downloaded the knowledge bank of each member into their android replacement.

Before they could ask any questions, I quickly informed them that the historical and emotional intelligence was not downloaded into these replacements. "They will introduce themselves to you as Dr. G, F, C, M or V. Even though the former Governor will be here in the center, I have given him a replacement android, as well."

"Wow! A big change!" Diana moved to stand up.

"A necessary last minute decision," I replied firmly. "We need to preserve the knowledge banks of the Group of 5 and what better way to do that than to provide replacements. If something happens to one of them on the outside, Reinhart can recreate them. She also saved their historical information—much of which they have not shared with us—but did not download it into the replacements."

There is no reason for these replacements to be privy to the past." I stopped for a moment to organize my thoughts. "In fact no one should inform this new series of the past—programming humans, revolutions, etc. They will have access to all scientific information, but will not be capable of analyzing and determining how things evolved in a relevant past." I took a deep breath to calm myself.

There was a long silence. "We have worked with equivalents for a long time—Drager, Jarrod and Fleming, who have scientific knowledge and whose knowledge of historical events can be accessed by Reinhart, and Reinhart alone." I cleared my throat. "More importantly Reinhart will be able to shut these androids down, even at a long distance."

"She suggests that Dr. M work with Ralph and Iris in the agricultural unit and replace Diana in the marine biology center, where she can also call upon Doctors F and G for advice. Dr. C and Dr. G should continue to participate in behavioral science projects and in the medical and genetic science departments, alongside Benjamin, Stanislas, Ruth and Sarah."

"All of these android replacements," she picked up rapidly, "are excellent in the vast field of physics, especially Dr. C and Dr. V, so, John, you can use them when you need them."

I paused to let that sink in. "You will find that having two Dr. V's will take a lot of administrative pressure off of you, as they will be able to oversee the proper functioning of the center, assigning and supervising the various scientific projects."

"Well, I am in favor of it," John announced. "I did worry about how I was going to manage certain tasks all alone. And," his eyes met mine, "Flanders' replacement will be able to monitor your baby, Pamela. I know nothing about that." My heart raced, I had forgotten that very important detail.

"I would just add that Fleming and Jarrod can help me with assignments for the 5 replacements, as can the former Governor." I nodded and John's eyes turned to the others. "Should we take a vote?"

"I think we all agree that Dr. Reinhart made the right decision." Ferdinand replied. Heads nodded, some more enthusiastically than others, but no one objected. "If you are listening, Dr. Reinhart, would you please remember to include us in future decisions?"

I could feel her energy surface. "I hope that you will be diplomatic, Mother," I said on a cerebral level.

"Yes, Ferdinand," she began, "you are absolutely right. I have admitted on several occasions that I should have consulted all of you before making important decisions. In the haste of planning for the exploration of the planet, I overlooked several very important, rather critical things, necessary for the future survival of our community. I needed to act rapidly to find the right solutions to resolve these matters. I promise to protect each and every one of you, but, for that, I ask for your indulgence."

'She touched the right chord.' Passed through my mind, as I observed my colleagues, their expressions changing from tight-lipped concern to utter calm, as they sat in serene silence.

I finally broke their silence. "Dr. Reinhart would like to spend a few minutes alone with you, Ruth, before I go off to meet with Jonathan." I said, adding that I would like to speak to Mathilda later about the children.

"See you all tomorrow," Joseph said, as the others followed behind him.

I stood alone with Ruth. "I hope that she is not upset with me," Ruth said, as she concentrated on smoothing out the folds in her robe.

"Not at all, Ruth," Dr. Reinhart replied. "I want to restore your youth." Her words uttered, suppressed tears streamed down Ruth's face. "I have watched your relationship with John move from that of a man in love to that of a young man seeking maternal guidance. Is your present relationship the one that you want to keep, or do you prefer... youth?"

"You are also a woman, Dr. Reinhart, so you must know the answer." She said through sobs.

"Then I shall give you what I would most want," Reinhart replied. She asked Ruth to accompany her to the inner circle. We entered into the medical unit. She asked Ruth to remove her robe and then motioned to her to lie down on the examination table. "You have nothing to worry about." Reinhart reassured Ruth before beginning the process.

I could feel Reinhart's energy growing stronger and stronger inside, as she prepared to rejuvenate Ruth. I knew Reinhart had reached her final stage of metamorphosis months ago; and that my human physical characteristics camouflaged from the view of others her high level of cerebral energy flowing inside of her section of my brain. She no longer needed her rejuvenation machine. With Ruth's DNA logged in, she could restore Ruth's youthful appearance.

She asked Ruth to open to her eyes wide. I then felt a burning sensation in my eyes as Reinhart's energy entered Ruth's body, moving rapidly, scanning all her organs, her skeletal muscular system, her aging physical and neurological cells, preparing to make the right changes.

When she was ready to rejuvenate Ruth, I felt the intensity of Reinhart's energy rise inside of me, a terrifying heat and luminosity like a corporal supernova, until my body released a stream of white light, capturing my mind as I swirled helplessly in a world of cyberspace, struggling to keep up with my Mentor, as she reconstructed Ruth's body painlessly and rapidly.

This was the first time that Reinhart dragged my consciousness along with hers when she rejuvenated a member of our team. I knew that I could not duplicate the procedure and was more relieved than disappointed with this truth. And yet I was pleased that my mind did eventually catch up with Reinhart's, accompanying her as she entered Ruth's body, giving new life to what were aged cells and organs, boosting her memory, reinforcing her cognitive skills, and adding aesthetically beautiful finishing touches to create a youthful body.

Within minutes, a young, vibrant woman, with long thick, black wavy hair, bold deep brown eyes, a slim nose, and full lips stood in front of me.

"You look wonderful, Ruth!" I was unable to hold back my enthusiasm, as I gazed upon her, someone whose nature and beauty had fallen into obscurity, now restored, reborn, as she embraced a new cycle of life.

She turned to observe her reflection in the mirror before rushing towards me, throwing her youthful arms around me as she screamed, "Thank you, Dr. Reinhart."

"It was my pleasure, Ruth. Now hurry and find the man you love!"

She dashed out of the inner circle going straight in the direction of John's lab.

Reinhart was relaxing, so I left for the music room. I found Jonathan and Imogene practicing together. Like the other musicians, they rarely dined with our group and never participated in the meetings. Passive participants, reaping inspiration from their observations of the world around them, was what the musicians in our center seemed to prefer.

"Pamela, what a great pleasure to see you!" Jonathan jumped up, rushed towards me, picked me up and spun me around until I felt dizzy.

"I wanted to see you both before I left for the exploration of the eastern region." He gently put me down, a wave of nostalgia sweeping over me when my eyes took in the splendor of the stage and the orchestra pit.

"We could open the audio system. A bit of music might be appreciated," he said. "It could have a soothing, calming effect." He rambled.

"I am ready," I giggled, in a childish way. "What do you have in mind?"

"Your choice," he insisted.

It took me several minutes to choose among all the splendid musical scores that passed through my mind. "Ok," I finally replied, "but in this order: 'Für Elise' by Beethoven, followed by 'Rhapsody for Clarinet and piano, op. 167' by Claude Debussy, and last, but not least, 'Fantasia,' Op. 66, by Chopin."

"Excellent. Love it!" He rushed to the side wall. "I am going to announce our short concert over the audio system. Maybe some people will come." He wiped his hands nervously on his sleeves. "It has been a long time since I played Debussy's Rhapsody, but, well, hopefully, no one will notice my mistakes."

"It has been even longer since I played the piano!" I pretended to shutter, wiggling on my piano bench. "But, I am certain that we will do just fine."

Even though it was late, our colleagues were still awake and entered the auditorium within minutes of the announcement. My cheering section, the Group of 5, with their replacements following close behind, took their usual places, next to the orchestra pit. My fingers, caressing the keys of my piano, and my mind miles away, recalling the musical scores, I did not hear Jonathan announce our choices. When I did look up, he was bowing in my direction, his right arm and hand extended in a royal gesture of honor. My lips parted, moving upward into a very broad smile.

I felt so alive as my hands moved so naturally over the keys, revealing, certainly, my extraordinary talent and my love for this magnificent instrument. The chemistry passed between us and Jonathan and I did honor to Debussy's Rhapsody. At the end, we playfully bowed to our applauding audience that was screaming for more. We finally conceded, playing Handel's 'Sarabande' for piano, with Jonathan on the violin and Imogene playing the kettle drums. It was a good way to end the concert, inspiring lots of energy and enthusiasm.

"Well thank you all for coming." Jonathan shouted over the voices and applauds of our colleagues. "The next concert is after your return from the northern hemisphere."

"See you all tomorrow morning." I said, before I said goodbye to Jonathan and Imogene.

Mathilda caught me as I left the auditorium. "You wanted to see me, Pamela."

"Oh, yes, Mathilda. I wanted to ask you to look after my daughter, in my absence. I don't think I shall be back before she is born." I looked straight into her eyes. "I know that I can trust you to take good care of her."

"Of course, Pamela. I shall protect her as if she were my own." We walked a few minutes together, before she broke the silence. "I saw Ruth. She looks fantastic and John is chasing after her, like in the good old days!"

"You will be ok, Mathilda?" I asked.

"Oh, Pamela, you don't have to worry about me. I shall find comfort with someone." She said, as she broke out into spontaneous laughter, catchy enough that I joined in. Randolph was waiting for me when we passed through into the inner circle.

"Wow, I didn't expect to see the two of you together." He said in a hoarse, throaty voice.

Mathilda did not seem to notice his anxiety, or decided to ignore it, preferring to rush into his arms and pull herself close up against him. "Let's go have some fun together, Randolph. It is going to be awhile before I see you again." She said, loud enough for me to hear.

Even though Randolph certainly saw my mouth drop open, I maintained a detached calm when I spoke. "Have fun! See you both tomorrow morning!"

"She needs him." I consoled myself. "And I should make one last visit now to see my little girl."

I turned away from them and continued down the corridor until I arrived at the right exit point for the birth center. She was sleeping. I closed my eyes, imagining my baby inside of me and my hands gently moving up and over my large belly, connecting with her. But I knew that the softness of my touch and the sweetness of my voice was being projected to my child by an elaborate machine. I could feel tears welling in my eyes.

"I hope, my child, that when I return you will recognize the loving tone in my voice and the comforting firmness of my touch which, today, only lightly stirs the serenity of your tiny world."

"There is always tomorrow!" Repeated over and over again in my mind, as I reluctantly walked away.

Chapter 11: Startling Discoveries

The exploration teams met in the transport unit, dressed in military fatigues, with a laser gun slung over our shoulders. "We look more like soldiers than explorers," crossed my mind.

"Remember we are on pacifistic missions!" I shouted over all their loud ruckus, and their heads turned in my direction. "Capture and collect, rather than kill and destroy, new life forms!" I pleaded.

"Understood!" Their unreserved enthusiasm shining through.

"Reports at the end of each day," I added.

Our members divided into the assigned group and entered into their respective aircraft. I was in the pilot seat with Randolph and Drager as co-pilots. Androids would pilot the aircraft for the second team, with Francis in the position of alternative co-pilot. Other android pilots, as well as the vast number of android crew, were in charge of the safe passage of the cargo planes, helicopters and smaller aircraft.

All the survival equipment, as well as vehicles, like dune buggies and land rovers, and other supplies, including tents were on board the cargo planes. Reinhart had forgotten nothing. She had even programmed the aircraft with the proper air routes and the landing sites to be visited and explored, one after the other, over the next month or so.

I had never piloted such a large aircraft and felt ill-at-east in the pilot seat. I turned to face Randolph. "We are off!" I shouted.

Even though clear skies accompanied us throughout a major part of the flight, I had to pass the aircraft over to Drager or Randolph from time to time, to relax a bit. I was in the pilot's seat when we got close to our destination, which turned out to be a good decision, for if we continued the violent fluctuations of air pressure on the outside would have forced us off our course.

Reinhart finally surfaced inside of me, as she took over, steadying the aircraft and bringing it down, in a rather dramatic landing, as the plane bucked, throwing us forward in our seats, before losing velocity, as she sent it spinning in large circles over the icy tundra. When it finally came to a halt, we waited on board for the cargo planes to land.

It was late in the day so I suggested that we put on our thermal suits and helmets, made for artic conditions, and stretch our legs.

"We shall go first." Miller spoke up. "We have adjusted our systems to withstand the cold and will send off a couple drones to take aerial photos of the region to make certain there are no dangerous life forms waiting up ahead."

"In the meantime, I shall contact our Group in the western region." I informed them. "They should be landing, or have already landed by now. We shall catch up with you very soon."

Francis, a member of the western region team, replied quickly, "We landed about 30 minutes ago. It is evening, so the desert air is rather fresh, cool not cold. Dr. Gordon and Dr. Crawford took a dune buggy for a quick tour of the area. You might be able to hear the sounds of the engines in the distance."

"Hi, Pamela," Joseph broke into the conversation. "We are just stretching our legs. "He said in a low, sleepy tone. "Nothing to report for the moment. There was no sign of life when we got off the plane. As there are no visible signs of tracks or indentations in the desert sand, I have the impression that no one has walked on its surface for thousands of years."

"Don't be so sure of yourself," Reinhart cautioned. "Desert winds wipe away foot prints very rapidly so what you are seeing may not be exact."

"Francis said that Gordon and Crawford left to investigate the area. Did the androids send out any drones to take photos?"

"Yes, Gordon and Crawford did that before leaving the encampment." He stopped abruptly. "I think that I see their vehicle returning." He hesitated. "Yes it is them. Perhaps you would like to speak to them."

Gordon and Crawford were now on the visual. "We saw nothing of any interest, but it is late in the evening, perhaps we shall be luckier tomorrow," Gordon said, moving aside to let Crawford speak.

"Dr. Reinhart," Crawford weighed in, "the drones have sent us some photos of the high mountains, located about 50 miles away. There is no sign of life, flora or fauna on the photos, but, we shall see better in the daytime," his voice without human emotion.

"Ok. Keep in touch. Over and out."

"Dr. Reinhart, come quickly," Miller called out. "I think that we found the remnants of an aircraft."

I took Drager's place in the snowmobile, alongside Flanders. Reinhart, still in command, drove at high speed in the direction of their find. When we arrived, she slowly examined the debris.

"Yes, it corresponds to an aircraft used by the non-intellectuals before the revolution broke out." She clicked her tongue. "They used these obsolete planes they found in a warehouse in an abandoned village to deliver supplies to their outlying communities, none of which were anywhere near the polar region." She studied the small pieces of the debris, manipulating the broken parts.

"Interesting. Perhaps some of these non-intellectuals actually did seek refuge in this polar region, hoping to ride out the revolution and return home later. But it is more likely that this damaged aircraft was thrust into the air, under the violence of the Doomsday explosion, eventually breaking into pieces, surfacing here."

"There is no sign of human life or robotic machines, just a wing and the cockpit of this old plane," Flanders mentioned, as he used his maximum force mode to lift the heavier pieces in search of the body of the aircraft.

"It appears that these pieces are all that is left of the aircraft, so we have to use our imaginations to give the aircraft a form," Reinhart commented. "I want you to have the android crew take the pieces back to the center for study."

We returned rather rapidly to the rest of the group. Reinhart downplayed the find, saying that it had very little relevance for our mission, when, to the contrary, I could feel her strong, fervent interest in this discovery rushing inside of me, charging my curiosity.

The android crew had a simple dinner of rehydrated rice and vegetables ready for us. Hungry, we served ourselves large portions of rice, topping it with carrots, broccoli, green beans and mushrooms.

"Come with me." I said, as I grabbed Randolph's hand. He and I were the first to slide across the icy surface. The others followed, pushing each other and laughing at the skids and falls of their friends.

I stopped sliding several times to study the splendor of the blackish blue sky, with traces of white luster, like floating lights and sparkles behind a smoky curtain. Only the North Star boldly stood illuminating our passage.

"There is something creepy about this arctic environment." Randolph's description made me smile.

"I think that we have to be very cautious," I replied.

I took a low level sleeper close to the cockpit, just in case we had to leave rapidly. Even though my claustrophobia seemed less pronounced than in the past, I still preferred to sleep with the compartment open.

Upon awakening, I grabbed a hot energy beverage that tasted bitter, and an energy bar reminiscent of my programmed days, before I took a stroll out on the ice. The sun filtered through a dark, grayish blue sky, in fine strands of yellow and orange. I decided that our team should head south, fly the plane in that direction, and leave this polar area behind.

"The airplane parts are being flown to the Center," Flanders called out to me. "Do you want to stay here, or move south?" he asked.

"South."

"Ok, I shall tell the androids to prepare the planes so we can leave as soon as the others have finished their breakfast."

A short move father south brought us to the boreal forests, very sparsely populated with small fir trees. The Balsam firs, Blue Spruces, and Douglas Firs, imposing in their size and splendor on Miller's slides, were but tiny, frail replicas of another time, bending in the wind, their branches skimming the thick snow surrounding them.

"Well, Dr. Miller," I spoke for our group, "you were right to warn us that the slide shows might not be a true representation of the area today." I paused. "But at least there are trees, small but sturdy, growing in this area. We shall have to take care of them so that we will see the return of a Boreal forest."

Shouting diverted my attention, but did not prepare me for the snowballs that Tirence, Rebecca, Basil and Birch were throwing at their elders, one of which hit me in the face, with a cold sting. I quickly grabbed some snow, throwing it at the closest target. Miller and Flanders, standing so officiously, were perfect targets as I jettisoned a few in their direction.

"Enough!" We all stopped abruptly. "You are here to explore this area. You are not here on vacation—to play like children in the snow!"

Flanders clapped his hands together, like a coach, getting his team back on track.

"Pamela," Miller called out to me. "There is a mountain in the distance. Perhaps there is animal life living in the caverns." She pointed to a small speck in the distant horizon.

I felt Reinhart's energy surface, practically stifling my breathing. "Yes, we shall have to inspect that area and for that I need a large vehicle, fully equipped with survival gear, exoskeleton suits for three humans, food, weapons, and lab computers and so forth."

My eyes strained, trying to visualize the terrain. "I want Miller, Drager, Flanders, Randolph, Diana and 3 android scouts to accompany me for a quick tour of the area."

I looked at the others. "The rest of you should take small samples of the trees and any shrubs you might uncover. I want a few androids to burrow in different areas in search of life forms." I looked at Jason. "I am putting you in command for the moment."

"With pleasure, Pamela. But, if you find anything interesting in the mountains, let us know." Tirence called out. "And, Be Careful!" I nodded.

Within 15 minutes the five of us left in a large vehicle equipped with weapons, exoskeleton suits, food, water, camping gear, a large mobile lab, medical equipment, computers and other survival equipment. There was even enough remaining space for containers and cages of varying sizes, in the hope of finding new life forms.

"How long will you be gone?" Jason's voice barely audible, as the motor of our vehicle began to turn.

"We shall be back tomorrow evening."

"Why are we rushing off like this?" Diana asked. "What does Reinhart expect to find?"

"I don't know, Diana. But, I feel her strong interest in exploring the area."

We traveled seemingly hundreds of miles over the snow with Reinhart driving fast, easily navigating through the treacherous, slippery terrain. She seemed determined to reach the mountain before nightfall. And we did, for we arrived at the base of the tall mountain as the sun began to sink behind its ridge. The evening sky came ablaze with vibrant shades of red and orange, catching our full attention.

When she jumped out of the car, I could feel the fervor of emotions suppressed for centuries, surface inside of me. "Miraculously, this old mountain survived the Doomsday explosion!"

Randolph's arms moved round my trembling body. "Dr. Reinhart, are you ok?"

"Yes, Randolph. I am just fine," she gently released his hands. "We must make camp." She finally said under gasps, as she gained full control of herself.

Flanders and Miller, who were still standing in a straight, formal posture, ordered Drager and the android assistants on board our vehicle to set up camp and make dinner.

We were huddled together in the warm tent eating rehydrated rice and vegetables, when Miller rushed towards us. "Dr. Reinhart, Jason is on the visual." She said, handing the portable system to Reinhart.

A strange creature that looked a bit like a mixture of a field mouse and a rabbit was on center screen. It had thick, white fluffy fur, long ears, a slim face with short whiskers and sharp little teeth on a pudgy face.

"A hybridized creature," she articulated slowly. "It is definitely not an evolutionary version of a new rabbit species because it is missing two very distinctive rabbit features, or 2 pairs of sharp incisors for front teeth and a round, fluffy tail. Look," she pointed to its lower backside, "it has a long, thin tail, like a rat, passing between its large powerful hind legs."

"It is inoffensive," Jason said. "Actually, the android crew dug up several of them and we are in the process of preparing to send them back to the Center to be studied."

"Granted, they are rather peculiar looking, mutated life forms," I replied slowly, wishing that Reinhart had not disappeared. "Finding even hybridized life forms is a good sign, at least, a lot more encouraging than finding petrified specimens of extinct animals." I continued. "Just be careful, though. They may not be so inoffensive and could be dangerous predators that feed off little creatures in the area."

The visual ended and we sat back down to finish the meal. "How do you know, Dr. Reinhart, that the mountain is old?" Randolph asked.

"Of course it is a supposition, Randolph, because the Doomsday explosion could have altered the normal development of mountains, causing them to age more rapidly. But young mountains, at least before the Doomsday explosion, had high, pointed, usually snow-capped peaks that could reach very high altitudes, of over 26,000 feet." She replied.

"With time," she picked up, "meaning thousands and thousands of years, these young mountains, with sharp, acute angles, suffered from erosion, caused principally by natural forces like wind and rain. They took on a different look as the aging process installed. The rounded peaks and heavy, compact body of the mountain in front of us, rising between 10 to 12,000 feet in height, is a mountain that has aged."

Everyone sat silently so she continued. "One good aspect about this is that its interior has probably fragmented, forming basins and caverns. Hopefully, there will be living creatures occupying the small and large interior caverns. That we shall discover tomorrow."

The first thing Reinhart did before breakfast was to order Drager, Flanders and Miller to put their strength up to maximum. "You will need to slip into covering of sorts, there are some military fatigues that should fit you in the box over there." She pointed to a supply box in the bedroom area. "And you will need to wear boots to protect your systems and make it easier for you to walk on treacherous mountain terrain."

I then sat down to sip a warm drink, packed with the day's vitamin and mineral requirements, and eat one of the dry, tasteless biscuits. "The kitchen staff did not prepare other food?"

"Sorry, Pamela," Flanders began, "we asked for healthy products. Actually, we thought that we would find berries, nuts and other such products growing here."

"I sent some androids to scout the area and find an easy path for us to climb." Reinhart said. "My exoskeleton suits are masterpieces of technology. I am glad you had time to train with them before we left the Main Center. To remind you, your exoskeleton suit has been adapted to your bio-physiological and skeletal muscular system. It is not bulky and adjusts like a second skin. It will enhance your skeletal muscular system, absorb shock and make it possible for you to run faster, perform hazardous work, and, even lift heavy loads.

The android scouts returned. "The cliff paths are very narrow, so you humans must be careful." He began. "We found several possible cavern entrances. Unfortunately, they are blocked. They must have suffered from varying degrees of turbulence, like land and rockslides. We will know more once we try to open up the entrances," the scout leader reported.

"How long will it take to dig out the entrances?" I asked, sitting back down on the bench.

"Difficult to calculate," the android replied. "We shall make every effort to open up the lower cavern area rapidly, taking precaution not to injure anyone, or damage these cavernous regions."

"We can explore the lowlands," I suggested, as the others followed me outside.

The air was fresh, no longer that bitter cold of the arctic zone. And, the clusters of small forests, with trees much smaller than those in the area our colleagues were exploring, sparked our enthusiasm. We packed ourselves into a large snowmobile with Reinhart driving.

The snowmobile stopped and we all jumped out. Even though I was struck by the absolute silence and the well-defined paths, I continued onward, following the others. We took small samples of the various fir trees that rose above us. It was evident that these trees were hybrids, by their needles, branches, trunk sizes, and medium heights. We meticulously inspected the five small forest areas that formed a uniform semi-circle against the horizon.

"I wonder if someone planted these trees and is pruning and caring for them," Flanders commented.

"Interesting that you should say that, because I have the same feeling," I replied.

"In that case, we must find the caretaker." I said.

"Well, the guardian is not here. That is for certain," Miller replied. "I don't detect any life form other than the three of you, and I don't feel any robotic energy either."

Flanders nodded.

"Ok, we shall have to look elsewhere," I said, as we returned to our snow mobile and headed back to the large tent.

There were energy bars and a hot beverage awaiting us. I decided to skip lunch and take a short tour of our immediate area, looking for animal prints or undergrowth. But even digging a good foot under the snow did not reveal any sign of life.

"Dr. Reinhart!" I turned and saw the scout leader rushing towards me. "We dug out one of the entrances. Come!" He took my hand. "The cavern is wide and there are a number of small chambers off the main entrance. Everything is intact. There is no risk of avalanches or falling debris."

"Wait, Dr. Reinhart!" Flanders rushed to catch up with me. "There is a problem in the western section. We have Joseph on the visual."

"You can't take care of it?" I asked.

"No, Pamela. Dr. Reinhart is needed."

I felt short waves of negative energy, like sparks of electricity, building up inside of me. "I think that you will have to work this out with Joseph." Reinhart replied in a firm tone.

"They are under attack, Dr. Reinhart!" Flanders screamed.

Reinhart tossed my head in annoyance and turned to the android. "Continue to evacuate the debris...open up other caverns," she ordered, before rushing over to the visual. Joseph was not in view. Instead, we saw android assistants and scouts, racing about in front of the cameras, as they meticulously surrounded the encampment with an impenetrable, vulcanized fiber barrier.

"Where are you, Joseph?" Reinhart cried out loudly into the audio system.

"I am here, Dr. Reinhart." His voice animated as he came into camera range. "We are under attack."

"Yes. I have been informed of that." Her voice strained. "So what is the nature of this attack?"

Joseph quickly showed her the photos that the androids took. "These creatures kept a safe distance from us for a good hour, during which time we naively took them for curious observers. We were fascinated by their appearance and took a number of photos."

He stopped to control his rapid breathing. "Even when they split up into small groups and began moving in an organized fashion in our direction, we did not feel threatened. I imagined that this was their natural way of studying a new species." Reinhart responded with an unpleasant, guttural sound that Joseph decided to ignore or simply didn't notice, preoccupied with his reporting.

"It was only when their eyes grew so large and focused, and they revealed their long, curving claws and razor-sharp teeth, that I realized that we were confronting dangerous predators," his voice shaky.

"I quickly ordered the android scouts to fire stun rays to stop their attack and then secure our encampment with the protective barrier. Clarence, who was now in view, agreed with me."

I sat straight, stiffening my back, waiting for Reinhart to finish studying the photos of the large sized animals that appeared to be a strange mixture of a grey wolf and a grizzly bear. She surged inside of me, ordering the android scout leader to send out drones to get close ups of the hybridized creatures.

"They are frightening—almost as frightening as WD was when we first encountered him," Randolph shouted in a hoarse, angry voice.

"Hybridized animals appeared throughout human history. Some were the result of artificial insemination, like the lion-tiger hybrid, and others natural cross-breeding of other species like the coyote-wolf hybrid. Cross species, like birds with mammals, were rare and the mutated offspring did not go on to proliferate their species." I said in a dry academic tone.

"How do you know this, Pamela?"

"She is making me privy to the mass of information running through her mind," I replied and he nodded. "Apparently, hybridizing with artificial insemination produced sterile off springs, while copulation between species sometimes created a new species. Fortunately, certain freaks of nature, like birds with insect features, did not survive."

"We have the close-ups." Joseph was back on his feet.

Reinhart returned, ready to tackle the problem. "Where are Gordon and Crawford?"

"They are supervising the android crew," Clarence replied.

"Convenient," She replied in a caustic tone. "Tell them I want to see them." Clarence rushed off.

"What do the two of you know about hybridized grizzly bears and wolves?" She addressed Gordon and Crawford.

"We were not involved in this," Crawford replied. "But the Governor did create the floral garden---the plants and animals."

"Of course. He must have hybridized a number of species, using the DNA of various species that he acquired from the preserved, dead animals in the Air and Space center," Gordon said. "By the way, the Governor is on-line now."

"We received the field mouse-rabbit specimen. Incredibly

interesting that these two creatures reproduced, but not that shocking, as they are very closely linked genetically." He took a deep breath. "By the way, we heard from Colonel Shannon and our three astronauts are in good health, their cryogenic suits functioning perfectly."

"Thank you for the up-dates, which are more positive than what we are facing now," she replied. "Do you know anything about this newly discovered, predatory species? Did you play around with the DNA of grizzly bears and wolves, by any chance?" She pressed for answers.

There was a very long silence. "Uh! Maybe?"

"Tell me what happened."

"Well, this is so long ago. Even though I doubted my research, I understand the absurdity and negligence of my actions. But...yes, I did create mutants."

"And?"

"They were not that unattractive physically, resembling more the grey wolf than the grizzly. Their ancestors had the head and facial features of a grey wolf, the greyish black furred body, and strong, very muscular hind legs, but like a Grizzly they had large paws with retractable, razor sharp claws, a large throat and broad shoulders, and the digestive system and enzymes of an omnivore. Their eyes were a glowing yellowish color when they were agitated...or maybe hungry. These creatures did not hide their natural aggressiveness, showing their large teeth and salivating; yes, big drops of water drooling from the corners of their mouths." He started to cough violently. "I find myself in a quandary."

"What do you mean?" Reinhart interrupted him.

"Well, my human emotional side is telling me to hide the truth of what happened, while my logical android side is refusing." He covered his mouth and coughed loudly. "I guess I have said too much, and have no choice now but to admit that a few of them escaped."

"How could they have escaped? The center is a labyrinth of corridors so it would have been difficult for them to find their way out rapidly."

"Yes, you humans, living in that small community in the cavern on the outside left your scent behind. They apparently found the exit by following your odor."

"Continue."

"The androids were ordered to sedate these hybridized creatures, who were in large cages in the storage area and then take them to the incineration unit," he said in a low voice, as if he were reliving the situation. "I didn't realize how intelligent, clear-headed and strong minded a wolf could be, especially one that positioned himself as the leader of the pack." He gritted his teeth.

As the wolves in the first cage collapsed instantly with the first laser stun," he continued, "the androids passed rapidly, initiating the same procedure with the rest of the hybridized creatures in other cages. The alpha males rolled rapidly over, avoiding the laser beam, the moment the Androids fired and laid still, giving the impression they were out cold." He stopped abruptly. "The androids did not detect any movement in any of the cages and had no reason to believe they had missed their targets."

"And?" She pressed for answers.

"When the androids opened the cages with the Alpha males to take them to the incinerators, they attacked the Androids, springing fast and violently, knocking them over. Their large jaws filled with razor sharp teeth and massive claws were more powerful than we realized. The androids moved close together, forming a barrier, but the hybrids did not back up; instead, they charged with a combined force, their mouths open and their claws projected outwards, as they toppled the Androids, damaging the android systems." He grimaced slightly.

"These creatures then rushed to the laboratory exit and sped through the corridors, eventually entering into the lower level and following the tunnels under the monorail."

"Their survival instinct was certainly a driving force, but they were also lucky, because a group of androids was entering through one of the outside doors, as this group of wolf-grizzlies arrived on scene. They trampled the androids and disappeared." He concluded.

Reinhart smiled and nodded. "Incredible! Amazing!" she screamed, as she clapped her hands together in what appeared to be...praise._

"We sent out scouts to find them and destroy them, but the scouts never found them dead or alive and so we eventually abandoned the search. By our calculations, there was a very low probability that they could survive on the outside. And, absolutely no risk they could procreate. They were all male." He rubbed his hands together in a slow, meticulous way. "Why did you ask me about them?"

"Take a look," she said, as she pointed to the recent photos taken by drones.

"I never imagined that they could have survived. But as they were all males, how could they have reproduced?"

"One of the most logical answers is that they found packs of wolves as they moved to the northern hemisphere. With their size and strength, they could easily take leadership and reproduce a new, stronger species of wolf-grizzly," Reinhart replied. "But it is also possible that some of them changed sex. Perhaps female hormones were more alive in some of them; or perhaps their instinct for survival accelerated gender changes. There were animals, most specifically birds, fish and insects that carried both female and male sex hormones and organs."

"But, as these were hybridized creatures, you," her eyes met those of the former Governor, "might take a closer look at your research because you may have created a hybridized species carrying male and female sexual organs and hormones."

"I shall do that. But, Dr. Reinhart, a grizzly lives in cold, not hot, environments."

"I don't agree. Bears, and grizzlies, did adapt to climate changes, moving to warmer climates to find food. There were black bears and grizzlies living in deserts at different periods of history. And as these animals appear to be more wolf than grizzly, wolves did adapt to hot climates."

She stopped to sift through her knowledge bank. "Yes, it is very possible that these animals live at higher elevations, or in the lower steps of the mountain range. But there are grasslands and scrublands, up ahead, where they might find shelter as well."

"Oh you must destroy them," his voice vibrating with human emotions.

"Get a hold of yourself," she ordered. "You are letting your new found emotional configuration influence you."

He closed his eyes for a moment, before continuing, "Their

ancestors were not friendly creatures. Quite the contrary, they were dangerous predators. I made a mistake creating this species. Just kill them!" He covered his eyes with his hands.

"They are life forms!" Reinhart screamed. "They cannot be annihilated!"

"No! This is foolish, Dr. Reinhart. They are not nature's creatures, they are my mistake!"

"Yes, they are your mistake. But their survival is scientifically interesting, so I want to study a certain number of these creatures." My eyes moved to the screen on which Gordon and Crawford stood at attention. "Order the androids to capture a few male and female adults and as many offspring as possible and fly them back in cages to our Center." Reinhart requested and then turned back to the Governor.

"I want your android replacement to study the behavior of these animals and provide them with food and water. They might actually feed off of the creatures that Gordon and Crawford sent back to you or the field mouse-rabbit hybrids, and innocently entered onto the encampment looking for their normal food source." She sighed, switching off the Governor and returning to Crawford and Gordon.

"Until we know more, I am going on the assumption that these are a highly intelligent species that live in a societal order." She sighed. I could feel her cerebral energy invading mine, running havoc through my mind.

"If today, these animals, descendants of the former Governor's experiments in hybridizing species, do not attack, or violently try to defend themselves, but retreat when the androids approach them, then you must let them resume their lives in peace. I trust you, Joseph, Dr. Gordon and Dr. Crawford, to treat them with respect and make a humanitarian decision by protecting this species, in my absence." She ordered.

"Understood," Crawford replied for the group, before he and Gordon bowed their heads in respect.

"I am sorry, but I have something else that I must take care of now," she said, "I shall get back to you later."

Randolph was still standing next to me when I switched off the audio-visual screens. "We better leave now, Randolph," I said.

He grabbed my arm as I stood up. "Dr. Reinhart was right to suggest that these wolf'-grizzly creatures might feed off of those strange look-ing rodents, but maybe their intentions were different, perhaps they wanted to make contact with our team members. Remember the dol-phins and WD and his family—they could actually communicate with us."

"I know what you are getting at, Randolph, but I don't believe that all animals are capable of communication in the language we use." I hesitated. "They might have been simply fascinated with the androids, and wanted to approach them. Reinhart is right, we have to learn more about this species. Up until now, they have not done more than ob-serve the group from a distance." I replied. "Let's see what happens."

"Where are we off to now?" Randolph asked

"Reinhart wants to explore the caverns." I turned to Randolph.

"Right. The android scouts discovered an entrance to one of the caverns," Reinhart surged inside of me.

Flaunting our exoskeleton suits, we walked in silence, carefully climbing the 300 foot narrow, steep, slippery, icy path, until we even-tually arrived in front of the first cavern opening. The androids had removed the large stones, placing them stylishly in the form of a high rising stone-wall, resembling a barbican tower, a short distance from the cavern's entrance. We marched in lockstep through this fortified gateway.

I stopped and watched as the others moved meticulously along the narrow, interior passage. The moss on the walls gave off a low light and the air was damp with a musky stench. My knees wobbled as memories of the hidden passage in the interior of our outside cavern surfaced, inciting those same trepidations that haltered my progres-sion in the past. I wanted to turn and leave, breathe in the fresh air and feel the freedom of open space, when Randolph gently took my hand in his and led me through this narrow passage to a large, open, circular cavern.

I watched Miller, Flanders and Drager working diligently, taking calcium carbonite samples from the icicle formations of stalagmites and stalactites, various glowing mosses and the sandy soil. But I wa-vered, until Reinhart's interest surged. She was aware of my fear of enclosed spaces and her presence helped me to overcome my claus-trophobia and appreciate the beauty of this cavernous world.

While Reinhart looked for secret entrances, which she did not find, my thoughts drifted. Reinhart and I had been living in a symbiotic relationship of mutual respect for many years. She made me privy to her research, educated me, and actually placed confidence in me, as a leader, by sending me instructions to deliver to members of our team. She also gave me freedom to make my own decisions and to learn from my own mistakes. We were two different people sharing the same body, occupying two different regions of my brain, in a mutually advantageous way. And, I was happy just knowing that she there to guide me when I needed guidance, to praise and respect me when I succeeded, and to protect me and others from danger.

After hours of exploring and collecting specimens Reinhart lost interest and disappeared to meditate. I suggested that we leave and return in the morning.

Just as we were beginning our retreat, Reinhart resurfaced asking the android scout leader if there was a cavern just below the one we were in.

"If there is, there is no visible entry," he replied.

"And the other entries, will they be open soon?"

"They might take more time. The crew is working hard, but they have to remove much more debris."

"Ok, continue," she replied, and he immediately called out to the others to work as rapidly as possible.

The sun was beginning to set when we exited the cavern. I followed the others, Miller, Flanders, Drager, Randolph, and Diana back to our encampment for dinner.

"Unfortunately, Pamela, the menu has not changed. The androids were not able to find any eatable plants to add more flavor to the packaged meals," Crawford pointed out.

"No problem. I am so hungry that I could virtually eat almost anything." I said, as I plunged my fork into the rehydrated food.

"What does Reinhart hope to find?" Diana asked.

"I have absolutely no idea. I can't even guess what she might have in mind. All that I can say with certainty is that she wants to explore the various mountain caverns." I put my fork down. "If she does not find what she is looking for here, then my best guess is that there will be other mountains to climb."

"Joseph and Clarence are back on-line. They want to talk to Dr. Reinhart," Drager interrupted.

I got up and followed him. Joseph was not cowering behind the screen like earlier in the day. He was in a relaxed position, his body reclining on a bench. Clarence was sitting next to him, running his fingers over the prickly edges of his lower jaw. "Is everything ok?" Reinhart surged inside of me, punctuating her presence with her accent.

"Yes, things went much better than we expected," Joseph commented. "The androids captured a dozen females and a dozen males, as well as thirty or so young ones."

"And?"

"Oh, when the others awakened from their stunned sleep, they did not make any effort to attack the android guards, or rush our enclosure, like before. Instead, they slowly grouped together and left the area." Reinhart said nothing.

"So, what should we do?" Joseph asked, his voice lacking energy, like he was bored.

"You should continue to move on, explore other areas, and prepare yourself for another attack from these wolf-grizzlies," she huffed.

"You don't honestly believe they are going to attack again?"

"Yes. Think about it and you will figure out their motives," she replied. "You will come to understand that this was a clever subterfuge of sorts, orchestrated by seemingly wild, savage, irrational creatures, led by several alpha males, whose level of intelligence may be superior to that of an average human."

"For what reason would they want to attack us again?" Joseph insisted.

"Food." She snickered. "You might have appeared to be quite appetizing, Joseph."

"So why did they back off?" He pressed for answers.

"This is pure conjecture on my part, because these are hybridized creatures. A grizzly would have used its force, more so than cunning, to take down its prey. So a grizzly would have probably continued its charge. Whereas a wolf would rather conserve its energy, even stay hungry, if its prey was temporarily beyond reach. So they would back off and wait for another opportunity." She took a deep breath. "It would appear that both their instinct and reasoning is more wolf than grizzly."

"I agree with Dr. Reinhart." Gordon broke into the conversation. "These animals, seemed quite clever. Dr. Crawford and I discussed their hierarchical organization, with team work, noticeable in their rapid division into units. There is definitely one or more leaders and it appears that the pack was called back to conserve their energy for a later attack."

"Ok. We shall break camp early tomorrow and head west," Joseph said, his eyes blazing. "Do we have your permission to shoot to kill?"

"Only if there is no other solution. It appears that this desert is their homeland and we must respect their right to occupy it. Of course they may do their hunting later in the day, when their prey would be off-guard." My eyes penetrated theirs.

"For the moment, you only kill to save your lives. Stay inside the dune buggies which are well equipped with everything you need. Send the drones to scan the area, and then follow up with android scouts, before you venture into new territory. There could be grasslands and even small, rolling hills up ahead. But, do not take any unnecessary risks. And at night, make certain the androids set up the impenetrable enclosures. Talk to you tomorrow," Reinhart instructed.

"Did you receive any information about our captives from the Governor?" I asked Crawford.

"No. I believe that they have not yet stirred. I know that the androids administered a high dose, not enough to kill them, but enough to put them under for a long time." He insisted.

"Ok. Keep me informed. I am going to get some sleep," I replied. Before I retired, I contacted the rest of my group to make certain that everything was going well. Tirence and Rebecca were still awake and answered my call.

"We spent the day exploring this area, but have not found anything of interest. Perhaps we should approach your camp?" Rebecca suggested.

"No, stay where you are for the moment. You can take the snow mobiles and venture a few miles away from the encampment, but take android scouts and drones with you. Do not approach any animals until the androids have confirmed they are friendly, not hostile, creatures."

"Ok. When will you be back?" her voice, shaky.

"Don't be afraid, Rebecca. Tirence will protect you. He has a lot of combat experience and is a seasoned explorer. We shall return as soon as possible," I said in a soft and tender tone.

"Yes, I shall take care of her and will keep you informed," Tirence reassured me.

I switched off the communication system. I was all alone in the communications room. Randolph and Diana had gone to bed, Miller and Flanders were checking on the androids, and I did not sense Reinhart's energy; she had disappeared deep inside of me.

"I wonder what she expects to find hidden in one of those caverns." I spoke softly enough for my ears only.

As I got up to leave, the communications system started flashing and I quickly answered.

"Pamela," I recognized John's voice, "we have some strange news from our team on board the inflatable space lab," his voice, an urgent, staccato tone.

"Ok, John, tell me about it." Reinhart replaced me.

"Yes, it is better that I report directly to you, Dr. Reinhart." He took a deep breath. "Mathieu told me that he, Isabel and James were informed today by Captain Robert Cray that Colonel Shannon, who is in command of the Spaceship *Benevolence,* sent small android-piloted spaceships to move the space lab farther away from Earth and the departure date for our members' return to Earth was moved several months forward. She explained to them that this decision was made in their interest."

"I am listening," Reinhart replied.

"Apparently, members of her scientific team detected movement of space debris that was headed in the direction of the space lab. To protect the space lab and ensure the safety of the humans on board, a decision was made to move the facility and crew members into deeper space. She did not give us any idea of when our group would return to earth." He stopped to let that sink in. "She said she would be willing to explain this in more detail if you wanted to contact her."

"Did you tell her anything about where I was and what I was doing?"

"I simply said that you were not available for the moment and that I would pass on her message the next time you contacted me," he replied.

I could feel her hot waves of anger rushing through me as I sat staring at John, whose eyes were focused on his desk top. He eventually raised his head and added, "I hope that I did not say too much."

"No, John, you did well," she replied. "Did you notice anything unusual about Colonel Shannon's behavior?" Reinhart asked,

"Well, that is not an easy question to answer. She always gives the impression that she is hiding something. But it could just be her shyness or uneasiness when dealing with us Earthlings," he replied.

"Yes, I know what you mean. It is like she is reading a script and cannot digress from the wording." Reinhart replied.

"That might be it. This time she was certainly uneasy about what she reported. Her voice was rising and falling involuntarily," he replied.

"I want you to contact Colonel Shannon—but keep the communication system open so that I can see her and hear what she says."

"Ok. I can do that. But, what do you want me to tell her?"

"You say the following: Dr. Reinhart is vacationing and will not be available for a conference call for a few weeks. She would like you, Colonel Shannon, to inform the High Commissioners of her gratitude with the following message: 'I am very pleased that you have taken proper measures to protect my scientific team and rely upon you to continue to act in their interests.'"

"And," she continued, "I want you to inform Captain Cray that Dr. Reinhart has a message that she would like you to communicate in private to Mathieu, Isabel and James," she said in a strong voice and the Governor nodded.

"My message: 'Be patient. This is only one of perhaps many slight missteps in our determined and measured progression into a glorious and memorable future in space travel and colonization.'"

"I know Cray will be listening in on this message, which is meant to confuse him. I want to be able to see their faces and hear any remarks they might make regarding their situation. Remember, this is a private message—we will be able to see if it is being monitored and transmitted by Captain Cray to Colonel Shannon."

"Are you worried, Dr. Reinhart?"

"John, I don't want you to tell anyone else about this. I will bring this up with the Group of 5 later on. I am not worried. Things that I suspect, but cannot reveal right now, are developing faster than I anticipated, but time is still on our side."

"Will our team understand your message, because, admittedly, I don't?"

"Oh, don't worry, the message is really not for them."

"I am not certain that I am following you well, but I promise to keep the contents of our discussion to myself." He replied. "Are you ready for me to contact the parties concerned?"

"Yes, I am camouflaged on your screen, so please contact Colonel Shannon now."

"John to Colonel Shannon," she answered rapidly

"Is Dr. Reinhart available?" She asked, her shrill voice registering a high level of stress.

"No, but she asked me to give you the following message," he replied.

Reinhart registered the voice inflections and facial expressions of Colonel Shannon, while John relayed Reinhart's messages, which would be transmitted by her to the High Commissioners. Colonel Shannon's eyes moved rapidly and the corners of her mouth twitched involuntarily. "Is that all that she said?" Colonel Shannon asked, her eyes drifting from side to side.

"Yes. That is the entire message." John replied, before turning off the communication system.

"Very well done, John. Now contact our team."

Captain Cray answered, asking whether John had news from Dr. Reinhart. John went on to explain that he had a message from her for her crew. "I don't understand why this is a private message. We are working together and my life, as well as theirs, is in danger."

"I am sorry, Captain Cray, but she was very specific." John replied. Dr. Reinhart heard him switch on an outside captor, as John repeated her message.

"Was he listening, Dr. Reinhart?"

"Yes," she replied, under heavy laughter. "Everything went like I wanted. You did very well."

"No one asked any questions. Instead, they pretended to understand your strange messages."

"Yes." I replied, in a voice tautened from laughter. "Shannon, Cray and the six android Commissioners understand from Reinhart's messages that she does not trust them. And, she is giving them a chance to prove otherwise, show their allegiance to her, before she confronts them in a more radical, decisive... final way." John nodded.

Chapter 12: A Falcon Rises

I woke up feeling good, knowing that Reinhart was watching over all the astronauts, and that the safety and survival of Peter, Frederic and Stuart, was assured. I rushed through an icy cold shower and then ran through the hot drying system, before putting on the tightfitting undergarments that would further insulate my body when I later entered into the exoskeleton suit. I felt alive and ready to start the day.

I heard Diana and Randolph stirring when I collected my gear and left for breakfast.

"The android scouts found several varieties of wild berries and a small number of Maple trees. They drilled a hole into the bark of several Maple trees and inserted a faucet. The sap is now oozing from the metal faucets into fibrous sacks." Flanders uttered under his breath, as he served me the dry energy biscuits and hot, tasteless drink.

"We sent the sap and berries off to the center to be analyzed. Hopefully, you will soon be able to add a touch of maple syrup to your dry biscuit and bite into blueberries." He added.

"That is excellent news. Were these bushes and trees close by?"

"A few miles from here, so we can collect these food sources if they are eatable, before we return to the other members of our group."

"I'll let you supervise this, but, for the moment I need you to accompany me." He nodded.

She wanted to continue the exploration so I left with Flanders, Miller and Drager, knowing that Diana and Randolph would catch up with us soon. The scout leader led me to the next, partially open cavern. "As I mentioned yesterday, it will take time to clear out these entrances, but the crew is working rapidly."

Flanders moved closer to the excavated area. "We could probably venture inside. The entrance is small, but nothing seems to be obstructing the passage."

"It is risky, Dr. Flanders." The scout leader cautioned. "There could be rock slides, when you enter. Let me go with you and Drager. We shall come back to get Dr. Reinhart and Dr. Miller, if the area is safe," he suggested.

I sensed Reinhart's energy rise, giving me the impression that she did not want Flanders to enter this cavern first, but I had no idea why. So I led the way as we all squeezed through the small hole, tumbling onto a sandy path. Flanders was right, only the entrance itself had been sealed off. The interior passage was wide and luminous—a strange amber colored, florescent beam of artificial light guiding us as we made our way into a large, dome-shaped chamber.

"Is this a burial chamber?" Flanders asked, as he stopped in his tracks, giving the impression he was frightened.

"Perhaps all of you should let me proceed alone," Reinhart ordered. "I shall call for you if I need your help." No one protested.

She was controlling my body as she marched forward, pulling my shoulders back and holding my head high. The light grew stronger and stronger, making my eyes water, in spite of all of her efforts to keep them clear and focused.

I felt someone or something grab me. "Let go!" she ordered.

"Dr. Reinhart, it is you?" A metallic voice spoke.

"Yes, where is he?" She asked.

"He has been moved to another level."

"Explain."

"There was moisture seeping into this cavern and we were programmed to keep him in a dry environment, so we moved him farther inside the cavern." A very primitive robot, with a large, square, heavy metallic body, advanced slowly on tiny wheels in our direction, as its long tubular arms moved in an uncoordinated, disjointed fashion. It had no outer covering hiding its metallic structure and its face had no mobile parts—its eyes and mouth appeared to be carved into a block of metal. I found its appearance appalling and wanted to cover my eyes, but Reinhart was in command.

Its voice was being projected by a tiny computer system with audio and visual accessories, embedded in its chest area. Only its programming seemed to be at a highly advanced level.

"Can we access this new chamber?"

"I was left behind as the guardian of this vaulted area. I have five other robots working for me and we were, up and until a few weeks ago, planting and cultivating trees and plants." It stopped, making a grinding sound as it uploaded more information. "We are also programmed to protect him from his enemies who might try to enter into his private quarters."

"You will let me into his private quarters now!" Reinhart ordered.

"I cannot reach the others and the wall is sealed," The robot replied.

"Show me where the entrance is and I shall open it."

"Your voice, Dr. Reinhart, as you know, is registered in my system, so you are authorized to enter his private chamber. Nonetheless, Dr. Reinhart, you must give me the password." It replied, before its systems went on standby mode.

"Flanders!" she cried out.

"Dr. Reinhart, are you alright?" His voice modulating, as he approached her.

"Where is Drager? I want him now!" I noticed that Miller and Flanders moved aside, putting Drager in the limelight.

"The password. What is it?" my voice still very agitated.

"I don't know." He whimpered. "I might be able to find it but you will have to give me the right clue, or the right order." He bowed his head.

"The right clue? Are you playing games with me?" she asked, as she turned in circles, throwing my arms violently in the air. "You are not cooperating." She grabbed Drager and pushed him with all my strength, Flanders catching him before he fell.

"Dr. Reinhart, perhaps we can be of help. Who are you looking for?" Flanders asked.

"Who do you think? Are you incapable of reasoning now that you have emotional intelligence?"

"Murdoc?" Miller said under her breath.

All of us stood our ground, our mouths dropping open.

'Was Miller right? Could he have survived the Dooms Day explosion? Why did it take her so long to find him then?' these questions passed rapidly through my mind, as I turned to the others. Randolph and Diana were standing still, their faces, a pasty white.

Reinhart sent me a wave of positive energy, before she addressed me. "Everything is fine, my child."

"Why were you given a password?" Flanders asked, taking the initiative, as he approached the robot. Its systems reactivated.

"Because he is an ancient God and must be protected."

"What ancient God is he?" Flanders insisted.

"Apollo," the robot replied

Flanders moved next to Reinhart and whispered in her ear. "Elisabeth, try the word "*wisdom.*""

She grabbed his arm and looked deep into his android eyes. "Of course. Oh, thank you, Edward."

She called out to the robot to approach her. It advanced in such a rudimentary, sluggish fashion that I finally appreciated how truly incredible our androids were. "*Wisdom,*" she said in a clear voice.

The robot moved instantly to the wall. It spent a long moment drawing a strange anagram composed of geometric structures that formed the word, *wisdom*, in some unknown, exotic language. The wall opened. "Only you can enter, Dr. Reinhart. The wall will close behind you. To leave the chamber, you must compose the same anagram. It does not matter where on the wall, so long as it is the same." The robot stopped. "You have registered it in your system?"

"Yes. I have registered it," she replied. She turned to her team of androids. "I shall need your help later." Their heads were bowed. "You have nothing to fear from him. I will protect you," she called out, as she passed through the opening in the wall.

The same amber light that guided her down the first passage was ablaze in the small chamber. A dozen or more robots moved in her direction, their laser weapons pointed, ready to fire. "Who are you? How did you know the password?"

"I am Dr. Elisabeth Reinhart and I have come to save Dr. Aegir Murdoc," she spoke in a firm, authoritative voice that the robots recognized instantly as that of Dr. Elisabeth Reinhart. They bowed their heads. "You must let me approach him. Move to the other side of the room," she ordered, and they scurried away.

She slowly approached the archaic cryogenic tube connected

to a nuclear power system, all of which was resting on a mobile structure. She spent a long moment studying the functioning of the cryogenic tube and observing its occupant.

"Pamela," she spoke to me on a cerebral level. "Dr. Murdoc is alive, but in bad condition. I need a few minutes to recuperate his DNA so I can restore his physical, as well as his cognitive and emotional intelligence. I shall rejuvenate him, using the same method I did with Ruth, and bring him up-to-date on everything that has happened since his absence. I won't be long," she said, before vanishing inside of me, leaving me facing Murdoc.

I stood immobile, my eyes focused on Murdoc. His naked body had aged badly. His greyish skin, sagging from deteriorated, crumbling bones, their brittle edges poking through his thin skin, and his facial features, limp and droopy, all withered from time and weariness, sent qualms of absolute horror through me.

Shuddering, I covered my eyes, hoping that what I saw was not real and that there was hope for him, but when I unwrapped my eyes and gazed upon him for a second time, I shrank back in face of this horror.

I imagined Murdoc's putrid odors suffocating me and his sticky, rotting skin clinging to mine, when the tube would finally open. I forced myself to stand up, trying in vain to fend off my raging fears. But instead, my vision blurred and I doubled over in violent spasms that ended only when I spewed forth the dry, tasteless morning biscuits.

Reinhart returned rapidly. "You mustn't worry, Pamela," she said softly, as she took control of my body, preventing me from collapsing again.

I listened while she instructed the robots to be ready to clean up the liquid content from the cryogenic tube along with the fragmented tube and dispose of everything, burying it 30 feet under the sandy soil, in order to neutralize the contents of the cryogenic tube and its exterior, preventing any chemical and material contamination in this chamber.

"I cannot open the tube because it is sealed on the inside, so I have no choice but to force its explosion," she explained. "You must protect yourselves by staying close to the wall until Dr. Murdoc is revived." They nodded

She sent me a cerebral message, asking me to try to follow and understand her rejuvenation of Murdoc, before wrapping my body around the tube and connecting with his mind, forcing him to open his eyes wide enough for her to enter them. I struggled to stay alert, as the minds of these two intellectually superior beings came together in an aura of cerebral power.

But my mind, and with it my very essence, floated about helplessly, until I lost consciousness, only to be awakened when the cryogenic tube exploded, and we were swept up in a gush of rushing liquid, eventually leaving us flopping about on the cavern floor.

Reinhart was exhausted and needed time to recover from the extraordinary efforts she exerted in bringing Murdoc back. I didn't move for a long moment, the time I needed to come to terms with the reality of my situation. I heard Murdoc groan. I lay prostate, pretending to be unconscious, keeping my breathing slow and at a practically inaudible level.

Eventually, I heard his slow, rhythmic breathing. He was definitely alive. But, I was not ready to confront him. And so I chose to let my curiosity guide me, as I slowly opened my eyelids. The first thing I saw was the robots rushing about, cleaning up all the debris and digging deep holes to bury it.

My eyes drifted more to the right and I saw him sitting with his back towards me in a lotus position. He seemed unaware of me, so I studied him from a distance, watching him as he stood up, stretched and turned in my direction. His youthful, chiseled face, deep brown eyes and long curly blond hair displayed that same Adonis-like handsomeness of Randolph.

'She had definitely rejuvenated him physically and mentally. Murdoc, very tall, robust, with large sculptured muscles in both his upper and lower body, was, like his son, certainly endowed with Herculean strength. And, I wondered if he was as mean and cruel as the Group of 5 claimed he was.'

Occupied with these thoughts I did not see his eyes move in my direction and I didn't close mine fast enough. He had already sensed my awakening. "Hello, Pamela," he chortled with amusement. "I know that you have been observing me for quite some

135

time." I opened my eyes and saw his lips quirk upwards in a half-smile, as he moved in my direction.

He stopped for an instance and ordered one of the robots to request clothes for him. I heard him chuckle under his breath.

He hovered over me. "Where is Elisabeth?" his voice sounded raspy.

"I don't know. She probably needed time to recover. You were in very bad shape."

"You are identical to her physically, but much different from her intellectually, and yet you appear to have great potential." He said in a low, mellow, solemn voice, filled with regret. He stretched out alongside of me and gazed up at the ceiling.

While he lay in absence, my mind focused first on his fragrance, which was neither rotten nor putrid. His breath exhaled vibrant scents of wild berries, punctuated with the sweetness of honey, and his body was a perfumed masculinity of sandalwood, alive with that piney, erotic odor of freshly cut trees.

His full lips were the single, visibly distinguishable, facial difference between him and his son, whose upper lip was slightly thinner. I considered his eyes, the portals to his mind.

They were not Randolph's happy, dancing, playful, big, brown eyes that could turn cold, even intense, when in deep thought, but rather solemn, dark brown, mysteriously alluring eyes that dared or tempted the most brilliant to pass through these gateways to his mind, only to discover their intellectual inferiority.

"Was that the reason he stared so deeply into my eyes? Did he want me to believe he discovered only mediocrity, when I had the potential to be brilliant?" I wondered.

'His quick judgment of my intellectual competence, expressed in a remorseful tone, strongly impacted on me, because I knew differently. I was not simply stocking all the information that Reinhart was sending to me. I understood and assimilated it. I was capable of using it in her absence. She was educating me, helping me to evolve on a higher level. With time my mind and my intellect would shine in harmony with theirs,' I told myself.

My thoughts stopped abruptly, when he gently ran his fingers through my long wavy hair and lightly brushed his cheeks up against mine. "Do you mind, Pamela, if I try to revive Elisabeth now. I know she was tired after rejuvenating me and bringing me up to date on everything that happened on this planet during my years of absence. I shall need her with me when I leave this sanctuary." He whispered in my ear, sending sparkling chills of desire running through my body.

Leery of becoming too comfortable in the arms of this seducer, I agreed, taking myself out of his erotic world, by saying, "I think that she is waiting for you."

"Thank you, Pamela." I could feel his words spoken on my lips as his mouth met mine in an irresistible, tenderly warm and titillating kiss. "Are we still learning how to make love, when another generation mastered it?" I wondered, before Elisabeth pushed me aside, plunging me into a profound sleep. She awakened me only when the robot entered with Murdoc's exoskeleton suit, so that I could follow their conversation.

"A masterpiece of technology!" Murdoc jumped up from the sandy floor, his enthusiasm bubbling over. "It is incredible. With this suit, I am now ready to meet any genetically modified or hybridized life form."

"I agree. I am brilliant," she vaunted.

"Yes, no doubt about that. But, you are not always right, Dr. Reinhart." He said, grabbing my arm firmly and holding me in place. "As you brought me up-to-date on everything, I do believe I have the right to comment and I shall. I know, Elisabeth," he continued, "that you believe that all the members of the Group of 5 are our true allies. More worrisome, you recently downloaded emotional intelligence or the personalities of their human opposites, into them, because you believe that we will need them to help us today, and in the future. I am warning you, though, that I shall never be able to embrace them as friends. I shall keep my distance and, Elisabeth, I shall destroy them one by one if I suspect anyone of them of foul play."

"Relax, Murdoc. I have put very complicated programs in them that will prevent them from trying to take control. And if they eventually succeed in overriding my programs and, thus, vie for power, they will ignite the ultimate, irresistible virus that will shut them down permanently."

"Right, but I will remain vigilant," he said, showing me that he was not afraid of her. "Actually we should be very pleased with ourselves. We did it, Elisabeth. We are back, just like you promised me, so very long ago," his voice echoing off the walls.

"But it was so risky. Even though I followed your instructions and left you clues in Drager's system, when I entered into that cryogenic tube, I honestly believed I was never going to wake up again."

"Were you ill?" she asked. "I saw videos in Drager's system that frightened me. I was actually worried at one point that you did not survive."

"No, I was not ill. But when I learned that that miserable Crawford had killed you, I decided I had to stop the Group of 5's search for me by pretending that I was critically ill. I had Drager broadcast my death. I even had him play a film showing my body being incinerated." He laughed mockingly.

"I set up a system of passwords in Drager," he continued, "that only you could decipher, if ever you reappeared, which did not seem probable." He paced back and forth. "We lost a lot of time." He huffed. "And, to complicate things, I have to compromise my natural desires for you today because you share a body with someone else." He pulled me close up to him. "I love you, Elisabeth."

"Pamela is listening. I want her to be alert when we leave this chamber," Reinhart commented and he nodded.

Yes, I was listening and his slight pause gave me time to think. Things were becoming very clear. Reinhart left instructions with Murdoc to ensure his survival, just as she stored her intellectual and emotional intelligence on DNA strands. Their survival was assured and finding each other in the future was inevitable.

"I know," he replied brusquely. "Do you know that Pamela is a hypersexual creature?"

"Yes. She is like us." I felt a long-winded sigh seeping from between my lips. "There is a viable solution to our problem waiting for us at the main center. You must be patient," she pleaded.

"Ok, what is this solution?"

"A surprise!"

"You know that I hate surprises." His replied brusquely. "Fortunately, there are other important things to do." He blinked teasingly. "And I love scientific and military challenges. So let's get on with building a new world!"

He took my hand and together we passed through the wall to meet the others.

Flanders, Miller, and Drager were standing in the front line, the android scouts lined up behind them, with Diana and Randolph in the back range.

"So nice to have you back amongst us, Dr. Murdoc," Flanders said vigorously.

"Good try, Flanders," he replied. "Thank you, Drager. You were perfect."

"I am a programmed machine, Dr. Murdoc, and only carried out your orders." The sound of a jovial laugh slipped through Murdoc's tight lips.

"You are looking good and... very tall, Dr. Miller." He raised his eyebrows suggestively, informing her that he was aware of her accident, her years in a heavy metallic robotic body and Reinhart's eventual reconstruction of her android body and insertion of longer legs.

I noticed that Flanders and Miller nodded slowly, acknowledging that Murdoc was aware of everything that happened during his long years of absence.

He pushed his way through the android line. Randolph and Diana stood at attention, a distance from him. "Dr. Diana Ming." He pronounced her name slowly, letting his eyes study her physical appearance. "You and the others did a good job, Flanders. These young ones, Pamela, Diana, and Randolph, are identical physical versions of their predecessors, but are they as intelligent?"

Dr. Flanders coughed, like he was choking on Murdoc's words. "Only you and Dr. Reinhart can answer that question."

"Well, in that case, I shall start my study... today."

Randolph's long, confident strides, moved in Murdoc's direction. "You don't have a great reputation, Dr. Murdoc." He said, when he was close to him. "I succeeded, on occasion, to argue that not everything about you was bad, but I can assure you that it was not easy," his eyes and spirit melding with his wide grin.

"Well, that is enough for me." Murdoc said as he threw his arms around his son. "Are you ready to work with a father that looks your age?" They both laughed

We slowly descended the narrow mountain path. I was glad when we arrived at our camp grounds. Murdoc instantly grabbed one of the snowmobiles and Randolph jumped in. "Give me a couple of those laser rifles. I would like a couple surveillance drones. I shall program them myself. I also need a few android scouts to lead the way," Murdoc ordered, and the scout leader acted rapidly.

I waved goodbye as they sped off in the direction of the newly discovered berry bushes and maple trees.

"Do you need anything, Pamela?" Flanders took my hand in his.

"Actually, I think I might just have something warm to drink and then contact the main center and the rest of our group to bring them all up-to-date."

"Good idea." He hesitated. "I thought perhaps Dr. Miller, Drager and some of the android scouts could accompany me. I would like to see if there are any animals, insects, birds, actually, any life forms, inhabiting the higher level caverns in the mountain."

He left and I sat sipping my hot drink. "I want you to be nice to him." I heard Reinhart, initiating a cerebral conversation.

"I will be, but like Murdoc insinuated, my body cannot be a constant playground for the two of you."

She hesitated then said, "It won't be. You and others believed that I was incapable of love. You know now that all of you were wrong. But my first love is intellect, even though I do enjoy the physical side." An understatement that sparked laughter in the confines of our cerebral cavity.

"Dr. Reinhart, you have a call coming through." The android technician overseeing the communications systems called out.

I was there in a flash. "We have some interesting information on the hybrids." Eugene, the former Governor, announced: "Actually, the hare-field mouse hybrid is a rather affectionate species. They like to cuddle up in one's arms. Evidence of vegetation and small insects was found in their feces. This is promising. I suggest that Joseph continue to explore for low, growing plants, maybe root plants, and scrape the sandy surface for insects."

"Excellent idea." Reinhart replied. "And the wolf-grizzly?"

"Right. The very young ones are not aggressive. They behave like dogs, former house pets. We tested them. They actually like to run after balls. Some of my assistants reported that these animals liked to be petted and have their heads scratched." He cleared his throat. "The young adults, though, have the sly, unpredictable behavior of a wolf. The grizzly personality is absent, but an omnivore diet is visible in their feces. We did not receive any older, adult versions of these animals or, more precisely, an alpha male or female."

"Keep studying them. Remember not to frighten them and don't let them escape," she replied. "Now, Eugene, I want to share some good news, from my standpoint, with you."

"Ok." He replied.

"I detected nuclear activity in a mountain in the Eastern region, the reason why I wanted to explore this section," she said. "I found Dr. Murdoc, protected by programmed robots, alive in a cryogenic state in a cavern in the low, lying mountain we were exploring. I awakened and rejuvenated him. I also brought him up-to-date on everything that has happened since the Dooms Day explosion, and shared all my scientific knowledge with him. I hope you, like Flanders, Miller and Drager will work well with him."

"I know how much you loved him, even though you did not always agree with him politically. We, the Group of 5, were your creations so we naturally prioritized your safety over his when the explosion took place," he replied.

"I am grateful you saved me."

"My ultimate allegiance is to you, Dr. Reinhart, but I shall make a concerted effort to work well with him, if that is what you want."

"Thank you, Eugene. That is what I expect and what I want," she replied. "He and his son, Randolph, just left for a short discovery trip in the area where wild berry bushes and maple trees were discovered yesterday by some of the android scouts."

"Is there anything else?" he asked

"I'll call tomorrow," she said

"With pleasure...Dr. Reinhart." He articulated his words slowly. "Is John next to you?"

"I shall go get him." She didn't wait more than a few minutes.

"Dr. Reinhart, your timing is perfect. I just received a message from Colonel Shannon, who received the following response from the High Commissioners: "We are pleased to learn of your highly ambitious projects and are ready to offer whatever assistance we can in the future." He hesitated. "Do you want me to send a reply?"

"Well, that was a rather audacious confirmation of their interception of my private message to Mathieu, Isabel and James." He sat patiently, while she cogitated on a plan of action.

"We shall not answer their message," she finally replied. "Let them think that we are worried."

"Agreed."

"By the way, I want to announce some good news. I have found Dr. Murdoc."

"This is wonderful news, Dr. Reinhart. He will be our "secret weapon." His eyes lit up under a broad smile. "We certainly do not want the High Commissioners to know about his return. We distrusted Murdoc because of his political position, but the High Commissioners really hated him because of his close relationship with you."

"Yes, we must absolutely keep this information secret, so do not mention this to our astronauts." He nodded. "You should, though, tell everyone else at the Center about Murdoc's return. By the way, how are the Group of 5's replacements working out?"

"Very well. They are very cooperative. There is no rivalry. I believe that their lack of a fragmented emotional configuration, like that of the Group of 5 in the past, makes it easier for us to communicate with them," John replied, reflectively.

"That is exactly what I was hoping for. Will talk to you tomorrow," she said, as she signed off.

She then called the desert team. Joseph answered. She gave him an up-date on the animals, telling him that the feces of both species had residues of vegetable and insect life.

"That is excellent news. I guess that we must look more actively for food sources." He made a gurgling sound. "We are perhaps moving too slowly. I planned to go about 20 miles tomorrow, but will perhaps go further."

He stopped to collect his thoughts. "Hopefully, we will find more life forms, vegetation, animals and insects inhabiting this planet. I shall send the scouts out to dig in different areas and ask them to send out drones to take photos of the areas farther ahead." His eyes drifted in thought. "Oh yes, the androids are fortifying the encampment every night now and standing guard during the daytime hours."

"Good news. You must be careful," she replied politely. "Again, you should also look for small lizards, snakes, and the like. They resist desert heat very well." She took a deep breath, before adding that they should be very careful when coming into contact with new life forms.

"I forgot about the reptiles, the snakes, and, of course, the lizards. They probably do support the heat better than us reptilian humans," he commented. "I shall pass on your warning about poisonous insects and will call if we have any problems. Otherwise, I'll talk to you tomorrow."

"Wait!" she called out. "I want to speak to Dr. Gordon and Dr. Crawford. You should stay on-line and listen."

"I'll get them."

"Is everything under control?" Crawford asked.

"Yes, the information that I received from the Governor was very positive."

"I shall give you all the details later," Joseph intervened.

"Thank you, Joseph. Now I want to inform you of a new arrival." She paused. "I found Dr. Murdoc in a cavern in a low, lying mountain in the area our small group is exploring. He was still alive, but in a cryogenic state. I rejuvenated him. He just left to explore the outlying area with his son, Randolph. Dr. Flanders and Dr. Miller who are showing their loyalty to me in supporting Dr. Murdoc."

"Great!" Joseph's enthusiasm visible in his howling lizard tone.

"Ah...this is...very... good...news." Said Dr. Crawford. Gordon nodded. "You can count on us to work well with Dr. Murdoc. Do give Dr. Murdoc our best."

"I shall do that." She said. 'I heard her say in a very low voice, time changes everything.' A smile spread my lips as I rejoiced in her happiness.

She then contacted the other members of our group who were very happy with the news. Rebecca and Tirence both mentioned they were looking forward to meeting Dr. Murdoc.

"We shall stay another couple days in this area. If you have any problems, let us know."

I sensed Reinhart's energy leaving me as she disappeared either to rest or meditate. I was back in control of my mind and body, so I decided to take a tour on my own. I wanted to revisit the fir trees that the robots cultivated. I picked up a couple of laser guns, programmed a few drones to take photos of the area, and took two android scouts with me in my snowmobile. Once we got to the fir trees, I launched the drones and ordered the scouts to explore up ahead.

I was digging in the snow, looking for other signs of life, when an adrenaline surged instinct for survival caused my shoulder muscles to tighten and the hair on the back of my neck to stand up high. Something was observing me at close range. I slowly drew my laser gun from my inside pocket. Once it was secure in my hand, I rolled onto my back and prepared to shoot.

The predator, which I easily identified as a medium sized Bengal tiger because I saw this animal on Gordon's films, was advancing slowly, but was still a safe distance from me. I wondered if it was just curious, or if it was actually hunting me. It was soon close enough for me to perceive its legs quivering as it advanced inches at a time in my direction, waiting for the right moment to spring.

I fired the laser in its direction, purposely avoiding a direct hit, hoping to scare it away. Instead it leaped very quickly out of range. I fired again, as I jumped to my feet, and ran rapidly in zigzags over the 30 feet that separated me from the safety of the large trunk of a tall fir tree. I screamed hoping that the android scouts were close by and would come to my rescue.

Through the low lying branches of the fir tree, I still had a view of the animal. My exoskeleton suit kept my heart beat at an even pace, reminding that I could increase my running speed and leap high, if ever the animal rushed or lunged at me. So I watched and studied the animal's behavior, registering its method of attack, as it continued to advance in my direction. It was only when it got close enough that I could see its bright, bold yellow eyes and almost smell its breath seeping from within its wide open mouth, fortified with sharp teeth and large canines, that I pulled the trigger, releasing a high powered stun that toppled the animal instantly.

The animal lay between me and the snowmobile. 'I should have taken the communicator with me. Why did I leave it in the snowmobile?' I reproached myself.

"Dr. Reinhart."

I jumped at least a foot in the air when I heard the android's voice behind me. It took a few minutes for me to regain my composure before I answered. "No, I am Pamela."

"We came as fast as we could," the android continued.

"The Bengal tiger is out cold between us and the snowmobile. I don't know how long it will stay immobile, but I want to capture this animal alive," I ordered.

"The second scout is arriving. He is just over there." I turned and followed its pointed finger.

"I shall go now and get the snowmobile," the android said, as it rushed off.

"I signaled the drones to return," the second scout reported. "Do you want me to examine the creature laying there in the snow?" it asked.

"It is only stunned. It could awaken at any moment."

"If you would give me the order to go into maximum strength, that animal would be no problem for me."

Only humans could authorize these androids to move to maximum strength, a safety measure to prevent androids from gaining control over us humans. I hesitated an instance, long enough for Reinhart to surface. "Ok, upgrade your system to maximum force." Her voice had a different effect on the android than mine. It bowed obediently and maximized its force.

"Would that android have injured me?" I asked, when the android was too far away to hear me.

"No. It is not capable of independent thinking. It indicated its capacity to upgrade its force, but would not have used that force against you. But, you were right to hesitate," she commented.

The Bengal Tiger began to stir when the android approached it. Reinhart fired on it before it could regain its equilibrium and attack. The other android arrived with the snowmobile, the drones on board. It opened a large compartment underneath the vehicle and removed the pieces of what became a large, metal cage. The two androids moved the tiger into the cage and hooked the cage up to the back of the vehicle.

"I think we should leave now, Dr. Reinhart," the two androids said in unison.

We arrived after Murdoc and Randolph, who rushed towards us. "A Bengal Tiger!" Murdoc applauded. "It appears to be pure bred, which means that at least one ancient species has not been hybridized. But it is smaller than the original Bengal Tiger. Perhaps it is just young."

"You know," he continued, "tigers don't live in groups, they are solitary animals. But male tigers do have their own territory. There might be a female with cubs close by. Perhaps we should take another look tomorrow."

"I don't know if it is young, but I know that it is hungry." I pulled back my lips. "It stalked me. I was lucky that I sensed its presence and that I had a laser stun pistol with me."

"Where was Dr. Reinhart?" Randolph asked.

"She was working, or sleeping, or just not interested. She appeared when the android scouts returned." I didn't like the way Randolph and Murdoc made reference to Reinhart as my savior, like I was incapable of taking care of myself.

"Well, you are alive, Pamela. This was a good learning experience for you," Murdoc commented. That was a slight dig but I chose not to respond to it. "We should contact John and tell him we are sending a Bengal Tiger for him to examine." His eyes quickly scanned our encampment. "But we don't have a plane?"

"Oh, that is not a problem. I shall contact the rest of our group and give them our position. They can send an android-piloted craft that will deliver the goods to John."

I was ready to tackle that project, a good excuse to get away from the two of them, when I heard the voices of Flanders and Miller in the distance.

"We found some unusual creatures in the cavern at the very top of the mountain. We caught a dozen and caged them."

"Where are they?" Murdoc asked.

"The android scouts are carrying them. They are just behind us. We should probably let them pass in front of us so that they can deposit their load."

"Are they birds?" I asked, catching a glimpse of the winged creatures as they passed by me.

"Hybridized birds," Flanders insisted. "They look like a mixture of a Bat, a flying mammal, and an Eagle, a large predatory bird. Their wings and wing span are very large, like that of a Baldheaded Eagle. Before caging them, I noticed that bat wing cartilage was absent and feathers present."

Even though they have that small, brown, furred dog-like mammalian body," he lectured, "they do not have a bat's nose, jaw or mouth, with tiny, sharp teeth. Instead their heads are covered with white feathers, from which protrude the large, hooked beak of a Baldheaded Eagle." He scoffed.

"They were actually hanging upside down, their large eagle claws gripping the ceiling, and their wings, drooping like long-feathered cloaks." He stopped and scratched his head, mimicking his human opposite, reminding us that he had the emotional intelligence and personality of his human opposite.

We waited while he gathered his thoughts. "They attacked us. I think that our android bodies, lacking bitable flesh, confused them. But, my quick study of their method of attack confirmed my suspicions. They definitely have the very keen vision of an Eagle and the echolocation, or super powered volume system of a Bat which makes it easy for them locate their prey. We had a difficult time avoiding the onslaughts of their powerful wings." He looked me straight in the eyes. "Perhaps we should have taken some laser guns with us."

"Yes...obviously," Reinhart replied pensively. "Next time one of us humans will accompany you," she added.

Arriving at our encampment, a quick glimpse at the creatures in the cages gave credibility to Flanders' study of their hybridized origins. "Oh, I forgot to mention. We found insect life!"

"Did you collect any of them?" Reinhart's voice lacked emotion.

"Yes, we captured different kinds of species. They do not seem to be hybridized. We found millipede, centipede, beetles, as well as relatively small spiders, some hiding in cracks and others overseeing their webs. We also dug up worms, at least that is what they looked like to me. I am not an expert on these life forms, but we collected a number of these creatures. They obviously serve as a food source for birds. Do you want to see them?"

"No, I don't need to. Rudolph will inform me of their characteristics and behavior," Reinhart replied.

"Tirence is on-line." The android communication technician screamed, putting an end to the discussion.

We all rushed to the screen. "We sent an android-piloted aircraft to pick up the animals and take them back to the center." He rubbed his hand over his chin, as if in thought. "Actually, a couple of android scouts found a female black bear and two cubs hibernating in a very small cavern. They stunned the animals and brought them back to our camp. With your permission, we would like to send these animals to John and the Governor to study."

"You have my permission," I replied, taking command. "Were they hybridized?"

"They looked like the pictures of black bears on Dr. Miller's educational tapes."

"This is very good news. Looks like animals from the past have survived in their original form. Keep us informed," I heard Murdoc comment. I realized he was not someone who respected protocol.

"Will you be returning soon?" Tirence asked.

"Tomorrow," I signed off.

"Good news!"

"I am starving," Murdoc announced, changing the subject, as he got up to leave.

We all headed to the dining hall.

In route, Diana mentioned: "I called the Center during your absence and spoke to Mathilda. The children are doing well. She said that Rhea is very active and that Flanders' android replacement believes that her birthday is only months away.

"Thank you for the news." I replied sheepishly, embarrassed that I hadn't yet asked about my child.

"Why didn't you invite me to accompany you when you returned to the fir trees?" She asked.

"I don't know. But, I am sorry. In retrospect, I should have asked you."

"He bothers you?" she asked, when we were outside earshot of the others.

"I don't know how."

She grabbed my shoulders and turned me in her direction. "Pamela, he is not Randolph!" she said brashly. "What I mean is that Randolph appears to be a team- player, but Murdoc is like Reinhart. They are both leaders, in their own ways."

She quickly changed her tone. "I like Murdoc's personality."

"Why?" I asked, surprised.

"I like strong-minded men, like Stuart. I also like those who are sensitive and kind, like Jonathan," Diana replied. "Murdoc fascinates me like no other man ever did."

"You don't consider Randolph strong-minded?" I ignored her last comment.

"He hides it. He is manipulative. Murdoc is direct—something I appreciate. I like to know where I stand with men and women."

"But, Randolph is direct with me." I replied vehemently.

"From what I observe, he is very adept at getting you to agree with him." Her normally serious, intense look changed, as her lips moved up into a glistening smile. "He uses a soft touch."

"Maybe with you, but, at least not with me." I answered brusquely. "Randolph and I discuss the alternatives. He is not the kind of person who needs to control."

"Whatever. If you feel on equal terms with Randolph that is all that counts." She threw her hands up in the air.

"Murdoc is the perfect match for Reinhart. He is tough, sure of himself, ready to defy her, convince her that she is wrong and even seek ultimate control, something that seems impossible," Diana continued. "He sees you as her equal, something that you don't understand. If I were you, I would feel flattered. Stop feeling threatened by him."

"Next time you decide to explore an area, ask me to come with you." She added and I nodded, as we entered the dining area.

There was a seat waiting for me between Murdoc and Randolph. They coaxed me over and Diana took the seat in front of me. It seemed natural for Murdoc to seek Elisabeth's companionship and Randolph's mine. Unfortunately for Murdoc, Elisabeth was busy working on her projects.

"I heard you say we would be leaving tomorrow, Pamela," Murdoc mentioned, between gulps of food. "I am starving." He blurted out, between bites. "What do the rest of you think?" He looked at the androids. "I am talking to you, Flanders and Miller, as well. Get over here and join in," he ordered.

"And Dr. Reinhart, what does she think?" Flanders asked, hiding behind Reinhart's skirt.

"Who cares?" Murdoc replied. "Stop pretending that you are something you never were, or someone who takes orders from their superiors. Need I remind you about the treacherous things you did in the past."

"Ok, that is enough, Dr. Murdoc. The past is the past. You have to accept the fact that we are all living in a different era," I replied, in a firm voice, Diana nodding in approval.

He slapped me so hard on my back that my head fell forward. "That is the way I like to see a woman think." He shook with laughter.

"We are running out of supplies, so it is probably a good time to leave," Flanders mentioned.

"Actually, I think I would like to fly farther south," I said boldly. "I am ready to leave the cold, boreal forests and venture into the deciduous forest area." I paused. "Does anyone know what season it is father south?"

"It should be springtime," Miller replied. "Moving on is an excellent idea, Pamela. We have found animal life in this area and can send androids to continue to scout for other specimens. But will Dr. Reinhart agree?"

"I don't see why she would object," I got up and left. I wanted to be alone. I walked to the edge of our campsite and sat on a small bench, leaning my head back to study the sky. The stars, barely visible behind a thick veil of a cloudy mist, intensified my sadness. "I miss you, Peter," my voice barely audible.

"It is cold out here." His voice startled me and I turned quickly, only to see Murdoc sit down next to me "I should have been kinder, more considerate with you, because you are not like your Mother.

You are more sensitive and emotional than she is—something I find quite charming."

I felt his arm move around me and I let my head rest on his shoulder. "You mustn't worry, Pamela, Elisabeth and I shall save your family."

"How can you be so sure?" Hoping to provoke him. "The two of you lost everything in the past."

"Because what happened in the past was our plan."

I didn't even have the strength to push him away, something that made it easier for him to pull me even more tightly into his arms. "Get a hold of yourself and try to think clearly," his voice low and firm, as he maintained his grip. "If it hadn't been planned, then why are Elisabeth and I here today? It was not an accident or clever move by the Group of 5." He chuckled. "They were programmed to bring her back and she would later come for me."

He released me like he was throwing away a wet rag. I watched him pace back and forth. "Can you keep a secret?" he finally asked, in a calm voice.

"I think so," I replied.

"You must never tell anyone what I am going to tell you. Promise me!"

"I promise," I said hesitating, wondering if I could keep the secret. I was more vulnerable, more human, than him or Reinhart.

"You know I was in touch with the non-intellectuals and even lived among them on occasion," I nodded. "I could honestly understand their pain and frustration, but as my rational side is far more dominant than my emotional side, I was able to keep my distance. Even though Elisabeth claimed, and continues to claim, she feels guilty because she blew up that spaceship, she avoids emotional attachments." He sat on the bench and looked up at the heavens.

"You know she loves you." The words just slipped out.

"And so she does," he said, turning towards me and lifting his eyebrows suggestively, making me laugh. "We go back a long time," his voice sober, "and our love has grown stronger with time."

"The living conditions of the non-intellectuals," he picked up where he left off, "were despicable, but bringing them into the center to live was impossible especially due to_their numbers." He cleared his throat. "Strangely enough, as Reinhart's disappointment with the intellectuals was less intense than her abhorrence for the non-intellectuals, she convinced me that annihilation of the human race was the best solution. So we designed an ingenious plan."

He took a deep breath. "I appeared during her final address to the intellectuals and promised them a victory, usurping the power of Reinhart, throwing her into the hands of the Group of 5. I then added a very primitive military programming to the android fighting force, and programmed others to kill humans. I downloaded programs in Drager that Reinhart could access if she needed to neutralize any android military force in the future." A slight smile touched his lips. "It was a good thing that I did that because the Captain was apparently a real danger."

"Why didn't you just fight and destroy the non-intellectuals and then take power yourselves?"

"Because, Pamela, as I just mentioned, Reinhart wanted all human life to be destroyed." He sighed. "Even if that had not been her most profound desire, Reinhart was destined to die---and, I guess, I was too, regardless of which group won the revolution. So it was better for us to sabotage them and save ourselves for the future, which is what we did," he replied in a cold, detached tone.

"But it took thousands or more years before you reappeared. You consider that to be a victory."

"Yes," he replied adamantly. "Because we took a big risk and... we won!" He thundered.

"Did you expect Crawford to kill Reinhart? Did you imagine that the Group of 5 would set off the Doomsday explosion and then begin a cruel and inhumane process of programming humans, exploiting them and then disposing of them at a predetermined date?"

"We both knew that Reinhart would be executed, but, of course, we thought it would be the humans who would carry it out." He gritted his teeth. "Crawford actually offered her a kinder death, although I won't tell him that."

He paused. "The Group of 5 was worshipped by the non-intellectuals and the intellectuals, so we both knew they would survive, even if one of the groups actually won and humanity continued. What neither group of humans understood was that the Group of

5 was faithful only to Reinhart and they would have found a way to bring her back—something they were programmed to do anyway-- by whatever means was at their disposal."

"And the fate of other humans that they created?"

"Well, I didn't program them to do that. But maybe Reinhart did. The Doomsday explosion was an extraordinary risk, but I have to compliment them on their decision. It achieved our objective in a single move." He cleared his throat. "As for the inhumane treatment of humans, well, like it or not, Pamela, Reinhart and I can hold no grudge because they accomplished their mission and brought her back and then, indirectly, helped to bring me back. It was all a big risk and the Group of 5's participation was critical," he repeated himself.

"And to save my family, is that a big risk that could take thousands of years?"

A slim smile tainted his lips. "Of course, nothing is a certitude, Pamela. That is why we have to be well prepared and ready to change our game plan, if necessary. And, most importantly, we have to stay focused and never become overconfident," he sighed.

"Yes, it is a calculated risk, but I plan to enjoy the win this time, when I take down my enemies! It should be interesting, amusing, annoying, and eventually, fulfilling, working with you, Pamela."

He stood up, leaving me. My only thought was: "I understand why Diana is so infatuated by this man."

Chapter 13: Unveilings

I woke up feeling confident. "Some of Murdoc's self-confidence, spilling over onto me." I thought, as I jumped up and rushed through my morning routine.

"The snowmobiles are packed and ready to leave," Miller announced, as she served a plate of dry biscuits surrounded with wild berries dotted with maple syrup. She noticed my hesitation. "We spoke to John this morning. He informed us that Ralph confirmed these products are edible."

We dug in, enjoying the succulent flavors of these natural berries, lightly covered in maple syrup.

"Do you have a first name, Dr. Murdoc?" Diana asked, between bites.

"Good question." He laid down his spoon. "Everyone called me Murdoc, just Murdoc, before I entered into the academy of sciences." He picked up his spoon and pushed the berries around. "One of my professors called me Artturi, all the others called me Aegir." After I graduated and began to work with Dr. Reinhart, I introduced myself as Dr. Murdoc. "

"And your parents, why didn't they give you a first name?" Diana pried.

"Because I had no parents—at least, no father or mother that I ever knew. But, parenting was not in vogue when I was born." He squinted, as if he were remembering something painful.

"So which name do you prefer, Arturri or Aegir?" Diana continued to probe for answers.

"And you?"

"Aegir."

"So you can call me Aegir if you prefer that to Murdoc," he replied in a gruff voice.

After the androids loaded the main tent with all the living accessories, like showers, beds and dryers, onto the large transporter,

154

Murdoc jumped into the driver's seat. I felt Reinhart's energy surface rapidly, as she argued with him over which one of them was going to drive that large, heavily equipped vehicle, while the androids took off in the smaller ones. In the end, Murdoc relented, moved over and let Reinhart take the wheel. She sped past the smaller vehicles, making certain that ours would be the first to arrive.

"Are you ok, Dr. Murdoc?" I asked, when I found him alone.

"Why wouldn't I be?"

"I thought you had a hard day, but I guess that I was wrong." I blushed unwittingly.

"Are you referring to Diana or Elisabeth?" He asked.

"Both."

"Give me a minute to find the right words." His eyes moved pensively from side to side. "Ok. There are moments when one has to be tough and uncompromising and there are other moments when even the embarrassment of conceding something that may not necessarily be negligible, is more effortless and more rational than arguing." He approached me and stared into my eyes. "Did you understand?" I nodded.

"So which first name do you prefer?" I quickly changed the subject.

"Ok. Aegir because it is an informal name. And you?"

"The same."

"But to be perfectly honest, though," he replied in a soft, distant voice, "I don't prefer, a first name basis. So call me by my last name, Murdoc, because it has been associated by some with my determination and strength, and has been known to inspire fear in others. So if you don't mind, I would rather avoid the first name basis." I nodded obligingly.

"Hello, Dr. Murdoc." Jason pushed his way between us. "Do you remember me?"

"Should I?"

"I was Dr. Reinhart's experiment in cryogenics. She recruited me from among the non-intellectuals and I was the only one that survived. The Group of 5 opened my tank, or tube, or whatever you call it, and I escaped from the Center, becoming an explorer, living for short periods of time with one outside community after another."

"Dr. Reinhart brought me up-to-date on everything and everyone, including you, Jason. You were definitely one of her experiments." He swallowed slowly. "I know, like me, she rejuvenated you, Jason. We both returned from the dead—you, many years ago and me, less than 24 hours ago. Having this in common is and will also be our binding force." Their faces lit up with complicity.

Jason turned quickly, motioning to Ludovic to join them. "Ludovic is the last of the people of many colors."

"My sincere regrets for the annihilation of your family and friends," Murdoc replied, in a low voice. "I am happy you survived and I look forward to working with you." He reached out and shook his hand.

Randolph introduced his father to Rebecca and Tirence who, in turn, introduced him to Birch and Basil. I was expecting him to be pretentious, to react, like he did with us, the young versions of the illustrious scientists that he collaborated with in the past, and then flaunt his intellectual superiority. Instead, he reached out to them, shaking their hands. He smiled as he spoke, situating them as his equals, complementing them on their scientific acumen, mentioning how much he was looking forward to working with them, and encouraging them to continue to progress.

He gained their allegiance instantly and the small group followed him, continuing to recount their lives, adventures, and the various projects they were working on at the moment. Certainly he was not only what he pretended to be, or sensitive to the misery of the non-intellectuals making him capable of showing great empathy, but also an undoubtedly accomplished manipulator.

It was late in the evening, after all the excitement of our reunion ended and we were ready to get some sleep, when Murdoc took me aside and asked to be alone with Reinhart. Reinhart sensed my agreement, but replaced me only partially, letting me eavesdrop in the beginning on parts of their conversation by keeping my cerebral consciousness alert.

He was not interested in conversation. Instead, he took my hand and led us to a small alcove that served as a passage between the two main tents, where he had moved a large mat at some point during the evening. "What do you think, Elisabeth?" I felt my body collapse in his arms, as he lifted me so easily, pulling me close up against him, his desire mounting as he breathed in Reinhart's natural, rich, vibrant sexual pheromones, emitting an intoxicating, vanilla scent.

His steps faltered both under the odor of her heightened sexuality and her warm, moist kisses as she moved my body closer up in his arms. His legs trembled as he struggled to gently place my body on the low lying mat. She cuddled up against him, rubbing my face up against his chest, breathing in his fresh male sexual pheromones doused with the deep, woody, balsamic scent of sandalwood, sending shivers of desire rushing through my body, becoming stronger and stronger, revealing my heightened sexuality, as I reached out to him, drawing him closer to me. And then, in an instance, when I so wanted to be a partner in their love, I was absent.

When I awakened, I was in a cot between Murdoc and Randolph. I noticed that Randolph was in a sound, peaceful sleep. When I turned in Murdoc's direction, his shining eyes met mine. "Thank you, Pamela," he whispered.

The androids had breakfast ready when I arrived. Murdoc had already finished eating and I could hear him calling out orders and giving instructions to the android crew, on where to load the different material onto the aircraft.

"Hi, Pamela," Randolph said, startling me, as he came up behind me, breaking into my thoughts. I forced a smile.

"They were together last night," he commented. "So where were you?"

"My system was shut down," I said and he feigned a chuckle.

"Are there any other surprises that Reinhart has in mind for us?" he asked, as he swallowed a big gulp of freshly squeezed berry juice.

"She was very patient with me all these years, giving me the privacy I needed so that I could be with Peter and you." I replied in a low, distant voice before shaking off memories and turning to his question. "Surprises. I don't know."

"I agree that she was indulgent with you but she had no desire to seek emotional, or even physical, satisfaction and certainly not, vicariously!" His voice rose an octave. "She focused on resolving practical matters and working on scientific projects." He shrugged his shoulders, put down his spoon, and got up to leave.

I rushed after him. "Wait! We can take a walk if you want."

"Why not," he said enthusiastically, as he grabbed my hand and led me to a secluded space.

Sitting on the hard, ice-covered snow, my head resting against his shoulder, thoughts flickered through my mind. 'Why didn't she put me in a deep sleep sooner? Why did she want me to feel her fervor of love?' And then the answer came to me. "She wanted me to know that she was capable of receiving and giving profound love in all its splendor when she was in the arms of Murdoc."

When Randolph's mouth meet mine, jarring me from my emotional quandary, that tingling, sparkling energy of Murdoc's lips against mine the night before was missing and I felt deep frustration. "I think that we better get back to the others," I said, as I moved abruptly out of his arms and stood up.

"What is the matter? Are you attracted to him?"

"No, Randolph." I said as tears formed that I couldn't prevent.

"This is crazy, Pamela."

"They are another generation..." I pushed past him. "I am a bit confused."

"He does not have the right to play with your emotions," his voice deepened. "I am going to talk to him. He can have Reinhart, but not you!"

"Reinhart said that there was a solution to this problem waiting for us at the Center."

"What did she mean?"

"I don't know. Just please be patient."

We walked back in silence.

"Where have you been?" Diana called out. "We are ready to leave."

This time, Reinhart did not ask Murdoc to let her pilot the plane. She sat in the co-pilot seat, with Randolph and Drager occupying the seats behind us.

"You are not alone, Dr. Murdoc, so please don't resort to aerial acrobatics," Miller called out, as he revved up the motor.

The plane sped down the short icy runway, tilting to the right as he lifted it and steered it sharply off to the south.

He flew low so that we could see the fine, and then wider, cracks that appeared on the icy, snowy surface, forming cobwebs of streams, as they fed into a vast wasteland of dark, muddy, brown soil that added a certain monotony to the flight, putting everyone but Murdoc and I to sleep.

"So what happened out there between you and Randolph?" he asked, breaking the silence. "He is sound asleep. He can't hear you," he added.

I turned to make sure that Randolph was asleep. His eyes were closed and he was leaning back in his sleep, so I replied softly. "Nothing really."

"He loves you, Pamela. I can tell when a man is in love."

"But, not like you love Elisabeth." The words just slipped out.

There was a long silence. "He can't love you like I love Elisabeth, for many reasons, the most important of which is that you don't love him exclusively. You also love Peter."

"I forgot that Reinhart brought you up-to-date on everything that happened during your years of absence, including details on all of our lives. So you know about Peter?"

"Yes, she brought me up-to-date about everything, but you also told me about your love for him the other night when you were sitting studying the stars." He replied.

"So, it is my fault?"

"To a certain extent, yes, you are at fault." He stopped to adjust the flight pattern. "But, quite frankly, the real problem has to do with the way in which your emotions came to life. There was no competition for Peter in that small outside community. You both needed each other and found happiness together. He protected you when you were with him and you certainly love each other. Elisabeth has confirmed that." He paused.

"You and Randolph began your relationship inside the center where defying the system, outwitting the Group of 5 and organizing a revolt animated your relationship and you became playmates, hiding feelings and just enjoying sex. Today it is evident that your love for him is sincere, but that makes you feel guilty. You hold your feelings back... so he does the same." He spoke like a friend, showing me he cared about me and his son.

"So what should I do?"

"You can't do anything for the moment. And you should stop looking for the same sensations with him that I share with Elisabeth. We go back a long time."

"Look over there." He said, as he pointed to the tall trees in the distance. "We might actually have the pleasure of some long walks in a blooming forest and fall under its mesmerizing, intoxicating odors of springtime." He landed the plane 20 meters from the forest entrance and the android piloted supply planes landed alongside.

The androids immediately began to set up camp. "I want to contact Joseph and John." Reinhart was back. "It is late. The flight was longer than I expected." She added, looking Murdoc straight in the eyes. He shrugged his shoulders and left to oversee the androids.

Joseph answered quickly. "We stumbled upon the burrows of that rabbit-field mouse hybrid. Their burrows were next to what might be considered an oasis. A pool of water with grass, long-stemmed weeds and different low shrubs, some of which could be a kind of cactus." He stopped to catch his breath. "We sent samples back to Ralph to study."

"Excellent."

"We are now approaching the area with large sand dunes. And the android scouts reported finding strange, very round, hard surfaced mounds in a circular formation about 30 miles up ahead." He moved into a reclining position. "I think that we shall investigate that area tomorrow."

"Make certain you have laser guns with you and that you are wearing protective gear, or your exoskeleton suits, when you are exploring." Reinhart ordered.

"We have been very cautious since our run in with those wolf-grizzly animals." His globular eyes swelled as he stared into mine. "As I mentioned to you once before, Clarence and Linda support the heat better than my species, but that does not affect our high level of enthusiasm," he added, punctuating his species impediment.

"The exoskeleton suits will adjust your body temperature so

that you can support very hot and very cold environments," she replied pedantically. "Are you wearing them?"

"Not all the time." Joseph lowered his eyes. "I shall inform all the reptilian humans to wear the suits regularly. I didn't know..."

"Well, I know that I mentioned this. Perhaps you were not listening to me. Anyway, you know now. So wear them," she ordered. "And, Joseph, wait until Dr. Gordon visits the hard, round domed site and reports back to me. Stay with Dr. Crawford for the moment."

"Hello, Dr. Reinhart." Dr. Gordon and Dr. Crawford said in unison.

"I am pleased with your cooperation and engagement in the exploration of the region." They nodded. "I would like you to split up today. Dr. Crawford, I believe that you should stay with Joseph and his group and continue to explore the area you are in, joining Dr. Gordon and her group, only after she has had time to study the hard domes and confirm that the area will pose no danger for the humans and reptilian humans."

"We shall carry out thorough investigations and give you detailed reports." Crawford spoke for the both of them.

"You should probably leave now, Dr. Gordon, with the last group of androids moving into that area." Joseph added.

Reinhart then placed a call to the main center. John was with the former Governor, when he answered my call. They were both on the screen. "There is so much happening that we can hardly keep up with everything. We are still studying the various animal and plant species coming from your area and the western region. The android replacements of the group of 5 are working very well. Their participation is critical." John replied.

"Almost forgot—we heard from the Captain late last evening. They have not encountered any navigational difficulty. WD and Weldon are making an excellent team, even though they have not found any new marine life." He cleared his throat huskily.

"The Captain sent us samples of different species of birds-seagulls, pelicans, and several varieties of albatross," he continued. "Sarah, Ralph and Ruth examined them this morning. They mentioned that although they are physiologically identical to their ancestors, there are noticeable anatomical differences. For example, all new species are twice the size of their ancestors, with larger, more powerful wingspans of 4, 8 and 12 feet, in the order in which the species were mentioned."

"Ralph should continue his research. I am particularly interested in the reason why these species have doubled in size."

"No, just a minute." He raised his hand. I heard him ask the Governor to check with Ralph about any other species that might have arrived.

When he left the room, John told Reinhart that he received another message from Colonel Shannon, asking when he could speak with her. "I noticed right away that her hair was disheveled and her vest only half buttoned, a real contrast with her normal, proper military appearance. When she spoke in a brittle, cracking voice, I understood that she was under extreme pressure to get a reaction from you. I actually felt sorry for her."

He swallowed hard. "She has always been very cooperative with us, but, things have changed. So I told her I was not sure when I might hear back from you."

"Thanks, John! Keep her, and the others, wondering."

Murdoc heard the end of the conversation. Their faces sparked the same smile of complicity the moment Elisabeth switched off the communication system. "Do you think that we can do it—win another battle this time against six deranged Commissioners, with the crew of the *Benevolence* acting under their command?" She nodded.

"You said that the spaceship was in apparent good condition?" He continued.

"Yes, but the systems have to be examined closely. Moreover we need crew and android soldiers. And, we shall have to program androids to win a war and not lose a war, like in the past."

"No problem with that. It was actually much more difficult to program them to lose. We shall do it. Let Shannon and her crew and those deranged Commissioners panic and make some mistakes. They are becoming impatient and, as we both know, impatience breeds carelessness."

"So we continue to explore this area?"

"Elisabeth, let's go have a nice dinner of dried food smothered in berries. And then enjoy an evening together." She nodded.

I was still alert when they left for a stroll. "There are things that I need more answers to...or, just need to understand better, Elisabeth."

"Like what?"

"The emotional configurations, or emotional intelligence. The emotional configuration is the programming and the emotional intelligence is the way in which their former personalities evolved within the context of the program."

"Oh, Aegir, I made mistakes." She interrupted him, revealing her first name preference for Murdoc.

"No, I am not talking about the androids. Generations and generations of so-called brilliant scientists made mistakes on artificial intelligence. They believed that artificial intelligence would save the human race." He laughed mockingly.

"They were even...so fascinated with artificial intelligence and, at the same time, impressed, enamored with themselves, for creating it." He continued. "In spite of warnings from a minority of scientists, referred to as negative thinkers, the human race naively believed that they could control androids through complicated, inhibiting algorithms, principally viruses. But it didn't happen. Those scientists were not intelligent or competent enough to succeed in ensuring their survival by creating androids identical to themselves in all aspects, physical, emotional, intellectual, to name a few."

He stared deeply into my eyes. "Amazing that you found the right programming solutions."

"Yes, creating my android opposite was a high-risk project. I needed to design a program that would give me control over the knowledge bank I installed in her. And, I wanted her to develop emotional intelligence that would reflect my own cognitive emotional processing." My throat tightened as her memories surfaced.

"Even though humans and androids have often times compared me to a machine, imagining that I am only cold-blooded and insensitive, I do have feelings. And I discovered to what extent I have feelings when I came face to face with my android opposite." She paused.

"I was surprised by the way in which my android opposite selected only dominant aspects of my personality, interpreting and applying them in a purely logical fashion, ignoring human sensitivity at even the most basic level. And, worse, my android opposite misread my true personality, thus resorting to lying and manipulation to gain power."

"But like all machines," she continued "she assumed that her genius surpassed mine, which was not the case. She realized at the very last instance the power I had over her. Even pleading and begging me to give her another chance was useless. I actually felt a certain pleasure when I released that hidden, undetectable virus that forced her to self-destruct."

"Yes, you refreshed my memory about that when you rejuvenated me. And, Elisabeth, even though human stupidity in the past leaves me dumbstruck, I am in awe of your genius!" He smiled, before adding. "But, this does not answer my question: Why did the Group of 5 program humans? That is where I am confused."

"The reason goes back in time and is based on a combination of the following hypotheses, keeping in mind the control that I continued to have over them, even in my absence," she began. "The Group of 5 was alert and understood that they could not develop emotional intelligence through their own free will, because my programming prevented that. They also feared that they, like my android opposite, carried viruses, one of which would activate and shut them down, if ever they did, even accidentally, find a way to install an emotional configuration." She replied.

"And they were certainly aware of the risk that they might encounter, if they tried to neutralize my viral backups. The only way for them to have, let's say, the right, to develop emotional intelligence, to either replace humans completely or use humans to serve them, was to bring me back. That became their ultimate project. But, rational creatures, they knew that they had to first test their skill in reproducing humans."

"Ok, but something is missing..."

"Please, be patient." She interrupted him. "Another more general reason is that being surrounded by humans and serving or working with them was so deeply imbedded in their system, that having humans working with them was inextricable from their overall raison d'être." She stopped for a split second to observe him.

"Moreover, the Group of 5 was, and probably still is, convinced they are superior to me, their creator, but to prove their superiority, if we reason like a machine using pure logic, their absence of emotional intelligence does not place them on the same level as me or humans in general." She drew a deep breath.

"For example, they will not question or adapt a logical decision by taking into consideration its humanitarian nature, or integrating ideas like love, affection, concern, anger, frustration, and other such emotional elements. And, as they cannot integrate emotional elements, they cannot predict how humans may reason and react. So, to prove their superiority they decided they had to be both intellectually more brilliant and also better able to master emotional intelligence than humans and eventually me." She sighed.

"Apparently my programming reinforced their own obsessive need to reproduce humans and study humans with and without emotional intelligence. They compared the control group, or the programmed humans in the Center, to the small community living on the outside, whose decisions were based upon logic and emotions; each person having their own personalities and convictions integrated into their decisions." She stopped.

"I still don't get it. Why program humans?" He insisted.

"Because humans are unpredictable, or were, up until now, for the Group of 5. They used the same method that I did with the non-intellectuals. Programming humans to see a rosy colored world gave the Group of 5 ultimate control. This way they could exploit the humans, like humans did androids, and dispose of them when they became redundant."

"I never agreed with your programming humans. I found it revolting, Elisabeth," he protested.

"I know, but that is because you saw this as degrading, when in fact I used it to make their lives more euphoric. You lived with them, for short periods at a time and understood their pain, suffering, and frustrations. You spent time with them in their sub-standard housing or in their underground caverns where you were exposed on a regular basis to physically debilitating levels of pollution in air, water and everything they touched." She sighed.

"The centers," she picked up, "where the intellectuals were

living, were unpolluted, dome-covered and protected, but they were not large enough to receive the vast number of humans living on the outside."

"I realized too late that my programming was not foolproof and that extraneous elements, like electric shocks or extreme emotional reactions, or even the malfunctioning of their visual receptors could neutralize the non-intellectuals programming and they would see the real world they were living in."

"Dehumanization is a human condition," she continued. "Human history is replete with examples, discrimination on physical and intellectual levels, exploitation of the poor by the rich, torture, slavery...need I go on?"

"No. I find that part of human nature revolting." Murdoc replied. "I despised the rich with their attitudes of superiority. If I could have saved the non-intellectuals I would have, but it was impossible. The masses were under the influence of violent, irrational leaders who resorted to satanic forms of manipulation. I lost interest in them when they resorted to cannibalism."

"These non-intellectuals were a constant reminder of how easily humans can be manipulated. Before they were programmed, they sought meaning, because existing was simply not enough for them." Murdoc coughed violently, as if he were choking on her words. She just ignored him.

"Elisabeth, I do remember my role in helping the non-intellectuals and in orchestrating the revolution and, what we discussed earlier, assuring our return in the future. But, I was not yet born, or very young, when certain events took place. And, it is interesting to learn why you distrusted the intellectuals."

"The past and present generations of humans spoke of different, invisible forces ---some evil, others kind---that they called Gods, Devils, Supernatural creatures, and so forth. They worshipped, sought to appease these creatures they believed would protect and guide them and, eventually, offer them a better world—whether a high flying spiritual existence after death or a return to Earth as evil spirits with extraordinary powers so that they could wreak havoc and torture the living." She stopped abruptly.

"Elisabeth, these non-intellectuals were just lost, confused, un-happy, desperate people."

"Perhaps, you are right. But. I don't agree with you," she pro-tested. "They were all just fundamentally human!" she said, in an outburst of rage, smothered in contemptuous sarcasm.

"Just like humans in the past they looked for leaders, who they referred to as prophets, revolutionaries, visionaries, ideologists, dark spirits, to mention a few—that would show them how to live and obey an ideology which favored either peace or war, but would eventually lead to the killing and torturing of others in order to im-pose their beliefs and thus give meaning to their lives."

She stared off into the distance, before adding, "How could pro-gramming these irrational individuals to be happy and believe that their lives had meaning be worse than what they would naturally seek? At least they were not killing and torturing each other."-

"But, to return to your original question, regarding the Group of 5," she mocked, "after years of experimenting in recreating our scientific team, they achieved the seemingly unachievable, bringing back physically identical members of my original team, with the same intellectual capacity or IQ. Not all of them, though, appeared at the same time, which is why I had to rejuvenate or make younger, certain members recently."

She paced back and forth. "I used a machine in the center to re-juvenate members before evolving and being capable of rejuvenat-ing someone by entering into the individual's body and mind, like I did with you."

"The Group of 5 knew that these members of my team were physically perfect replicas, but needed to test the emotional de-velopment of these humans to be certain they had the same per-sonalities and emotional intelligence. So they arranged for their deprogramming."

"The Group of 5 agreed to let John, the self-proclaimed leader of the Group of humans, live in a cavern outside the large center, and promised to feed and clothe them. In this way, the Group of 5 ac-complished what they wanted. They were able to observe and study the emotional development of the humans on a daily basis. And the Group of 5 was more than competent enough to carry out this study. Eventually the Group of 5 concluded that, in all cases, their emotional configurations compared favorably to their ancestors."

"So everything that happened was planned!" Murdoc replied with fervor. "But, Stuart and Randolph never left the Center."

"That is true," she said slowly. "But, Stuart and Randolph were the control Group. The Group of 5 compared emotional development in a presumably free zone to emotional development in a programmed environment. While Randolph, Stuart and John worked together with the other humans living in the outside community to organize a revolution, overthrow the Group of 5 and put power back in the hands of humans." Murdoc did not reply, so she continued.

"Then reality set in when The Group of 5 feared they might lose control. They began to recognize the danger of not being able to anticipate and defend against humans seeking power and the right to determine their own destiny. As such, they brought me back. Fortunately, Pamela Series 13 was at the right age to interest me and was the perfect depository for me, because she had never studied any of the sciences."

"Ok, you don't have to say more," Murdoc broke in. "You did not want someone getting involved in your projects or challenging you."

Her eyes narrowed. "Just to remind you, I let the Group of 5 serve me over the last few years, refusing to give them what they wanted, or an emotional configuration. And yet, as you know, their strong allegiance to me is unwavering because it is integrated into their programming at every level. They cannot resist worshipping me which of course gives me absolute control over them. And recently, I added other elements that give me the power to force one or all of them to shut down."

Murdoc hesitated, pondering and slowly choosing his words, "Yes. Your distrust of both humans and machines is a formidable aspect of your character that carries over into the way that you interact with both humans and machines."

"Dr. Murdoc, it is not simply distrust that influences my actions and reactions to humans and machines, it is my ability to see the whole picture and my acute understanding of humans and androids that makes it possible for me to surpass them both," she sighed.

"I am by nature, cold and calculating; but even more so, I am determined to succeed in my ultimate mission, which I have not yet revealed to anyone, simply because I do not remember my very distant past." She forced a smile.

"So...," he stuttered, realizing that he had gone too far, "humans without emotions were like primitive androids," He said returning to the previous discussion. "The Group of 5 did not feel threatened by them. Even worse, they did not feel worshipped or even respected by them either," he said, and she nodded.

"Well, I am now able to follow their logic. It all makes sense. They were patient, focused and, much as I despise saying this, contrived a brilliant strategy which was also a virtual miracle for us humans," he admitted.

"Don't say anything laudatory to them, Murdoc, and don't be so nice to them. I can see that they feel more comfortable around you, sense a comradery, when it would be better to stand firm." She hesitated. "Treat them like you did in the past."

"Understood," he remarked. "I didn't realize that I was being nice," he snickered.

"I guess that we should get some sleep," Reinhart said, moving in the direction of the tent.

"Oh, by the way, do you know, Elisabeth, that Pamela is uncomfortable about your sharing her body intimately with me. And she thinks that my son is not as skillful a lover as I am," his voice floating on self-esteem.

Turn me off, my mind was pleading, but she pretended that she did not hear me, "I know," she replied nonchalantly. "I shall put her to sleep earlier from now on...

"But tonight," she continued, "let's just get a good night's sleep. I don't know what we might find in the deciduous forest, so we have to be alert," she said, as she disappeared, leaving me holding Murdoc's hand.

"Hi, Pamela," he said as he continued to look straight ahead.

'Amazing how everything about her, -voice, touch, ideas, dominance, and more- was remarkably absent when she turned off.' With these thoughts smoldering inside of me, I struggled to release his grip.

"I am glad that you and Elisabeth are not the same. It would be very sad to have you an identical replica of her."

"Thank you, Dr. Murdoc," I replied, in an officious tone, keeping myself on guard with this accomplished seducer.

The bed between Murdoc and Randolph was waiting for me. Diana, in the bed across from me, was not yet asleep and discretely waved goodnight. I lay awake for a long moment.

I pondered Murdoc's quick summary of my emotional attachments to Peter and Randolph, his words repeating over and over again in my mind. Even though none of us were faithful in the old-fashioned definition of coupling and didn't really expect fidelity, each of us had one person with whom we felt the most emotionally, or perhaps just psychologically, entwined. In the end, memories of Peter soothed me and helped my eyes to gently close.

It seemed that I was just drifting, when Flanders abruptly shouted. "Time to wake up. The android scouts have already left and will hopefully send us data soon. We have the vehicles ready, although it would be better for all of you to hike."

"You miserable machine, that is no way to wake people up!" Murdoc sending Flanders scurrying out of the room.

We got up and rushed to get dressed, only to sit down to a healthy, but tasteless breakfast.

"Dr. Flanders and I will stay here and oversee the construction of a tent to receive the various life forms you might capture or collect." Dr. Miller mentioned and no one objected.

The forest, covering a large land mass, was within walking distance. The android scouts, under the supervision of Drager, had already started to clear a narrow path through the dense, thick underbrush, cutting and sweeping aside the shoulder high thickets to prevent any entanglement or injury to any of us humans. Our team now included Rebecca, Tirence, Jason, Ludovic, Basil and Birch. In a single file, we followed, behind Randolph and Murdoc, who warned us of any holes, stumps or fallen branches, encumbering our passage.

As it was just the beginning of springtime, only buds and blossoms covered the compact layers of branches stemming from the tall, thick trunked Maple, Oak and Beech trees, letting the sunlight peek through their heavily populated quarters, in a bedimmed haze of visibility. The humid, woody odor of the moist, humus soil covered with lichens, fungi and mosses rose from the forest floor, attenuating as it blended from time to time with the sweet smell of honeysuckle, the pungent odors of thyme and rosemary or the musky odor of Balsam Poplar.

There were moments when I was certain that I heard the rapid tapping of a woodpecker, the chirping of crickets, the loud, shrill cry of a crow, or the whiny call of a robin. Movements under the forest canopy gave me the impression that there might be other life forms following or escaping our heavy footsteps.

Perhaps there were reptiles, like snakes and lizards, as well as squirrels and chipmunks, or even worms, caterpillars and slugs, as well as grasshoppers and ants underfoot. But, their true form was indiscernible. Even the low growing shrubs were hidden from our view, and yet we could see the blue, yellow, pink and white petals of wild flowers peeking through, reminding us of their existence, as they laid buried deep within the density of this forest.

We trudged onward for several hours along this narrow, slippery corridor, reaching 5 miles within the forest, hoping for an open space, but there was none. The high, dense walls of prickly vegetation and sharp, thorny branches, on both sides of us impeded efforts to meticulously explore the area and even gather specimens. We finally arrived at the thick patches of evergreens that forced us to halt. Drager motioned to us to go back.

We turned obligingly. My earlier excitement vanished and I began to see the forest from a different angle. I wanted to push forward rapidly to reach the exit, but the uneven, rugged path made it necessary for all of us to be cautious and alert.

Heavy darkness fell on us. I clutched Jason's shoulders. I wondered if he shared my anxieties, enhanced while imagining the exit would close before we arrived and the walls of vegetation would fold around us until we could no longer move or breathe. 'It is my claustrophobia,' I reminded myself. Fortunately, Reinhart intervened, pushing me to take long firm strides, and in turn pushing Jason and the others, until we eventually reached our original point of entry.

Randolph and Murdoc, at the back of the line, maintained a comfortable distance from the group, arriving a good 15 minutes after us.

Reinhart disappeared with their arrival, leaving me with a palpitating heart and perspiration shining my face.

"Perhaps we should take a small plane and fly over the area this afternoon," Diana commented.

"Good Idea, Diana. Plodding along **a** narrow path was a waste of time," Murdoc replied. "Actually, I am starving. I hope that Flanders and Miller have something better than dried biscuits to offer us."

"Dr. Reinhart," I turned to see Drager rushing towards me. "I thought perhaps we should clear out a larger path. I could use heavier equipment to cut down trees and thickets to widen the path and then remove some of the evergreens that impeded our advancement. We could always let the wood dry in the storage tent and use it for firewood later."

"Drager, I prefer that you wait until tomorrow, after we have gotten an aerial view of the forest," Reinhart replied, and he nodded. "After which, we shall meticulously select the trees and plants that should be removed to widen the path and open up the evergreen section. We must respect the environment by using ecological methods, like we did with the ocean plants. And, of course, we must send samples of all plants that we remove back to the main center, before piling the rest here for future use."

"Understood," he said in a low voice.

"Thank you," I replied.

"I am at your service, Pamela," he answered, showing me that his voice recognition was working.

"We are going to have lunch now." I replied.

We left after lunch in a medium size helicopter, so that the entire group could be on board. Diana took photos, as Murdoc and Reinhart took turns flying the plane. This relatively small, very compact, forest formed a perfect circle, measuring 100,000 acres, or 156.25 square miles. Through infrared, and other forms of thermographic, telescopic equipment, Rebecca captured images of a significant number of isolated finger-like streams, varying in length and width that emptied into stagnant ponds. Their origins were uncertain. They could have been formed from the melting snow of the Boreal forests descending through the tundra and forming intricate, small waterways; or, they could simply have been natural to the area.

Other photos revealed multi-level vegetation, in which tall, medium and small trees growing in a tight formation were all intricately entwined together by thick-stemmed vines that sprouted from thick bushes and dense layers of prickly undergrowth. It would take time to carve a trail without cutting down a significant number of trees to remove the massive, thick vines and prickly sharp undergrowth.

High flying birds, identifiably large Eagles, Falcons, Alpine Chough, as well as tiny sparrows, followed our plane at a distance, their curiosity apparently stronger, than their survival instinct. After giving them a good chase to wear themselves out, Murdoc reduced the speed of the plane, giving Diana and Randolph the opportunity to use their pistols to stun a considerable number of the different species of birds, at the same time that Basil and Birch released the nets in compartments on the outside of the plane, catching them at exactly the right moment.

"Don't you find it is strange that the forest is a perfect circle of 360 degrees?" Randolph asked the question that plagued all of us.

We sat in silence for a long moment, before Murdoc replied. "Elisabeth, you must remember those descriptions of dangerous, haunting Gothic castles and forests." He paused, hoping for a reaction, but none was forthcoming. "Anyway, this forest is so thick with vegetation that it almost makes you feel like you are entering into a sunless, supernatural environment where demonic creatures could possess you and just drive you to the brink of madness, even though..."

"I agree," Randolph broke in. "Walking with vegetation on both sides of a precariously slippery, narrow path, I had the eerie feeling that I would eventually enter a labyrinth from which I would never escape. There is, as you said, something demonic about this forest." He paused. "And now, observing its perfect circular formation makes me wonder if someone, or some evil force, created this alluring, seductive forest to attract and capture its prey."

"Wow!" Murdoc broke into heavy laughter, as the plane bounced up and down. I quickly took control, bringing the plane to a smooth landing.

"I would not be so sure about a gruesome monster, but by the perfect circle it seems it's been orchestrated. And, I do agree that this forest is well-groomed and cared for by someone."

Murdoc and I then stood observing our catch. The birds were ripping the netting and violently flapping their wings in an effort to escape, so we used our laser pistols, stunning them again, before placing them in individual cages.

Reinhart announced that there were no obvious hybridized physical characteristics in any of the species of birds, but that further study would naturally have to be conducted. The cages were placed on board a small plane and an android pilot left immediately for the main center, with the cargo.

It was already dark.

Only Murdoc and I stayed awake for the evening calls.

"It has been a crazy day!" Joseph announced, in a throaty voice. "The natural dunes were of different sizes and shapes. When we arrived, the androids had finished digging deep inside the dunes that turned out to be nothing more than wind-swept piles of desert sand. They did not find any animals or birds, but they did find a number of reptiles, like rattle snakes, which we avoided, some 4 feet long, yellowish brown colored spiny tail iguanas with keel scales covering their backs, as well as a dozen small greyish yellow lizards with greyish white spots running down their backs and decorating their sides." He stopped for a minute. "Dr. Crawford said they resembled the Sonoran collared lizard, native to this region in the past."

"And," he continued, "insects, principally beetles, roaches and ants, from what Dr. Crawford said. The scouts collected around 15 members of an arachnid species measuring at least a foot in length, with elongated bodies and a narrow segmented tail terminating in a dart, or stinger. The scouts suggest they are scorpions and humans, including reptilian humans, should avoid them."

That news sent shivers through my body. "Anyway, we have already sent these samples back to the main center for testing," he added.

"Insects," Reinhart repeated the word slowly. "These miserable life forms are very resistant, but I suppose they do serve a vital purpose."

"I gave my team the day off." He continued, ignoring her comment. "We drove buggies and motorcycles over the dunes. It was so exhilarating!" He bellowed into the audio system.

"Hi, Dr. Reinhart." Clarence moved onto the screen. "We had a day of fun."

"One needs that from time to time," she commented. "Where is Dr. Crawford?"

"I am here." He shouted from a distance. "I can confirm what Joseph and Clarence have reported. By the way, a desert sunset is a phenomenal blend of earthy colors. And the landscape with those marvelous, natural sand dunes was so picturesque, at least they were before the android scouts dug deep holes, but, as you know, these holes will fill in rapidly as the rough wind picks up at the end of the day."

"Did you hear from Dr. Gordon?"

"No. She has a terminal with her, so you should try calling her." He replied, before adding. "I imagine that she needs more time to determine the origin of those domes."

"I shall call her now," Reinhart replied.

"What do you think, Elisabeth?" Murdoc asked, after she signed off.

"I am happy that life forms did survive, but...well, insects are not my preferred species."

"And, why is that?"

"I was born with an aversion to these life forms and have never been able to understand why." She shrugged her shoulders.

"We should call Dr. Gordon," Murdoc suggested.

Dr. Gordon replied quickly. "How is everything going on your side?" Reinhart asked.

"My emotional configurations violently surfaced when I arrived in this area," her voice unsteady.

"What are you talking about? Snap out of it!" Reinhart ordered.

"There are actually a dozen hard, round disk-shaped, artificial covers that form a perfect circle. And we have no idea what they are. They could be explosives." Her eyes widened.

Another perfect circle passed through my thoughts, as Reinhart continued the conversation. "Did the android scouts open the covers?"

"They are trying to, but, as I mentioned to them many times now, I believe these covers are locked and that they have to find and neutralize the locking mechanism." She fidgeted. "They refuse to take this order from me."

"Ok. Send the Group leader to me." Gordon moved out of view to find the leader.

"What do you think, Elisabeth?" Murdoc nudged her.

"Oh, I can imagine many different scenarios, like, for example, that these covers are entrances to underground tunnels constructed by a group of visionaries, living amongst the renegade intellectuals, who wanted a safe place to hide should a revolution break out. Or they are space vessels that crash-landed on Earth."

"That is real science fiction, Elisabeth, but, going back to the crashing vessel scenario, why would crashing space vessels appear in a perfect circle?"

"Because the Group of 5 ordered Drager and his team to organize and bury them deep in the sand." Anticipating Murdoc's next question, she continued. "The constant wind on the open desert over all the thousands or more years has eventually revealed these ships. This scenario would best explain why Gordon is so flustered."

We sat in silence until the android leader, standing at attention, came into view. "What have you discovered so far?"

"The material, an unidentifiable substance, is very resistant and none of our explosives or high-technological equipment have been able to make even a dent in the surface," he replied, in a grinding android voice.

"I want you to take close-up photos of all the covers from all different angles, paying particular attention to the part of the cover resting on the desert surface." He nodded. "I also want you to send me samples of the sand next to these covers and in the surrounding areas."

He saluted and left.

"Dr. Gordon."

"I was waiting in the sidelines," she said, as she came into view.

"I want you to supervise the projects and get back to me at

any time, if you have questions or concerns. I shall ask Miller and Flanders to check in with you during the night." She nodded, and the conversation ended.

Elisabeth then contacted John. Ruth and Sarah were in center screen with him, while Ralph and Mathilda were on the sidelines.

"How is everything?" Reinhart asked.

"We are using the zoo to house the animals and study their behavior in a larger environment," Ruth began. "Some of them, like the Siberian Tiger and the wolf-grizzlies, cannot share space with others, so we are obliged to keep them in large cages." She paused. "Actually, we are now using the artificial tropical forest in the zoo for the birds."

"We are feeding them various berries and nuts and have added some tofu, smelling of raw flesh, for the carnivorous birds." Sarah interposed.

"Do you think that the tropical garden would be a good alternative for some of them?" John asked.

"That might be an interesting alternative for some, like the lizards, reptiles, insects and the hybridized rabbit field-mouse. I also recommend that we keep a limited number of all the different animals for observation at the Center and insert tracking devices in the ones that we intend to release in their natural habitats." This inspired a round of yeses.

"By the way, Mathilda, how is Rhea doing?"

"Flanders' android replacement has everything under control. Rhea should be able to continue in the artificial uterus a bit longer," she said in a deep reassuring tone. "By the way, Dr. Reinhart, Ralph and I would like permission to reproduce," she added, changing the subject so abruptly that Reinhart choked on my saliva.

"I was unaware of your emotional attachment to each other," Reinhart replied, taking a long moment to evaluate the request, before giving her unequivocal approval. "As you know, you cannot carry a pregnancy to term, Mathilda, so you will, eventually, have to transfer the baby to the artificial uterus. You must discuss this with Flanders' replacement." Reinhart smiled unwittingly, admiring how physically successful her rejuvenation of Ralph was many years ago now.

"Thank you!" their response peppered with loud, juvenile laughter.

"Where is the former Governor, John? I would like to speak to him?"

"I don't know where he is." He turned to the others. "Can you find him or call him over the intercom system."

When they were gone, Reinhart asked John whether he had any other messages from Colonel Shannon.

"I didn't want to mention this in front of the others, but she contacted me early this morning and told me that the personnel on board the inflatable space lab were in good health, but that the High Commissioners did not yet authorize their return to the Earth, pretending it was still dangerous—too much space debris, as she put it---for the lab to be moved back to its original location." His brows lifted for an instance. "She did not mention Peter, Frederic or Stuart."

"Let them worry, John," I said, before the former Governor arrived.

"If you don't mind, John, I would like a few minutes alone with the former Governor. I need to confirm some information and will bring you all up-to-date later," he nodded

"Eugene, a dozen, large, hard, round covers forming a perfect circle were discovered today in the desert in the western region. Do you know anything about this find?"

He sat down on one of the chairs, his hands moving into a steeple position as his elbows rested on the desk top. "You know, Dr. Reinhart that we intercepted spacecraft launched off the Mother ship, now under Colonel Shannon's command, over a long period of time. Regrettably, we killed the human pilots, sometimes saving the spaceships. The only excuse that I can give you for this behavior is that their arrivals were not only a potential threat to our long-term projects, but a nuisance."

There was a long pause before he picked up the conversation. "Incredible," he announced, as his hands unraveled. I detect potentially elucidating information in my secondary storage unit but I can't upload it. I don't know why."

"Eugene, I shall help you." Reinhart replied. "I am connecting with you now." Since her final metamorphosis, Reinhart was capable of entering into any human or android mind, recuperating knowledge, frequently through direct eye contact. I could feel her energy level rise and rush through me. As always, she pulled my mind alongside hers so that I could learn. "You have nothing to fear, Eugene. I shall not initiate any self-destruct program. You must look into my eyes. Do you understand?"

"Yes. I trust you, Dr. Reinhart." He replied, as his wide eyes fixed on mine.

"I felt my mind following hers as she sifted through layers of outdated data until she finally located the right file, which she immediately uploaded. "I have skimmed it, but I want you to explain this to me in more detail."

After examining it he continued: "The file goes back many years, even before our reactivation. The Earth's surface was hostile—too hostile for us to reactivate and too hostile for life forms to return. The leader of the cleanup crew, those primitive robots that walked the Earth's surface after the Dooms Day explosion, spoke of an invasion, contaminated air, violent volcanic activities, and earthquakes that ripped through the Earth's surface, while destructive ocean waves effaced coastal and low-lying lands. The leader asked for permission to shut down. I agreed and programmed all the android crew to awaken regularly every hundred years, to check on the evolution of the Earth and reactivate us if and when the Earth became habitable for androids and humans."

"Yes, I know that, actually, we all know that and have discussed it so many times. I am fed up with listening to and repeating the same things. I had to spend time bringing Murdoc up-to-date, answering his annoying questions the last few days." She screamed. "So please get on with it. Tell me what I, what we, don't know!" Reinhart said impatiently.

"They informed me that a large number, I believe more than 50, spacecraft had entered into the Earth's atmosphere, effectuated an easy, safe landing before the ships burrowed deep into the Earth's hot, molten liquid surface, precipitating an incredible cooling of that area, creating a vast section of sandy soil. These androids claimed that this section of the Earth had been given new life."

After asking them if they had investigated the area, they told me that high flames appeared within days, encircling the site, preventing them from accessing the area. They did not know if there was a safe zone on the other side. Instead, they asked for permission to fire missiles in an attempt to destroy these buried objects that might cause even more damage to the Earth's surface. Naturally, I gave them permission."

He sighed. "When the clean-up crew finally awakened us, they never mentioned this incident, perhaps it was erased from their memories. But apparently I did save this discussion." His eyes narrowed. "Dr. Reinhart, I believe that you found this in my secondary storage, or even my trash box after someone had tried to delete the information, but failed. Do you know why this information was "top secret?" He shrugged his shoulders.

"Have you ever intercepted messages from that region?" She pried.

He began another search of his memory banks, but Reinhart, losing patience, interrupted him. "Yes, you were aware of signals coming from this region but you associated them, right or wrong, with vessels sent from Colonel Shannon's ship." She observed him for an instance.

"Anyway, thank you, Eugene."

"For what?" He asked.

"For the work you are doing in the Center," she replied.

"Talk to you tomorrow, Dr. Reinhart." John said, as he entered the office.

"What did you do, Elisabeth?" Murdoc took my chin, turning my face in his direction to study her expression.

"I put the information back in his trash bin," she replied.

"You know who arrived?" Murdoc asked.

"Maybe." She looked him straight in his eyes. "Don't mention this to anyone."

"I never planned to," he replied.

They walked in silence back to the tent. She turned off and I appeared.

"You were listening, Pamela?" he asked in a cool, detached tone, pretending that he was not all that interested.

"To what?" I replied, feigning ignorance.

Reinhart took Miller and Flanders aside, just before we left in the land rovers to explore the outside of the forest. "I am going to leave at the end of the day with Dr. Murdoc for the western region. We shall take a quick look at the outskirts of the forest now. I want the two of you, though, to oversee the exploration of the forest in my absence. You can count on Drager and Jason to help you. We shall only be gone for a couple of days."

"I don't understand." Flanders desperately blocked her passage.

"I shall explain everything to you and the others on my return. I absolutely need to closely examine the hard, round covers that form a perfect circle in the desert."

"You know what they are?" He held his place.

We separated into three groups. Murdoc, Randolph, Diana, with Reinhart driving took the lead rover; Jason, two android scouts with Drager driving, took the second rover followed by Birch, Basil, Rebecca, with Tirence driving. We proceeded rapidly along a smooth dirt road.

Reinhart concluded that it would take a long time to open up passages in this thickly populated forest. When we stopped and got out, we came upon a 100 foot deep, 1 mile wide, trench that separated us from the forest, forcing us to stop in our tracks.

"There was no large trench at the forest entrance...yesterday," Basil's voice trembled slightly.

"Apparently someone wanted us to enter this forest yesterday and hold us captive, like I mentioned in the plane, while you all laughed," Randolph said, kicking up the dry, brown dirt.

"Perhaps this is where the streams empty out," Rebecca replied, proposing a reasonable scientific explanation.

"So, what do you think, Dr. Reinhart?" Jason asked.

"There is certainly a rational reason for all of this. Let's take some soil samples for analysis," she said, as she lowered the infrared lenses on the helmet and adjusted the focusing to get a closer view of the trees in front of us.

"What I don't understand," Tirence began, "is why we didn't realize that this wide trench separated us from the forest until we got out of the rovers and moved closer to it."

"Its absence was a visual illusion," Reinhart replied, as she walked slowly along the edge of the trench, studying the forest from different angles. "The rest of you should take pictures and gather samples!" she ordered.

Murdoc joined Reinhart, using the same optic equipment. "It looks like the large, thick vines were wrapped around the trees and underbrush, like a ribbon around a package." Reinhart looked full at him and boldly chuckled.

"I don't see anything funny," his gaze, steady and commanding, bringing her laughter to a quick end. "But, the possible moving of this, deeply rooted, massive forest is unfathomable."

"The roots are no deeper than the 100 foot trench," she said.

"Do you know something about this?" he questioned.

"No. But, this forest and the hard, dome-shaped covers in the desert may have been the work of the same visitors. We shall know more tomorrow." She approached him, her warm breath against his cheeks.

"By the way," she continued, turning away, "I informed Gordon and Crawford that we will be arriving tomorrow morning—we are leaving tonight--- to take a closer look at the circular formation, so we must resolve the forest issue today."

"What?"

The others were in the land rovers ready to continue, when Murdoc and I arrived. I moved aside and let him drive. "Where is she, Pamela?"

"Studying the problem, I guess."

We continued to move rapidly, stopping from time to time to collect soil samples and take pictures of the forest. We stopped halfway around the forest, or on the 180 degree line, which placed us, directly, opposite the forest entrance.

We turned abruptly when we heard a distant, melodic voice repeating several times the words: "I am the caretaker."

A female android came into view, as we got closer. She walked towards us. She had a slender, tall body and long, silky black hair, draping naturally the contours of her radiant, expresso brown face and partially exposed shoulders, eventually falling gracefully below her waist. Her vibrant ocean-blue eyes, with fluttering long lashes and perfectly curved, bold black brows, combined with her

rosy-colored lips, with a slight cupid's bow, gave her an air of seductive innocence.

"Who are you?" Reinhart's voice broke the trance we seemed to
be in.

"I am the caretaker." She answered.

"Please define that for me?"

"I am responsible for this package." She said, in a giddy, childish
tone, as she pointed to the forest.

"And who put this package in your care?"

"Maybe you did," she said, feigning innocence.

"In that case, you will send it now to its destination," Reinhart
retorted.

"I need time to boost up my power," she protested.

"Do it. Power up!" Reinhart ordered.

"I have problems." Her voice screeched and her body jarred, revealing the existence of a primitive robotic interior shielded behind
an immaculate exterior, most probably a version identical to that of
her creator's.

"We are in a hurry," Reinhart pressured.

"I can't. I can't. I..." She spun round and round, her formerly
graceful arms now moving in lunatic spastic gestures, which led
to an explosion of her metallic body parts, flying haphazardly in all
directions. We withdrew to a safe distance, about 50 yards away
from the metal storm flogging the ground.

Reinhart searched among the debris until she found a single
computer chip, the only visible element still intact after the blast.
"Hopefully, this contains the program that kept this android monitoring this area for maybe thousands of years." She paused. "It is
imperative we collect all the debris and study it, just in case her
program was hidden elsewhere."

"Some of these metallic parts indicate she was a primitive robot," Murdoc commented. "I don't understand how she could have
had such a high-tech appearance, when her basic components are
so primitive?"

"Dr. Reinhart, do you know why?" Diana asked.

"As you all know, I am more critical than indulgent with past generations of humans who vaunted genius. Humans also placed too much

value on appearance---their own, those of others, and what they created. Having a robot that was as sublime physically as the one that just
exploded, must have been considered, at the time, more of an achievement than endowing it with superior intelligence, if they were scientifically capable of that. By our standards, we can conclude that this
android's outer crust, or its body, was a technological success, but its
inner circuitry and performance were major failures."

"Dr. Reinhart," Randolph weighed in, "why is the female robot
always so much better looking than the males?"

"We have too many good-looking men in our human scientific
community," Rebecca remarked unabashedly.

Reinhart took her time before replying, as she spent a moment
focusing on Rebecca's mediocre appearance. Her pale, round face,
framed with long, thick, curly, mousy brown hair and her slight features, small brown eyes, a pudgy nose and slim lips, wondering if
she should give this young woman's face more life, before letting
her thoughts move on.

She was medium height, with muscular, shapely arms and legs.
Her torso was a haven of desire, her tight-fitting exoskeleton suit
accentuating her large breasts and the rounder of her firm hips.

"Do you have a problem, Rebecca?" Reinhart asked.

"Well..." she stammered.

"You see men and women, Rebecca, but I see only scientists with
very good minds." Rebecca backed away from Reinhart's immutable
gaze. "Nonetheless, let me expand on what you said in another way,
by confirming that the female robot that self-destructed is an example of how a man might perceive a physically perfect female body."

"Feminist movements surged and resurged throughout human
history." She glanced at Murdoc, whose eyes widened. "There were
many horrifying cases of sexual abuse throughout human history,
as well as other forms of discrimination against women, for example with respect to higher education and salaries—or payment
for production, something that was abandoned at my time--, career
opportunities, life-styles—the list is long and, fortunately, of no relevance today."

"But why was there discrimination against women?" Rebecca
probed.

"Even though I divided society into intellectuals and non-intellectuals, I did this with a detached, indifference to the individual—their appearance, the color of their skin, their sex, their sexual preferences, convictions and what not. But based upon my observations, during the hundreds of years that I worked alongside humans, I do believe that discrimination is learned, not inbred."

After a long pause, she picked up. "In a pure, viral sense, I place female rivalry as the principle reason why women were unable to take and maintain a climate of equality. Their need to be more physically appealing took precedent over the real booster for equality, or respect for the person regardless of their sex and physical attributes."

She hesitated. "For instance, even during the period when women were seeking to eradicate sexism, they were infatuated and flattered by beautifully conceived and fabricated females and female machines, like the one we saw today."

"Perhaps you should stop now, Dr. Reinhart," Murdoc said, in a loud, firm voice.

She pretended not to hear him and concluded. "Personally, I didn't understand, let alone identify with, any of the feminist movements, because of their inherent contradictions, but, worse, I found my generation of women embarrassing, because they actually flaunted and used their bodies to acquire power, while pretending that this was their new wave feminist movement."

"You did the same," Rebecca challenged.

"Not at all." She threw my head back in one of her earth-shaking laughs. "Your impertinence is amusing."

"Yes, men were attracted to me," Reinhart admitted, "but they also feared me. I used my mind, not my body, to gain power. I am a scientist before anything else and my team-members were and still are scientists. As you have a problem with the number of males and females on this scientific team, Rebecca, perhaps you should return to the Center, because I have no patience with insecure people."

"I am sorry that I brought up the subject," Rebecca said in a whisper. "I like being part of this team, but, well, Dr. Gordon mentioned your preference for male scientists over female scientists." She lowered her head. "I remember Dr. Gordon mentioning, as well, your intellectual preference for men over women after one of those learning tapes."

"I shall speak to her about that, but, yes, as I said, discrimination was---hopefully never will be again---a human condition." Reinhart's voice calmed. "I have no problem with your being aware of the harsh and unjust effects of dividing society ...cataloguing people by physical appearance, including the color of one's skin, intelligence, gender, including transgender, sexual preferences, and so forth."

"I sincerely regret bringing up this matter," Rebecca vociferated between sobs, her face wet with tears.

"As I mentioned, you have the right to know about this subject." Reinhart adjusted her voice to a soothing tone. "I am pleased you are aware of the abusiveness of discrimination in all its forms. I however despise hypocrisy on all levels, and am offended by those who use their physical appearance, including their sex, to gain recognition and power, something that existed in the past and was presented to us today."

She turned to Randolph. "Did I answer your question?"

"I guess, but it doesn't matter. I am ready to continue fumbling through the debris," he replied, avoiding eye contact.

The group resumed a thorough search, collecting all the particles, while Reinhart contacted Miller to ask her to send an android crew to collect the debris.

"Elisabeth, you really must try to be more diplomatic," Murdoc said, as he pulled me aside. "People like delicacy, tenderness, soft, understanding speech, not your brutal, direct rhetoric."

"She is gone for the moment. I believe that the conversations bored her and she now wants to concentrate on the 'invasion' issue," I said.

"Sorry, Pamela," he turned and walked away.

Murdoc's remarks, along with my growing impatience over controversy, sent my thoughts in another direction and I found myself wondering why Dr. Reinhart made concerted efforts to disassociate herself from past generations of humans. Perhaps it is because she is not human, or if she is human, she is not of this universe.

Chapter 14: Unleashing

"Dr. Reinhart," Miller dashed in her direction, on arrival, "we received photos as well as videos of those hard dome-shaped objects."

"Excellent." She turned to Murdoc. "Do you want to accompany me?" He nodded energetically.

Videos of androids' attempts to pierce through the hard surface and their determined efforts to explode these dome-shaped covers were in vain. Reinhart carefully studied the close up photos of the domes, slowly passing from one to another, confirming they were identical in size, texture and appearance. She was certain they were fabricated from the same, smooth, seemingly impenetrable substance. She motioned to Miller and Flanders to leave her alone.

"These are not spaceships that landed in a circular formation. They are organically webbed, dome-shaped covers that were fabricated, transported and neatly installed." She closed my eyes in thought but I remained privy to her analyses.

"Do you know what they are made of and what their purpose is, Elisabeth?"

"I believe I know the answers to both of your questions." She stood up and moved in the direction of the others, Murdoc close behind her. To my dismay, she stopped abruptly and turned to face him. "Don't ever intervene in one of my discussions in the future," sadness, more than anger, resonating through her reply.

"What do you mean?"

"Today, with Rebecca..."

"I am sorry, but she is so young and innocent...," he interrupted.

"How do you think that I stayed alive for hundreds of years?"

"I don't understand what you are talking about." His naivety sounded sincere.

"I stayed alive because I know who I can trust." She breathed very deeply. "I know when someone stands in admiration of me and when someone is trying to discredit me."

"But, she did not discredit you, Elisabeth. She was just acting her age, looking for answers."

"And, so, you don't see it?" she asked. "But I do. Look at you, you are already defending her and accusing me of being insensitive and...." He reached out, but she kept her distance.

"You are perhaps right," he conceded. "Admittedly, I didn't see it that way. I only wanted to protect you—yes, that is it, prevent you from being too cruel to her. You know that you can be critically indifferent to humans."

"I don't need your help!" she insisted. "Look at yourself, how easily you can be manipulated ---in this case by an adolescent who inherited her father's spirit for leadership." I could feel the heat of her anger rushing through me, enflaming my eyes. "Don't make me regret bringing you back."

"Are you hungry? The others have already eaten," Miller called out to us, ending the heated discussion.

Half way through the meal, Murdoc addressed me. "It is you, Pamela?" I nodded.

"I didn't realize that I was compromising her power. I was worried she would say something..." he hesitated, snapping his index finger against his thumb several times, searching for the right word, "cruel."

"Strange, Dr. Murdoc, even I understood after Reinhart disappeared inside of me that Rebecca is power-hungry and can't be trusted. Perhaps you need more time to really wake up and regain all your intuitive powers."

His eyes lost their luster and his brows contracted. "We better get started. I wonder which one of us is flying the small plane."

I followed behind him, sitting down in the co-pilot's seat, thus answering his question. "I see that the flight plan has been registered. I guess she expects me to fly the 10 hours, more or less, to the western region."

I didn't answer.

"Where is she? I am not going anywhere until she comes back?" He hesitated, then said firmly, like he was on a run. "Did you hear me, Elisabeth? I am not your slave!"

"Oh calm down, Aegir. I have been mediating. What happened

earlier is over and done. I have moved on. So let's get this plane up in the air."

"I am taking off," he replied in a loud, agitated voice, which amused her. A low chuckle caused him to turn in my direction. The plane bobbed up and down along the rough, dirt runway, as he burst into loud, spontaneous laughter, bringing an end to their dispute.

"Stop! What is that up ahead?" She shouted. "Slow down."

Randolph and Diana jumped out of a land rover, Drager in the driver's seat. They were waving their hands and running towards us. Murdoc brought the plane to a stop and lowered the stairs.

"You can't leave without us. The four of us are a team!" Diana exclaimed, as the two of them boarded the plane and fastened their seatbelts.

"Welcome aboard!" Murdoc replied, preparing for a second takeoff.

Once in the air, discussion broke out. "We asked Miller and Flanders to supervise the others. Apparently they had done a bit of exploring on their own and found a few low-lying mountains that they claim might have animal life," Randolph said.

"That sounds like an excellent idea," Reinhart commented.

"Sorry about this morning, Dr. Reinhart," Diana said spontaneously.

"Thanks, Diana." Reinhart reached out and squeezed Diana's hand.

"So what are those dome-shaped covers, Dr. Reinhart?" Randolph asked.

"She is now resting," I answered.

"Nice to have you back with us, Pamela."

Murdoc woke me after a few hours of flying to take over the controls and later Randolph replaced me. It seemed like only minutes, instead of hours, when Randolph woke us, asking for help.

"I can't keep the plane on course. The wind shifted." He rambled. "There are strong undercurrents. The plane is jolting up and down and veering off in different directions. There are no storm clouds on the horizon, only high mountains looming in front of us. We are going to crash!" panic looming in his screechy voice. "The plane is out of control. It is ready to dive!" He made a dramatic, rash, last minute effort to stabilize the plane.

"Move out of the seat!" Reinhart ordered, as she grabbed his shoulders. "It is not going to enter into a free spin."

"It is too late." He shoved her away.

"Take my co-pilot seat. I'll take care of him," Murdoc yelled, as he rushed towards Randolph, pulling him out of his seat and away from the controls.

Reinhart, with her supernatural calm, stabilized the plane, moving it gradually to the right altitude, while turning it back in the direction of the mountains.

"What are you doing, Dr. Reinhart? We are all going to die! There is no way to pass between those peaks," Diana's high-pitched cries adding to the stress.-

"We are going forward," she replied. Take your seats, fasten your seat belts and close your eyes. Trust me. Joseph, Gordon and Crawford told me that maneuvering through these narrow passages was treacherous and required extraordinary skill. Don't worry, I love this kind of challenge!"

She quickly adjusted my vision, while explaining to me on a cerebral level that the high, snow-covered, tightly knit clusters of mountain peaks, like any visual illusion, confounded my mental perceptions, giving me, as well as the other crew members, the impression there was no plausible navigational route between the peaks.

Reinhart continued explaining to me that the androids that piloted the planes for our western team were not susceptible to this phenomenon and recognized that these steeple-shaped chimneys, sprouting from flat, high mountains, were spaced far enough apart for a plane to pass through.

Everything became clear. I understood that without her intervention, I would have experienced visual illusions, very similar to those caused when wearing virtual-reality helmets, and would not have been able to distinguish between the virtual world and the real world. With my eyes properly adjusted, I was seeing clearly. I hoped, though, she could easily pilot the plane through the various treacherous, narrow passages.

After Randolph and Murdoc were back in their seats and all seat belts were fastened, she quickly scanned the corridors available, before pushing the throttle to maximum speed, as she tilted the plane 90 degrees. Skillfully piloting the craft through a very narrow passage between two towering, jagged mountain peaks. She proceeded along a roller coaster course, the plane, lifting, dropping, and inclining as she carefully negotiated winding curves with sharp, pointed projectiles, resisting the erratic changes in wind and air pressure, that could have sent the plane into a spiral spin. With a composed effort, she chose, at the last possible moment, the right upper or lower corridor.

Her concentration at a maximum, she initially ignored the incessant, high, shrill, piercing cries coming from her three passengers, before bringing the plane into clear, open skies. A ride that seemed like an eternity was a mere 30 minutes.

"I feel ill." Diana was the first to speak. "Can you bring the plane down for a few minutes, Dr. Reinhart?" she pleaded.

"I see a clearing up ahead. Anyone else feeling sick." Yeses from Randolph and Murdoc were forthcoming.

She landed the plane gently on a hard dirt surface and the crew rushed out of the plane to empty their stomachs. "What happened?" Murdoc asked, when he was feeling better.

"Visual illusions, similar to our initial imperceptibility of the wide trench surrounding the forest, confounding our reasoning. These visual illusions distorted your perception and made you feel dizzy and nauseous," she repeated what she had already told me.

"We can't stay too long because it is getting late, but we can take the time we need to collect a few soil samples. It will be good, anyway, for all of you to move around a bit," she added.

"Visual illusions." Murdoc repeated the word. "Were they natural or fabricated?"

I felt the pressure to say something. "She is mediating for the moment and I don't know any more about the subject than you do."

"Elisabeth, why do you always disappear when we need answers?" he reproached.

"What is that up ahead? I see something in my visual. It looks like a pool of water...and there are fir trees surrounding it." Diana spoke.

"We have time to take a look." Reinhart was back. "It can't be more than a mile away." We all began jogging in that direction.

Another circular formation came into plain view, this time a beautifully alluring single row of fir trees, surrounding a clear, blue pool of water. "Don't drink or even touch the water," she warned, as the group rushed to the lake. "Keep your hands and faces protected and use the filtering system in your helmet to protect you from any invisible gases," she cautioned.

Even though we didn't have time to take the 3 mile tour around the lake, we collected water and fir tree samples to send back to the main center for analysis. We were gathering up our gear when Diana broke the silence.

"Dr. Reinhart, this lake is really an enormous swimming pool. My equipment registers a water depth of only 50 feet. A hard, organic substance forms its sides and bottom. The trees are actually planted in a circular trough with rich, organic soil. The trough is equipped with a regulated seepage, or irrigation system, that provides a constant flow of water for the trees."

"So this too is like a package, like the circular forest, to be lifted and then delivered. But where?" Reinhart commented, rubbing my right hand slowly over my chin.

"Rather mysterious," an uneasiness in Diana's voice.

"We must get back to the plane," Reinhart instructed, without further comment on Diana's discovery.

When we finally boarded the aircraft, Murdoc took over the controls, landing a few hours later next to the western region encampment. I was surprised to see that Gordon and Crawford were waiting for us outside the encampment.

They approached Murdoc, their heads bowed officiously. "We are so pleased, Dr. Murdoc, that you survived and are now back with us. And we are honored to be able to work closely with you and Dr. Reinhart," they said in perfect harmony.

"Let the past be the past," he said, as he threw his right arm around Crawford's shoulder and took Gordon's hand.

I wondered why Reinhart did not seem bothered by the fact Gordon had abandoned the android scouts, letting them continue to gather up soil samples and test the durability of the dome covers without her supervision. As she heard my thoughts and did not respond, I let my thoughts drop.

When we arrived at the encampment, Joseph spoke for everyone. "It is an honor for all of us to meet you, Dr. Murdoc. For us new breed humans, your name is almost as legendary as that of Dr. Reinhart." He motioned to the others to come forward and introduce themselves.

And our royal welcome did not end there, for our friends spoiled us with local gastronomical wonders of oasis green, leafy vegetables and the sumptuous fruit of the Prickly Pear Cactus, piled on top of a large dish of rice. Joseph, advised us that the products had been sent back to the main center for analysis and were safe to eat.

"Dr. Reinhart, you must know something about the circular sites." Dr. Gordon commented.

"Just suppositions...for the moment. Yes, just suppositions that need verification."

"We might be able to brainstorm this together, if you give us a clue," Crawford's shaky voice brought a slight grin to Murdoc's face.

"Are you having difficulty controlling your emotions, Dr. Crawford?" Reinhart asked.

"No! I am just fine," he insisted.

Reinhart nodded and then turned to the western team. "You have accomplished so much in such a short period of time. I am very pleased."

"I was worried that you might say the contrary," Joseph replied.

"I don't understand."

"Well, we did lose time in the beginning---pondering a safe way to escape from the grizzly-wolves."

"You took the proper precautions. And, it takes time to explore an area in detail." She paused. "If it is ok with you, Joseph, I would like Dr. Crawford and Dr. Gordon to go with us tomorrow to examine those dome-shaped formations," he nodded.

"By the way, Dr. Reinhart, we had news from John who had a long conversation with the Captain and WD," Crawford mentioned.

"So, tell me what is happening?"

"WD sounded disappointed that neither he nor Weldon encountered any different species," Gordon said dryly. "I do believe that you are aware of the fact that they passed by common species, like salmon and tuna. They captured several of these fish for study, even though WD believes that they are identical in every aspect except in size---being much larger than their ancestors."

"No, I was not aware of this." Reinhart paused. "Anything else?"

"Yes, something very interesting. The Captain sent android divers into deep ocean waters in protected cages, a necessary precaution." Crawford commented. "Like in the past, a number of different prehistoric fish, which they characterized as very unattractive and aggressive, approached their cages."

"You do know that these cages are equipped with long, tunnel-like traps." She nodded. "After the predators entered into the high pressure spherical traps, the entrances closed behind them." Reinhart nodded again. "These traps were slowly raised from the ocean depths upwards to the surface. The environmental conditions did not remain stable."

"Some of these predator fish," he continued, "could support neither the slight fluctuation in air pressure and luminosity, nor water temperature and died before arrival on board the ship. Those that survived were sedated and placed in aquariums, replicating their natural deep sea environment, for shipment back to the Main center. Unfortunately, very few survived the flight." His eyes moved rapidly in their sockets. "John mentioned that Ruth and Sarah are assisting Ralph in identifying these fish."

"This is very good news. It is remarkable that these species of predatory fish exist today. And this confirms our theories that oceans are havens, replete with a large variety of life forms," she said. "By the way, are they identical to the predatory fish that were captured during earlier expeditions?" she queried.

"As John mentioned, all deep sea species look like they are descendants from the dinosaurian period. We shall know more after they have been examined," Crawford spoke and Reinhart ended on that note.

"We shall have everything ready to leave in the morning," Gordon said, changing the subject.

"Well, I think we need to get some sleep." Reinhart stood up and motioned to Murdoc, Diana and Randolph to follow her example.

"You are right. It is late," Joseph replied, before asking one of the androids to show us to our tent.

The tent was rather large, with two, intimate alcoves, each with a separate shower. I smiled as I watched Randolph and Diana leave together.

"Should we follow their example, Elisabeth?" The warm, rapidity of his whisper sending chills through my body.

"I want to solve the 3 circle enigma, so I shall leave you, Aegir, to Pamela, who seems interested in replacing me," her voice projecting a light touch of amusement.

"I shall take the first shower—and alone." I replied adamantly and he stepped back, the palms of his hands raised. I wondered if Reinhart was testing us.

When we were both feeling clean and relaxed, we laid down on the large cot, our backs turned to each other.

"It is annoying, Elisabeth, how you want to control everything." Murdoc commented before asking me if I was asleep.

"I am trying to sleep," I said bluntly, his arms already around me, drawing me close up against him.

"I don't want to be a player in your or Reinhart's game, Dr. Murdoc," I protested, as I elbowed him.

"You are not curious, Pamela, what kind of lovers we might make." His words annoyed me, but his alluring voice, began breaking down my resistance.

"Not really," I replied, but I feared my rapid breathing would betray me.

He slowly turned me in his direction, gently caressing my face, his fingers lingering playfully over my lips, until my mouth opened slowly and I was sucking. My body began to crave more, and I pulled him closer, his strong arms cradling me, as his warm, titillating lips brushed up against mine. I hesitated, expecting a wet, perfunctory kiss.

And then my body stiffened as I wondered. 'Was she alongside of me, alert, participating, making me feel almost crazy with desire? Was she the source of my longing for him? Did she want me to be humiliated? But, I did not sense her presence. She was definitely absent.'

He tenderly took my face between his hands, forcing my eyes to meet his, drawing us naturally towards each other, until his warm, soft lips met mine, dissipating my inhibitions and doubts, as I then savored the fiery, intense sensations of his kisses, possessing me, making me long for more.

But instead of running his hands along the contours of my body in a quest for intimacy, he lightly pushed me away and sat up straight in the bed, his eyes taking on the melancholy of a blind stare.

"I am sorry, Pamela." He gently pulled me back into his arms, this time fondling me like a child, his fingers running casually through my long, thick hair.

"You love her."

"I am sorry," he repeated.

"I am not as beautiful, exciting, interesting, seductive..."

"Stop. You are her equal in almost every way, but...you are not her, Pamela, and Elisabeth and I go back a long time." He sighed heavily. I wanted to believe him, both in deference to her and in resignation to our impossible love.

"She was testing me—perhaps testing us. That was cruel, but that is also Elisabeth." He added.

'She must have sensed our attraction to each other and decided to give us an opportunity to live it,' passed through my mind, as he kissed the top of my head in a pleasingly paternal way, consoling me.

"She would have been jealous so that is why you stopped?" I asked.

"She would have been angry with me for defiling her daughter. But, she would not have been jealous," he replied convincingly.

"She knows we are not meant for each other." I spoke softly. "And, she just wanted me to know that."

"I promise you I shall protect you and those you love until my last breath, Pamela." His voice strained with emotion. "Now, let's get some sleep."

I felt tears, not tears of humiliation but those of lost love, streaming down my face. I finally cuddled up close to him, finding warmth and comfort in his arms, and eventually fell into a deep, relaxing sleep.

"Time to wake up!" Crawford sounded the alarm.

"You still act like a crazy machine!" Murdoc retorted, as we all jumped out of bed and dashed to ready ourselves for the day.

"So, what happened between you and Murdoc?" Randolph asked brashly, as he pulled me aside.

"Nothing. But, I believe that you and Diana did not sleep much." I pushed him out of my way.

"Dr. Murdoc," Elisabeth broke in, "we shall need to leave now. I arranged for several android scouts to accompany us in a second vehicle. The four of us will follow close behind."

"Last night..."

She stopped him in midstream. "Thank you for treating my daughter with kindness and respect. Now, let's get on with more important projects."

He raised his eyebrows several times like he was sending a coded message, and she spilled over in giddy, childish laughter that continued as they ran off hand in hand to the rover.

Gordon and Crawford took a second rover and the 4 android scouts jumped into a larger vehicle, carrying tents and supplies so that we could stay in the area for a few days.

"We have another audio-visual system with us, if you prefer privacy. There is equipment already in place," Gordon raised her voice above the noise of the motors and Reinhart acknowledged her with a wave of the hand.

"Why don't we use a more sophisticated communication system, like holograms?" Randolph was the first to break the silence.

"Oh yes, holograms, those three dimensional images, using laser light for illuminating the subject." My brows corrugated. "We don't need to have this full body imaging. It makes sense, perhaps, in an interstellar context. But, personally, I prefer to observe the individual in his or her surroundings and have a clear picture of the person's facial expressions."

"So we shall never use them," he said, with a hint of sarcasm in his tone.

"I didn't say that," she retorted. "Holograms are simply not a priority for me at the moment."

From a distance, we could observe the androids busy collecting soil, rocks and dry, bush weed. On arrival, they approached us, offering their help to unload the cars.

"How do you want to proceed?" Gordon asked.

"I shall go with Diana, Randolph and Murdoc and take a look at the domes."

"You already know what they are, I presume?" Gordon said sarcastically.

Reinhart pretended not to hear her and we left immediately to examine the objects. "We need photos, but first I want to show you something." She approached the domes and then ran my hands slowly, gently, along the periphery of the dome, from its center to its circumference, until my hands fell upon the spot that registered my body heat and the dome gave way.

As my hands slid inside, I felt the same gelatin-like substance imbedded in the outside walls of the inner circle in our Center. The wall, with its integrated bio-physiological readers, only gave passage into the inner circle to humans and hybridized human species with dominate human DNA. But she was more prudent, startling and disappointing me when she quickly pulled my hands out of the substance.

"That is true, but we must be cautious," she read my thoughts. "We don't know what lies below the domes' covers," Reinhart replied. "I am in the process of studying it." It took her a matter of minutes, before she said, it was safe for us to pass through.

"What kind of life forms conceived these domes?" Randolph stuttered.

"Now that is the real question." She puckered up my lips and then turned to Crawford and Gordon. "For the moment, I want the two of you to stand guard. I shall enter first and, if it is safe, I shall return for Murdoc, who will later return to instruct Diana and Randolph to join us. If I have any problems, I shall contact you." She paused. "Actually, we shall all be carrying transmitters and will contact you if we run into difficulty. Just be patient and wait for us to return."

Her eyes met those of Murdoc, Randolph and Diana. "Our exoskeleton suits are in the rover, along with helmets, visors, laser guns, gloves, boots...all we need."

"Wait," Murdoc replied. "Do you know what is in there?

"I am pondering various scenarios." She replied, as she entered into the exoskeleton suit. "But, I don't have time now to recount them!" tension in her voice. "What I can say with certitude is that aliens who inhabited this planet in the past used volcanically carved tunnels, or lava tubes, to construct the underground city we will be visiting today. I believe the cities are partially or completely intact."

"That is all?" Murdoc pressured.

"For the moment, although I could add that I don't believe that the aliens are still inhabiting this underground city. They must have run into difficulties, forcing them to leave in haste, so they never had time to destroy what they built."

Reinhart, ignoring Murdoc, reiterated: "So again, I'll go first to make sure it is safe!"

"No way. I go with you or you don't go at all," Murdoc insisted.

They stood in the Center of the Dome for a few seconds, while the bio-physiological readers imbedded in the upper surface of the dome verified they were humans and not machines, before letting them slide slowly hand in hand through the outer shell, landing upright on a mobile platform.

They rapidly adjusted their flashlights until they had a clear view of their environment. There were other mobile platforms behind them, all without doors or windows; only a safety rail to cling onto. A large guidance system, similar to that on a spaceship, was in the center of the platform. There was no steering device and it seemed they needed to activate the guidance system if they wanted to explore the area.

"Do you know how to activate this panel? Perhaps it can be voice-activated?" Murdoc asked.

"We can try, but there must be a security system in place—perhaps a password is necessary?" I felt her trembling, something that I never expected from her. She was worried, and so was I. "We are stuck here. We would need to move the platform closer to the dome to get out!"

"Ok. We have been in difficult situations before, Elisabeth," Murdoc replied firmly trying to instill confidence in them. "I am going to study the panel. Maybe we just have to push one of these buttons or lift one of the switches to activate the system, but which one? The panel appears to be as complex as the guidance system in a spaceship."

"I am going to search my memory banks, perhaps I, like the former Governor, put this information in my cerebral trash bin."

While he stared at all the levers and buttons, before randomly pushing them, she searched her memory. At one point he touched something that sent off ear-splitting sirens, causing the platform to tilt 180 degrees on its side. "Now look what you have done!" Reinhart's anger burst forth in a loud howl, as she, like Murdoc, slid off the platform, clinging to its edge.

"Do you know what to do?" his voice calm and measured.

"Yes. But I have to get onto the platform," her voice shaky.

"Ok. Move closer to me," he suggested.

She ignored him. I felt the exoskeleton suit respond to her supernatural energy, as she reinforced my body's physical force. "Hang on, Murdoc," she said as she swung my body into the middle of the tilted platform, gripping her way along the grooves in the platform, until she reached the control panel. It took a few seconds for her to identify the switch Murdoc had activated. The switch resisted, like it was stuck, making my heart beat rapidly. And then a new burst of supernatural energy rushed through me, giving her the force to push the recalcitrant lever back into place.

"Ok, Murdoc, climb aboard," she called out.

He swung his body onto the platform and was standing behind us in a few seconds.

"Move over, Murdoc! Give me some room!" She ordered. "I know what to do. I found the code in the attic of my mind."

She opened a trap door under the panel, revealing an entry code box with letters and numbers on it, a replica of security devices used to access buildings, labs, and other private areas in the very distant past. She entered a long, complicated code into the entry system and the platform jolted, as bright lights began to flicker off the walls. She rubbed my eyes vigorously to adjust to the sudden luminosity. We already had a view of our environment. There was a deep tunnel, or tube that would take us where?

"Do you know how to steer this platform, Elisabeth?" he asked, as he touched one of the switches sending the platform spinning around.

"Stop touching things!" She slapped his hand, like he was a child.

"Well explain to me how you had information buried in your mind."

"Actually, it was beginning to surface, but not fast enough, apparently," she replied. "I had to pry it out."

"But the Governor received information about these dome-shaped covers when the clean-up crew reported to him. You were already dead, Elisabeth. So how could you have known of their existence?"

"Because I was in contact with aliens before the revolution." His eyes bulged under her declaration. "But, I don't know whether the aliens I was in contact with are the same ones that placed the domes. We shall find out soon."

"You never told me about aliens."

"Why would I?" she asked provocatively.

"Because..."

"I had no obligation to make you privy to everything and there were moments when your commitment to the non-intellectuals put a strain on our relationship and made me very suspicious of your intentions with respect to me and my scientific team."

I noticed that his face flushed.

"Their civilization was much more advanced than ours," she paused. "When the revolution broke out, I was hoping that they would arrive early enough to save me, and, of course, you, and, to the extent possible, our civilization. In the last message I received from them, they informed me that their mother ship had been damaged by cosmic debris and that they had to return to the Mother ship for repairs."

"So they couldn't help us."

"I doubted the authenticity of their message." She clacked my tongue. "I was convinced that they did not want to take sides in a rebellion, because they believed in peace and good will." She took a deep breath. "They were in contact with me on a cerebral level, so I have no idea what physical appearance, if any, they have."

"So before the revolution broke out, they tried to erase the knowledge of their existence from your mind?" Murdoc asked.

"I am very suspicious by nature, so I moved my contact with them out of my present memory, so they thought I had forgotten about them. I hid all this in my cerebral "trash bin.""

"But they landed and then created an underground civilization?"

"My best guess is that they never intended to change their original plans and that exploring this planet was a priority, in spite of what they communicated to me."

"So there are aliens more brilliant than you, Elisabeth?" He smiled sardonically. "Should we take a look at what they did?"

"Yes, but before we move forward, I want Diana and Randolph to enter the area. I believe that they should be privy to our discoveries."

She contacted Gordon on the communications system and asked her to tell Randolph and Diana to pass through the dome. She mentioned it was safe for them to enter.

She already understood how to use the control panel and opened the operating unit. A quick move of her finger and the platform moved upwards and the dome-shaped cover opened wide enough for Randolph and Diana to slide in and land directly on the platform.

Reinhart quickly brought them up-to-date on everything, before she lowered the platform and activated the drive. The platform converted into a monorail and we plunged slowly into the depths of the Earth, eventually reaching our destination, the underground city.

"It is an exact replica of the domed city we lived in before the explosion. Elisabeth," Murdoc's breath, coming, in spurts, "it is almost as if they saved our world for us!"

Her laughter was soft and low, fitting for someone with her power.

Her laughter stopped and she perused the scene silently, then exclaimed: "They must have reinforced the ceiling in the lava tubes."

"True," Murdoc replied. "If not, as you rightly conjectured, the Earth's gravity might have forced the ceiling to collapse."

"We need to study and to identify the substance they used to reinforce the tubes. Hopefully, the substance can be reproduced," she added. "The oxygen is pure and the temperature a constant 79 degrees Fahrenheit. Look," she pointed, "there is a fountain, from which trickles water, just up ahead. But don't drink it!" She warned. "We must take a sample and have it tested."

"So this is the kind of city that your generation, Dr. Reinhart, lived and worked in?" Randolph did not wait for an answer. Instead, he jogged down one of the long, floral bordered paths.

Diana went in a different direction, crisscrossing the various walkways until she reached the towering monument in the center. We followed close behind her, stopping from time to time to touch the rose petals, breathe in the captivating fragrances of lilacs and lavender, and reach out to caress the branches of tall Maple, Cedar and Weeping Willow trees.

When we caught up with her, Reinhart was staring at a life-like sculpture of herself dressed in a long, tight fitting, black robe. The statue did justice to Reinhart's immaculate beauty, highlighting her captivatingly vibrant green eyes, luscious, full lips, high cheeks bones, and refined, yet prominent, nose. Her long, wavy, reddish brown hair sensually draped her shoulders, accentuating her firm, round breasts. Two very tall, imposing figures, with the body of a human and the face of an animal stood behind her.

Reinhart said under her breath. "These creatures are very similar to drawings and sculptures of Egyptian Gods." She stared at Diana and Murdoc. "You may not be familiar with them?"

"I read about them," Diana replied.

"They look strange." Randolph added.

"Then you know that historians, archeologists, even members of the scientific communities, imagined that these creatures— with a human body and an animal head—were aliens, and that the Egyptian culture, and other cultures in the Mesopotamian region, benefited from the knowledge that these presumed alien creatures, worshipped like Gods, transmitted to them."

She finally caught her breath. "From the human side, their bodies resemble the etchings and sculptures of Egyptian warriors. Even their attire is strangely familiar. They are both wearing short skirts that reveal their well-built, attractive, olive colored legs, with slim, yet muscular calves and thighs." She chuckled softly to herself, before revealing something infinitely intriguing. "These marvelous symbols and exotic figures engraved in their jewelry and decorating their clothes are complex mathematical formulae."

"They have the face of... a rat?" Randolph's voice grating like that of an android. "These were despicable creatures. Mean, aggressive rodents that attacked humans, transmitted diseases and stole their food. As such, they cannot be trusted," he warned.

"Take a closer look at their thin, regal, refined, black faces, Randolph," Reinhart interrupted, correcting him. "And, their large, clear, dark brown, rather than black or red, eyes that sparkle a serenity."

"I don't see it." He protested.

"It is true that the rat was not worshipped by the Egyptians, but it was placed in high esteem in other cultures, like Asian cultures, and even had a sacred or respectable place in certain religions, like Buddhism and Hinduism. The rat was considered to be more than a ruthless survivor. It lived in organized communities. In some cultures, it became a symbol of fertility, wealth, and an emblem of good luck. In Hinduism the rat was worshipped for being the most powerful of demons because it was blessed with foresight and prudence."

She stepped back to observe the statues. "Yes, these figures remind me of the Egyptian Goddess, Maat, or the Goddess of truth, order, balance, justice and freedom, who wore a single, tall Ostrich feather attached by a headband."

"Did the Ostrich feather have any real significance?" Randolph asked.

"Yes, actually it did. Maat would weigh the deceased's heart against the Ostrich feather on a balance, a kind of scale with a beam supported freely in the center with two plates of equal weight suspended from its sides. The heart of the deceased was placed in one plate and the ostrich feather in the other. The heart had to weigh less than or equal to the weight of the ostrich feather in order for the soul, or non-corporal energy, of the deceased to enter into another, non-corporal existence."

"Do you believe all that?" Diana giggled slightly.

"I respect righteous beliefs... even if I do not necessarily embrace them." She replied, trying to be diplomatic

"I wonder if these statues are representative of the aliens that recreated our city," Murdoc broke in. "Do they have such perfect bodies and rat faces? Do they have a pacifistic nature?"

"The animal appearance of a given God in the Egyptian culture was representative of the personality, the inner strength, or the spirit of the God. As I mentioned, the rat has many virtues. Let's hope these aliens have taken on the virtues of the rat and the Goddess, Maat."

"I am very curious as to why they would have engraved such complex mathematical formulae in their ornaments, unless..." He took a deep breath..."their existence was threatened?" Murdoc questioned.

"No!" Reinhart replied adamantly. "They were not fleeing from an enemy."

"But..."He began.

"I am sorry, Dr. Murdoc, but Dr. Reinhart is now meditating."

"She disappeared again in the middle of the discussion." He exhaled a slow stream of air. "Well, let's explore the city." He replied brusquely, as he marched forward. We followed closely behind him.

When we exited the garden, the path opened up onto a long avenue lined with small buildings which Murdoc referred to as shops. He briefly recapped what we already knew regarding the use of currency to purchase exotic products in the world he lived in. We already knew about currency and purchasing power from the games we played when we lived in the outside community after our deprogramming.

"We all received the basic clothing, or long white robes, and meals, delivered to our living quarters, or available in the main dining room. If someone wanted to eat something that was produced in limited amounts, cook their own food, stylize their look with a different garment, etc. then that individual had to have currency to pay." Murdoc said.

"Unlike earlier generations of humans," he continued, "we did not receive currency for our day to day work. We received a bonus in the form of currency for exceptional contributions. This bonus encouraged competitiveness, as well as...how can I explain this," he hesitated, looking for the right words, "a willingness and desire to contribute more for the benefits of everyone like working more hours, treating more patients, doing more-research, and so forth."

"So there was a disparity among members of your elite society?" Randolph asked.

"Yes, there was and will always be disparity between members of society when currency exists. Money, the common name, breeds arrogance, contempt, jealousy, and injustice, but also, as I just mentioned, can encourage creativity, inventions, progress and more."

"Did Dr. Reinhart take money?" Diana asked.

"No. She seemed quite happy with the simplicity of life." He paused. "She did not socialize. She invested all her time and energy in her work, but never took monetary compensation for her innumerable scientific achievements and inventions."

"But, she had beautiful clothes," Diana pried.

"Yes. They were gifts from her many admirers."

"Admirers or lovers." Diana grinned.

"Admirers," he replied firmly.

"So she accepted gifts from admirers, but gave them nothing in return," she replied, as she continued her inquiry. "Is that true, Pamela?"

"It surprises you, huh, Diana," Reinhart replied in her firm, commanding tone.

"I am sorry, Dr. Reinhart. I got a bit carried away." Diana lowered her head.

"So, should we keep going in the direction of what might be our former living quarters, Elisabeth?" Murdoc changed the subject.

"Yes. I don't understand why they went to so much trouble to duplicate our domed city," her gaze shifting reflectively over the contours of the city.

She began taking long confident strides, like she was returning home. We followed behind her. We finally arrived at a large parking lot, small planes floating in the air a few feet above the ground.

"We used these aero-mobiles, or flying cars, to reach those circular buildings that rest upon metal stilts," she pointed in that direction, "which are exact replicas of our living and working quarters. It's so strange," she said in a low tone.

"I think that it is eerie, Elisabeth, to stumble onto our past, in this abandoned, underground structure, resembling a gigantic doll house! They may have succeeded in luring us into a trap. We should stay alert, ready to defend ourselves and maybe leave immediately!" Murdoc's voice began to shake with concern.

She ignored his warning. "Diana, you come with me."

I could feel Reinhart's energy rushing through me, moving from high-spirited enthusiasm to uneasiness and trepidation, as we approached the aero-mobile.

She first ran my fingers slowly over the sleek, teardrop-shaped front end of this hybrid machine, before opening the doors and verifying that the equipment was functioning and that the seats were properly adapted for land cruising and flight. She inspected the structure and systems in the rather wide, but compact middle region, verifying that the aircraft wings would be released on command and verified the rear end.

She then spent a long moment cogitating the utility of the very long, rear tail wing that projected upwards. She mentioned to Diana that it looked very much like the tail of a bird, more specifically that of the Meves's Glossy Starling, native to the southern region of the former African continent.

"Are you ready, Aegir?" she asked.

"Yes, everything looks fine here," he replied. "I don't understand the utility of the long tail. Do you?"

"It must just be decorative, because the rest of the aircraft's design and systems are the same as those we used in the past." She shrugged my shoulders. "Let's get on with the visit," she called out, as she boarded the aero-mobile, with Diana in the co-pilot seat.

Both Reinhart and Murdoc converted the aero-mobile into an airplane rapidly, taking a quick spin in and around the tall towers built in a circular formation, before landing on the large, suspended airstrip.

Elisabeth and Murdoc led the way. Elisabeth then randomly opened the doors of different living quarters, apartments, as she referred to them. Diana, Randolph and I were fascinated by the size and complexity of these apartments that had a large, comfortably furnished lounge with floor-to-ceiling bay windows opening onto a balcony decorated with potted plants and flowers, a cozy low-lit dining room, and a small kitchen with high tech equipment for easy cooking and storage of food.

A long corridor off the dining room led to a bathroom complete with a large basin, toilet, shower, whirlpool bath and sauna. At the far end of the apartment lay a vast bedroom, furnished with an imposing king-size suspension bed, graced with tall cabinets on either side. At the rear of the bedroom suite was an anteroom, complete with cozy couches, mirrored walls and a very large walk-in closet.

"Where was your apartment?" Diana asked.

"I shall show you, but I don't believe it will be any different from what you have already seen," she replied.

We followed her to the next level. She stopped in front of the apartment bearing the number 13. I felt her tremble when she opened the door. The sterile white walls with white linens, towels and cushions of the preceding apartments, were now in various shades of blue.

She smiled as she proceeded nonchalantly through the salon, dining-room and bathroom as if she were showing us an apartment she was still living in. Her eyes lit up when she noticed that the thick, fluffy quilts and pillows on the large, suspended bed were enveloped in covers of azure blue.

But alas, she stepped back when she entered the wardrobe and found it filled with her clothes, including jewelry and shoes she had worn when she had lived there, so very long ago.

"I am starting to feel the hair on the back of my neck rise," Murdoc commented.

"Let's just continue the visit. I wonder if your former quarters are also personalized," she added.

We passed by the other apartments, going directly to number 48. When Murdoc opened the door, he stopped in his tracks. The walls and furnishing were in various shades of brown and grey.

"Let's just check the closet," Reinhart said, as she pushed past him.

"Incredible. It is not only as disorganized as my closet always was, but it is full of all of my favorite things, backpacks, safari jackets and trousers...look, Elisabeth." He dislodged his machete with a riveted wooden handle, causing both his travel canteen, canvased tent and calf belt with double buckles to fall.

"This is definitely weird!" he said, as he opened several drawers, tossing his t-shirts and underwear on the floor, until he found what he wanted, the antique compass and binoculars he had found buried in one of the caverns occupied by the non-intellectuals.

"Right! We should now visit the labs and the auditorium," Reinhart said firmly.

"You are right. I can take another look at my closet later."

"It is time for us to move on. I want to visit my laboratory," Reinhart said.

We followed her. She opened a side door that led onto a long, glass corridor, connecting one building to another. We stopped to take in the captivating view of the vastness of this building, more floors overhead and twenty or more below us, before continuing in the direction of the Science and Technology Center. When we entered, the first door on our right bore her name, Dr. Elisabeth Reinhart.

She pushed open the door, "it is identical to the laboratory I used before my death."

The others followed closely behind her until she stopped abruptly in front of a white board. "The equations for my final research are on this white board, as if patiently waiting all these years for me to solve them." I felt my body stumble backwards. Murdoc rushed forward, preventing me from falling.

"I wonder if we did more, Elisabeth, than penetrate the Earth. I feel like this is a parallel universe," Randolph suggested.

"Interesting idea, Randolph. But we are not in a parallel universe." Elisabeth commented, as she erased the white board. "They are flattering us, or just me, in a strange way. I think we should leave this section."

We turned and retraced our steps until we were back to our landing site, this time we walked a good twenty minutes in the direction of another building which housed the auditorium.

The auditorium was filled with hundreds of seats placed in rising rows in a semi-circular formation. An imposing, large, circular stage was positioned so that the audience could easily see the performers, whether actors or politicians, from any angle and any one of the auditorium seats. The podium behind which Reinhart addressed the members of the intellectual class on many occasions was absent, replaced with twelve small tables arranged in a semi-circular formation, in center stage. Even from the rear of the auditorium, we had a clear view of the table tops, glowing with the intensity of smoldering embers.

"What kind of substance is on those tables?" Randolph asked, as he backed up against the auditorium doors.

"You asked about holograms, Randolph. Well, perhaps you are about to see now how they function today."

Reinhart led the way, slowly climbing the high stairway onto the stage. As we moved inside the semi-circle, approaching the tables, beams of coherent light instantly illuminated three dimensional images, holograms, of life forms identical to the sculptures in the garden. The four of us instinctively moved close together, turning slowly in a tight formation, as our eyes met one by one the twelve, 7 feet in height, holographic figures, graced in an aura of divine light emulating their immortality, encircling us.

"Dr. Reinhart," she moved away from us to confront the speaker, "we are very pleased that you are alive and well and hope you appreciate the underground living quarters that we created for you."

"Created for me?" Her eyes swept the group. "Why did you do this?"

After a long silence, another figure occupying center position spoke up. "You have lost nothing of your grandeur and self-confidence, Dr. Reinhart."

"We could not help you," came a soft voice from another figure. "Our mission was to observe and study your planet and its inhabitants."

Reinhart's dauntless green eyes met theirs before she turned and walked past the various holograms, moving in the direction of the stairway, preparing to leave. "Wait!" The strained voice of an elderly member of the Group brought her to a halt. "We want to help you."

Reinhart stopped and turned towards them. One said, "We have not treated you with proper respect, Dr. Reinhart."

"You are playing games with me and my team. If you have something to say of any importance, say it now."

"We want to help you rebuild your civilization." The voice of a young man came up behind Reinhart, startling her, as she turned rapidly in his direction.

"I had asked you for help in the past and you refused it. You in fact had ulterior motives!" she replied.

"We are unable to lie." The young man replied. "Our explorers were obliged to return to the Mother ship to make repairs," he replied.

I could feel her instant camouflaging of her cerebral activity and a change of strategy, designed to provoke them. "It is an excuse, like any other!" Not getting a reaction she_proceeded. "And there are other ways to interpret your message, maybe even_intentional interference in the natural development of a given society was... unauthorized."

"You wanted this planet for you, your people. Our revolution was an unexpected blessing, because we were in the midst of destroying ourselves. Maybe you even wanted to eradicate us. But what you did not expect was the irrational behavior of the Group of 5 who set off the Doomsday explosion." The holograms flickered. "The most that you could do was to prevent the total devastation and, effectively, the disappearance of a planet that you wanted to inhabit."

She moved slowly past each of the holograms before she spoke again. "Unfortunately for you, the Earth was no longer habitable. You were forced to change your plans, look for new worlds to conquer. But before you left you encircled this large parcel of uncontaminated land with an impenetrable wall of flames, in order to save this land for the future. And you built this underground city much later, using the cooled down lava tubes, useful remnants of the Doomsday explosion."

Reinhart stepped back and met their gazes. "I can just imagine your frustration with the Group of 5."

Their flickering presences began to vividly glow, inciting Reinhart to continue. "When you contacted me, on the verge of the revolution, it was in the hope that I would help you with your plans to annihilate the human race. You naively believed that I was so caught up in the horror of this impending revolution that I was unable to decipher your true objectives." She chuckled. "You should never have underestimated me. You must be very disappointed that we humans are now back in control," she said, punctuating the last few words.

"Stop!" an elderly woman cried out. "First, our ancestors never sought to destroy your species. They sought to educate you...something that proved to be an almost insurmountable task, the reason why they formally left your planet, returning from time to time to evaluate your progress," she confessed. "You are right about some things, like our ultimate refusal to intervene in your war, but we had no desire to colonize your planet. Actually, when you contacted our ancestors, the Elders had already made the decision to remain neutral. They determined it was impossible to decide which side to support. And, Dr. Reinhart, we believed that you would be able to arrange for your survival without our help." Her eyes lost their luster.

"You are right," she continued, "we never expected the dramatic explosion that ended all life." My eyes held her rodent gaze. "We did, as you mentioned, set up an impenetrable wall of flames and did create this underground city much later.

"We also sent two packages," she picked up, "the forest and the large pond that you recently discovered. And, we removed the wall of flames so your western team could find and study the circular mounds. We wanted you to come to us."

She paused for instance. "But what you unreasonably ignore is that we used our scientific and technological skills to prevent a total destruction of this planet and to accelerate its recovery. And we did this, not just for our use but for your use as well."

"Did you need to make repairs on your vessel, or was that just an excuse?" Reinhart asked.

"Yes, our vessel was damaged and repairs were necessary. But, Dr. Reinhart," came the voice of a young man, "you surprised our ancestors. With the help of Dr. Murdoc, you saved various centers, replete with advanced technology. Programming the Group of 5, as you refer to them, was ingenious. You assured your return, Dr. Murdoc's return, the return of your most trusted scientific community and, most importantly, the return of the human race. We thus consider you to be our equal and endeavored to honor you and Dr. Murdoc by recreating your city."

Reinhart did not reply, she turned slowly, studying each of the 12 figures, before they disappeared.

"This is really weird, Elisabeth," Murdoc had time to say, before real life figures of a man and woman appeared.

"We have no defined leaders. Instead we have more respected members. We refer to them as the Elders. How can we be of help to you?"

"If these Elders are as intelligent as they appear to be then they know what I want! Are you willing to help me?"

"We will naturally have to discuss this but we shall be at your side," they said in unison, before disappearing.

"I wonder if we were just hallucinating from...lack of oxygen." Randolph's words provoked spontaneous laughter.

"What do you think, Elisabeth?" he asked, before adding, "It is apparent you knew of their existence."

"Yes... but I never met them before," she responded. "Let's get out of here. We can invite the others for a tour tomorrow." She said, shattering frozen faces.

We retraced our steps and were next to our planes in a matter of minutes. Murdoc had left his safari memorabilia next to his plane. He began to randomly press various buttons under the steering wheel, hoping to open the trunk, before moving to the rear of the plane, and looking under the strange tail Feather.

"Reinhart, something is wrong. The tail feather is changing form."

"It is a missile!" Run!" She bellowed the order. "When you hear the blast, throw yourselves on the ground and cover your heads with your arms!"

She moved a good thirty feet away, watching the tail feather change form, unveiling a short range cruise missile, programmed to follow a given launch trajectory. She rapidly calculated the launch trajectory and speed. Turning my head in the right direction, she locked my wide-open eyes on the missile. At the moment of launch a white laser light radiated outwards from my eyes, hitting the missile straight on and blasting it into pieces. My eyes were burning from the intensity of the blast, when she turned them in another direction, targeting the debris, disintegrating and reducing it to tiny pieces of ashy dust.

"It is safe. I removed bacterial and toxic substances from the dusty remains of the missile, so you can breathe freely," I heard her steady voice.

"My eyes are burning!" I shrieked hysterically.

"Pamela," she spoke on a cerebral level. "I didn't have time to explain. Your vision will recover completely in the next couple seconds." And, it did.

One by one the group got up and moved back to the vehicle. "We could have died?" Diana's face glazed like she was still in a trance.

"Do you know what button you pressed, Murdoc?"

"No!" He shouted. "I am still trying to recover my calm."

She headed in the direction of the other plane and examined the mechanism under the bird's tail wing, before opening up the door of the driver's seat and studying the panel. "Ok, I found it." She called the group over and showed them a tiny switch, the launcher, on the steering column. "We shall have to be careful not to touch it. It is a very sensitive switch."

"Well, at least we know why that tail feather is on this hybrid land rover, aero-mobile," Murdoc huffed.

We were already retracing our footprints through the garden, when Reinhart spoke again. "I shall show all of you how to activate the monorail system and then move it upwards vertically, so you can exit this underground without me."

"Can we really trust those Aliens?" Diana interrupted, her combative spirit returning.

"Trust them? Can we trust anyone?" she asked. "The real question is... do we need to trust them?"

"Of course we do!" Diana replied unequivocally.

"No, we don't! We only need to rely on ourselves."

She changed the subject, turning to practical matters, as she explained how the systems function so that anyone of us could enter the right codes to activate the monorail. She eventually moved the platform high enough that our bodies automatically passed through the dome covers and into the outside world.

"Well, you were gone for quite a long time." Gordon spoke with folded arms.

"We were naturally worried, but stood our place, as ordered, hoping that you were ok." Crawford added.

"Yes, you are right, but the underground city is much larger than I expected."

"I imagine we cannot enter this underground wonderland." An underlining tone of sadness in the melancholy of his voice.

"That is not true!" Reinhart replied energetically, knowing that she could adjust their systems to fool the bio-readers in the dome's surface. "I am not yet ready to trust you. I want more proof that you are our devoted allies."

"I don't know what more we can do!" Gordon scoffed, as she threw her hands up in the air.

"I know you will be loyal to me, but I'm not sure you will be loyal to other humans," Reinhart's gaze met Gordon's eyes.

"Understood, Dr. Reinhart," she replied with downcast eyes.

Reinhart ignored Gordon's humble posture, turning her attention for a long moment to a sky shrouded in darkness. "I am hungry," she announced surrealistically, as she started to walk rapidly in the direction of the small encampment, Gordon and Crawford following meekly behind her.

"I am going to ask Joseph and Clarence to meet us here in the morning. As the aliens have human and animal morphology, the bio-readers in the domes should respond like the wall in the inner circle at the main center, permitting our reptilian humans to enter," she began.

"I also want to contact John to get more information about the ocean creatures and hopefully, some news concerning our astronauts," she said, leaning back in her chair, appearing rather relaxed. "What do think? Do any of you have any questions or suggestions?"

"I think that we should also contact Miller and Flanders," Murdoc replied.

"Why not?"

"How long are we going to stay here?" A touch of urgency was in Randolph's voice.

"Are you worried, Randolph?" Reinhart asked softly.

"Yes and No." He gripped the table. "Actually, Dr. Reinhart, I would like to know more about your future plans. What I mean is that I want to know if Diana and I are going to be accompanying the two of you on future missions. I think we make a great team!"

"You are right and I intend to take the two of you with us." She left and walked to the communications tent to contact the main center.

John answered straight away informing her that the android

divers plunged into the deepest and darkest depths of the ocean, using spherical traps to catch a number of different species all of which resembled prehistoric life forms. Some of which were actually inhabiting these deep ocean waters hundreds of years before our generation arrived.

He continued, "For example, WD encountered a Black Marlin close to the continental shelf where the water is warmer. These fish are apex predators and feed off small tuna, squid and octopods, samples of which are here at the center. Black Marlins were known in the past for being the fastest fish in the world, reaching speeds of 80 miles an hour and capable of diving to depths of 2,000 feet."

"The one that was sent back, however, weighed 2,500 pounds and was 20 feet in length. WD told me that these new breed Black Marlins are not only bigger and more rapid than their predecessors, but additionally their formerly dangerous predatory nature seems to have evolved, making them more aggressive and fearless. Also it seems that our specimen's slim, pointed bill is twice the size of that of its ancestors." John concluded.

"Is it alive?"

"No."

"What happened?"

"Well, first of all, WD told me that if he had known that this species was still roaming the oceans, he would never have strayed so far away from the ship. Apparently the Black Marlin was not intimidated by WD's size and charged him. WD could not outrun it so he stood his ground, hoping to confuse and eventually tire it by taking deep, long dives. But when the Black Marlin continued the hunt, WD had no other choice but to charge and kill it before it killed him. At the right moment, he sank his large walrus's tusks into the body of the fish, forcing it to bleed out." He stopped to collect his thoughts. "At least he did drag it back to the ship."

"Ok. Continue to keep me up-to-date on that," she replied brusquely. "Anything else?"

"We have no news from Colonel Shannon and have lost all contact with the inflatable space station as well." He continued, anticipating her question.

"Did you try to reach Colonel Shannon?"

"No. I thought that it might be better for us to give her and the High Commissioners the impression that we trusted them. We are however very worried about the safety of our crew members."

"You are probably right, John." She took a deep breath, before bringing him up-to-date on everything that was happening in the western region, skimming over our encounter with the aliens, while insisting upon our need to work with them. "They have technology we need. And, even though I understand how to create this technology, we need to be operational now!"

"This is incredibly fascinating, Dr. Reinhart. It makes me wish I were there." He paused.

"You will have the opportunity to explore later, but for the moment you are the only person that I have confidence in to coordinate everything and interface with Shannon, should she contact you in the near future." She paused. "Diana, Randolph, Murdoc and I, as well as others will be returning to the Center over the next few days."

"Great!" He took a deep breath, before adding. "Can we make an alliance with the Aliens?"

"Yes. Actually, we have no choice. We need to be operational over the next month."

"Ok, send me those photos. I shall be back to you tomorrow," I added.

"Wait, Dr. Reinhart. Can I speak to you?" Ruth asked, as she shoved John out of her way.

"A problem?"

"Rebecca was in touch with me and gave me her version of your recent, apparently animated, exchange," her voice trembling.

"And?"

"She has always admired you, Dr. Reinhart and is very close to Pamela, and she asked me to tell you how embarrassed and ashamed she is about her lack of proper protocol." Ruth continued to plead on behalf of her daughter. "Can you please forgive and forget?" she finally asked in a low, humble tone.

"I can forgive, but, unfortunately, I cannot forget," Reinhart replied. "I shall, nonetheless, at some point in time, give her another opportunity to prove to me that she is not going to be a constant thorn in my side."

"Thank you. By the way, I am sending the photos of the ocean creatures now. If you have a few minutes, I can give you more details about them, our research has moved forward rather rapidly." She added enthusiastically and Reinhart nodded.

"Abysmal marine life was never known for its beauty, but rather respected for its perseverance in a world shrouded in darkness, in extremely cold waters and under intense pressure. The five different specimens resemble in certain ways their prehistoric ancestors. But, if I can be so presumptuous as to propose a neologism, it would be more accurate to refer to them as neo-prehistoric marine life."

"Please go on."

"As there is a natural lack of food supply in the deep ocean, it is not surprising that many of the life forms are small. And yet, I believe that the specimens we are studying now are newborns and that they will eventually reach sizes greater than their ancestors. That, of course, has to be confirmed."

"Ok, Ruth, I like your reasoning. And, would like to pursue this discussion with you, but not now." Reinhart declared.

"No problem," Ruth answered, mentioning that she would download her research on disks and forward them to Reinhart to consult later.

There was a long pause before Reinhart, ignoring Ruth's enthusiasm over the spider fish, asked what she was feeding the fish.

"We have naturally separated the different species so they will not attack each other. But as abyssal marine life will resort to cannibalism, we have to be careful to provide the different species with a large amount of nourishing food. We are using an edible, powdery substance, rich in marine snowflakes. The real challenge for us was not finding a viable food source, but rather finding a way to maintain the intense, deep sea pressure that they need to survive."

"I assume you have done that?"

"Yes."

"I do believe that I was informed by the Captain about the capture of deep ocean creatures by android divers---that is a while ago now. I think that the android divers used much the same equipment to capture the specimens that you are studying today."

"To my knowledge, none of them were live specimens. There are some rather unusual fish in large jars in the inner circle and in the marine biology lab. I know the equipment and techniques the androids used to capture the live specimens, now in my possession, were not used previously." Ruth's eyes drifted off in thought. "Yes, this is the first time we are actually studying live abysmal life forms."

"Thank you, Ruth, for this information and for managing these projects," she said, slowly stroking my chin. "Continue to keep me up-to-date on all research in the main center, including that of Stanislas, Benjamin, Ralph, and others. It would appear that research in existing flora and fauna is progressing rapidly. This is excellent news." They exchanged smiles, before signing off.

"Yes, yes, of course," she replied adamantly.

"We shall return to the encampment tomorrow," Reinhart reassured her.

Joseph and Clarence were awaiting her call. She gave them a quick update and asked them to meet us early in the morning with a small android team.

"Interestingly, we anticipated your request and are ready to leave early tomorrow." Joseph's iguana lips smoothed into a slim, yet pleasant, smile.

I collapsed on the bed next to Murdoc. He studied me for a short moment, assuring himself that Reinhart was meditating, before he turned his back to me.

I lay awake for what seemed like hours until, eventually, the deep, rhythmic breathing of my friends lulled me into a confused sleep. I awoke as beads of perspiration crawled down my cheek. I recalled a strange dream in which I stumbled along a labyrinth of intricately conceived passageways that seemed to lead nowhere, until I tumbled violently through a concealed entrance, falling face down in the middle of a large conference room.

In my nightmare, I pulled myself up and stared into the dark, piercing ruby black rodent eyes of the aliens, seated behind a large, semi-circular conference table. I pleaded vigorously for the release of my friends and colleagues, who stood obediently behind them, smiles of euphoric servitude etched on their faces. Between waves of silent laughter, the reigning figure asked me if I wanted to join my friends.

I trembled as I backed away from them but their brain waves dragged me towards them like a tidal undertow. I somehow pulled myself away from their clutches and dashed back into the chaotic confines of the labyrinth.

"Pamela, time to wake up." Randolph was there. "You had a nightmare. I heard you scream."

"I don't know what you are talking about," I replied. "I want to take a quick shower."

The warm water slid slowly over my body, like a healing ointment, dissipating the images of my nightmare and invigorating me.

"Did you precipitate this nightmare?" I asked Reinhart.

"No. I was not in contact with you during the night."

"Do you want me to tell you about it?"

"That is not necessary. I have already visited your subconscious."

"And...?"

"You are just too sensitive, Pamela. They are not going to enslave us. I spent the night analyzing all my past correspondence, principally verbal, with them and am now convinced that we need each other. Even though our immediate objectives are probably not the same, there is no doubt that our futures are so intricately entwined that we must become strong allies."

"Thank you for making me feel foolish."

"You are not foolish, Pamela," Her voice wavered. "Your concern for others is very touching. Strangely, if I could be jealous of anyone, I would be jealous of you for I strongly admire your very righteous and sensitive human side." She instantly retreated inside of me.

I concluded that whether her words were sincere or not didn't matter, because I felt my self-confidence rushing back. I strode into the dining room, my arms swinging at my sides.

"Glad to see that you recovered," Randolph commented, and I tapped him lightly on his shoulder.

"Pamela, what is Elisabeth planning to visit today?" Murdoc asked.

"I don't know. But, I don't think she wants to collect any memorabilia from her former apartment." He nodded.

"I don't feel comfortable with the hybridized Aliens," Randolph said. "Reinhart seems so fascinated with their rat heads. I wonder if they were born like that or a mad scientist created them to wipe out other civilizations."

"I got the impression these Aliens could be friends one day and enemies the next," Diana commented. "And you, Murdoc?"

"There is an unearthly serenity that surrounds them, either because they are incredibly brilliant or they are manipulative, or a combination of the two." He replied. But if she…"

"We are ready to leave," Clarence and Joseph said in unison, as they arrived, bringing our discussion to an abrupt end and leaving us with the impression that danger was lurking.

Chapter 15: Transformed

"Are you absolutely certain, Dr. Reinhart, we won't suffer any internal injuries or be harmed in any way, when we pass through these domes?" Joseph's voice trembled with concern.

"Your apprehension is misplaced," Reinhart replied.

"Ok. But you go first."

"No problem."

We had just arrived on the platform when Joseph and Clarence passed through, hand in hand, their faces drained of color.

"You were right, Dr. Reinhart." Joseph spoke for the two of them. "It was like passing into the inner circle."

She nodded absently, motioning to them to follow her, so she could demonstrate how to operate the monorail. We left together to visit the underground city.

Once underground, we meandered off in different directions. Murdoc expressed strong interest in exploring his walk-in closet and Diana and Randolph offered to give Clarence and Joseph a guided tour. We took the aero-mobiles, Clarence and Joseph taking the back seat in Murdoc's vehicle.

Reinhart mentioned that she wanted to visit her lab. Instead, she went to the auditorium.

When she entered the auditorium, the holograms began to flicker.

"Do you know where my astronauts are?" her habitual arrogance and pride, succumbing to humility, as she slowly lowered my head.

"Yes." The word resonated in unison.

"We can help you," came a soft, reassuring, elderly voice.

"What happened to them?"

"The inflatable lab is moving slowly, hiding in natural dark spaces where there are no stars or other celestial bodies giving off light, eluding your equipment," the elderly woman replied. "And your family is getting closer to the *Benevolence*. But as you probably suspect, they are not going to be received as dignitaries."

"Yes, I know now that I made a mistake trusting Shannon," Reinhart confessed.

"We all make mistakes, Dr. Reinhart," she replied.

"Do you know where the High Commissioners are?" She queried.

"Neither the High Commissioners nor the crew of the *Benevolence* are located in the Wolf or Gliese constellations. The High Commissioners are located in a humid, somber cavern on a small planet hostile to life forms and the *Benevolence* is stationed a short distance from them." Her voice vibrated and Reinhart stepped back with clenched fists.

"But then why did Shannon claim the contrary?" she pressed for answers.

"Simply because they wrongly believe that they are in the Gliese constellation."

Reinhart unclenched her fists.

"Can I save my family and the members of the space lab?" Reinhart's voice calm and clear.

I shuddered. Reinhart was worried that Peter, Frederic and Stuart would probably be captured and... killed.

"Is time still on our side?" Reinhart pressed for answers.

"We have been encouraged by the Elders to offer whatever assistance is necessary," she replied convincingly. "We thus offer to move the inflatable space station back to its original position. We shall then upgrade your operating systems on Earth so that the renegade android scientists will be apprised of Earth's improved and superior technology. Imagining you have a technological advantage might encourage them to alter their original plans and make peace."

Reinhart's cerebral activity pounded my skull pushing my mind to the brink. She felt my anxieties and put me to sleep, awakening me only after she had studied the pros and cons of the Aliens' proposal.

She finally replied. "If I have rightly identified the androids in power, they are more diabolical than clever. There is every reason to believe that they might resort to more brutal behavior, at least with respect to my family members."

"What do you suggest?"

"I believe we have to focus on Captain Robert Cray." She gritted my teeth. "He must fall severely ill. With him out of commission, my crew will be forced to take command and return to Earth, so Cray can receive immediate medical care." She paused.

"Your assistance in both upgrading our Earth-based technology and piloting the spaceship docked on the space lab is indispensable." She cleared my throat very loudly. "You must camouflage, the best word I can come up with, this upgraded technology from these renegade androids. I want them to believe that the crew members on board the inflatable lab were very lucky to save themselves and Cray."

The Aliens discussed the problem in low voices. Then the elderly woman spoke: "We can easily introduce a virus that will affect all the crew members. Once they fall unconscious, we shall revive only your crew members, sequestering Cray." She proposed.

"In the meantime," she continued, "we shall upgrade your Earth-based technology so that one of your trusted technicians on board can enter into the space lab's operating systems, piloting it to the proper distance from the Earth's atmosphere. Or we could just move it ourselves to a safe distance and then awaken your crew."

"I like the second option." Reinhart replied as the images flickered again.

"It will take a few days for us to accomplish this. Certainly, once the lab is close enough to the Earth's atmosphere, your crew will be instructed to use their spaceship to effectuate their return. The ship is situated in the lower section of the lab."

She held her hands in a steeple position, vaunting a position of power. "They will be given the proper program and coordinates to enter into the craft's guidance system to assure a safe landing. They should not run into any difficulties. And, naturally, we shall revive Cray once he is in the Main Center."

The young man who spoke before interrupted. "You want those androids to think that your technology is very basic and that in the event of war, they will be superior."

"Naturally, I shall need time to get my ship ready for space travel, so I can save my family and confront the renegade androids, or, as they refer to themselves, the High Commissioners. We have the cryogenic skin for a long space voyage, but we don't have a crew that can pilot the spaceship."

"I am capable of making the trip without a cryogenic suit. I think that you know that." She added.

"Yes, Dr. Reinhart, we are very much aware of your powers, which we would like to study and maybe even acquire," said the young man, as my stomach muscles tightened.

Reinhart pried for more information. "I don't understand, actually, how the members of the spaceship *Benevolence* have survived all these years in a non-cryogenic state, considering the vessel's very basic level of technology.

"Because," the elderly member intervened, "to save the human race, we used our technology to create the right atmospheric and gravitational environment for Earthlings to live and reproduce on board the spaceship *Benevolence*." She sighed. "In retrospect, it was perhaps a mistake for us to take this initiative, but then we were unaware at that time of your survival."

She pulled her slim, rat lips back into a tight smile. "I still believe that even if our direct involvement was a mistake, we did assure the survival of many generations of humans on board the *Benevolence*." She paused. "There are no habitable planets in the area so their extinction would have been inevitable."

"So you could do that for our spaceship?" Reinhart asked.

"Yes. And, we are ready to do that as soon as you return to the Center. We shall also upgrade the ship's technology, operating and communication systems and more, so that it can move at much greater speeds and we shall give you the right coordinates to reach the *Benevolence* very rapidly."

Another member who had remained silent until now spoke. His voice was filled with youthful energy and enthusiasm. "You have sufficient small fighter vessels on board your ship and, of course, our fleet will be at your side"

"This is all very reassuring, but I know there is either a condition to your offer of assistance or another reason why you want to join forces with us. Perhaps it is time for you to reveal your ultimate plans." Reinhart noted firmly.

"First, we want your promise that you shall never again divide society, on any level, and that Earthlings will live in peace and harmony."

"I know you." Reinhart quickly responded.

"I led the non-intellectuals into battle," he replied. "I was saved by my own people, but not before I saw the horrors of war." His eyes widened. "You must promise us that you will avoid war between and among humans at all costs. If you cannot promise this, we cannot have an agreement."

"I do not agree that what I did was wrong." She paced back and forth. "I must accomplish that which I am destined to do. So, anyone or anything that stands in my way is at risk. I cannot make promises I might not be able to keep. What I can promise you is that I shall save the human race from extinction."

No response forthcoming, she added, "If this is not enough for you, I shall go it alone," her strong voice resonating her disdain.

Messages passed inaudibly from alien to alien.

"It is not what we hoped for," the young man began, "but it is reasonable." His voice quivered. "Nonetheless, I would have preferred a more humanitarian response, but then, as you point out regularly, you are a very rational, logical person." He shrugged his shoulders.

"You are young, so I shall overlook your lack of tact and diplomacy in the interest of compromise." She answered firmly.

"As you rightly concluded, Dr. Reinhart, we will certainly need your assistance in the future," the elderly woman confessed, breaking the tension.

"We shall initiate procedures to protect your crew on board the space lab and our various technical teams will be ready to assist when you return to the Main Center," the elderly woman promised.

The holograms disappeared before Reinhart could respond.

With an energetic, confident stride, she left the auditorium.

"We are saved, Pamela. Their cooperation, as I mentioned, is imperative."

"They are determined to help us," she insisted. "I know what they want because I can I read their minds!" She strained my vocal chords with her laughter. "They do not yet realize who I am."

226

"What does that mean?"

"Another, and hopefully, final metamorphosis, Pamela, is approaching. It will take no more than one Earth day. It will be like in the past, our symbiotic relationship will always remain intact, but you will not be able to reach me before my metamorphosis is complete."

"I hate your absences," I replied.

"Listen closely," she insisted. "Like in the past, my knowledge will remain stored in the part of your brain I have been occupying for a very long time. Should anyone threaten my existence, you will be able to access that information and bring me back. No one will be able to force you to either erase my existence or otherwise interfere with you accessing my knowledge."

"But, Elisabeth, if something happens to you, it will happen to me. I won't be alive either."

"This is not true, Pamela. I shall be leaving your body soon."

I felt my legs weaken. "Where are you going to go?"

"Into my clone," she said firmly.

"What clone?" I virtually

"The one I created in my image and is now ready to receive me. It is in a semi-cryogenic state in the Main Center."

"I don't want you to leave me," I protested. "I can't live without you!"

"Don't be ridiculous. I am part of you and will always be. Trust me, you can access my knowledge and even feign my personality if you so desire. I shall even continue to reach out to you and educate you on a cerebral level. We shall stay linked."

"But I must leave your body in order to protect you," she continued. "I am the one that those foolish androids, those ignoble High Commissioners, want. So, if something happens, our symbiotic relationship will save me."

"Well I hope that nothing happens to you. I still don't understand why I can't just become you?"

"Because, Pamela, we are not the same. You can't be me, and, believe me, you don't want to be me." She replied, slowly and calmly.

And then, her gears shifted and I could feel intense, vibrant waves of laughter building and rushing inside of me, as if there was something humorous in what she said. She dramatically threw my head back, dragging me along in her folly, as she let her high spirited, euphoric laughter explode, filling the air with positive vibes.

My body still aching from the pains of laughter, she disappeared, leaving me to fly the aero-mobile back to the parking, where the others were waiting for us.

"Well you finally arrived?" Murdoc said, a tone of annoyance in his voice. I watched as he continued to shove his special collection of safari gear into the large backpack he would use to carry these items back to the monorail.

Our Group, Diana, Randolph, Joseph, Clarence, Murdoc and I, were ready to return to the surface. The monorail functioned like a charm. It was late when we exited the domes.

I ordered the androids to break camp. Gordon joined us humans and reptilian humans, as we left for the western region encampment, leaving the primitive robots to guard the domes.

We were directed to the mess tent. Over a digestive drink, a warm herbal tea, Reinhart's energy suffused me, pushing me aside.

It was clear their hybridized human-reptilian bodies adjusted very well to the hot days and cold nights and that living in wide open spaces appealed to them. They expressed their strong interest in continuing to move onwards towards the ocean where they would eventually meet up with WD, Weldon and the rest of the Captain's crew.

Eventually, the group broke up, wandering off in their own directions. Only Joseph and Clarence remained behind.

Joseph and Clarence turned in the direction of Reinhart's voice, "we shall be leaving late tonight, and will be returning to the Main Center over the next 24 hours."

"Because of the aliens?" Joseph asked, his eyes avoiding mine.

"I have not shared everything with you about the eastern region and/or events taking place," she began.

"Is something wrong?" Joseph kept his calm.

"I am worried. The inflatable space lab has drifted into a dark zone. I am worried about the safety of Frederic, Peter and Stuart." She mentioned how important it was for our Group to work in conjunction with the aliens to secure the safe return of our astronauts.

"The renegade android opposites of my former scientific team are unpredictable," she added, avoiding details, like her former contact with the aliens, her military strategies, and her personal projects.

"I want to go with you." Joseph slapped his large lizard hand down hard, rocking the table.

"Me too," Clarence blurted out.

"I have confidence in both of you to carry out this mission and to meet the Captain and WD, when they arrive on the western seaboard? No one could replace you."

"Adam could." Joseph proposed.

"No, he is not your equal. I need you and Clarence to accomplish this mission." She stared off into the distance. "Should we need more help, I shall send for you."

"Besides, Murdoc, Randolph, Diana, as well as, Dr. Gordon, Dr. Crawford, Dr. Miller, Dr. Flanders, Jason, Tirence and Drager will be accompanying me." She said under her breath.

"Why do you want those androids?" Joseph and Clarence asked.

"Because they know the renegade androids. Their human opposites worked with the human opposites of these renegade androids. I am relying upon them to use their emotional intelligence to anticipate the actions of these ruthless renegades."

"You understand that decisions based on emotional intelligence, sometimes referred to in general terms as the personality traits of an individual, are more difficult to anticipate when processed by an android." They nodded.

"And, from another practical standpoint, I cannot leave them alone, outside of my surveillance. There is always the risk that their fully developed emotional intelligence will lead them to initiate another "coup d'état", or seizure of power."

"And, Dr. Venderkof, the former Governor, must be leaving as well," Clarence replied.

"Yes, I am taking him with me." She took a deep breath. "I would also like to take John, if I can find someone who can replace him. I shall make the decision at the last minute, after consulting with Murdoc," she replied.

"If Tirence goes, I go too!" Joseph's vile lizard howl, blasting my eardrums.

"You and Tirence go back a long time and you both accompanied me in the past." She turned to Clarence. "Can you handle this on your own?"

"Actually, I don't see why not. Adam can replace Joseph." Clarence replied.

"Well, prepare then to leave with us in a few hours, Joseph," she replied. "And, Clarence, you will be in charge of exploration, with Adam as your second in command. If you have problems, you must contact the main center for reinforcement."

"And, I shall ask Birch, Basil and Ludovic and, maybe, Rebecca to join your group," she added.

Murdoc, who had been lingering outside the dining room, grabbed my arm as I passed by him. "What is the matter?" Reinhart asked.

"Rebecca—if you take Tirence, you must take her. Otherwise, there is a strong risk she could turn vindictive and try to take command, or sabotage the exploratory mission."

"I am sending her back to the Main Center. Ruth promised me she would oversee her activities."

"Foolish! Really foolish, Elisabeth! Someone like her needs to be under your command. You don't need our human society to fall into the hands of an immature young woman, vying for power." He stopped short. "At least, that is the impression that you have given me of her."

"You are right, Murdoc," she huffed. "I cannot trust her and she could easily manipulate her Mother. But, she is a pest, a nuisance, a thorn in my side... and more!" her voice building in volume with each consecutive word.

"You will have to assign her to a section where she cannot cause problems. Give her a lot of boring work!" He forced a smile.

She played with my fingers. "Do you like my idea of merging the two regional exploratory teams?" She changed the subject.

"Excellent. But, how are they going to get here?" Murdoc asked.

"The androids can fly the planes, remember I mentioned that their vision is not confounded by the visual illusions." He nodded. "Actually I will need androids to fly the second plane today."

Reinhart shook my brain, and I wondered what she was predicting.

Hours later we were preparing to board the planes for the eastern region. Android pilots would carry Joseph, Gordon and Crawford on their plane. Reinhart suggested that we all stay seated and let her fly the plane until she passed through the mountain range. Randolph and Murdoc could take turns flying after that.

"I already notified Birch, Basil and Ludovic of their transfer tomorrow morning to the western region." She took a long, deep breath. "Miller told me that a plane with newly discovered animal life left an hour ago for the main center. The androids are loading the carts and equipment onto the large transporters, for transfer to the western region. Things are moving ahead smoothly," she rambled on, as we approached the aircraft.

Our plane took off first. She was piloting, so I had time to think. In spite of our earlier reassuring discussion, I was still worried about my future. I felt distraught, reflecting on when she would leave my body, knowing I would have to rely exclusively upon myself.

A deep sadness invaded me. 'How could I survive without her energy, power, and genius? Depressed, I faltered in the past when she left me without warning for an exceptionally long period of metamorphosis. John took power and ostracized me from the others. Even Peter kept a distance.'

'But, I aligned myself with Randolph, with whom I found a binding love, and my brother Stuart. And when she returned from her metamorphosis, power shifted back to her and I was again treated with respect.'

'But, as we are physically identical, would the others see me more like her shadow than her protégé?' my thoughts continued.

"Stop these wretched thoughts, Pamela," she said on a cerebral level. "You are my daughter, with qualities I would have been honored to possess. You will always be respected and admired by your colleagues, not just for your genius, but for your personality. I am feared, Pamela, but you are loved." There was a long pause.

"Pull yourself together. I have to concentrate on flying this plane!" Our broad smile spread my lips.

I must have drowsed off for an hour, when I heard her. "Wake up, Murdoc. We are getting close to the mountains. Keep the plane steady while I choose the best route to take." She quickly analyzed and then chose the safest available passage.

"The android's plane is at the right distance behind us," he commented.

She shared her thoughts with me. I was so pleased that I understood why she selected the narrow passage that was just slightly off to our right.

"I am ready to take over now, Murdoc," she said, as she grabbed the controls, forcing the plane to maximum speed, tilting it 180 degrees, as she steered it through this very narrow passage, with sharp, rock clusters protruding on both sides. When the passage widened, she flipped the plane upside down several times while maintaining the speed as she proceeded ahead, selecting at the last possible minute the least treacherous upper or lower corridor to engage. When we were safely on the other side, her crew members opened their eyes.

"Does anyone feel sick?"

No one answered, so she continued the flight.

"I suppose you are now adjusted to this high speed flying through treacherous, narrow zones, where a plane can turn 180 degrees on its side or flip the 360 degrees several times in a row." Reinhart mocked, before she asked her co-pilot, Murdoc, to take over the piloting of the plane.

It was close to midnight when Murdoc landed our plane, with the android pilots landing behind us. We were escorted to the main tent.

"I assume everyone knows that we are going to abandon the exploration of the eastern region for a few months or more. Birch, Basil and Ludovic, you will be leaving tomorrow for the western region. I believe that you will be very happy working with our dynamic western group."

"I have a favor," Jason spoke up.

"You don't want to leave with us?"

"Of course I want to leave with you. This will be the greatest exploratory mission of my life," his voice thundering. "But I humbly request permission to bring Ludovic with me. He is my...how can I say this...yes, my trusted friend, Dr. Reinhart."

"Is that what you want, Ludovic?" He nodded. "We will be confronting much danger and any timidity on your part could be a handicap for us," she replied firmly.

"I have grown emotionally strong and I always had exceptional physical force. I am ready to confront danger."

"You, Ludovic—and this concerns all of you---will be under constant pressure to perform at all levels, especially intellectually, scientifically, strategically, and physically. We need to leave soon. Anyone who becomes a handicap for me and this mission, will be left behind." She stopped to let her words sink in. "Anyone who is not certain that they will be able to cope with constant pressure should step forward."

No one spoke out. "Ok, Ludovic, welcome aboard."

We were beginning to disperse, ready to get some sleep, when Rebecca approached me. "Dr. Reinhart, are you really taking me with you?" She asked, in a delicate, feeble, childlike voice.

"Yes, you will be accompanying us, but, as you are young and inexperienced, you will have to take orders from your superiors."

"I know that I still have a lot to learn. I want to show my worth and am happy you are going to give me this chance." Reinhart disappeared when Rebecca rushed towards me, ingratiating herself in my outstretched arms, while Tirence hovered in the background.

"Elisabeth." I released Rebecca and sent her back to Tirence.

"Yes, Aegir," his arms now moved around me. "I did what you suggested, but I don't like the idea," she confessed.

"Believe me, you did the right thing inviting her to join us," he said, his eyes focused on something outside the tent. "What is that?" He pointed to a bright image.

She immediately rushed out, coming face to face with six young aliens flaunting the same hybridized appearance as the Aliens we encountered in the underground city.

The rat's body was dissimulated under a large headscarf so only the ruby-red eyes and slender nose were visible. Their olive colored human bodies, rising to 15 feet in height, were much taller than ours. To Reinhart's dismay, I stepped back when I saw them, something they interpreted as fear.

"Sorry if we frightened you. We just wanted to inform you that we intercepted the space lab and released the virus. We shall monitor and, if necessary, further upgrade the small spaceship's systems to withstand a rapid, smooth entry into the Earth's atmosphere. We shall be reviving your crew in a few hours." There was a long silence. "We thought it would be better for you to be present when your crew arrives."

"Excellent. Thank you." Reinhart replied. "This is good news. I thought it would take you more time to accomplish that."

Their eyes took on a very deep, reddish luster. "But, Dr. Reinhart, as you well know, there was very little for us to do, apart from releasing the virus."

"You had already up-graded the systems, or rather entered into the space lab's guidance system, and that of the small spacecraft, before you left for the eastern region." He added.

"Yes, I was testing you. So you read my mind..."

"Like you read ours."

"I do rely upon your continued help. My astronauts might need your assistance in piloting their small spacecraft."

"We have our technicians ready to assure their safe landing," he replied. "Our fleet is regrouping to accompany your space ship. If the mere size of this space ship will be enough to dethrone the hostile, deviant, android Commissioners, then no one will die."

"They will not be alone," Reinhart replied. "Your enemies have probably already joined forces with them and are moving into place. I cannot disclose more. But, I can assure you that we still have time to build a winning strategy."

"How can you be certain that our enemies are united against us?" The leader of the group struggled to maintain his calm.

"Because I know." A slim smile of contentment across my lips. "For the record, your enemies are also our enemies so we shall be fighting side by side."

"As you know this must be taken up with the High Council. I must bring this up with them," a dark, somber sadness radiated his eyes, turning them from ruby-red to pitch black. "Thank you for this information. We shall discuss strategy with you very soon." They stepped out of view.

"You just forgot to tell me everything, Elisabeth?" Murdoc interrupted the silence.

"You must keep this to yourself. I do not want anyone else to know that I have been doing things on my own."

"What else have you done?"

She shrugged my shoulders. "It is late, Aegir. We both need sleep."

"Sleep?" He asked, as he pulled Elisabeth, who was replacing me, up close to him. They dashed back to a small tent, their private quarters for the night. He grabbed my waist and drew my body close to his, as he gently unzipped the exoskeleton suit, before stepping back, watching it slide over my shoulders and onto the floor.

I was still alert and could feel my body shimmer as his warm, moist breath flowed in erotic tingles over my naked shoulders. My blood rushing and my desire mounting, I had no intentions of holding back. But, Reinhart saw things differently and pushed me aside, locking me outside her emotional zone, putting me to sleep, as she surrendered to him. Like a child standing in front of a closed door, I imagined with envy, the intensity of their love, pigmented with lustful pleasures, before falling into a deep sleep.

Reinhart was cerebrating when I awakened. I shoved Murdoc's naked body, still entwined with mine, away from me. "Well, Elisabeth," I began, as I snarled and sprang to my feet, rushing in the direction of the shower, "once you enter your clone, I won't have to offer my body to you and Murdoc for orgasmic pleasure."

"Well said, Pamela," she replied. "And, I won't have to hide from yours!"

Just after breakfast, the androids left for the western region with Birch and Basil and we left for the main center, in three separate planes. After living on the outside for months, the comfort of the Center was a welcomed change and I was looking forward to sleeping in that big bed I shared in the past with Peter.

Over lunch, Reinhart announced that she wanted to meet with everyone in the late afternoon to bring them up-to-date.

"How much are you going to tell them?" Murdoc asked, when everyone had left the dining room.

"Everything that has happened, or, more precisely, everything that I mentioned to Joseph and Clarence. There is no reason for me to hide this from the others." She replied calmly. "Needless to say, I shall not reveal any of our future strategy."

"Be careful," he warned.

"What do you mean?"

"I wouldn't mention to them that you had met the aliens in the past, for instance."

"You are right," she said softly.

"Well, one thing is certain, you are the only person that can assure the survival of the human race for a second time!" He replied emphatically in a firm, forceful tone.

Reinhart wanted to relax, so the big bed seemed like the right place for it. I could feel her rhythmed cerebral activity and smiled to myself. I would miss these moments, in a few days.

"Pamela." I opened my eyes to find Randolph leaning over me. I quickly moved to a sitting position.

"Is Dr. Reinhart alert?" he asked.

"She is absent for the moment." I replied. "Is something bothering you?"

"Do you mind if I lie down next to you?"

"Why?"

"Because I don't want to be alone."

"Is something bothering you, Randolph?"

"Apart from the fact that I love you, Pamela, and that Rhea is our child, something I promised to keep secret." He replied.

"I am tired. Let's get some sleep," I said, as I moved into a reclining position and cuddled up next to him, pulling his comforting arms around me. I didn't know that he was still awake when I said in a natural, easy whisper, "I love you too."

"What are you doing here, Randolph?" I heard Reinhart awakening me. "What time is it?" She asked.

"I don't know what time it is." He jumped up to check the clock. "Oh, we still have an hour before the meeting. I came by to check on Pamela and I fell asleep."

"Well, now that you are rested, perhaps you can start to round up the others. We can always begin this meeting a bit earlier."

He dashed out of the room to carry out her orders.

"Nothing happened," I protested.

"Oh, I don't care!" She laughed quietly. "I just enjoy kidding Randolph, in my own way. He would make a good comic-actor, if we did not need his scientific skills."

The conference room was overflowing. Ferdinand ordered the android maintenance crew to bring more chairs. John, Ruth, Sarah, Samuel, Stanislas, Benjamin, Mathilda, Tirence and Rebecca sat on the far side of the table. The group of 5 stood obediently behind Reinhart, who sat in the large, presidential chair, with Ferdinand directly in front of her. Murdoc was seated at her right, followed by Randolph, Diana, Joseph, Ludovic, Jason, Ralph, Jonathan and Imogen.

"For those of you who have not yet met Dr. Murdoc, I would like to take this opportunity to introduce you to him," she said, opening the meeting. He stood up.

"You and Randolph look like twins." John commented.

"Physically, John." Murdoc replied. "Just like you and others in this room are identical versions of your ancestors." There was a moment of tension, everyone repositioning themselves in their seats, like they were preparing for a quick exit. "I know that my reputation may disturb some of you who have not yet had the opportunity to work with me."

"It is true that I don't tolerate any forms of deception but I have a strong sense of justice, and in the past worked for the defense of human rights. And, as Randolph," he gave his son a fatherly tap on his shoulder, "Diana, and others with whom I have been working closely can attest I am a relatively easy-going person. At least a lot easier-going than my Elisabeth." This broke the tension, followed by nervous laughter.

"Thank you, Dr. Murdoc," Reinhart replied. "You can be seated," she said in a dry tone. He covered his mouth to stifle his laughter, as he quickly sat down.

She began her presentation. "I want to thank John for being not just my liaison with this center, the spaceship *Benevolence* and the Space lab, but for his effective supervision of scientific projects here at the Center during our recent absence

"I want to thank those of you who chose to remain at the Center while we left to explore parts of the northern hemisphere: John for his vital role as a liaison with the spaceship *Benevolence* and the Space Lab; Ruth, Sarah, Samuel, Ralph, Stanislas and Benjamin for keeping me up-to-date on the various research projects, especially those relating to newly discovered life forms, animal and plant, that were sent back to the Center for study.

"I want to give a special thanks to Ferdinand and Johnathan and others for continuing to disseminate political and historical knowledge and promote the arts, most specifically, music, and Mathilda for assuring the education of new generations."

You will have the opportunity to meet our Alien friends, over the next couple weeks. They are in the process of assuring the safe return of James, Mathieu and Isabel and will remain with us, helping to upgrade our spaceship's technology so we can save the lives of Peter, Frederic and Stuart."

"Did you know anything about these aliens before a few days ago, Dr. Reinhart?" Benjamin asked.

"Alien life was science fiction for a long time in human history, but there was no convincing evidence of alien life before the Doomsday explosion." She lied.

"How did you know that Dr. Murdoc was still alive?" Mathilda asked.

"I didn't know that Dr. Murdoc was still alive, but was hoping he was," she replied. "He ingeniously masterminded his survival by programming a select group of androids to help him escape, enter into a cryogenic state, and move his cryogenic tank to a safe region, away from the Group of 5, just before the Doomsday explosion took place. I noticed a flickering beam deep inside a mountain range in the eastern region on the radar and thermal imagining screens and followed the flickering beam to its origins. It was a miracle he survived."

She drew a deep breath and continued, "Amazingly, he had the foresight to program three of our Centers, already floating just above land level, to lift off, much like a spaceship, and ride out the shock waves precipitated by the Doomsday explosion. It was ingenious."

"Mathilda, do you have any other questions?" She asked, breaking a long silence.

"No, Dr. Reinhart."

"How are we going to save Frederic, Peter and Stuart?" Sarah asked.

"We are going to use the spaceship that I designed, built, constructed, and fabricated before the Doomsday explosion to recuperate my family members."

She ignored the members' startled gasps and continued. "The spaceship with android personnel on board is at the Air and Space Center. The ship is hidden from view under a veil of invisibility, or cloaking device that I created in the past," she said. "I visited the ship before we left for the exploration of the eastern region and it is in excellent condition. The different android units must be reprogrammed to make the spaceship more efficient." Muffled sounds filled the room.

"Relax. Everything is under control. But, as I mentioned, our Alien allies will help us upgrade and replace our older outdated technology. And they will introduce more advanced technology, like creating a viable atmospheric and gravitational environment on board the ship so humans will not have to enter into a cryogenic state."

She stopped to let that sink in, before continuing. "They also have the proper source of energy to fuel the ship and can increase the ship's thrust power, so it can move at excessively high speeds. Most importantly, they know the right paths, or worm holes, to take so that we can arrive safely and rapidly. We will be able to save Frederic, Peter and Stuart."

"There are always risks associated with even what appear to be simple rescue missions." She drew a deep breath. "In our case, we will not be able to avoid war."

Her voice did not falter. "If we don't fight this war in space alongside our Alien Allies, the war will eventually come to us. We have the advantage now so we must act rapidly. Our future and that of our descendants is in our hands."

A long silence followed her talk. Murdoc's hand grabbed mine, reminding her she was not alone.

Finally, John stood up and spoke. "I am ready to take down an Empire to save my children and my friends."

His words struck the right chord as they all joined in, their voices reverberating their support in their own way.

"One last point," their eyes were on me, "the Group of 5, as you know, will be going with us. Their assistance, particularly in deactivating the hostile androids is fundamental."-

A heavy knock on the door silenced everyone. Ferdinand opened the door to greet an android from the communication's department.

"Dr. Reinhart, Colonel Shannon wants to speak to John."

"Do you want to take it, Dr. Reinhart?" John asked.

"Tell her that John is in the middle of an experiment and that he will contact her later," she ordered and the android rushed off.

"I want to know if our returning astronauts are close to Earth before communicating with Colonel Shannon," she replied. "If anyone wants to come with me, you are welcome."

Everyone followed me to the communications center. "Do you have a direct line with the spaceship and/or space lab, John?"

"She sent me updated communication coordinates a few days ago, but told me that it would be impossible for me to reach them because they were in a "dark zone," whatever that means. I should not have trusted her." He lamented.

"No problem. Just give me the coordinates she gave you."

"Dr. Reinhart to James, Mathieu and Isabel," she repeated several times.

"Is that really you, Dr. Reinhart?" She recognized James' voice and smiled approvingly at John.

"Yes, James. Are you ok?"

"Yes and No," his voice wavering, like he was confused. "It has been very strange ever since our lab drifted off into a deep, pitch-black space. Captain Cray, unable to make contact with Colonel Shannon, ordered us to stop floating outside picking up space particles and remain inside the spaceship."

"Eventually," he continued, "Cray accused us of sabotaging the mission and threatened to have us arrested, if ever his people recovered the inflatable space lab. About 5 days ago, he barged into our sleeping quarters, pointing an enormous laser gun at us and ordering us to follow him. He locked us up in one of the small research labs, where he had already placed enough food and water to keep us alive."

"Go on."

"A few days ago, the three of us fell very ill." He gridded his teeth. "We had high fevers and convulsive vomiting. Mathieu told us that we either caught a virus or were poisoned by Cray, and that, without immediate medical care, we would eventually die."

"How are you now?"

"I am feeling fine now. We all experienced a form of delirium when we were ill and might still be under its effects." She listened patiently. "For example, irrational as it might sound to you, we are convinced that we have been interacting with very strange creatures, with muscular human bodies and rat faces."

"They appeared first as holograms, before taking on tangible forms." Isabel grimaced. "Delusionary from high fevers when they arrived, their appearance was particularly disturbing." She sighed.

"Well, I was feeling very weak and dizzy when they appeared and actually tried to put up a fight. They were stronger than me and forced me," James growled, "to swallow a vile potion. I watched as they gave the same substance to Mathieu and Isabel. I thought that we were all going to die."

"And?" Reinhart asked, a hint of amusement in her voice.

"We recovered rapidly." He raised his hands in denial. "It was a miracle."

"What happened then?"

"Well, we followed them obediently to the lower section of the space lab. They told us to sit down in the flight seats. I argued that we needed to enter into our cryogenic suits. The spokesperson, or leader, replied in a calm, convincing voice that there was no need for us to take any precautions," he stopped abruptly.

"The following are his exact words which remained imprinted in my mind: 'We have adjusted your spaceship for a rapid and comfortable return to Earth, so strap yourselves in, sit back and relax. Your ship has been programmed for a safe entry into the Earth's atmosphere and a smooth landing outside your Main Center. Captain Cray is locked up in the small supply closet. Stay away from him, he is very ill,' the alien creature warned."

"I understood that they would not be hanging around, making this trip with us, so I tried to get more information from them before they disappeared. Strangely enough, they told me that they were friends of yours, Dr. Reinhart." James' eyes looked like they were popping out of their sockets. "I am sorry, we must sound confused and irrational."

"Calm down. You were not and are not delusionary. These aliens exist and they are our friends and allies."

"So we aren't going mad from space travel," James broke out in giddy laughter, as he slumped down in his seat

"We are breaking the atmosphere now," Mathieu called out.

"I have them," Murdoc replied calmly. "They are coming in at the right speed for a smooth landing--- just outside the center." He grabbed Randolph and John. "Come with me. I shall need your help."

"Did you hear what they said, James?" Mathieu asked.

"Yes."

"We are saved! We landed!" Isabel cried out and the others chimed in

"James, listen to me, did the aliens give you some medication for Cray."

"Yes. They shoved it in my pocket," he said, as he touched his vest pocket. "It is still there."

"Do not let Cray out of the closet. Once you are safely in the car with Dr. Murdoc, Randolph and John, the android medical staff will get Cray and bring him to the Center."

I was at the medical center waiting for them. Flanders carried out the tests. He quarantined Cray and then verified the health of our three astronauts. "They are in perfect health," he began, "but I would like to keep them under observation for 24 hours, in case there are secondary effects from the virus."

"Good idea. I think that they need a few days anyway to recover from everything they have been through," Reinhart replied.

"I am going to inject the solution into Cray, because he has lost consciousness and cannot swallow it," Flanders stated. "I shall keep him under constant observation."

"Keep his door locked," Reinhart added.

"I shall be back later to get your impressions." She said to James, Isabel and Mathieu. "Just before you arrived, we had a call from Colonel Shannon. I knew that the Aliens were going to help you, but wanted to be sure that you were with us, here on Earth, before talking to her. I shall keep you informed, but for the moment I want you to shower, have something light to eat, and then relax." They rushed towards her and threw their arms around her, as she tapped them lightly on their shoulders and smiled.

She told them she was very pleased with the results of their mission and very impressed with their undisputable courage, before she left to call Shannon.

Within minutes, Colonel Shannon was in view. "Dr. Gunther, I don't see you."

"Do you see me?" Reinhart asked as she moved onto the screen.

"Dr. Reinhart. I thought you were off exploring the planet."

"I was, but I came back to the Center for a few days. I understand that you have been refusing Dr. Gunther's calls recently."

She was unable to hide her trembling hands and puffy eyes. "We had problems with our communication system. Everything is working properly now." Her voice sounded strained.

"So, do you have any news from my family and my scientists on board the inflatable space lab?"

"Your family is still a distance from our ship. We anticipate their arrival in several, more like two months." Her voice cracked and she quickly sipped some water. "But, the space lab has disappeared from our radar. This is very disturbing."

"What measures have you taken to locate the lab?" Reinhart asked in a firm tone.

"Dr. Reinhart, the High Commissioners and I are very concerned. I am under extreme pressure to find your crew. We have no vessels close to the region where the space lab drifted, and they are not replying to our calls. The High Commissioners are worried that this incident could adversely affect our heretofore relationship of confidence."

"If you hear from them, would you please inform me directly?" she pleaded.

"Do you have any idea in which direction the space lab drifted?" Reinhart asked.

Colonel Shannon began to choke, a minute elapsed before she could calm down. "Our last communication with Captain Cray was difficult to understand. His message was so cryptic—broken—that we could not make any sense out of it." She feigned ignorance.

"Did he perhaps mention their hiding in a deep, dark zone?" Reinhart waited for a response.

"I know nothing about deep, dark zones," she lowered her head a few minutes to avoid eye contact, before adding, "I shall be right back," in a voice now steady and clear.

"What do you think?" John asked.

"I think that she wants to tell us the truth, but is frightened," she replied, after turning off the sound in case someone was listening.

We waited a long moment before Shannon was back on line. "I am sorry. I have no idea where these deep, dark zones are," she confirmed.

"I have very good news for you." Reinhart spoke. "Our astronauts have just landed on Earth. Apparently, Captain Cray fell ill. Dr. Flanders is treating him. He caught a virus—perhaps inevitable due to invasive microscopic organisms that probably flourish in the dark zone."

Shannon's eyes narrowed. "How did they pilot the ship and return so rapidly?" She asked impulsively. The moment she spoke, she realized her mistake. Her face turned white and her hand moved quickly up over her mouth. Yes, she disobeyed orders from the Commissioners, by acknowledging the vessel's great distance from Earth.

"Where they were and how they got there is of no importance. We are just pleased they are back on Earth," Reinhart replied. "Would you please transmit this message to the High Commissioners?"

"Yes, of course."

"Tell them that human ingenuity, cognitive powers, and courage, to name a few qualities and virtues specific to humans, will always be superior to those of any and all humanoid machines."

"I shall give them the message." Her teeth clenched involuntarily. "And, Captain Cray?"

"Oh he will spend some quality time with us," Reinhart replied.

"I know that you will take good care of him," she replied with enthusiasm, hoping to break the tension. "I shall keep you informed about your son, Stuart, and grandson, Frederic, as well as, Pamela's partner, Peter."

"Thank you, Colonel Shannon," Reinhart switched off the screen.

"I have always had a very good rapport with Colonel Shannon." John commented. "Her treachery and deceptive practices were not evident. We misread her intentions."

"Dr. Reinhart is right, the High Commissioners, those detestable, power-hungry, disturbed group of androids, were listening." Crawford entered the conversation. "You were perfect, though, Dr. Reinhart. You gave them the impression that humans alone were capable of achieving the impossible. Excellent!" He exclaimed in delight.

"But," he continued, "even though they may wonder about, even reflect on, the possibility of humans wielding superior power, they are machines, like me, and, will ultimately determine that humans are inferior. This will inevitably turn out to be their biggest mistake, because even machines should never imagine that they are invincible. Invincibility is a human flaw that emotional intelligence, from what I sense happening inside of me, accentuates."

He stopped to rub his hands together. "I am beginning to see better how we, the Group of 5, can force them to shut down," he said.

"Wow, Elisabeth, I think that Crawford gave you a real compliment," Murdoc chuckled.

One by one we got up to leave. I was heading in the direction of the medical unit when Mathilda came up behind me. "You are close to the Birthing Center. Don't you want to visit Rhea?"

I could feel my cheeks flush with guilt at having temporarily forgotten my child? "Yes, Mathilda," I replied, grabbing her hand.

"She will be born, leaving the artificial uterus in a few day, Pamela," she mentioned, as she led me to the Birthing Center. "With luck you will be the first to hold her."

Warm tears of happiness flowed slowly down my cheeks as I gazed upon my little girl, moving energetically inside her closed quarters. I felt Reinhart's presence. She too admired her perfection, physically resembling, more her father, Randolph, than her mother.

"It is probably better that the Reinhart characteristics remain with you and me," I replied on a cerebral level. "She will be able to hide from our enemies."

I heard Reinhart laugh with amusement. "Everything will be fine, Pamela."

"Are you ok?" Mathilda placed her comforting hand on my shoulder. I smiled reassuringly.

"Come now." She said, as her hand took mine. "We have to visit the medical unit."

As might have been expected, Captain Cray had recovered. He tapped on the circular window on the door of his isolation chamber and I turned obligingly, acknowledging him with a slight nod of my head.

"Dr. Reinhart!" his cries muffled by the cushioned walls and door. "Let me out!" He ordered.

"Oh, I shall activate the audio system in his room, if you want me to." Flanders proposed.

"Ok. Perhaps he is in the mood to confide in me, tell me what he knows." Reinhart said.

The ensuing conversation was tainted with unnecessary accusations on his part. Initially there was no doubt in my mind or that of Reinhart that he had been manipulated by his superiors.

"I was warned over and over again I was being sent on a dangerous mission and that I should not trust anyone, human or machine." He rushed towards the door, pulling and jerking it with all his force. "You think you are so smart, Dr. Reinhart. We did more than train your astronauts, we spied on them! We even planted listening devices on them to gather information."

I felt my body stiffen, almost solidify, as if turning to steel. Reinhart showed her super strength, as she knocked down the door and grabbed him, flinging him across the room, before scooping up his unconscious body and strapping him in a chair. "Wake up, you slimy creature!" She slapped his face vigorously until his eyes finally opened.

"I won't tell you anything." There was hysteria in his voice.

"You don't have to tell me anything because I am going to enter your mind." She said as she connected with his eyes.

I was still with her, something that surprised me. She skimmed his memory banks, like she was using a computer. He woke up on board the Spaceship *Benevolence.* He was not programmed like us humans to see a world in rosy colors. He had a euphoric childhood, a balanced schedule of learning, recreational and combat sports, as well as social activities, like gaming, dancing, and music. He was young, only 21 when he was sent to us, but he was one of the best trained astronauts. His studies also included technical training in intelligence gathering and the artfulness of resolving complicated puzzles and enigmas. And, moreover, he was brainwashed to believe that Dr. Reinhart was an evil scientist who hated humans and machines alike."

She stepped back for minute. "There is something wrong. I detected gaps and contradictions in his past memory. It would appear the real memory of his childhood and past was erased. I don't know why." She sighed.

"Does it matter?" I asked.

"It does not matter for the moment who he was. His present mission is what interests me." She said, as she re-entered his mind.

"Now what were they supposed to do here at this Center." I heard her say to herself as she moved rapidly forward in his memory bank, stopping the moment he was chosen for Mission Earth.

"Apparently he and Jennifer Marshall were to plant, like he mentioned, listening devices in various places, principally in our many different science labs and communication centers, as well as in your private quarters, Pamela, and those of the Group of 5." She stated.

"Do you remember that he and Captain Marshall spent the first few days after their arrival locked inside their different bedrooms?"

"Yes. It was strange. I remember being worried about their health."

"Whatever." She snapped. "They were studying the layout of the center, expecting to be able to easily complete their espionage mission, but what they discovered was that we were spying on them, for they found our surveillance equipment, installed in their bedrooms and in the various labs they worked in."

She snickered. "It must have been incredibly frustrating for them. Obviously, their training was too one sided. They were taught how to plant surveillance equipment but they were not taught how to sabotage another system of surveillance. When they realized we were observing them, they were afraid that they would not be able to carry out their mission, because they were incapable of gaining access to our research and development." Her voice sounded relaxed.

"Rather than admit to Shannon they were unable to carry out their espionage activities. They decided to lie."

"But, it is clear that fear was their motivating force. So, as they were unable to access our research and development, they made the decision to send messages indicating that we Earthlings were far behind their own people in all fields of sciences and were even using very basic levels of technology. They described the Group of 5 as primitive robots, claiming that they had been stripped completely of all their former capacities."

"So in the few messages that he sent from Earth," she continued, "and later from the space lab, he underlined his disappointment with the mediocrity of Earthlings today. Excellent!" she shouted, my ears ringing for a long time afterwards.

"Should we let him go now?" I asked.

"Yes. I am going to release him." She said, before adding, "He is more pathetic than dangerous."

"You are evil, Dr. Reinhart," his voice vacillating involuntarily.

"I don't care what you think of me. Evil is as good a description as any." She flicked my finger, like she was brushing away a fly. "Do you prefer to stay here with us or do you want to return to the *Benevolence* and face the consequences of your mission failures?"

"I hate you and everyone else in this center," he replied, in a forlorn attempt to save pride, before coming to terms with the reality of his situation. "I could always try to get over hating you, Dr. Reinhart, and even pledge my allegiance to you, if you promise to protect me. You seem to be even more powerful than our Commissioners."

She spent a moment observing him. "For the record, I am the one who decides the terms and conditions." She stood up and paced back and forth, before turning her eyes on him. "I have decided to give you the opportunity to show me you are worthy of my protection."

His eyes rolled. "How can I do that? That could be dangerous for me?"

"Stop whining." She huffed.

"You will make contact with your superior, tell that individual that you have negotiated your freedom to circulate—mentioning that Dr. Reinhart is more humanitarian or understanding than they realize, and then confirm your commitment to their cause. You will explain that your unconditional freedom to circulate and participate with scientists and technicians on their various projects puts you in an excellent position to continue your former mission, or espionage activities." She replied, before adding, "But, you will not be circulating, instead you will be sending the information that I give you to send."

When he regained his composure, she continued. "Your faithful cooperation in this mission could buy you your freedom. I am promising nothing. Do you want time to think about it?"

"No. I don't need to ponder your offer. I am more afraid to face reprisals if I return to the *Benevolence* than to work with you."

"Once we are certain that you have fully recovered from the effects of the virus, we shall move you to more comfortable facilities."

She turned and exited. The Group of 5 along with my entire team were packed in the hallway. They had listened to everything.

"Did you enter his mind, Dr. Reinhart?" Crawford asked.

"Yes."

"But, how could you do that, you are not a machine, you are human," he insisted,

"Are you really human, Dr. Reinhart?" John asked for the umpteenth time.

"Actually your question, John, is redundant. We all know that you are more evolved, Elisabeth." Murdoc snarled. "So you moved through his brain, like you were scanning the memory of a machine, a computer."

"So we can confuse those androids, send them the information that they want or are hoping for?" John asked.

"We have to be cagey. The Group of 5 will come up with the right mixture of android logic and emotions to convince their counterparts on that distant planet that we are far behind them technologically and are no real threat."

"It will be our pleasure, Dr. Reinhart." They replied in unison, underscoring their combined loyalty.

"Does anyone have any other questions?" Reinhart waited a few minutes.

"I am hungry," Diana said, putting an end to dialogue as we rushed off to the dining room.

I left straight after dinner, hoping to get a good night's sleep. Even though Reinhart was resting when I arrived in my bedroom, I was still too mentally and physically wound up to jump into bed and decided to pamper myself with a long, hot shower, before dosing off. I turned on the shower and stood back, mesmerized by the gushing stream of water, the odor of the hot vapors forming and engulfing me. I could have stayed like that for hours, and yet...I would have regretted missing what happened next.

"I love you, Pamela," his voice riding on misty water, as he turned me in his direction, taking my head tenderly between his hands, his lips touching mine.

"I want you, Randolph," was rushing through my mind. "Hold me, caress me, do whatever you want to me; I am yours for tonight and forever." I uttered aloud. His eyes met mine. "I love you, Randolph!"

Flickering morning lights, awakened me. His arms were still tightly around me, comforting me, and... I snuggled up even closer.

Reinhart, indifferent to what I was doing, broke into my sublime thoughts of blissful happiness to inform me that she would be back in 24 hours.

"Oh!" I sighed, awakening Randolph.

"What happened?"

"Reinhart is leaving me for her final, cerebral metamorphosis," I replied. "She warned me of this a few days ago."

"Now? We need her." He jumped up.

"She will only be gone for 24 hours, but her timing is bad"

"Don't worry? We shall tell Murdoc. Let him handle things, Pamela." He replied, as he pulled me up out of bed. "We have to get dressed and find him."

When we opened the door, Murdoc was on the other side. "She left," he said, pushing us both back into the room.

"How did you know?" I asked.

"Mental telepathy," he uttered. "Listen to me...both of you," he said emphatically. "No one else should be informed for the moment. We don't need unnecessary panic. From your perspective, Pamela, she is mediating."

"Well, I thought that only certain insects and amphibians metamorphose," Randolph continued. "And, she admits having passed through different stages of metamorphosis." He drew a long breath. "And, strangely, she despises insects. But would she be insulted, being compared to amphibians, which do like us have a backbone." He slumped into the bedside chair. "Nothing about Dr. Reinhart makes sense."

Murdoc sat down on the bed. "She is neither an insect nor an amphibian. I met her hundreds of years after she arrived on Earth. She was young and has remained ageless".

"She took an interest in me," he confided, "the reason why she increased and accelerated my learning capacities. I often wonder if she did that to make herself complete, imagining that if she could merge with me she would become an invincible hybrid, male/female creature." He chuckled.

"Actually, Dr. Murdoc, I see you as her equal." His eyes met mine in a cold, Reinhart stare.

"That is flattering, but untrue," he confessed. "She is intellectually superior to me. She defies the laws of science in so many different ways, like entering into the human physiological and biological systems to rejuvenate the individual or diving into someone's brain and roaming through their memory banks—something I didn't know she could do before yesterday." He sighed.

"How can you explain then that she loves you?"

"Because she is human in every sense of the word. She has needs and desires, just like the two of you. Our love for each other has survived time." He sighed. "But, what is important now is that we make the right decisions in her absence. So get up and get dressed. I need you both by my side today!"

Chapter 16: Dilemma

As it was, Reinhart did not surface during the night, but woke me around 5 in the morning. "I told you that I only needed 24 hours, and if my internal clock is exact, it is precisely 24 hours since I left."

"Elisabeth, I am glad you are back."

"Pamela, sit up and try to stay relaxed. All of my knowledge and emotional intelligence is now in my, should I say, reserved section of your consciousness." I felt my heart begin to beat rapidly and my hands grow moist.

"Please don't worry. But, in my absence, you will have access to my knowledge and can feign my personality to maintain power over others. We might get separated. You might have to take command."

"You mean that your clone could be arrested by the renegade androids?" I replied, in a groggy voice.

"Exactly!" The high-pitched, unrestrained tone, so unnatural to Reinhart, perturbed me. I was now very alert. "I shall have to resist all their efforts to gain access to my knowledge." She paused. "I know that they will not be able to break me down, but they might otherwise dispose of me—imprison or execute me. That is when you will take command."

"How am I going to do that?"

"You are going to reactivate me by repeating the following code, but not out loud," she warned, "rather on a cerebral level!" she insisted. "Here is the code: erh33. Continue to repeat the code, as you connect with me on a cerebral level, until all my memory banks open and my personality reappears. Only you can activate me, so it is in your interest to protect yourself and stay alive."

"By activating the code, we will return to a symbiotic relationship?"

"Effectively."

"How will I know that I should activate you?"

"I will make contact with you on a subliminal level. Even though I shall be in a separate body, I shall continue to interact with you on a subliminal level, using, like today, telepathic communication," she sighed. ""So don't do anything drastic, even if I disappear for a long time, unless and until I contact you."

She hesitated. "And, even if these crazy androids tell you that they are torturing me you must remember that I can fortify myself and, if need be, repair any damage they may inflict on me physically. I shall only contact you for assistance if I am in an irreparably weakened condition or if my execution is imminent." Her voice was filled with enthusiasm rather than despair.

"So you will you be able to control the actions and reactions of your clone, the time that you need to pass over as my symbiote?" I asked.

"Pamela, what we are discussing now, will probably never happen. But, it is important to prepare for all scenarios, including the most bizarre and horrific ones," she repeated herself, easing my mind. "Now to answer your question, the moment that I know that you have initiated the code and activated my return as your symbiote, I shall abandon my clone. She will be but an empty shell, a kind of rubber doll, void of knowledge and unable to communicate."

"They will come for me in that case."

"Maybe," she sighed. "Even if they do, you will be protected by others," she said in a low voice." And, Pamela, tomorrow, I am going to reregister your personality and knowledge on empty DNA strands, and do the same for myself because my various stages of metamorphoses have augmented my knowledge bank. They will be stored in a vitreous state. The Group of 5 knows how to rehydrate these DNA strands and knows my method of downloading them."

There was a long silence. "There is nothing to worry about. And, no matter what happens, the Group of 5 will bring us back!" she said with conviction.

"Do I have your permission to confide in Randolph or Murdoc?" I asked.

"No, we have to count on each other," she replied firmly. "Hopefully, we will soon rid ourselves of our enemies!"

"Dr. Reinhart...Elisabeth?" She didn't answer. I was moving like a lifeless automaton when I left for breakfast. 'She is overestimating me,' I thought. 'I am not like her. I don't like danger. And yet...'

"Pamela, you look like a zombie." Randolph grabbed me from behind. "What happened?" He turned me in his direction.

His silly, innocent smile added levity to this desperate situation. I had to smile.

"I didn't sleep very well."

He grabbed my hand and we engaged in a lively jog to the dining room. My enthusiasm returned when I saw Mathieu, Isabel and James sitting at the long table.

"Glad to see you, Pamela," James called out to me. "You haven't missed anything."

I sat down, ready to listen intently, as they recounted their adventures.

"We really didn't discover anything special during the mission, but we did learn the techniques used in asteroid mining," James was the first to speak. "We actually disembarked on several small asteroids and a spent comet, explored the rubble in the deserted mines and took specimens from amongst the debris." James drew a deep breath.

"As incredible as it might sound, we were able to activate some of the abandoned mining equipment, and uncover more deeply encrusted minerals." James seemed to relive his adventure as his eyes drifted away.

"As I mentioned, we were only allowed to collect and conduct experiments on the surface samples that we found in the various mines. And as you know, we were unable to bring any specimens back with us."

"The training that we had at the Air and Space Center in simulated anti-gravity conditions made us operational. We had no difficulties moving through the space lab or conducting exercises or repairs on the outside of the lab. Additionally, the protective space suits and helmets were less bulky and more comfortable than those we used for training." James added.

"Were you able to deal with the "containment" aspect of the space lab, or did you find yourselves going stir crazy?" Reinhart asked.

"I was worried I might become claustrophobic living in such a confined space, but I didn't." Mathieu replied. "I actually lost the sense of time while I had lots of energy." He paused. "We were very active--there were even exercise rooms and lounges on board. And in the first weeks, we gathered up—collected—other small inflatable labs, attaching them to ours, like we were building an enormous puzzle. We eventually had a lot of space, with recreational centers."

"I am a bit confused. You were floating in anti-gravity conditions in the beginning?" John interrupted.

"Yes, in the beginning," James replied.

"Ok, explain to me, to all of us, what happened." Reinhart pressed for answers.

"Yes," Mathieu continued, "there was a package outside the space lab. Even Cray seemed to be a bit surprised when we discovered this package, which we thought was —food or other supplies—drifting close behind the main, central space lab. We had no idea who sent the package."

When we prepared to go outside to examine its contents," he picked up, "the exit door got stuck and we were unable to close it completely. So we slid back inside the space lab to solve the problem. We were actually in the process of testing the system, when this container just drifted on board. To our surprise, the door shut immediately upon its entry and continued to function perfectly thereafter."

"It was like someone was sending us a gift and making certain it was delivered." Isabel interjected. "And, whoever it was, was able to activate the cargo unit door, because we never had any problems after that."

"Upon opening the container, which to clarify the timing, arrived within the first ten days, a small mechanism floated out and attached itself, like it was alive, to the wall. Immediately thereafter, we started to sense a slow, building gravitational pull," James recounted. "We could feel our bodies move into easy standing positions, as we ran through the corridors, eventually running up the steps to the control room."

His eyes met his colleagues. "Cray had been watching what was happening. He accused us of severe negligence in letting that container follow us into the loading area. But when he finally came to terms with the fact that we had an artificial gravitational system in place, he claimed that it must have been sent to us by Colonel Shannon."

"No matter," Mathieu spoke, "once the artificial gravity system was activated, our physiological systems functioned at an optimum and I felt great!"

"Do you know who sent the package?" Isabel asked.

"Yes. Our Allies, the Rat-Human aliens, were looking out for you," Reinhart replied.

"Is that when the lab began to drift off into that deep, dark zone?" Reinhart asked.

"No, as James mentioned, all of this happened in the very beginning of our mission. At that time we were moving in a very slow, orderly fashion," Isabel confirmed.

"It was months later Cray mentioned that he was losing control of the space lab and thought that it was because we had collected and incorporated too many floating modules." Mathieu replied.

"Actually, we all agreed that his conclusion made sense. We collected more than 30 modules, perhaps more than our ship could safely carry." Mathieu explained.

"Soon after that," James picked up, "I noticed that Cray was acting strangely. In the beginning, I thought it was a space-related syndrome that we might all eventually experience. But as we weren't affected by it, I started to worry."

"He was always looking over his shoulder like he didn't trust us," James continued. "I heard him talking to himself as he passed through the corridors. I kept a close eye on him. But when I inadvertently heard him on a number of occasions speaking in a low voice over the communications systems to Shannon, I began to worry."

He hesitated. "So when he rounded us up and locked us up in that little room, I was certain that he was carrying out orders." He took a deep breath. "I can assure you that Cray was not showing any signs of delusion or acting like he was in a trance, when he came to kill us. He must have been ordered to dispose of us at a given point in time and he decided to do just that." He hesitated. "Whatever, we were lucky that the Aliens intervened."

"Well, he was trained to follow orders," she replied. "As Colonel

Shannon didn't know where you were, I believe that Cray confronted a dilemma. He was supposed to eliminate you, but he was troubled by having lost control of the guidance system. He could no longer reach Colonel Shannon." She sighed. "Fortunately, your spaceship was under the control of the Aliens."

"So why didn't the Aliens tell us that they sent the Space Lab off course, letting it drift into a dark zone?" Murdoc asked.

"Does it matter?" She replied.

"But that means that we can't trust them!" he said in an authoritative tone.

"Dr. Murdoc, there is another way to see this," she protested. "They undeniably delivered the gravitational system months and months ago and later saved our crew. But, naturally, we shall stay alert."

"Cray asked me if he could have something to read. He claims that he is bored." Crawford changed the subject.

"I don't care if he is bored. He is not our guest. He is our prisoner. Keep a close eye on him, though," she replied, before turning to the group. "I have something urgent to take care of so I shall see everyone later today." She stood up to leave, grabbing Murdoc by his hand, nodding discretely in the direction of the Group of 5.

When they were out of the range of the others, she asked Flanders to get the empty DNA strands, he nodded. "Please meet me at our habitual entrance into the inner circle."

After they rushed off, Murdoc confronted her, reminding her that the inner circle should not be accessible to the Group of 5. "I have no choice, because my clone is located in a secret room in that inner circle." She sighed. "I am ready to transfer into it. I need the Group of 5 to supervise my transfer and the downloading of my knowledge and emotional intelligence, as well as that of Pamela, on these DNA strands."

"Why?"

"Because they helped in the past—they coveted my very essence and they brought me back, even though one might argue that they only did what they were programmed to do. They of course did a lot of despicable things during their reign—the Doomsday explosion, programming and executing humans, creating hybrids, engaging in genetic research, and so forth--but I need them today and in the future. If they defy me, I shall destroy them and they know that."

"We can't pass through the wall, Dr. Reinhart," the former Governor insisted on arrival. "The bio-readers."

She passed slowly in front of each of them, maintaining an intense moment of eye contact, connecting with their individual systems, like she did a few times in the past "Now you can, but I shall remove your capacity to pass through the wall afterwards."

They hesitated. "Go! This is an order!"

"Just follow me!" Reinhart called out.

We walked down empty corridors until we arrived at a back wall. "We have to slide through this wall now," she said, as she pointed to the Group of 5 to go first. Her clone had reached the age of maturity and was resting comfortably in a cryogenic tank. She began the awakening process, slowly elevating the temperature as the solution drained, drop by drop into a reservoir.

"It will take some time for her body to be receptive to me, so in the meantime, I want you to simply supervise—that means intervene only if necessary—as I record my knowledge bank and emotional intelligence on DNA strands." She placed a tight -fitting helmet, similar to the helmets we wore when we downloaded the learning cassettes, on my head and hers.

She painlessly entered into the section of my brain she had occupied for a long time, as I experienced low waves of energy passing through me. I wondered if I was asleep, dreaming that I was floating in a world filled with colorful diagrams and figures, surrounded with a thick, spongy substance.

"Ok, Pamela, it is your turn," I heard her say, as she entered into another corner of my brain. "I felt a tingling inside my head, as my knowledge and experiences, even feelings, moved easily on to the empty DNA strands. I smiled, as images of people and places were gently released, becoming nothing more than a long stream of bright light."

"Pamela, it is over," I heard her say. "The transfers were a success. You can get up now," she said, as she hovered over me.

"Reach for me inside your brain," she requested, when I was sitting straight. "Can you find me?

"Yes. Yes, I can. You are still there," I said, finally opening my eyes. "And, surprisingly, my neocortex region is still intact!" my awestruck admiration of her broken by her low, gentle laughter.

"Perfect. You certainly know what I must do now. I cannot do it on my own." She was speaking to me on the subliminal level. "You will transfer me to my clone," her voice soft and maternal. "I have verified the DNA strands for both of us and they are perfect repro- ductions. It is time for us to install all of me—my knowledge and my emotional intelligence---into my clone." I held back my tears.

"From today onwards you will be Pamela and I will no longer be your symbiote. But we shall continue to communicate on a sub- liminal or telepathic level. We shall always remain connected." We smiled in complicity.

I stood up and looked around the room. Murdoc's face was as listless as those of the androids' who huddled together.

"I will always need you," my voice trembled.

"We are ready," Dr. Flanders replied in a very warm, paternal tone, as he left the huddle. "I know that you can do it, Pamela."

And so I followed her instructions. I lay down on the bed and took the lifeless hand of a lifeless body, an exact replica of Reinhart, into mine. Its closed eyes and hand, cold as ice, made me tremble. It could have been a doll, if it didn't have human flesh and blood. I took a deep breath, closing off my own thoughts, letting Reinhart make the transfer, this time into her new body."

When the transfer was complete, I turned my head slowly in the direction of her clone. I could see the changes, as they happened, from the moment her mind entered her clone's body. She exerted the right amount of cerebral energy, acting like a defibrillator, send- ing shock waves, activating her heart, as the clone's body arched upwards, several times. I could hear her breathing, deep and raspy in the beginning, slowly taking on a calm, even rhythm, as her skin turned her natural pale brown tone.

She stretched, before moving into a sitting position. I shud- dered when the clone stood up in that Reinhart style, her shoulders pulled back and her head held high. For the first time in all these years, I was gazing upon my Mother, my flesh and blood Mother.

She approached me and pulled me up into her arms. I knew, like those closest to her, that she had feelings and that she could be kind and gentle as easily as she could be stoic and ruthless. "Thank you, my child. We shall make a formidable team."

"I know," I replied.

"By the way, Pamela, you still feel my presence," a strange anxiety in her voice.

"Yes, I can feel your presence. Your knowledge and emotional configuration are still in the part of my brain you occupied for years. You can always reach me on a cerebral level and even return to your former symbiotic state." I replied.

"And, so it worked," she said. "And, Pamela, you will always be able to access me as I can access you."

"Look at me. I am standing naked!" Reinhart exclaimed in disbelief, as if we were responsible for her oversight.

"I shall be right back with a uniform," I replied, as I passed through the wall and sprinted down the hall, returning in a couple of minutes.

"Do we look the same, Aegir?" she asked, teasingly.

"I see no physical difference." He contemplated. "There definitely is a difference, though, in the energy that you emit, Elisabeth. Your eyes are a fiery green and your skin lusters. You have an aura around you that is fascinatingly beautiful, as it radiates your invincibility, reminding all of us that you are not exactly human."

"Excellent!" she replied.

"Maybe...," he began, before she interrupted him.

"Aegir, you sound sad. Don't be sad. Be happy for me. I am back and we can be together." She pulled herself close up against him, drawing his arms around her. The Group of 5 cleared their throats loudly, reminding Reinhart of their presence at this awkward moment.

"But, Elisabeth, I don't remember you like that," he said in a low, somber tone.

"Of course, you don't. I have metamorphosed," she replied moving away from him and strutting in front of us, like she was examining her troops. "I shall temper my glow, the aura of light surrounding me, when it is necessary to do so. But for the moment, it will help all of you to recognize whether you are interacting with Pamela or with me."

"I don't think that anyone will have a problem identifying which one of us is you," I said wistfully, which spurred nervous laughter.

"I should have taken the time to download your musical talent. A serious oversight on my part," she tormented.

"I think that we should leave. We have spent the entire day here. I believe that it is already dinner time," I said, as I turned my back to her, hiding my smile. The Group of 5 was directly behind me, with Reinhart and Murdoc bringing up the rear.

The moment we passed through the wall into the main corridor, she asked the Group of 5 to line up in front of her. Her eyes flashed a bright light as she passed by each of them, entering their android bodies and deactivating the biological and physiological reader she installed in them, removing their ability to access the inner circle

When we entered the dining-room, we were not met with varying degrees of surprise, shock, or gestures of incredulity, from laughter to screams to wide eyes and dropping mouths, instead, one by one, everyone at the table rose and stood at attention.

I watched my mentor, my mother, my friend, and my former symbiote take center. It was almost like a solemn ceremony.

Randolph motioned to me to take the seat next to him and Reinhart and Murdoc took the two empty seats opposite us. I wondered if Randolph had the same strange sensation as I did, like I was seeing my own reflection in a looking glass. She must have sensed my appraisal, for her eyes, so vibrant and profound, captured mine, reminding me that we were different and that I could never express her gaze or reproduce the power behind her glare.

"Well," she finally spoke, "time is running out. I want everyone to send me complete reports before the end of the day regarding your research in progress, because I shall have to assign other competent members to replace those who will be accompanying me on this long voyage to the spaceship *Benevolence*." She skimmed the group, her eyes eventually fixing on mine. "Those already chosen for this mission, and those who would like to be part of it, should meet with me in the conference room tomorrow morning. Any questions?"

No one replied.

Reinhart and Murdoc meandered down the corridor, passing

through the wall in front of me. They headed in the direction of Murdoc's quarters, or those that Stuart occupied before his departure.

I opened my bedroom door and let myself drop half-heartedly on the side of my bed. 'She is still inside of me, but inaccessible,' repeated several times, as big, warm tears began to flow, zigzagging as they rushed over my cheeks and dribbling off the end of my nose. I missed her active presence.

In the bathroom, I threw cold water over my swelling eyes and red nose. I looked in the mirror and saw his reflection.

"Randolph...," he took me in his arms, carried me back to the bed and sat down in the comfortable armchair; hovering over me, while I curled up in a tight ball.

"I am glad that you are no longer under her power," he said in a soft, mellow tone. "Remember the fun we had organizing the revolution: your role as double agent? Our crazy plans to pass information to the outside community—even putting messages inside Jonathan's clarinet case? Remember how we kept that crazy Group of 5 at a distance. Do you remember how easily you learned how to fight under Diana's instructions, and, how you saved my life and Stuart's when James, a programmed human at that time, attacked us? I was wounded and Stuart was out cold. You jumped on James's back and kept him occupied, punching his neck and shoulders, even pulling his hair, until Stuart regained consciousness and took him down."

I sat up. "Yes, the good old days!"

"Reinhart was not present before the end of the revolution. You may have sensed her presence, which is still inside of you, but we relied upon you and you alone. You were our guiding light then and during that long year of her first metamorphosis."

"Yes, Randolph, but..?"

'There are no buts!" he replied emphatically. "I am not Murdoc and I don't really want to be. I like having my sense of humor and sometimes just being an immature kid. I don't want to carry their burdens on my shoulders. I like being who I am and that is what I expect from you. You don't need her!"

"I have come to rely upon her" I confessed. "And, I felt special because she was part of me."

"I see it differently, Pamela," he replied. "Your respect for her did not change your true nature or your own brilliant mind. And she knows that you don't need her. She is expecting you to show her that because she wants you to be strong and determined."

I lay pondering what he said before finally replying. "How can a farceur like you, Randolph, be so wise?" I teased, as I reached up and pulled him down next to me. "Don't leave me, Randolph. Please don't ever leave me."

I enjoyed just being in his arms, listening to his steady breathing and the strong beat of his heart. "Tell me some gossip, the kinds of crazy things that would have inspired Reinhart's scorn," I pleaded.

"You know Mathilda is very interested in Murdoc."

"Oh wow! Mathilda is treading on dangerous turf," I blurted out. "Reinhart won't share Murdoc with anyone."

"Not even you?"

"I know that you don't believe me but he made it very clear to me that I could never be anything more to him than his child."

"Do you really want me to believe that?" he asked, before returning to the original discussion. "If Murdoc had an affair with Mathilda's ancestor, he might be easily seduced." He raised his eyebrows suggestively.

"Even if he did, I don't see how that could be of any importance today," I replied firmly.

"Do you think that Reinhart would be jealous?"

"Not of infidelity on a physical level, but of the risk of something more profound...like a risk of infidelity on an intellectual level, like disclosing her projects."

"You mean that Murdoc is like her intellectual soul-mate?"

"If you like," I replied contemplatively.

"Anyway, Ok, understood. I shall tell Mathilda that she should keep looking," he chuckled.

"Why not you?" I suggested.

"No, Pamela. I want...I long....to be only with you."

Chapter 17: Mission Readiness

Reinhart was pacing back and forth on the stage when we arrived. Wearing a long, sleek, tightfitting, black robe, her long, auburn hair hanging loose and her emerald green eyes sparkling, she quickly took her place behind the podium.

"Fortunately, we have friends, true Allies. I will introduce them to you later. And when you meet them, look past their physical appearance and remember that they brought James, Mathieu and Isabel back to Earth safely and are ready to join forces with us to save Peter, Frederic and Stuart."

"What actually happened to all members of the original crew of humans traveling in a cryogenic state on board the *Benevolence* is pure speculation. Some of them were certainly awakened at the end of their long space voyage and others were killed or died natural death, during the voyage. A small number, that I calculate to be 6, of the android opposites of my former scientific team took command and have been in command ever since."

"These androids, who organized the death of those whose existence could have been a threat to them, call themselves the High Commissioners." Her eyes drifted, as if she was watching the scene.

"The massive purging of this population on board the *Benevolence* most likely took place while the individuals were in a cryogenic state." She paused. "Clearly, the android opposites of the elite members of my scientific team, who met their deaths before awakening, were either destroyed or shut down by the High Commissioners."

"Humans were mesmerized by robots, androids, humanoid machines—whatever name you prefer-believing that they could outthink these machines and control them. They were wrong." Her voice strong.

"I am still a bit lost. Why did these androids receive the emotional intelligence of their human opposites?" Stanislas asked.

"The humans wanted eternal life," she replied.

"I did not program these High Commissioners." She continued. "They were programmed by their human opposites, who neither respected my warnings nor my programming protocol. Unfortunately, this space team left before I created my android opposite. I added protective measures, giving me ultimate control over my android opposite. Fortunately, I later introduced the same protective measures into the Group of 5."

"But, as I have said so many times, giving an android, which lacks a basic sense of morality, the right to integrate emotional intelligence, or use and adjust emotions to obtain its objectives is dangerous. For that reason, I strongly believe that the members of the Group of 5 are the only ones that can track and target the objectives of these renegade androids and accurately communicate their intentions to us."

"The Group of 5 will be able to decipher and understand how their emotional intelligence has infected their logical thinking, and find the weak spots in their systems, to force them to shut down," she added.

She turned her head in the direction of the Group of 5. "And, Stanislas, the Group of 5 knows if they defy me I can destroy them!" she added, bringing their moment of glory to an end.

"Today we must prepare for a rapid, and I mean, rapid military engagement, if necessary, to defend ourselves. I don't like war..."she smiled in derision, "but, our enemies, have decided otherwise."

"We don't have time to discuss and debate the logistics of this deep-space mission so I will make the decisions," she said. "But first I want to introduce two distinguished Alien Emissaries, Anaton and Martra".

"We have come in peace,"Anaton spoke. "We are here to offer our unconditional assistance, to fight alongside of you and to destroy your enemies."

"We are ready," Martra intervened, "to share our knowhow and technology that will help you defy and defeat those who threaten you. Our only interest is to protect and save the human race and, in so doing, save the planet Earth and the generations to come." She lowered her eyes. "We hope that we will become strong allies."

Everyone applauded and the meeting ended. Reinhart and I accompanied the Aliens to their departure point.

"Do we still have time to save them?" Reinhart asked.

"You have nothing to worry about. We have detected a great deal of confusion over this issue on the part of the High Commissioners and Colonel Shannon. Your calculations are accurate, the spaceship with your family aboard is still 3 months from its destination. One day is enough time for us to improve your vessel and install the proper coordinates so that you will arrive very rapidly." Anaton replied.

"But, you must prepare to leave in a week's time," Martra added.

"See you tomorrow at the Air and Space Center," Reinhart replied.

We watched them vaporize and disappear.

"What happened?" I asked.

"They were either physically transported through a kind of time-space funneling system to their home base, or their holograms were so life-like that we had the impression that they were physically present, that is until the holographic communication was turned off." Reinhart commented.

"Admittedly," she continued, "these Aliens are more advanced in certain areas than we are."

Following the meeting, she broadcasted our immediate assignments over the Intercom System. Murdoc and Randolph would be responsible for programming a certain number of our elite androids in the Main center to accompany us on this mission, before leaving for the Air and Space Center and to upgrade the programming in a large number of android pilots and fighter pilots to engage in aerial attacks, if necessary. She also wanted them to insert a safety valve system in these fighter pilots' memories, so that if they were caught by our enemies they would deactivate.

She told everyone that I would be accompanying her to the Air and Space. "We will be working directly with our Alien Allies to upgrade the technology in our immense spaceship, equipped with android support engineers and technicians as well as service staff," she added.-

"Please pay attention now to your future assignments and responsibilities."

"I shall occupy the position of Commander."

"Dr. Flanders, even though I agree that you are a very talented doctor and surgeon," she continued, "I am conceding this position to someone else, simply because I prefer to have humans at high level positions."

"Rebecca has excellent medical training. I tested her skill. She is familiar with medications and can calmly and rationally carry out hands on emergency procedures. She has experience in simulated surgical procedure and knows how to replace limbs, and even organs, with bionic parts, and knows how to program and use robotic assisted surgical techniques."

"Naturally, Flanders, Gordon and Crawford, you will assist, if necessary."

"But, Dr. Reinhart," Flanders' voice broke in on the intercom system. "I am the most competent to command this unit. And, my logical android side will certainly give way to human emotional intelligence in life and death situations. I do not believe that I will casually dispose of human lives," Flanders protested.

"You are making a good point, Dr. Flanders, but I shall be needing you and the other members of the Group of 5 to interface with Shannon and later the renegade androids. I need to have someone else capable of taking charge of this unit so that you are free to assist all of us, at any time and in any manner, in other tasks."

"Rational."

"And, Dr. Flanders, even though I agree that you are a very talented doctor and surgeon, I want to set the record straight. I am the most qualified in surgical procedures." Ripples of low laughter filled the air.

"Nonetheless," she continued, "I am giving this position to Rebecca, simply because I believe that I should occupy the position of Commander. Pamela is capable of overseeing complicated surgery as well, but, again I prefer that she, along with Dr. Murdoc, both of whom I have named Lieutenant Commanders, be available to replace me when necessary."

"We are a limited number of humans, with a large android support group, so it was not easy to determine who should be in charge of what." She continued, showing some degree of humility. "And even though there might be alien members on board, I want us humans to be in charge.

"Lt. Randolph Murdoc, I am naming you my Chief Engineer with James, Samuel and Tirence under your command. Drager will also be part of your team."

"Lt. Diana Ming, I am naming you to the position of Navigator. You will not only be responsible for navigation, but also for maintaining accurate charts of the different sectors that we pass through. Jason and Ludovic will be your assistants."

"Thank you," her voice full of energy came through the intercom.

"Lieutenants Isabel and Mathieu, you will be the Officers in charge of monitoring and calibrating Tactical sensory systems, short flight missions, and effectuating repairs, if necessary, on the outside of the ship." Their enthusiasm in their yeses.

"And what about me?" Joseph's voice coming through the intercom system loud and clear.

"I saved the best for last, Joseph. You shall be my Communications Officer."

"Thank you for your confidence, Dr. Reinhart."

"I am counting on the Group of 5 to provide assistance and advice, to intervene when necessary to maintain efficient performance of the ship, and to assign android staff accordingly." They bowed.

"Dr. Murdoc and Pamela both Lieutenant Commanders will also be available to assist at all levels," she added.

"The name of the Spaceship, Dr. Reinhart." I whispered in her ear. "Perhaps we should pass it by all of them now?"

"Yes, Pamela and I have come up with a name for our Spaceship. What do you think of the name, *The Redeemer*?" She asked. Enthusiastic cries came over the intercom systems giving Reinhart the confirmation she needed.

"What are you going to do with Cray, Dr. Reinhart?" Murdoc asked.

"I shall share this with all of you. Feel free to comment," she began. "I am going to have Cray send two different messages to Colonel Shannon. In the first message, he will tell her that we are treating him like a dignitary and he is free to move around the vessel and spy on us."

"In the second message, very shortly thereafter," she continued, "he will tell her that the viral infection has resurfaced and that he will have to be placed in isolation. He will add that he is in a life-threatening situation. I shall keep you informed."

Everyone voiced their confidence in her and her method over the intercom system.

"Pamela and I will be meeting with John now."

I left with her. I was still obsessed with the timing, worried about whether or not we would be able to save Peter, Frederic and Stuart. But when we reviewed all the messages, from the moment my family left, their spaceship was still 3 months from its destination.

"Will we make it on time?" I asked, as we walked rapidly in the direction of John's office.

"Space travel is not always exact, as the Aliens pointed out," she said in a whisper. "Sometimes the ship is pulled off course and sometimes it spins into a vacuum that accelerates its movement. Five months was a relatively optimistic travel time, but as they have been sending astronauts back to our planet for many years now and have certainly made improvements in both their ship's speed and navigational routes, they may have given us a longer than usual time frame in order to have an advantage, or...simply to cover themselves."

We arrived in John's office. "Are you disappointed, John, you won't be with us on this trip?" She put him on the spot.

"Very, even though I do agree that I am the right or, simply, the most experienced person to run the center and interface with Shannon; not to mention keeping in contact with you and the rest of the exploratory teams, whose members fortunately work well with me."

"There will be a next time, John."

"I know. Actually I am very happy that you are taking Samuel and Rebecca." His eyes drifted. "I would like to apologize to you for

Rebecca's behavior. She likes controversy, a bit of a rebel from her childhood onwards. She started to argue with me at an early age. I guess that this can be considered a positive quality in some situations, but not in all. I also had a long talk with her."

"I heard how you intend to use Cray to confuse Shannon," John continued, a wide grin splitting his lips.

"I prepared a reassuring message for him to send to Shannon. He will tell her that he is being treated like a dignitary. He can circulate freely." She replied. "I want to study her response to that." She hesitated. "He will send another, less reassuring message, shortly thereafter. John, you will be listening in on both messages."

She stopped to let her words sink in. "If we attack the ship, should that be necessary, saving the lives of Peter, Frederic and Stuart must be our priority. Once our members are safely on board the *Redeemer*, we can rid ourselves of the High Commissioners, those despicable renegade androids, and their Alien allies, who will certainly be fighting alongside of them." She sighed. "Of course, we have time to consider and reconsider the best strategy.

We began to get up to leave, when a call came through from the Captain. "John...Hi Doctor Reinhart and....Pamela?"

WD and Weldon rushed into the ship's control room, just as Reinhart began to tell the Captain that we were no longer symbiotes.

"Great news for you, Pamela," WD burst out in his exaggerated British accent. "Believe it or not, the only visible physical difference between the two of you is in the eyes. Yours, Dr. Reinhart, are definitely cold and austere."

"Enough flattery, WD. What's happening in the high seas?"

"We are moving closer to the coastline." The Captain interrupted. "We are ahead of schedule, so we shall drop anchor and explore the outer limits of the continental shelf close to our meeting place."

"Remember to report regularly to John."

"We know about the space voyage," WD vaunted, and Reinhart looked at John.

"I had to tell them, after all they are part of our team." She nodded.

"Just wanted to wish you good luck," WD replied, bowing his head.

"Thank you," her lips edging upwards in a tight smile. "If we find water, we might bring you with us on our next voyage."

"Not so fast—I am getting older." He tapped the floor with his large walrus flipper.

"No problem, I can always rejuvenate you," she tormented.

He dropped into a sitting position. "Why not?" His walrus tusks drooped.

"I am very happy with what you, Weldon and the Captain are accomplishing, so keep up the good work," she said, raising her hand to wave goodbye.

"By the way, Dr. Reinhart," WD spoke hesitantly, "did you have my female inseminated? Is she pregnant?"

"Yes. I thought that I already gave you the good news," her gaze drifting in thought. "Anyway, you have a baby girl on the way!" she replied, in a voice filled with gaiety, while WD flapped his flippers on the hard floor.

"It is time to deal with Cray," she called out, as she left the room.

The guards opened the door and Dr. Reinhart and I entered into my former quarters to meet with Cray.

"So now you are twins and I suppose that you expect me to guess which one of you is Dr. Reinhart." He doubled over, with what sounded like rehearsed laughter.

"Shut up!" Reinhart retorted and he stepped back cowardly.

We stood observing him for a long moment, his head lowered and his eyes immutably focused on the floor. "How are you feeling, Captain Cray?" she asked.

When he raised his head, his eyes caught mine. 'Is he hoping for pity from me or is he defying Reinhart?' passed through my thoughts, as Reinhart repeated her question.

"Better," he finally replied.

"Good." she turned to leave.

"Dr. Reinhart," he called out, "please don't leave yet."

"Are you ready to talk?" She asked and he nodded. "Ok, tell me who gave you the order to kill my scientists?"

"It was not a direct order," his voice shaky. "Do you mind if I sit down?" She nodded. "The order was certainly subliminal—must have been planted in my brain like you deduced. What I remember are growing waves of anxiety that confounded my reasoning. I start-ed to worry that your team was going to kill me," his voice shaky.

"I am not certain I understand."

"Actually, I don't either." He sighed. "Normally, I am a very calm person and not easily rattled." She nodded.

"I was worried when I lost control over the space lab, because it was drifting off into dark regions that I could not locate on my chart. I was also unable to contact Colonel Shannon. I noticed that your crew was very calm. They either thought or pretended that what was happening was normal." His hands began to tremble.

"Dr. Reinhart, you don't actually have the best reputation with our human community on board the *Benevolence*. We have been led to believe that you are a scientific genius, who lacks human com-passion on even the most basic level. For that reason, I began to wonder if you hadn't programmed your crew to eliminate me," he replied in a high voice, the whites of his eyes showing.

"I had no control over myself. I gathered them up and locked them in a room with food and water. I sat for days rocking back and forth in a lounge chair. I don't remember having a single thought. And then one day I picked up a large, laser gun and..." He stopped.

"Well, Captain Cray, I would like to believe that you were pro-grammed to kill my crew, because that would relieve you of liabil-ity for your behavior on board the space lab. Unfortunately, that, in and of itself, does not change your present situation. Actually, it complicates things in that it highlights the potential depth of your programming." She sighed.

"If you don't remember," she continued, "whether you were pro-grammed to kill my crew, then there is a risk that you could have another subliminal high—for lack of a better expression—and rush about this center killing my friends. So we shall continue to observe and evaluate your allegiance to us. And that said, your first test is to send a message to Colonel Shannon." He nodded slowly, starting to understand.

She opened up the communication terminal. "You will deliver the message that appears on the screen next to you, in a convincing, normal voice tone."

"Maybe I should read it first, so that it sounds natural."

"Good idea." He read the short message several times.

"I hope I can do this convincingly, Dr. Reinhart. I am a bit nervous."

"Look at me." Eye contact with her calmed him instantly and we quickly stepped out of visual range.

"Captain Cray to Colonel Shannon." She appeared immediately.

"Are you alone? Are you feeling better?"

"Yes, I am alone and everything is fine. I am being treated like a dignitary, even Dr. Reinhart is nice to me. I am free to go wherever I want and have already visited different labs." He replied.

"She trusts you?"

"Yes. And, interestingly, there is no surveillance equipment in my private quarters."

"You are certain?"

"I did a thorough search." He stopped for a second. "That was not the case when Jennifer and I arrived here months ago. We were definitely being monitored at that time."

"The High Commissioners will be happy with this news." Her voice seemed calmer. "And their research?"

"On first glance, it appears to be ages behind ours, but then this planet was destroyed during their revolution." He swallowed hard. "Believe it or not, they are much more interested in exploring this planet—discovering new life forms—than voyaging in outer space. Dr. Reinhart told me that space exploration is for the distant future."

"That seems strange?" She sat straight in her chair. "She has sent me some menacing messages over the last few months for me to transmit to the High Commissioners." She hesitated. "And, she told me," she stopped short, Cray's comments muddling her mind, rendering her voice unnaturally stern, "she is worried that her family will not be treated as dignitaries."

"Malicious." Reinhart communicated subliminally to me.

"I don't know what to say," he improvised. "Dr. Reinhart is cold as ice, but Pamela, her symbiote is sweet and natural. Pamela does not seem to be worried about her family and is looking forward to hearing from them when they arrive."

"Well, please continue your espionage activities. Be careful how you interact with Dr. Reinhart. I shall inform the High Commissioners of all of this."

He quickly switched off the screen.

"Well done," Reinhart said. "You changed the script a bit, but maintained the spirit of the message."

"I don't think she believed me."

"Of course she didn't. But then playing mind games, making them wonder and worry, was my objective." Reinhart cracked a laugh.

"Now," she continued, "I want you to give me the exact coordinates that your astronauts use to reach the planet Earth from the *Benevolence,* which I assume, is in a stationary position."

"This is an enormous compromise for me. If they find out, I could be executed." His hands were shaking as he typed in the coordinates.

"You have nothing to worry about, because you will probably never be returning to the *Benevolence,* Captain Cray," she replied mockingly. "Your objective should be to feel free in our world, and for that, you must win our confidence."

When Reinhart was inside of me, I didn't feel guilty putting pressure on others, even threatening their lives, but today I felt sorry for Cray, a prisoner, alone with humans who didn't and might never trust him. She saw my pouting look and grabbed my arm, leading me out of the room.

"Stop feeling sorry for him, Pamela," she ordered. "Where are your loyalties? Are they to him or your family?"

"You are right, Elisabeth. I must learn to be more...practical." I sulked.

I followed behind her alongside the Group of 5 as she set off for the inner circle. "We have to pack a large assortment of medical supplies. Even though the medical facility on board the *Redeemer* is equipped with state of the art technology, I want to take more android replacement parts, surgical equipment and bionic parts for humans," she said, as she filled a dozen large containers with medicine, bionic parts for humans, surgical equipment, monitors, IV tubes, and other general medical supplies. And I want to bring enough of this plant based substance with us in case we have to fabricate more cryogenic skin."

"Agreed. It seems like you have things under control," Crawford spoke for himself and the other members of the Group of 5, as they picked up the containers. Reinhart deactivated the human component she entered into their systems after they passed through the wall. We left together.

"Actually, Pamela, I am going to put Cray in a cryogenic state because he could be useful to us when we get near the *Benevolence*. He knows the layout of the ship and can help us locate Stuart, Frederic and Peter." She confided in me on a cerebral level.

"If we attack the ship, should that be necessary, saving the lives of Peter, Frederic and Stuart must be our priority. Once our members are safely on board the *Redeemer*, we can engage in a battle to rid ourselves of the High Commissioners, those despicable renegade, androids, and their Alien allies, who will certainly be fighting alongside of them." She sighed.

"Are we going with you tomorrow?" The Group of 5 asked in unison, breaking into our private discussion.

"Yes. You are members of my space team," she replied derisively, and then to confuse them she smiled, as a soft, tender glow flushed her eyes.

"We shall have the aircraft ready and will be waiting for you in the terminal for an early morning departure," Flanders replied in a dry administrative tone, as they left to carry out their mission.

"Perfect," she replied, as we left to meet with Murdoc, Randolph and the others who would be accompanying us in the morning. Apart from Samuel, a new member, the Main Center staff remained unchanged. Stanislas, Benjamin, Ruth, Sarah, Mathilda, Ralph, Iris, Jonathan, Ferdinand, Imogene, Jarod, Fleming, and the android replacements for the Group of 5 would stay on the planet to assist John.

Murdoc, Randolph and Drager had already finished upgrading the programming in our elite group of androids, and selected a 100 different androids programmed to assist in the maintenance of the vessel and the preparation of mission surveillance and flights. There were a 100 other androids programmed to carry out other necessary, sometimes menial, tasks.

We were leaving the area, when Murdoc showed up. "Everyone is asking the same question. Did Cray send the first message?"

"Yes." She replied. "In a few hours I shall have him send another prepared message for Shannon. You should bring the others to the auditorium so you can listen. I'll ask John to broadcast it. Just pay attention, he will signal you before it starts so you will all have time to arrive."

"Good Luck," he smiled. "By the way, we are ready to upgrade the programming in the android fighter pilots so that they will be operational to defend our vessel or attack on command." Murdoc replied. "How many of these pilots do you want?"-

"It will depend upon how many the aliens have given us and what additional numbers they recommend to me later, so start with 100," she replied. "I already have a crew on board the ship. Order the android pilots at the Air and Space Center to move at least 400 combat androids and a couple hundred more of the inactive superior class androids to our vessel as well. We can put them in storage and program them if we need them."

"Anything else you forgot to mention?" Murdoc pushed for more information.

"We have our Allies, the Rat-Human Aliens and the High Commissioners have their Allies, another Alien race. As you must have surmised by now, the Aliens that have joined forces with our enemies, the High Commissioners, are not just our enemies. They are also the enemies of our Allies. Saving the lives of Frederic, Peter and Stuart is our principle objective." She stopped to let that sink in. "If we are attacked, we can defend ourselves. But, we are not leaving Earth to engage in a Galactic War unless the renegade androids and their Allies leave us no other alternative."

"Agreed," he replied.

"And, I am not certain that my family will be arrested, and, if so, if they will be imprisoned on the *Benevolence*, or sent elsewhere. So, I am covering myself by taking Cray with us, in a cryogenic state. He knows the layout of the ship and can help us locate my family, if necessary.

"I am going to say goodbye to Rhea," I called out and they waved to me.

Mathilda was in the nursery when I arrived. "Don't worry, Pamela. I shall look after her. You will be her heroine, her model, and her extraordinary Mother. And, I promise to set aside time for you and Rhea on the communications system." She smiled at me reassuringly.

"Thank you, Mathilda." I reached out and took Mathilda in my arms. We stayed like that for a long moment. "So, Sisters we are and shall always be," I repeated several times, until I accepted the lucidity of her offer.

"He is not for you, Mathilda, and neither is Murdoc," I said in a low voice. "What about your project with Ralph? He looks very good since Reinhart rejuvenated him and he is so nice and caring."

"Yes, Pamela," a touch of gaiety in her voice, "I shall keep you informed about that project."

"Pamela," Reinhart contacted me telepathically as I was saying goodbye to Mathilda. "I have prepared another message for Captain Cray to send so meet me in Cray's quarters." I rushed off.

"John, I want you to contact Colonel Shannon from the main communications center and tell her that Captain Cray has asked to speak to her in private. You will then pass the call to this room." She ordered, at the moment the three of us, Murdoc, Elisabeth and I arrived.

"After Cray has spoken to her, he will send her back to you. She will naturally ask to speak to me. I shall be close by, but, to make her request appear unexpected, you will send a message for me to come to the communications center."

"Ok. I hope it works." He called out as he left the room.

"I shall be observing you, Captain Cray. The makeup I put on you gives you a very sickly appearance. She will certainly be worried about your survival." Reinhart's lips moved into a gleaming smile.

John's voice came through. "Colonel Shannon is on-line for you, Captain Cray. Are you available to receive her?"

Cray replied in a practically inaudible voice, "Yes," as he approached the screen in a slow, lifeless manner.

"You look very ill!" We observed her from a discrete angle. The blood drained instantly from her face and her trembling hands reached for a glass of water. "What happened? I thought that they, or rather Dr. Reinhart, had found a cure."

"I don't know," he replied, his words coming in long, languished breaths. "I collapsed." He stopped. "I have so much pain. I am afraid to die," he replied, adding more emotionally charged words to his script.

"Do you trust her?"

"Who? Dr. Reinhart?" he asked, his eyes rolling backwards, as if he were drifting into unconsciousness.

"Yes. Who else would I be talking about?" She snapped.

"Of course." He whispered so low that she had to lean closer to the sound system.

"John told me she has proposed a solution," her voice now firm and aggressive. "What is it?"

"She needs time to...find the cure for this...virus, or...disease." His words coming in painful, stuttering sounds.

"How much time?" She tapped her fingers on the desk top.

"I don't know." He slumped forward, leaning onto the terminal. "I am scared...I might be dying!" He pained.

"Ok," she replied calmly. "What is she going to do?"

"She is going to...." He spent a few minutes gasping for breath "... put me in a cryogenic state until... she has the cure."

"You sound terrible," her pupils large. "I am worried. Can I speak to her?"

"Ask...John," he replied, as he let his head drop hard on the table. The communication switched off automatically.

"You missed your calling, Captain Cray!" Reinhart screamed. "You should have been an actor."

"You may be right. But I can assure you that I can never return to the *Benevolence*," he replied.

"But we are not your enemies!" Reinhart replied in a firm voice. "Your enemies are the High Commissioners."

"Colonel Shannon would like to speak to you in the communications room."

"I am on my way," she replied, knowing that John was letting Shannon listen in.

"Dr. Reinhart," she began, "I have just spoken to Captain Cray. He has fallen ill again?" her voice strained.

"Yes. He has had a relapse," Reinhart replied in a monotone voice.

"He mentioned a cryogenic state."

"His vital organs are weakening, so yes, putting him in a cryogenic state will prevent the disease from progressing and give us the time we need to find an effective cure," she lectured. "And as we don't know how he contracted this disease, he needs to be isolated from the rest of us. Better that he sleeps during his isolation."

"So, you are not...you are really not, planning on visiting our ship in the near future?" she asked, befuddled.

"What made you think I ever had the intention of visiting your ship, Colonel Shannon?" Reinhart added, in an effort to confuse her.

Shannon straightened up. "But, I thought that you..." She stopped in the middle of the sentence, reluctant to provoke Reinhart. "We shall keep you posted regarding your family's trip and contact you on their arrival."

"Yes, please keep in touch. I shall let you know when I have found a cure. In the meantime, I shall be moving back and forth to check on our exploratory teams in the northern hemisphere, so you should pass your messages to me through John."

Shannon forced a smile and signed off. She sat in a catatonic state, a single, preoccupying thought, 'Oh, this is not good news,' rushed through her mind, making her whole body tremble.

"Are you pleased with what happened?" John asked, probably more out of curiosity than concern.

"Absolutely," she replied. "She is worried and completely confused. Marvelous!" she exclaimed.

"But of course we shall probably need her help in the future, or when we get close to the *Benevolence*. But for the moment, it is better that she does not know too much, because she reports to the High Commissioners. We want our arrival to be a real surprise." She paused.

"Certainly, Cray, whether he likes us or not, is playing his cards favorably with his offer to cooperate with us. Nonetheless, I believe he needs to do more than perform in front of us, for there is always the risk that he could change sides at the last minute." She stroked her chin. "I would rather put him in a cryogenic state until we get close enough to the *Benevolence* that he won't be able to sabotage our mission, and will find it in his interest to cooperate." They nodded.

She returned to Captain Cray, who was sitting in a lotus position, meditating his fate. She told me later that he told her that he found her decision reprehensible, but understood why she wanted to take precautions. She programmed the cryogenic skin for him. He obediently slid inside, when we boarded the aircraft for the Air and Space Center the following morning.

Chapter 18: The Redeemer

Reinhart grouped all of us together. "The vessel, as some of you already know," her eyes connected with mine, "is hidden and protected under a veil of invisibility, a cloaking device, extending beyond the limits of this Center. Nonetheless, we can only access it by passing through a wall, embedded with bio-readers located at the far end of the lower level where, as you know, other sophisticated, but smaller, spacecraft are located."

"Anaton, Marta and other members of their scientific and technological teams have installed a more highly developed artificial gravity system in our spaceship, and they are presently up-dating other technology on board." Reinhart spoke as she led us to the lower level and indicated that we climb into the transport vehicles and follow her.

When we were at the right location, she rapidly adjusted the systems of the Group of 5, so that they could pass through the wall, with the rest of us.

"When? How did you manufacture this enormous spaceship without our guidance and participation?" Crawford's voice energized, as he stared in utter surprise.

"Oh, your lack of humility, Dr. Crawford, astonishes me. This ship was under construction before you were created." This inspired a round of laughter.

"It is a magnificent spaceship, Dr. Reinhart," Martra said. "And we have marveled over the highly advanced systems and technology that you installed thousands of years ago. Perhaps your crew would like to meet ours and learn more about how this ship functions." Reinhart signaled her team to follow Martra and Anaton, while Murdoc, Randolph and I stayed behind.

We moved in a tight circle. The living quarters of the ship resembled those of the inner circle—spacious with large comfortable beds and fully equipped individual bathrooms. "Did you introduce a water filtering system, to evacuate excrement, converting it to a dry, powdery substance? I believe that is what we were working on," Murdoc interposed.

"Yes. But instead of disposing of excrement, I designed a refining unit that can convert and purify the residue so it can be used safely as fertilizer. And," she snapped her fingers…"there is a very large agricultural unit on board. Ralph is in the process of selecting different vegetables, including staple products like potatoes, as well as fruit-bearing plants. He will also give us seeds so we can continue to cultivate different plants. We will need rice and grains, along with a large quantity of dehydrated food."

"High tech! Never saw anything like this before! It outdoes all my expectations, and is more advanced than the Alien technology in the underground city!" He exclaimed. "I am a bit confused, though. I did work alongside of you, and was privy to your technology. I had studied previous spaceship designs like those of the *Benevolence*. You were programming androids to pilot the spaceships and engage worm holes as fast paths in space. Artificial gravity already existed, so…"

"Aegir," she interrupted. "I admit that I hid this project, the *Redeemer*, from you." He shrugged his shoulders. "It was not the right moment for me to reveal my spaceship because the revolutionary movement was gaining moment." She paused.

"My artificial gravity system," she continued, "was still not refined enough to prevent organ damage to humans during a long voyage, which is why I opted for cryogenic tanks. The cryogenic skin that was developed by the High Commissioners, and their scientific team, was an impressive move forward and, admittedly, this technology astounded me."

"Ok. But, I thought that it was impossible for a spaceship this size to break through the Earth's gravitational force and that it had to be built or assembled in space," I said, pretending to be very familiar with spaceship construction.

"Yes, that was the case in the very distant past. And, I encountered difficulties, in my early years, launching large spacecraft." She raised one eyebrow. "Even when a launch was successful, a number of ships disintegrated before they reached their destination." She muttered her discontent.

"I realized at one point" she continued, "that I had to abandon my projects until I passed through a number of significant phases of intellectual metamorphosis." Her eyes bore down on mine. "Even though I was intellectually more gifted than humans, from the moment of my creation, I needed time to develop my talents, expand my knowledge base and eventually test my theories."

"As you know, the Aliens discretely introduced the design for cryogenic skin and upgraded the artificial gravity unit on board the *Benevolence*, like they have done for us today, to ensure a consistent and proper level of gravitational force to guarantee healthy organ functioning in humans for prolonged periods of time in space." She waited for questions.

"The *Redeemer* can move at higher than warp speeds, without damage, because the Aliens have fortified the ship's exterior with a strong, resistant material natural to their planet. They have installed state of the art technology in our various systems, like guidance, transport, communication, and so forth."

"I visited this center with you in the past and spent time alone in the command center of one of those less sophisticated spacecraft, while you sent me visual images and information about former space exploration," I said, changing the subject.

"Yes. That is true." She replied. "It was rather cryptic, though, because, curious as you were, your mind was less highly developed for cerebral messaging than today."

"Well, there are two things that you did not mention at that time. You did not mention by name the *Benevolence*, or the many ships you sent into outer space. And, you never explained the lava tube experiments by former humans on Mars and the Moon."

"I am replaying that conversation and you are right," she said. "But, I sent these images to inspire your curiosity in science," she sighed before adding that lava tube cities were envisaged and even constructed, but, they did not make it any easier for humans to live on either Mars or the Moon."

Her eyes met mine. "I believe the real problem, Pamela, was producing enough oxygen rich air and water."

"I like the design of the *Redeemer*, with its integrating three large sections attached to wide, high supports that act as stairways leading to a number of lower levels, each equipped with long, slim side wings?" Murdoc spoke.

"Yes. It is amazing!" She puffed her own genius. "Actually it does look a lot like some of the spaceships that were used in science fiction films in the distant past. The real difference is that the *Redeemer* can take us to our destination, carry military forces, fighter crafts, and secure our victory," she vaunted. "Now let's take a look at the breadth of this ship."

"Why don't we begin the construction of another one?" Murdoc asked.

"Good question," she replied insipidly. "I don't know if we can find the raw materials that I used to build this ship, which was built with a light, heat resistant metal mined on asteroids. I used nano-technology to fortify and add flexibility and thermal protection to substances like aluminum, lithium, and titanium alloys, to name a few, that were natural to this planet. Perhaps I should program androids to explore for natural resources on Earth today."

I followed her through the various corridors, while she pointed out and explained the use of different technology. In reality she uploaded this information into me, so that I could replace her if ever she was captured. "By tomorrow morning, everything that I have passed onto you will make sense," she said, after she finished the tour.

"I am certain of that. But, Elisabeth, I am not convinced that I understand the layout of the spaceship," I declared vehemently. "You know that I lack a natural sense of direction. And, quite frankly, this ship is directionally challenging not only because the corridors frequently crisscross, but also because the design of the corridors differ from one level to another."

She huffed. "Ok, look at me. I shall send you the exact layout of the ship and try my best to give you a workable sense of orientation." As the future would confirm, she did exactly that.

We took a few minutes to check on Murdoc and Randolph, who were still in the Command Center, and explain to them that they were now in control of the ship and its crew, including the Aliens, for the rest of the day.

I flew the plane back to the main center while Reinhart

meditated and Drager went into sleep mode, landing the plane in a firm touchdown and taxing into the terminal where androids were awaiting our arrival. 'I have become an accomplished pilot,' I thought to myself, as I caught the smile of approval on Reinhart's face from the corner of my eye.

John, enthusiastic about her new project to find the same or comparable raw materials on Earth that she used to build former space vessels, accompanied us to the android elite section where Reinhart selected one hundred androids for programming. She downloaded the new program into Drager so that he could help her upload the program into the androids, ten at a time. In less than 2 hours the androids tested perfectly and were ready to take orders from John only.

"Send only 10 or 12 at a time into a given zone." She stroked her chin in thought. "You should review all the information they send back, to make certain that they are complying with your instructions, and, at least in the beginning, order their return after short intervals so that you can check their systems for compliance." He nodded.

"I have already given mission command to 6 of the androids, numbers 20, 30, 50, 70, 80 and 90, which translates into 6 exploration teams. Their numbers, as you can see, are visible on their backs." She cleared her throat. "If anything goes wrong, or you suspect foul play, you should just send my general order, which is in the voice registration part of the program. They will automatically shut down."

"I asked the Aliens to set up a holographic imaging system between the *Redeemer* and this Center so that we can communicate in a convivial context." She added.

"You can't do it yourself?"

"Yes. But, as they already have functional systems, I don't have to waste any of my precious time setting up the terminals. And, it is a way of ingratiating ourselves to them," she said, as she got up to leave. "The Aliens will be appearing soon with terminals and will explain to all of you how they function."

Reinhart took the pilot seat. "The holographic terminals are being installed on the *Redeemer*," she mentioned. "But surveillance of our environment will be limited to the conference room and lounge."

"Are we going to arrive on the *Benevolence* in time to save everyone?"

"Why is time so important for humans?" Slipped out, making me sit up very straight.

"Because you can change it?"

She titled her head in my direction. "Oh, Pamela, nothing is immutable, even though some things may be slightly more complicated to alter and adjust," she replied.

We sat in silence for the rest of the trip. The android crew opened the hangar when we landed.

"Everything is going forward so rapidly, Dr. Reinhart and Pamela," Crawford's voice screeching over the engine's last breath.

"Excellent." She took a moment to observe him. "I see that you are moving and speaking less and less like a machine."

"Isn't this what you wanted?" he asked.

"Nice to have you back, Rudolph."

"By the way, Dr. Reinhart, one of the Alien technical engineers asked me to inform you that the Alien High Council, some members of which you have already met, would like to speak to you. And, hologram terminals have been installed in the lounge area of the spaceship and the Command Center, as well as in the part of this Center where the spaceship is located," he quickly added and Reinhart activated the holographic system.

"Dr. Reinhart, rather Elisabeth," the elderly female Alien who chaired the discussions in the underground city answered. "We wanted to go over the military plan for your mission."

"I would like to know who you are," Reinhart replied, in a take charge manner.

"This is an unfortunate oversight on our part, because introductions are certainly in order. We do not have family names, only first names. I am Minerva. Starting from my right and moving around the table back to me, sit Thoth, Nemesis, Zelus, Kratos and Concordia."

"Am I to assume that your names represent your personalities? If so, please define them." She pleaded.

"Minerva is the Goddess of Wisdom; Thoth is the God of Knowledge, measurement, wisdom, alphabet, thought and intelligence; Nemesis is the Goddess of retributive justice; Zelus is the

God of zeal, rivalry and jealousy; Kratos is the God of strength and power; and Concordia is the Goddess of Agreement."

"I would like to know how your society is organized," Reinhart's voice an eerie monotone.

"We have a pyramidal society," Minerva replied.

"What does that mean?"

"We, the six of us, are at the pinnacle of the pyramid and are immortals. This upper pyramidal crust widens slightly as it descends to include, other intellectual elites encompassing a variety of fields from the sciences to the humanities, whose descendants are educated and trained to replace them. The pyramid continues to widen as another level of educated members appears. These individuals will rely upon their superiors for direction."

She took a deep breath, as her eyes fixed on Reinhart. "The base of the pyramid, includes the largest part of the population and can be compared to what humans refer to as the masses or, sometimes, the working class. Of course in ancient times, they were often slaves." She digressed.

"There is no mobility in our society. You are born into a class and will occupy the place of your parents and ancestors." She snarled, showing her sharp rat teeth. "We have never had conflict or rebellions."

"We have 3 major vessels with hundreds of medium and small surveillance and fighter ships on each vessel. You will be moving under what you refer to as a veil of invisibility and our ships have comparable shields."

"We would like to know the order of command, should something happen to you." She continued.

"Dr. Aegir Murdoc is the second in command, followed by Pamela Reinhart, Dr. Randolph Murdoc and Dr. Diana Ming." Reinhart replied. "Should all of us be out of reach, then the Group of 5 will be in command, in this order: Dr. Rudolph Crawford, Dr. Eugene Venderkof, Dr. Victoria Gordon, Dr. Edward Flanders and Dr. Agnes Miller."

"We are on the path to becoming strong Allies," Minerva replied firmly. "Once you have saved your family and the crew on board the *Benevolence*, we will need your assistance to reinstate an equilibrium, a genuine stability in the universe, by defeating our mutual enemies," she replied firmly.

"Of course. We will respect the Alliance." Heads nodded as the holograms slowly dissipated and we got up to leave for the dining room.

At the end of the meal, Reinhart asked for our attention. "I am leading the most incredibly competent team of humans that ever ventured into outer space. We shall accomplish our mission! We shall win! We shall become legends in our own time!"

Roars of self-admiration and victory filled the room, as we boasted our physical force through primitive, combative gestures, lashing our fists out hard at invisible enemies.

When we left the dining room to spend our last night on the planet Earth, we were ready to meet the trials and tribulations that would befall us. We were ready to meet the future.

But what future? Were we being manipulated by the Aliens?

Chapter 19: Troubleshooter

"Just a little something we came up with to properly honor all of you," the Group of 5 said in unison, startling us, as they entered the dining room, handing each of us three battleship grey uniforms with venetian red collars and navy blue cuffs along with lapel pins bearing our name and rank.

"Thank you!" Reinhart sprung to her feet, taking her pile and running her hands over the smooth material. "You outdid yourselves."

"We are honored to accompany you, Dr. Reinhart, and... your impressive team." Flanders' voice rising and falling in a futile attempt to mask his emotions. "We have also made similar uniforms for each of us and hope you will agree to let us wear them." He lowered his head, feigning submissiveness.

"Of course, Dr. Flanders, you and the other members of the Group of 5, are now our comrades in arms."

Our enthusiasm over these special uniforms, gifts of friendship designed by the Group of 5, tempered when an android officer rushed into the dining room. "John is on-line with an urgent call for you, Dr. Reinhart, from Colonel Shannon."

Reinhart dashed out of the dining room to the communications center. "Dr. Reinhart, I cannot speak too long. I am compromising my life for you only because my ancestors held you in high esteem." She spoke rapidly in a muffled voice. Her trusted officers Ranier and Trend were standing guard, just behind her.

"Why aren't you in your office?" Reinhart asked in a thin whisper.

"I do not want this message to be intercepted. I am taking an enormous risk, so I cannot talk long. But I must warn you. Your family is in serious danger." She kept her trembling voice at a muffle. "We are a small group of what you would call rebels on board the *Benevolence*, who will do everything we can to protect your family. I shall contact you when they arrive."

Colonel Shannon continued: "I thought that you understood that they were in danger and that you were on your way to save them. And yet your last communication inferred the contrary. Even though we are ready and willing to risk our lives to save your family and fight for a better world for all humans, we cannot promise a victory," she hesitated, "... without your help," her voice trembled with fear.

"Wait! When will they arrive?" Reinhart's voice barely audible.

"I just received information from one member of our group that the High Commissioners have the ship in a constant-thrust acceleration. For that reason, it will arrive sooner than we expected," Her face grew pale and the corners of her lips stiffened.

"Inform us of their arrival. Your allegiance to us will not go unrewarded." Reinhart turned to face the rest of us, her wide eyes searching the Group of 5.

"Tell her, Dr. Reinhart, that we are on our way. She is our friend and Ally." Crawford mouthed his words.

"We...," she hesitated, "I count on you to protect our crew when they arrive. Remember that we consider you, and your comrades, to be our most trusted friends and Allies."

"Thank you, Dr. Reinhart." She said, her voice trailing as she switched off the communication.

"Ok, let's get started," Reinhart ordered, her voice rising and falling, before she stopped abruptly in her tracks and turned back to observe us. "Her dramatic display of emotions seemed rehearsed and her message lacked sincerity, as well as, credibility." She replied firmly. "For that reason, I decided not to confirm our immediate departure. Put those uniforms on and meet me on board."

In 15 minutes, we were all strapped in our seats, and ready for takeoff. The Alien technicians had already taken their places in the control center and were ready to begin countdown. Several Earth Androids had been programmed to carry out the Aliens' orders and take turns tracking our vessel. Other Alien technicians and military specialists were onboard the *Redeemer*.

"Mission Control to Dr. Reinhart."

"We hear you," Joseph replied in her place.

"Count down in progress," the Alien Officer announced.

Our hands grabbed the arms of our seats, as we braced ourselves, expecting a jolting takeoff. Only Reinhart remained relaxed.

"Lift off in one minute," An Alien's voice rose above the loud, ear-splitting noise of the engines.

The lift off was smooth. The ship gained speed, tilting into an inclining, diagonal position, breaking the Earth's atmosphere in a matter of seconds, before shifting slightly to the right as it entered into the pathway that would take us rapidly to our destination.

Our departure, expedited, I had no time for second thoughts about space travel. In fact everything that happened within a matter of minutes seemed so uneventful that I felt like I had already boarded spaceships and traveled light years away.

Just before the *Redeemer* entered into the vastness of space, I caught a quick glimpse of the planet *Earth*, appearing like a round, polished, dark-blue marble, slight streams of white, misty clouds rising erratically from its surface, as it floated in the vastness of a pitch-black cosmic space. I engraved this beautiful image of *Earth* in my mind, placing it forever amongst my most treasured memories.

"Mission Control to Dr. Reinhart."

She switched on the communications. "Everything is perfect here. It was a smooth takeoff."

"Confirmation that the *Redeemer* has engaged the right pathway. We shall keep you on radar and adjust your route if and when that is necessary," the Alien replied. "Our ships are waiting for you up ahead. They will follow behind. Remember we are under your command. Have a safe trip. Over and out."

"It seems unimaginable that a ship this size could be launched from the planet Earth," Diana commented. "I thought, like Pamela, smaller models were launched from space stations."

"Diana, this ship would have lifted off without the Aliens' assistance, but, their updating our technology, adding gravitation units and all the rest has made this ship very resistant." She sighed. "The *Benevolence* was launched from Earth, thousands of years ago now, at a time when space travel was more prolific for Earthlings, even though we were using older technology, far from state of the art."

"Can we move around?" Murdoc asked.

"Yes, try your legs, if you want." She snickered. "Get up slowly so that you won't experience any nausea or weakness," she cautioned.

Reinhart stayed in the commander's seat, while Murdoc, Diana, Joseph, Jason,

Ludovic and I got up. The artificial gravity system was functioning perfectly. "Do you feel any weightlessness?" Reinhart asked.

"I feel the same as if I were walking on Earth," Murdoc commented.

"Excellent. I am going to ask the other members to move around," she said as she switched on the intercom system and notified the crew that they could circulate. She waited a few minutes before adding that if anyone experienced any difficulties, dizziness or nausea or other symptoms that could be associated with space flight, they should contact her. The crew members reported that they felt like they were still walking on *Earth.*

She asked Murdoc and me to accompany her as she visited the other members of our team who, following the orders of one or more of the members of the Group of 5, were monitoring the engineering systems as well as checking various technical equipment. The Aliens on board were explaining to others how to repair various spaceship components.

Reinhart returned to the Command Center, her preferred term for the Bridge, sat down in the Commander's seat, and reviewed the trajectory of our vessel. The programming was beyond reproach, but there was more space debris, like small asteroids, rock clusters, space dust, and old satellites appearing both on her radar screen and the large visual screen than she expected to encounter.

It was surprising she was not solicited to steer the ship which veered automatically, at the right moments, to avoid collision with these various objects.

"Do the Aliens know who you really are?" I pried.

She made a low gurgling sound and I shuddered after I said that, worried I had tread on delicate turf. "Most importantly, they know that I am human," she replied. "Now, let's take a close look at where we are heading and at what speed," her voice was steady.

"You could not have programmed the ship on your own?" my questions spilling forth.

"I don't know. But what I do know is that changing the past to bring about a better future is not that easy," she replied, before adding, "the reason why I am working on solving that problem." She turned to me. "Now stop asking so many annoying questions. I hate small talk. Let's just concentrate on winning a war!"

I slid down into my seat next to hers and stared out the large window. We were moving so fast that everything seemed to blend together.

"Up ahead, Pamela," she pointed. "Do you see that large hole that reminds you of a mammoth-sized, serpent's mouth?"

"Yes! It looks alive."

"You are so dramatic," she chuckled, as she reached for the controls and opened the intercom system. "Everyone, take your seats and strap yourselves in. We are entering into a worm hole. You will have the sensation that the ship is falling before it speeds up and exits." She waited to let that sink in. "I will let you know when you can move around again."

Everyone immediately strapped themselves into their seats. She then scanned the other levels to make certain that no one was moving about.

I quickly closed my eyes when we entered it, but could not block out an eerie sensation that the ship was being swallowed up. When I turned to observe the rest of our crew, only Reinhart looked alive. The others were white as ghosts, their mouths slightly open, and the veins in their necks and hands visible.

"Ok. We made it." Her calm irritated me. "The Alien ships are now behind us. They must have caught up with us, just as we entered the space tunnel. Perhaps they constructed it, using exotic matter."

"Dr. Reinhart," Joseph turned in her direction, "I am receiving a message from the Alien vessels."

"Put them on the screen."

The Commanders of the 3 Alien vessels appeared at the same time, introducing themselves as Nathan, Electra and Desmond. "We wanted to warn you about the space tunnel, or wormhole, but we were out of range." Electra spoke for the others. "We shall be encountering 2 more of the universe's shortcuts, as we refer to them, one after the other, over the next hour, so perhaps your crew should stay seated."

"These shortcuts will put us closer to your family's space-ship." Desmond entered the conversation. "We intercepted Colonel Shannon's communication with you. She is right. Our enemies have accelerated the vessel's drive system."

"Keep your shields up at all times, Dr. Reinhart," Nathan ordered. "Our enemies are unable to penetrate the shields, so they will not be able to signal your enemies of your arrival."

"Now be advised," he picked up, "that if we take the original pro-grammed course, your family will arrive a long time before our ship. That is why our High Council has chosen a more rapid, but more dan-gerous, route. You cannot rely upon the navigational system of the ship. You will have to take over the controls. Stay alert, Dr. Reinhart. You will encounter much space debris—large and small—from me-teorites to dying suns and dead planets. We shall lead the way."

"Be assured, Dr. Reinhart, that your family will not be harmed." Electra was back. "Your enemies only want you. Our mission is to save you, your family and all members on board the *Redeemer*. We will not disappoint you."

"Thank you for this information." Reinhart replied. "But you did not mention saving the humans on board the *Benevolence*. Was this just a momentary oversight?"" Reinhart queried.

"We have been given no orders regarding the humans on board the *Benevolence*." Electra's unemotional response mimicking Reinhart's style, making Reinhart laugh. "We are ready to engage the tunnel. Are you ready?"

"Yes, I am ready to pilot the ship. Please send me the coordi-nates in rapid sequence." Reinhart replied calmly._

"We shall lead the way, Dr. Reinhart. We will have to weave in and out, but you will have no difficulty duplicating our moves," Desmond replied.

"Prepare for the next series of shortcuts. We are very close," Nathan ordered.

"I am ready," she replied, before telling all crew members to rapidly take their seats and remain seated until she gave the order to get up.

"Are you ok, Elisabeth?" Murdoc's voice straining as he sought to hide his own rising emotions.

"Get ready to have some fun!" She shouted over the intercom system, before she turned to face me.

I shuddered involuntarily when the ship reached a kind of glutinous, expansive mouth that, in one enormous, enveloping gulp, swallowed our ship and crew. My claustrophobia heightened when the ship tumbled rapidly in a free spin, traveling through the worm's digestive tract, before being violently thrust upwards and ejected, into another part of the universe. I braced myself again, as there was less than 15 minutes between the two worm holes.

Like before, Reinhart smiled. 'She loves testing the limits of her endurance,' passed through my mind.

When the ship finally stabilized in another part of the galaxy, Nathan, Desmond and Electra appeared on the main screen. "Follow us, Dr. Reinhart." Electra said in a calm, reassuring tone.

"You have to keep the ship moving at high speeds for the next 24 hours. Will you be able to maintain that rhythm, Dr. Reinhart?" Desmond asked.

"No other human on board can replace me."

"We know that you are the only one of your human crew that can keep the ship on course," Nathan confirmed.

"Ok. In that case, I am going to request the Group of 5 join me here in the Command Center. If my concentration wanes, which it shouldn't, they will be able to carry out the right manoeuvers until I recover from any drowsiness."

"I could help!" Murdoc insisted.

"You have never done this before, Aegir," she replied.

"But, neither have you," he responded aggressively.

A smile creased her face. "If I need you, I shall let you know."

The Group of 5 arrived rapidly and she quickly informed them of the situation. "Crawford, approach me," she ordered, as she downloaded a new program in him. "You will replace me, if I need time to rest." He nodded obediently.

She then turned to Murdoc. "Unfortunately, Aegir, I cannot enter into your mind and program you, which is why I chose Crawford." A warm, inviting smile, spread her lips, disarming and appeasing Murdoc.

"Why didn't you use me?" I protested.

"To be able to properly replace me, you would have to connect with my mind and stay alert. 24 hours is a long time for us humans to remain focused. A machine doesn't need a break. So Crawford can replace me, when needed, with the programming I downloaded into him."

"Randolph is on line." Joseph informed her.

"Put him on visual," she requested.

Randolph was pacing back and forth, throwing his arms in the air, when her voice rang through putting a stop to his dramatics.

"Dr. Reinhart, is it normal that Alien engineers are adjusting our systems?"

"Yes," she sighed. "This was an oversight on my part, I should have informed you, but you should still remain seated. I didn't give orders for you to move around. Actually, everyone should stay seated for the next 24 hours."

"We are changing course," she continued, "and will be passing through a great deal of turbulence at very high speeds, so prepare yourselves for anything but a smooth ride. The ship might plunge rapidly, sway or even spin as much as 360 degrees, but don't worry. You are in safe hands. The androids will bring your meals, when you request them. And, the Alien officers will oversee the different departments."

She stopped to collect her thoughts. "Rebecca, keep your intercom open, if you have any emergencies, let me know."

"Understood," she replied.

"I shall keep in touch. This new pathway will get us to the *Benevolence* more rapidly. And even though this will not be a smooth ride, it will be an amazing experience for all of us!" She then turned to Joseph, asking him to contact the Alien Commanders.

Nathan, Desmond and Electra appeared instantly. "Are you ready, Dr. Reinhart?" they asked at the same time.

"Yes, I am ready," she replied.

I turned in her direction, hoping to make contact, but she was already preparing to move our ship out of a vortex of disequilibrium, caused by gas and dust swirling in rapid, circular motions, forming a vacuum in the center of a circle, drawing our spaceship towards its cavity. She accelerated the ship at the right moment and with the right speed, causing it to sway and buck, as it escaped undamaged.

Murdoc's eyes seemed to focus on the main viewing port, with its heat resistant shielding, and I followed his example. The seemingly harmless, sparkling lights that I had viewed at the beginning of our adventure, now took on the appearance of an enemy ship moving fast, ready to bear down on our spaceship. I turned quickly to check on Diana and her team, as well as Joseph. Their eyes seemed glued to the tabletops in front of them. When I turned back, the sparkling lights had disappeared.

The *Redeemer* was moving at such a high speed that my mind did not have time to register the rapid shifting of the craft, as she piloted the vessel, staying a short distance behind the Aliens' vessels. I had the impression the Aliens were pulling us with an invisible cord.

I spent a moment observing both Reinhart and Murdoc. They remained calm in stressful situations and I knew that even though they disagreed on occasion, they had confidence in each other. I wished I could remain as stoic as the two of them.

I focused on the main viewing port. There was a weird silence in the Command Center, especially with the rapid approach of gigantic, rocky masses, sometimes coming together in large clusters, making it even more difficult and dangerous to target and then engage the right pathway, The Aliens must have mastered this kind of intricate, demanding piloting of large space crafts over the years.

I suddenly realized I was sweating profusely, my uniform clinging in wet folds.-Embarrassed, I turned to see if anyone was reacting in the same way, as I mopped away the sweat on my forehead with my forearm.

Reinhart motioned to Crawford to take over. She activated his system and then closed her eyes.

"Why doesn't she contact me?" passed through my mind. "She could at least let me know that everything is going well," I thought.

And then I heard her voice inside of me. "Calm down. You are out of control. We are on a less hazardous path."

"Are you alright?" Murdoc asked, in a soft, paternal tone.

"I don't know. I am sweating a lot!"

I heard low chuckles. "We are back here as well!" Diana finally said. "We are lucky that the Group of 5 made us extra uniforms."

"Anyone know how long we have been flying?" I finally asked.

"Hours—more than 10 hours," Gordon replied.

"Pull yourselves together," Reinhart took back the controls.

Spontaneous laughter eventually brought back a normal, natural equilibrium to each of us.

"Did you get enough rest, Dr. Reinhart?" Crawford asked.

"I didn't sleep. I wanted time to study how they calculated the pathways. If ever we get separated, I shall be able to reach the final destination without their help," she answered. "And the rest of you, try to maintain the kind of discipline and self-control that one expects from high ranking officers," she said in an officious tone.

"Joseph, please contact the Aliens and tell them that I am back in the driver's seat," she ordered, in a lively voice.

The voyage immediately speeded up, and the ship rose, fell, side-swiped and somersaulted, as it raced through the onslaughts of debris in this part of the universe. I noticed that everyone except Joseph and I dosed off. Reinhart was in deep concentration and the members of the Group of 5, her faithful servants, were hovering over her.

Anger fumed inside of me, as my thoughts turned to Peter, Frederic and Stuart. I visualized the miserable Malwarian Androids and their Alien allies manhandling my loved ones. I stiffened as I worried they could even be tortured or worse. I began to prepare myself for war.

I wondered how Reinhart was going to react. "Would she surrender to them so they would free my family?' I pondered. 'Probably that was her strategy. As the Aliens mentioned, she is the one those androids want. But why?' I sighed.

'Maybe they believe,' my thoughts took a different direction, 'that she can make them more powerful. Maybe they are obsessed with her existence and cannot move forward until they have eliminated her? Maybe those Android commissioners even hope she will join forces with them? Maybe they actually worship her, like a God? Worse though, maybe they hope that her power will be their source of renewed energy?'

"What happened?" The crew was wide awake and curious. I bit my tongue and Reinhart shrugged her shoulders.

"Is everything alright?" Murdoc asked for clarification.

"Yes. We will be exiting this tumultuous area in less than 5 minutes," Reinhart said, over the intercom. "You will soon be able to stand up and even get something to eat."

We all reacted by applauding. Even the Group of 5 could not hold back their enthusiasm, as they stomped their feet.

"Dr. Reinhart, the Aliens are on the screen," Joseph reported.

"Excellent piloting, Dr. Reinhart." Desmond opened the conversation. "You definitely lived up to your reputation." His rat eyes twinkled.

Reinhart's face flushed, unwittingly. "How far away from my family are we?" She went straight to the point.

"As you will discover, we have reprogrammed the route. Our engineers have added even more speed to your spacecraft so that the engines will be able to reach our accelerated warp speed. Our speed, faster than warp speed, is very close to that of the speed of light but does not surpass it." Nathan replied.

"Do you have a strategy in mind?" Electra asked.

"Where is your planet located?" Reinhart pried, pursing information Electra had hidden from her.

"We are in a solar system, to use your terminology, situated near the edge, or seemingly at the edge of, what you refer to as the Milky Way Galaxy. Actually, one could almost say that we straddle two galaxies, the Milky Way and the Andromeda Galaxy," she replied. "Your technology was not capable of detecting the existence of our solar system."

"Does your solar system have a name?"

"No. We identify solar systems and constellations in terms of their mathematical coordinates. Only humans invented cute names for constellations and solar systems."

"Fair enough. But, does your planet have a name?"

"We call it, '*Vérité*,'" Desmond answered. "I believe that you have heard of it."

"Truth, in my language," Reinhart replied. "Yes, I have heard of your planet."

"And your enemies?"

"There are only two habitable planets in our solar system. *"Vérité* and that of our enemies. As ours is *"Vérité"*, they have taken on the name *"Illusion."*

"Dr. Reinhart, our enemies are not only treacherous creatures that don't respect other life forms; they are also the most hideous life forms that we have ever encountered. Their internal organs are encrusted in evil. I am telling you this so that you won't cringe, even vomit, when you first cast your eyes upon them."

"Do they have any human form?"

"No. And I might add, they do not resemble any animals, marine life, insects, spiders, or, any other life forms, big or very small, that existed on the planet *Earth* today or in the_past," Electra replied with a cold stare.

"So I'll simply ignore their exteriors," Reinhart replied. "But, their intelligence…

"Infinite," Electra screeched.

"Even for me?" she asked pretentiously.

"You could surpass all of us, but you have not yet understood that. And your last metamorphose has not been put to a final test, because you have not completely integrated it. So, it really depends upon how fast you evolve and how clear-minded you are when you confront them," Nathan commented.

"Your human side," he picked up, "is and will always be a detriment to you, both on an emotional and intellectual level. You must suppress it completely, at least when you confront these creatures. Otherwise, you will be no more effective than we are—the reason why we have no choice but to use military force to save our population," he said, in a very calm voice.

"Well, returning to the beginning of this conversation, thank you anyway for reprogramming and upgrading my ship," she said respectfully.

"What was that all about?" Murdoc asked.

"I have no idea what you are referring to."

"Perhaps it is time for you to tell us who you are," Murdoc replied.

Murdoc grabbed her arm as she turned to leave. "I am still waiting for an answer."

"You want an answer to a foolish question." She responded and he released his grip.

"But, then you are not an Earthling," he called after her.

"If being human is being an Earthling, then I am an Earthling," She said, with a cold indifference.

The android crew had prepared an assortment of dehydrated rice, with piles of freshly cut tomatoes, carrots and green, leafy vegetables, with potatoes on top.

"I think that we all need sleep." Reinhart spoke after dinner. "For that reason, I have put the Group of 5 in charge of the Command Center. There are several skilled Alien pilots with them. The engineering department, as well as other technical centers, and the medical unit are under Alien supervision. I would like to encourage all of you to return to your quarters now and get some rest."

We got up and left for our quarters. I noticed Reinhart and Murdoc headed for the same room. I stood outside my quarters until I saw Randolph approaching.

"I don't really want to be alone" I whispered.

"Me neither," he replied, comforting me.

I grabbed his hand and pulled him into the room. The shower had a timer on it, set for a single user, so we dashed in and soaped up rapidly, just having enough water to rinse off the residue of suds and sweat before the water stopped flowing.

When I reached for my gown, there were two. "Damn, the Group of 5, thought of_everything... even our staying together." He nodded.

I started to close my eyes the moment that I cuddled up next to him. "What was all that discussion about horrific-looking Aliens that are working with the Malwarian androids?" he asked, in a weak, strained voice.

"You heard it in the engineering room?" I asked.

"Yes. I think that the Aliens wanted all of us to be aware of everything," his voice, so lifeless. "After all, we are risking our lives, so she might owe us some explanations."

"You are probably right," I whispered. "They wanted to sound the alarm."

"You heard what she said to Murdoc. Do you believe her? Is she human, or not? Not that it makes any difference now," he rambled.

"Well, if she isn't human, neither am I." I joked.

"Maybe it is your alien side then that excites me," he said, his voice lacking enthusiasm. "But tonight, let's just get some sleep, Pamela." He pulled me closer and buried his head in my neck.

To our surprise, the Group of 5 had installed an alarm system in our bedrooms, like they did when we were programmed humans. This loud, clanging, wake-up call jolted us from our sleep. It was terrifying, but what happened next was virtually mystifying. Like programmed humans of the past, we jumped out of bed and reached for the clean uniform bearing our names and rank, lying on the chair in front of us.

"They delivered these during the night?" Randolph stammered.

We opened our door, only to find other team members moving like wound-up toys down the hallway, in the direction of the dining room. When we arrived, Reinhart was already seated and having a very animated discussion with the Group of 5.

"What is wrong with all of you?" I heard her shouting.

"We thought that waking you all at the same time with an alarm was an excellent idea," Flanders answered.

"Well it wasn't. Find some nice soothing music to replace your alarm." Reinhart ordered.

The Aliens left when the rest of us arrived at the Command Center. Reinhart, her eyes half-closed and her shoulders falling forward, was sitting in the commander's seat.

"Elisabeth, would you like to get some rest? You had a very grueling 24 hours," I suggested.

"Good Idea, Pamela," I think that I need to meditate for a short moment. I shall leave you and Aegir in command. The Aliens will notify you if there are any problems." She stood up slowly. "Call me, if you need me."

She stopped and turned back. "As the Group of 5 will also be with you in the Command Center, it is not necessary for both of you to be present at the same time. You should take turns moving around, relaxing or even working out in the gym." We nodded.

I looked from time to time at her empty seat next to mine and turned often to be certain that Murdoc was still there.

"It is a bit boring," I said. "There is nothing but emptiness in front of us. Is it because we are traveling so rapidly that our minds cannot register anything but the darkness?"

"I can't answer that question, even if I wanted to." Murdoc sounded bored.

"As Reinhart gave us permission, I would like to work out a bit in the gym, if you don't mind." I mentioned. "Physical exercise helps me to calm down."

"I am fine. Go relax a bit," he replied. "The Group of 5 is with me if I need help."

I stopped by the engineering department and Randolph motioned to me to enter and take a tour, as he pointed out the changes introduced by the Aliens. I left, heading towards the gym, when I caught a glimpse of Rebecca sitting alone in the medical unit. She told she was bored, which she said was actually a good sign.

She wanted to go with me to the gym, so I sent a message over the intercom requesting Flanders immediate assistance in the medical unit.

Arriving rapidly, imagining an emergency, Flanders seemed a bit disappointed that there was no challenging medical problem for him to resolve. But he quickly passed into a rather fatherly role, shewing us off and telling us to have some fun

To my surprise, we each had a special locker, with sportswear, toiletries, soap, towels, and a clean uniform, bearing our name and rank. The room had various exercise equipment, like stationary bikes, rowing and other cardio machines, weight and strength training equipment for body building, boxing bags and gloves, just to name a few. And, there were ropes suspended from the ceiling, walls for climbing, balls, disks, rackets, and other more specialized equipment. We spent a good hour working out, principally on the cardio machines and scaling walls.

"I feel much better," I said, new energy flowing through me. "I got a bit bored, and..."

"You did the right thing, Pamela. I think that we should all exercise once a day," Rebecca commented as we split up.

"We are moving too rapidly for our minds to register

displacement in space," Reinhart, appearing out of nowhere, addressed me in one of those lifeless academic tones. "And yet, Pamela, we are still far away from our destination," she added.

"Well, that is not surprising. The Aliens told us that we would be a bit late reaching the *Benevolence*."

"I am going to set up a meeting with everyone for tomorrow, at the end of the day," she confided.

"Is something bothering you?" I asked.

A slight smile stretched her lips. "Yes. I don't want any of our discussions with Colonel Shannon to be intercepted by our enemies."

"Just be at the meeting that the Group of 5 is setting up for me." She added.

"Dr. Reinhart, I am becoming more and more suspicious of all the players, from the Aliens to Shannon and even her crew." I said and Murdoc joined in.

"Actually I have not told the others, only because I don't want to alarm anyone, that I share your position. I am also receiving mixed messages. We must use caution with Shannon, try not to reveal our position. But now, we shall pay very close attention to her mannerisms and words."

"It seems risky for us to board the *Benevolence*, but it is the only viable solution, if we want to save our family and friends and rid ourselves of those wretched High Commissioners." I responded.

"You are absolutely right. I must make it very clear to everyone that we shall not board the *Benevolence* until I have resolved all that."

"I don't understand." Murdoc spoke.

"Shannon's very pronounced nervousness and excessive evasiveness is annoying me," she replied. "Besides, these renegade android High Commissioners seem to despise me even more than their human opposites did. Of course, their irrational behavior could be due to a break down in their emotional programming, but the problem may be even more extensive. If their programming has been manipulated through malware or reprogramming, then who is responsible for this and why?"

"And the Aliens?"

They are perhaps playing a vicious game with me, holding back information to maintain a strong hold over me. And yet they are our only hope of retrieving our friends and family." She turned to Murdoc, who was flanking her other side.

"Is there anything else that you want to tell me?" I rekindled the discussion.

"I believe that everyone is now aware, through daily interaction, that the emotional intelligence of the Group of 5 is fully developed. So they should be capable of recognizing and anticipating how the cognitive emotional intelligence of the Androids affects their logical reasoning."

"The Group of 5 should have a more detailed report for me by the end of the day. I might mention malware and see how they react to that," she said, as Murdoc and I took our seats, our eyes focused on the viewing port.

"Are you sending the Group of 5 to meet them?" I pried for information, communicating with her on a cerebral level.

"No, Pamela. As I have said on many occasions, I shall go alone to confront these androids, but the Group of 5 will not be far away."

"What does that mean?"

"Remember that my eventual transfer to you, should my existence be in peril, must stay between the two of us. Make no reference to this to anyone, even Murdoc."

"The Group of 5, accompanied by Alien warriors, will arrive in other parts of the cavern, when I send them the order, assuming that I will be in a situation to do so," her voice unemotional.

"So, what happened to my role in all of this?" I asked.

"Saving me, by activating the code erh33 I gave you. I shall return as your symbiote and my new body will disintegrate before their eyes. But, this transfer is the last resort."

"I would like to mention that these Malwarian Androids...," I stopped for a second. "What do you think of this name?"

"Excellent!" her brain waves vibrated.

"They could kill you before anyone, including myself, has a chance to destroy them and save you," I replied boldly.

"Yes, there are risks. But until they release our family, they must believe that I am alone and will remain their prisoner, if need be, until my family is safely aboard our vessel."

"Of course," she continued. "I have made it possible for our Alien Allies to read my mind, when I invite them to do so," she replied pensively. "While I am being interrogated by these Malwarian Androids...," she stopped abruptly, "Yes, I really like your choice of name!" We laughed in the confines of our minds.

"I shall send the Aliens, as well as the Group of 5, images of the cavern and the interactive behavior of these Androids so they can identify their programming problems," she concluded.

"How can you send images?" I pried, ignoring her last comment.

"In my spare time on board this vessel, I developed undetectable, thread-like strands of captors that are now imbedded in the uniform I shall be wearing when I meet these Malwarian Androids." She made a vulgar, rough sound. "Anticipating your next question, the Group of 5 redid my uniform, inserting these captors into the fabric."

"When did you have spare time?" my brain waves radiating outward.

"Recently, when you and Aegir were sharing command of the *Redeemer.*"

"Ok." I lowered my eyes, slightly embarrassed that I hadn't spent my time in research. "But, you know, they could strip you of your uniform and throw your naked body into a cage."

"This will signal the intervention of both the Group of 5 and our Alien Allies." She replied.

We sat in silence for several hours on Star Board before being replaced by six of our Alien Allies. The sound of our heavy footsteps echoed in the air, as we left together for the last meeting we would have for weeks.

Elisabeth repeated what she had told me, leaving out any reference to an eventual cerebral transfer to me.

"Elisabeth, what are we to do during your captivity, torture, etcetera, until our Alien Allies and the Group of 5 rescue you?" Murdoc queried.

"I am leaving, you, Dr. Murdoc, in command. So, I'll let you figure that out!" He nodded, his lips spreading in a sly smile.

"My surprise arrival will indicate that the *Redeemer* is close by," she continued. "The moment we get close enough to the

Benevolence, I shall board a small spacecraft, with the Group of 5, and head for their planet. The spaceship is capable of tunneling downwards, situating us close to their private, cavern quarters." Her eyes took on a distant look and we waited patiently.

"A larger spacecraft," she picked up, "piloted by androids, will arrive shortly after us, landing on the surface. Once the virus in the High Commissioners is neutralized, they will be given an order to shut down. The Group of 5 will load them onto the larger craft," she stopped abruptly, "commanded by Drager."

"The veil of invisibility will protect the *Redeemer*. They will not be able to locate the ship, even though they might be aware of our presence in the area."

"Ok. That is reassuring," Murdoc replied, and the others nodded. "What do you want us to do then?"

"Before I leave, I shall awaken Cray. He knows he will be executed as a spy, on the orders of the High Commissioners, if he returns to the *Benevolence* without our protection. He will certainly agree to lead a rescue team. He knows the layout of the ship and will know where Peter, Frederic and Stuart are being held."

"Can you really trust him?" I blurted out.

"If he wants to live, he has no choice but to help us."

"I am assigning the rescue mission for Stuart, Peter and Frederic to Murdoc, Diana, Randolph and Pamela, who will accompany Cray in a small spacecraft, and then join forces with the revolutionary group under the command of Colonel Shannon."

"I have arranged for members of our Alien allies to take technical command of the ship, during our absence. Not because I don't trust anyone else," she continued, "but because they have more experience in space travel."

She stopped to pace back and forth for a moment. "Yet, I want James, Mathieu, Isabel, and Joseph to take our places. There must be a human presence and I trust the four of you." They nodded. "If ever you suspect foul play, you must contact me. I shall leave you my coordinates before my departure."

"Please don't disappoint me!" She added.

No one said anything, so she continued. "Once I give the order to board the *Benevolence*, I want Mathieu and Isabel to be ready to board a larger rescue spacecraft. Your mission, Isabel and Mathieu, will be to recuperate the members of our crew and my family, as well as Shannon and her followers. Murdoc, Randolph, Diana and Pamela will open the loading dock and help with their transfer."

"Who will be replacing Isabel and Mathieu?" James queried.

"James, you will be the acting human commander and will have Joseph, Ludovic, Jason, Tirence and Samuel at your side. You will, as a group, assure the safe return of our rescue teams. The Aliens on board the *Redeemer* will assist you."

"Is there going to be a revolution on board the *Benevolence*?" Mathieu asked.

"Not if everything goes as planned, but... they might counter-attack."

"Naturally, if Shannon has amassed a large following, you will have to hide in waiting until the rest of us come to join in an all-out battle to take command of the ship."

"If the first scenario spells out, can't we just plant a bomb inside the *Benevolence* and get rid of the rest of the humans and androids, once we board our different space crafts?" Murdoc proposed.

"No!" she replied sharply. "It would be sad to destroy these direct descendants of Earthlings. We shall not abandon them either, simply because they have been brainwashed, or so indoctrinated that they are not free thinkers. We shall go back for them at a later time."

"Well, it doesn't sound like a real military plan. And we should rid ourselves of our enemies." Murdoc argued.

"I don't agree." She protested. "My hope is that once we have overthrown the High Commissioners, or Malwarian Androids, we can enter into an alliance with the members of the *Benevolence*. We can work and fight together. And I believe that the humans will accept an alliance with us, once we have destroyed the Malwarian Androids."

"I am also worried about your safety." He sighed. "I would rather be with you than with Pamela, Randolph, Diana and Cray on a fast pace mission to save Peter, Frederic, Stuart, and a band of revolutionaries." Murdoc protested.

"If I need you, Aegir, I shall call for you."

"How?"

"I can reach any one of you on a cerebral level, telepathically, if I need to. So, Dr. Murdoc, if I need you, I shall send for you."

John answered within seconds of her call. "Is everything going well for all of you?" unable to hide his anxiety.

"We are very close—a week to 10 days from our destination," she replied. "If you hear from Shannon, please tell her not to worry, but do not give her our exact location or how much time we need to reach them."

"I shall just tell them not to worry."

"Oh, you have visitors." John said.

"Hi, Pamela." Mathilda moved onto the screen. "Rhea was born a week ago and is doing very well."

As we were in the lounge, Reinhart passed to hologram imaging. "She is just...beautiful!" I exclaimed, as I felt Randolph take my hand in his, reminding me of his paternal right to be equally happy.

"Oh, I wish that I could take her in my arms." I felt tears of happiness, mixed with those of regret, running down my cheek

"Transfer calls from Colonel Shannon to me from now on, John. I shall keep you informed." He was still smiling when Reinhart gave her final order and ended the holographic discussion.

She turned to the rest of us. "I know that the next week or so will be uneventful, but it is important that all of us continue to exercise and prepare ourselves mentally for the final act in our adventure. Does anyone have any other questions?"

The ten days seemed like ten months, as our enthusiasm over our daily activities waned and boredom set in. 'We are like a generation of humans in the past, who went to work, did their job, rushed to the gym, and...'

I spent my nights with Randolph, just like Elisabeth with Aegir. Others enjoyed their solitude.

And then one evening over dinner, Reinhart informed us. "We are getting close to our destination," she said, in a pleasantly cheerful voice.

"A few days ago, upon the arrival of Peter, Frederic and Stuart, Shannon contacted me, relaying the following message, which I decided not to reveal until we were in close range of the *Benevolence*."

"The Malwarian Androids," her voice a deep, solemn tone, "sent her a message to read to Peter, Frederic and Stuart, after they boarded the *Benevolence*."

"Apparently, Shannon requested Lieutenant X to read it over the loudspeakers, as she discretely opened the communication system from the spaceship to Earth, so John could listen in on and record the message," she added before playing the message.

'In the name of the High Commissioners of the planet Gliese 581g, I hereby arrest Dr. Stuart Rever Reinhart, Dr. Peter Feragan and Dr. Frederic Feragan Reinhart for Crimes committed against our friends and allies, the Group of 5, which include, but are not limited to, their capture and enslavement, and for their Intended Acts of Espionage with the purpose of conquering and holding captive the High Commissioners and the Androids and Human Members of the Spaceship *Benevolence*.'

"Your trial will take place over the next few months. If found guilty, you will be executed in a manner that the High Commissioners decide proper."

We heard the muffled voice of Colonel Shannon saying that they should do whatever necessary to stay alive until Reinhart arrived.

I fainted, Randolph catching me before my head hit the floor, quickly sweeping me up in his arms and holding me until I recovered. Reinhart entered my mind, calming me and reminding me that we would save my family. When I regained my composure, I took my seat.

"It is a bit funny because they believe that we are either still on the planet *Earth*, or a very significant distance from the *Benevolence*. They certainly imagine our hysteria, our panic, our ineffectiveness, believing that we will have no choice but to meet all of their conditions or demands." She stifled her laugh.

At this moment, the Group of 5 entered the room, Joseph and Tirence at their sides. "What is the matter?" Crawford queried.

Reinhart ran the message for them. "Did you cavort with these High Commissioners?"

"Absolutely not!" Flanders' voice vibrated his disdain. "We have had no contact with them and have no intention of assisting them in any way."

"This is preposterous. They must be expecting our arrest and imprisonment, so that we will not be given the opportunity to confront them. And, they probably hope, you will deactivate us," Miller retorted.

"I won't even dignify their statement with a response." Gordon replied, as she threw her arms violently in the air.

"Their threats are outrageous!" The former Governor shouted.

Crawford ejaculated: "We-I- all of us—shall show them how foolish they are. We shall strip them of their power and drain them, empty them, of their essence." His eyes met Reinhart's. "They are not worth saving!"

We motioned to the Group of 5 to sit down alongside of us, as we sat in silence. "Where did they take them?" I finally asked.

"Cray will know. It is time for him to wake up," she replied, as she stood up to leave the room.

"Wait, Dr. Reinhart," Diana called out, pointing to the back wall.

"It must be our Alien Allies," Reinhart's eyes, like those of the rest of our group, fixed on the back wall. When the holograms took shape, we all gazed upon the ruling elite. The Alien High Council comprised of Minerva, Thoth, Nemesis, Zelus, Kratos, and Concordia introduced themselves.

"Dr. Reinhart, we are pleased that your trip went smoothly and we were impressed with your ability to manoeuver the ship so easily through treacherous zones," Minerva said, opening the meeting with a polite remark.

"Thank you. But I am certain that your presence today is not to applaud my prowess as a Commander."

"Yes you are right, Dr. Reinhart, we have come for another reason." Concordia spoke. "We know that you will stop at nothing to achieve your goals. And much as we admire you, we implore you to listen to our alternative strategy to confront, what you refer to as, the Malwarian Androids."

"Dr. Reinhart, will you do us the honor of contemplating our plan of action?" Kratos asked.

"Yes. I shall listen to your proposal."

"We suggest that you use Pamela, as a decoy, in the manner and for the reasons that we shall present." Zelus spoke.

"The High Commissioners of the humans and androids on board the Benevolence stand in awe of you, Dr. Reinhart." He began, pronouncing his words slowly. "They love you and hate you with the same intensity."

"I know that," Reinhart interrupted Zelus.

"Of course you do. But instead of defying them like you have always done, you are offering yourself to them," Nemesis picked up. "They are ready for you. They remember you, the cruel, indifferent, authoritarian Reinhart; the very person that you will have to be when you confront them. You cannot play innocent. That is why Pamela is the better interlocutor. She appears to be a sweet and compromising person. And, unaware of your newly cloned body, they will be very confused about how to interact with you."

"Wait!" Reinhart interrupted. "You are wrong. Cray already mentioned in his prepared statement to Shannon that I was now in a cloned body."

"True," she replied. "We overlooked that, but even so, she will avoid their games of logic, resorting to feelings, thus forcing them to reveal their own emotional sides. And their emotional intelligence is something that the Group of 5 needs to see so that they can identify problems in their cognitive emotional processing, and/or viruses in their programming."

"This is too dangerous for Pamela. She won't have the ability to…" Reinhart quickly uttered stepping back from the holograms.

"Dr. Reinhart, your battle is on two different fronts, both of which are critical." Zelus began. "The Malwarian Androids might even take pity on her, it will help us. Pamela's theatrics, playing nice and concerned, will buy us time. You will have resolved another problem and can save her."

"What problem?"

"Taking command of the *Benevolence* will be easy for you, Dr. Reinhart. You will have an android defense team on your side, and you are a legend for the humans; they will naturally bow down to you. There will be no real battle if you board the *Benevolence*."

Thoth paused, then continued, "But there would be a battle if Pamela were there.-Humans, in particular, need to follow an idol, a legend like you. The androids would have no fear of Pamela—their programming to fight and destroy enemies of the Malwarian Androids would remain unchanged and they would kill her."

Ripples of smothered laughter filled the air. But when she finally spoke, her voice was filled with determination. "You think of me as a cruel, indifferent person. Do you think that I like the role I have had to play?" she asked rhetorically. "I have a mission to accomplish. A mission that I failed to achieve in the past and must, absolutely must, achieve today. I have no choice but to remain coldly logical."

"You have told us nothing that we don't know." Minerva spoke. "And much as we admire you, Dr. Reinhart, I suggest a more appropriate and practical strategy."

"Yes. Yes, of course." She rushed to me and took me in her arms. "But she is my child and I love her! So, you must promise me that you will protect her in my absence." For that brief instance, powerful maternal love filled me.

"You will take control of the *Benevolence*," Concordia weighed in. "Once these Malwarian Androids discover this, they will threaten to torture and kill Pamela. The Group of 5 and our military force will then enter into the quarters of the High Commissioners and, after locating their malfunctioning systems, shut them down."

"Our military will then dispose of our Alien enemies, who are presently sharing space with the High Commissioners in a large, enclosed cavern, separated from the High Commissioners' quarters," she picked up.

"Even though the Aliens can enter the Commissioners private quarters, the Commissioners cannot gain access to those of the Aliens." Thoth hesitated. "We are capable of tracking, observing and approaching the installations of these Malwarian Aliens on the asteroid, as well as other planets, these Aliens have invaded."

"Pamela, you must get the High Commissioners to tell you where your family is being held, before they shut down, so we can rescue them," Kratos vociferated.

"Their Alien allies are visually hideous and exhume a suffocating, putrid stench," Minerva confirmed her previous description.

"What do they look like?" I asked.

"They rest in a liquid resembling a filthy, putrid, pool of reddish

313

brown stagnant water." She grimaced. "Their skeletal-muscular system, if we can call it that, is very special. They appear to have both plant-animal physical characteristics with a pile of organs, some recognizable, like the stomach and the large and small intestines, some not." She drew a deep breath. "I know that we mentioned some of this before."

She paused. "Their brains and bowels are grotesquely large. Depending upon their age, these creatures are capable of stretching their bodies upwards from a slumping position to as much as 20 feet in height. Their long stem can range in diameter from 3 to 5 feet," she paused, before adding, that their organs could be compared to fruits or flowers dangling from the low and high lying branches of a plant, swaying in perfect harmony with their forward strides.

"We have no knowledge about their longevity." Thoth commented.

"They are highly intelligent and communicate telepathically," Kratos intervened. "Their most shocking incongruous feature is their exposed brain, in the form of an umbrella-shaped mushroom cap with thin, wavering threads of brain tissue dangling like hair, moving in the direction of sound and light, amassing scientific, technological and other information from life forms, while gaining control over their thinking processes."

"It appears," Thoth weighed in, "that once these Aliens have absorbed the knowledge of other life forms and exploited them for their advantage, these populations become nothing more than a form of amusement for them. They seem to enjoy watching their orchestrated demise of what they consider to be inferior civilizations."

"They have no sense of morality. Their abhorrent antics remind me of what took place in the Roman Coliseum, alive with an unorthodox, including a despicable thirst for violence and death. I can still visualize the animated gestures and hear the resonating screams of Roman spectators, encouraging gladiators to fight for their lives," Concordia added.

"They feel superior to other life forms—perhaps because they are," Zelus said, in a soft admission. "They will even eat an ally as easily as an enemy."

"So their diet is limited to life forms," I queried, a wave of nausea passing through me.

"They will eat anything, Pamela," Zelus continued. "I suppose they would eat whatever is available. But no matter what they consume, they return to liquid form to digest it."

"I don't understand this liquid state," Reinhart broke into the discussion.

"We never tested the liquid. It is possible that the organs do remain intact but are camouflaged by an excessive secretion of digestive juices, so to speak. But the putrid odors and blinding gases, emanating from these pools, has made it impossible for us to examine the liquid. In fact, any equipment that we have used to penetrate the vapors has dissolved, virtually disintegrated, on contact. So, Pamela, do not approach the putrid pools of liquid, if there are any in the cavern." Concordia said.

"So they could eat the Malwarian Androids?" My eyes bulged.

"I don't know for certain that they would eat them, but they could destroy them," Zelus replied. "For the moment, these Malwarian Androids are important to them."

"I want to know more about the odor of this liquid. Would it compare to acid-rich, stagnant water?" Reinhart addressed her question to Zelus.

"Actually, in a way," he replied.

"Do you know if they eat plants or fruit from plants, or insects?" Reinhart continued.

"I don't know," he looked at the others, "Dr. Reinhart, if they eat plants or fruits, or insects." He admitted. "As was mentioned, they appear to eat almost anything."

"Are you suggesting that our enemies are more flora than fauna?" Nemesis asked.

"It is possible that these Aliens are a mixture of fauna and flora, as was mentioned. But, they may be more flora than fauna. Certain of their organs appear to be similar to ours---you mentioned the intestines, bowel, stomach, but you did not mention a circulatory system with a heart, and yet you were certain that they have no rigid skeletal-muscular system, as you defined their make-shift spinal column as excessively pliable." Reinhart weighed in.

"According to your observations," she continued, "they droop like plants, in an arid space, when they need nutriments, and after digesting these substances, they stretch upwards on a long, solid, or maybe even thick tubular, but definitely prominent, stem. From this stem, dangle an array of glittering organs, instead of green leaves, colorful flowers, berries, prickly and smooth fruits, cones, nuts, and other such male and female reproductive organs and spores." She paused.

"Precisely," Zelus replied, in a low pensive tone.

"Trees, highly intelligent life forms, communicated with members of their own species via their roots, limbs, and leaves," Reinhart changed the subject. "Normally, their messaging was for survival rather than for inspiring aggressive, destructive behavior. And, scientists discovered before my time that all plants were capable of at least primitive, but often, high level forms of telepathic communication, even sending general warnings to all members of the plant kingdom when danger, like natural disasters or human destructive activities, were approaching."

"Go on," Zelus replied.

"It is very possible that your aliens are a hybrid of a ruthless, intelligent carnivorous plant and a highly intelligent mixed humanoid animal, or ordinary animal, both presumably native to their home planet, *Illusion*." She lowered her eyes in thought.

"And yet, I am more inclined to believe that one of these life forms, animal or plant, originated on another planet in a close or distant galaxy, and propagated with an animal or plant living on the planet *Illusion*," Reinhart remarked and the word "hybridized" could be heard in the background.

"Please continue, Dr. Reinhart," Minerva spoke.

"I would add that the putrid stench of rotting, stagnant water is nothing more than, as was suggested, their digestive juices, gastric and enzyme, mixed with excrements from their hybrid digestive system."

"Even if you are right about their origins and their bio-physiological systems, we still need to prevent these creatures from reaping havoc in the universe. They present a clear danger to us and other pacifistic civilizations." Minerva protested. "In order to neutralize these creatures, we have to either kill, or at least sedate them, but we have not been able to do either," she said, with a sigh of exasperation.

"Look Dr. Reinhart," Thoth picked up. "Look for yourself," he said, as he displayed photos taken of the cavern on the Malwarian Androids planet occupied by the Plant-Animal Species.

The photos revealed twelve pools of a reddish brown liquid substance placed equidistant one from the other, forming a perfect 360 degree circle. The fumes rising from the blistering liquid appeared in the form of a white light, which turned into high flames emitting a green, gaseous substance when anything or anyone got within one foot of it.

There were a number of photos showing the violent explosion of objects as they approached these presumably acid-rich pools and others showing the melting of metallic objects as they were lowered down into the liquid.

"Do you believe us now?" Zelus asked.

"Do you have a close-up of what is in the center of these photos?" She asked in a low, pensive tone and he nodded, showing her close-ups from different angles.

"Thank you. These photos are more revelatory and confirm my convictions," she began, as she called our attention to the large, dark, circular land mass situated in the center, from which twelve, slightly elevated ridges, extending outwards, terminated in twelve acid rich pools of liquid.

"Imagine a large disc or saucer shaped spacecraft with twelve long appendages, spaced equidistantly, extending outwards, and terminating in twelve ball shaped objects measuring 50 feet or more in diameter."

"Of course," Minerva spoke.

"Logically," Reinhart pointing to the photo, "the control room, cafeteria, lounge, sports center, and so forth would be situated in the large cylindrical center of the spaceship.

"I propose," she continued, "that the crew members access their assigned pod, or sleeping quarters, when they are inside the spaceship by way of one of the twelve tunnels, or appendages and, when on the outside of the spaceship, by passing through cooled down, as you put it, lava pools, giving them direct access to their individual sleeping quarters."

She took a step back to observe us and the Rat-Human Aliens. "These compartments, or pods, are certainly designed to provide and maintain the proper temperature, humidity and protection for these hybridized plant-animal species when they need to rest and recuperate. And, the putrid lava pools discourage invaders."

She took a deep breath. "The crews on board these small spaceships are sent on exploratory missions, to meet and/or conquer and exploit new life forms," she continued. "The spaceship is programmed to land in a specific location that offers a soft crust surface so the spaceship can burrow or tunnel down, hiding the body of the ship from view, thus protecting the crew from outside invaders."

"And," she picked up, as a smile spread her lips, "the individual quarters for the crew remain slightly above ground, with basins filled with a liquid, taking on the appearance of lava pools. These lava pools apparently cool down rapidly so that these Aliens can easily enter or exit their quarters by passing through the lava pools, or sleeping quarter, and, if necessary, return to the control room."

"That makes sense but, if this is true, you have not solved another riddle. How do these hybridized plant-animal creatures enter directly into their sleeping quarters or pods when they must pass through a pool of hot, corrosive lava?" Minerva's voice shaky with impatience and heads nodded.

"There are different scenarios so give me a minute to explain them." Reinhart's eyes moved rapidly in their sockets. "Let's imagine that these reddish, brown acidic pools of liquid lava that bubble and spit white flames high into the air when the Aliens exit their pods, actually exist. If so, the material they used to create these shallow basins that could house flaming, liquid lava must be native to their planet, or a planet that they invaded."

"Or, more interesting for us, they developed a very effective form of insulation to surround these basins, protect them from spillover and devised a cooling system for the hot lava substance that would activate rapidly when the Aliens needed to access their individual pods or return to the control room." Her lips spread slightly upwards. "If that is the case we shall steal their scientific ingenuity later on."

"But," a smile animated her face, "after studying the photos you have shown me, I see things from another angle. I believe that the ring of fire, or high white flames, surrounding these so-called lava pools as well as the presumably acidic, corrosive, bubbling liquid inside the shallow basins above the pod hatches are very effective, visual illusions."

When no comment was forthcoming, she continued. "Think about it. It would take a long time for corrosive elements in liquid form that spit hot vapors and feed blazing flames to cool down. These aliens need to access their pods rapidly if their lives are in danger. And, as we are well aware, their bodies are exposed. They wear no protective clothing or gear." She replied firmly.

"But, Dr. Reinhart," Minerva interrupted, "some of our members have been scalded and burned when they approached these pods. Their presence activates the sensory system resulting in violent sprays of acidic liquid."

"Yes, I don't doubt they have been injured, but not by corrosive, acidic liquid or blazing flames, but by lasers fired on them by Aliens hidden from view," she answered.

"And if you are wrong?" Concordia broke the long, awkward silence.

"I am not wrong," she retorted. "But, the ship lodged in the cavern on the Malwarian Androids' planet requires a great deal of ingenuity to destroy. We don't know what material was used in its construction."

After another long silence, Reinhart spoke again. "I don't have all the answers. But I do know that if we can concoct a drilling system, like one used in mining operations but more rapid and silent than those used in the past, over the next 48 hours, we can plant missiles directly under the ship and blow it up while the Aliens are asleep."

"Of course this will be regarded as an act of War by the Alien community. It is a problem for the future, but not for the present," she said, adding that we will have saved my family, the members of the *Benevolence,* and put an end to Malwarian Android dominance of humans before another war breaks out.

"Dr. Reinhart, I hope you are right," Concordia spoke, "because I have just received confirmation from our engineering department. We have the proper drilling device on our ship. We can send a team to drill and install missiles, to be fired on your command."

"This must be done discretely and rapidly," Reinhart spoke. "Remember you must buffer the explosion."

"Right," Concordia replied. "We need a few hours, though, to prepare a sound-proof screening system." Concordia replied. "The Malwarian Androids will not know that they have no Alien support."

"What about the main ship? If we can destroy it, I suggest that the Plant-Animal aliens on the Malwarian androids' planet will surrender? And if they surrender, the Malwarian Androids will surrender as well." Thoth digressed.

"I am not looking for war," Reinhart lashed out.

"But, if our destruction of their, let's say, reconnaissance vessel is seen as an act of war, will we be able to defend ourselves?" Minerva retorted.

"For that reason, we must give them a chance to leave," Reinhart said through tight lips. "My objective is to rid ourselves of the Plant-Animal aliens on that small rock that the Malwarian Aliens call home." her green eyes narrowed.

"We will give the Plant-Animal Aliens time to surrender or leave. Are you all with me on this?" She asked and yeses seeped from behind the lips of Reinhart's crew and the slim lips of the Rat-Human aliens.

"Ok, let's plant those missiles," she ordered.

"Dr. Reinhart," Joseph interrupted, "John is on-line."

"Put him through."

"Dr. Reinhart, I see you have company." His eyebrows rose above a tight smile.

"It is ok, you can speak freely in front of everyone," she replied.

"A very strange thing happened. I found the android replacements of the group of 5 in the communications center. All five of them had shut down. I contacted the technicians to test their systems for any form of cyberattack. When they found nothing, I ordered them to reactivate."

"The Governor's replacement told me that his entire Group received a verbal order at the same time to meet together in the communications room. The order carried my voice tone." John added.

"Ok. You probably should have contacted me sooner, but well..." she waved him on.

"The party or parties that gave the order did not reveal their physical selves, but addressed each android by name, using voice tones similar to those of the different members of the Group of 5. This gave these replacement androids the impression that they were actually communicating with the original Group of 5."

"But," he continued, "when these parties requested information concerning their present activities on the planet Earth and communications they had directly with you, the androids told me that they told them they could not comply with their requests; mentioning that only you, Dr. Reinhart had access to this kind information and only you could adjust or override their programming."

"Apparently, these imposters were not convinced the androids were telling the truth and persisted in their quest for information, asking about their programming and, more specifically, about their cognitive emotional processing." His brows corrugated.

"The androids told me the imposters' questions confused them and they eventually experienced a system override, forcing them to shut down simultaneously. They reactivated 60 minutes later, seeking out my advice." John concluded.

"Are the androids close by?" she asked and he nodded.

"Pass each one of them in front of the screen one at a time," She instructed. In each case, a blast of white light flashed like a laser beam from behind the pupils of her eyes, as she verified the programming of each android from our distance, light years away, and confirmed that their systems were operating properly. When she finished, she asked them to resume their duties.

"So, everything is ok, Dr. Reinhart?" John's voice unusually screechy.

"Yes, John, you did the right thing to contact me. Even though my original programming and back-up systems were very effective,

I have upgraded their systems, so you have nothing to worry about. I will get back to you later. Over and out."

She turned to us. "I know that our Allies, the Rat-Humans are not trying to sabotage either my mission to confront the Malwarian Androids, or to save our astronauts."

"Will the Plant-Animal Aliens put up a real fight when you inform them that you want them to leave the planet?" Murdoc said in a huff, as Reinhart shrugged her shoulders.

"You mentioned that the Plant-Animal Aliens are able to control the High Commissioners, because they can enter their systems, maybe even reprogram them, but more importantly they can interact with them through their emotional intelligence," Murdoc continued.

"If the cognitive emotional processing of these Malwarian Androids reflects their human opposites, who were ruthless, unethical and power hungry, it might be in the interest of these Plant-Animal Aliens to defend them, rather than join forces with us." Murdoc proposed.

"I know we cannot negotiate with the Malwarian Androids. We shall have to overpower them. It will be both a battle of physical force and a battle of minds. And, Murdoc, the Plant-Animal aliens will make it more difficult, if not impossible, to take down the Malwarian Androids if they intervene."

"So..." Randolph intervened.

"Hopefully, things will become clearer with time, but, for the moment, we shall count only on ourselves," she replied, adding that she had also up-graded the hardware and software in the Group of 5's replacement androids.

"And the androids on the *Benevolence*?" I asked.

"It would appear that humans are in command," Reinhart replied. "But, they do have android personnel to fight alongside of them." She drew a deep breath. "We shall find out more from Cray when we awaken him."

"So the androids on the *Benevolence* will not attack us?" Murdoc asked.

"I didn't say that. They might have been reprogrammed by our enemies to fight against us, making it difficult for us to gain control of the *Benevolence*." She turned her attention to the Group of 5

"Now that I have given the 5 of you the cognitive emotional processing of your human opposites, I shall put another program inside of you that will prevent our Alien enemies from manipulating your cognitive emotional processing to adversely affect your rational decision-making and making you loyal to them rather than to us humans."

"This is something I believe they did to the Malwarian Androids," she sighed. "Hopefully, you will be able to detect each other's emotional weaknesses as well, and notify me, if you notice a change in behavior." The Group of 5 nodded.

"When do I leave on this terrifying mission?" I vociferated.

"There is nothing to worry about, Pamela." Reinhart replied. "The group of 5 and our Alien Allies from the planet *Verité* will succeed in protecting you from the Malwarian Androids." We sat in silence.

"Don't forget, Dr. Reinhart, that you will help us rid ourselves of our enemies." Minerva's voice, cold and austere, came over the loud speaker, ending our cerebrating.

"My promise is good." She turned to the rest of us. "Your enemies are our Enemies," she said forcefully.

We waited, as time ticked away before we received confirmation that the missiles were planted. "Can you give me the coordinates and the name of the spaceship for the Plant-Animal Aliens?" Reinhart asked Minerva.

"Why?"

"Because, as I mentioned, exploding their ship and killing their crew could be seen as an act of war. So, I must, in the name of humanity, follow protocol and give the Commander the right to save his crew."

"You are showing weakness, Dr. Reinhart."

"No, I am showing respect." Reinhart stated. Minerva nodded slowly, before passing her the coordinates along with the name of the space ship.

"Dr. Elisabeth Reinhart, Commanding office of the Earth Ship, *The Redeemer*, to the Commanding Officer of the spaceship, *Tracker 21*."

A very tall, hybridized plant-animal creature appeared on the visual, as gasping sounds seeped from officers and crew standing just behind Reinhart on Star Board. "Commander Jeffries at your service, Dr. Elisabeth Reinhart," he replied telepathically in perfect English.

"I have a technical problem to resolve. One of your reconnaissance vessels is occupying a cavern on a planet inhabited by six renegade androids from the planet Earth." She said and the Commander inclined his large mushroom shaped brain mass, in a slow nod. "I need to warn you that these androids might resist arrest and that the members of your spaceship could be inadvertently injured or harmed."

"We have an alliance with these Androids," the Commander's telepathic reply took on a firm, serious tone.

"Explosives have been planted in the ground around your ship and on my signal will be activated. You have less than 20 minutes, Earth time, to order the return of your ship and crew. Their lives are now in your hands."

"This could be considered an act of war, Dr. Reinhart."

"Call it whatever you want, an act of war or an offer of peace and security for your crew. The choice is yours Commander Jefferies." She said as she switched off the communications system.

We waited the 20 minutes. "Ignite the missiles," Reinhart ordered.

"Wait," Thoth screamed over the intercom system. "The ship is beginning its lift off, can we give them a few more minutes, Dr. Reinhart?"

"Let me know when they are far enough above the planet," she replied.

Minutes later the missiles exploded destroying the interior of the cavern, making a return visit by the Plant-Animal Aliens impossible and depriving the 6 Malwarian Androids of Alien intervention.

"In the interest of a future alliance with the Plant-Animal Aliens, they have sent me a copy of their last conversation with the Malwarian Androids which they believe will give you more insight into their personalities and objectives. I suggest you listen to the audio-visual, before sending Pamela to confront them." Minerva spoke.

"This gesture on the part of the Plant-Animal Aliens is very much appreciated. I shall do what you have suggested."

"It was a pleasure working with you, Dr. Reinhart," Minerva replied.

"Our Alliance is sealed," Reinhart declared.

"Onward to victory!" Minerva cried out.

Chapter 20: The Malwarian Androids

Reinhart invited all of us, including the Group of 5, to the conference room to listen to the audio-visual of the Malwarian Androids the Plant-Animal Aliens wanted to share with us. Our eyes were on the screen.

In the depths of a cavern on an uninhabitable planet for humans, oblivious to what Reinhart and her Allies were in the midst of contriving, the Malwarian Androids paced back and forth in front of their large stone conference table.

"We have no news from the *Benevolence* concerning Dr. Reinhart's arrival." Dorothy hit a sensitive note and the others turned their bright, android eyes on her. "Things are not going as expected. We no longer hold the advantage." She spoke with an ardor that surprised them.

"What advantage?" Jeremy Milhouse rigorously questioned.

"Our audacious plan to seduce, capture and hold Reinhart hostage the moment she enters our cavern," Dorothy Lansley retorted. "Apparently, neither the crew of the *Benevolence* nor any of us interest her at all."

"Dorothy, you are wrong. We are still one step ahead of her so our advantage is secure. We arrested her family," Elena Yung articulated, in a stentorian tone. "She will not let anything happen to them. She will come looking for us."

"It is not enough," Meredith Weber weighed in. "She is incapable of love," her voice moving in erratic waves. "We have always known that. We acted too rashly. Think about it," she pleaded. "Why would she risk her life, and those of others, to save three people whom she can probably genetically reproduce?"

"Of course, we never considered that," Graham Christenger shook his head. "Again, she has outwitted us!" His right hand, coming down so hard on the stone tabletop, alerted the Aliens.

Within minutes, three of the Aliens, residing in the deep, dark pit of the cavern, appeared. "Is something wrong?" They asked telepathically.

The Malwarian Androids, not able to cleverly hide their thoughts, replied in unison. "No, everything is fine."

"We are very intolerant of disobedience."

"Disobedience...," Charles Deringer replied calmly, "it is insulting to think you would question our allegiance."

"We received very strange, emotionally imbued vibrations coming from this room. We are never wrong."

"Oh. Like our human opposites," Dorothy broke in, "we sometimes disagree over silly, mundane things, like proper attire, hair styles, and so forth."

"If we discover that you have in any way deceived us, or are considering deceit as your best option, we shall not hesitate to rid ourselves of you!" The most robust of the group threatened.

"By the way, where is this Dr. Reinhart? When will she be arriving?" The Aliens telepathically transmitting the same questions simultaneously.

"She should have contacted your ship, the *"Benevolence."* The tallest member of the group continued. "She seems to be indifferent to our having captured her family, unless, of course, you are hiding things from us. Perhaps we should order the death of her family."

"No, don't do that. I assure you she will come for her family," Graham's voice radiating confidence. "She is considered to be both brilliant and invincible, but after years of working with you, we believe that you are more brilliant than she is," he adulated.

After the Aliens left, Graham suggested they contact Colonel Shannon for more information."

"The Aliens could be listening." Dorothy's quivering voice risked compromising the Group's security if the Aliens suspected foul play. Her comrades moved nervously in their seats.

"Perhaps we should wait awhile. Give ourselves time to think," Elena suggested.

The Aliens reappeared hours later.

"We have no news." Meredith spoke for the group.

"Our patience is running out and we have lost confidence in you.

We are even considering eliminating you and contacting Colonel Shannon directly."

"We shall do our best to satisfy your request," Jeremy replied enthusiastically. "We promise that you will soon meet Dr. Reinhart."

"Consider this to be our last warning!" The Aliens turned in the direction of the inner cavern and strutted off. The Androids looked at each other in silence.

"I searched my memory banks and have been unable to locate anything concerning our move from the *Benevolence* to this wretched planet." Dorothy finally spoke.

"It does not matter if we don't know why we are here," Charles' interjected. "The only logical answer is that Reinhart entered into our systems and erased parts of our past memory."

"Could be," Meredith sighed.

"She won't get away with this. We shall enslave her," Graham's voice full of energy.

"But why would she erase that part of our memory?" Elena pained.

"Because she has a deranged sense of humor," Jeremy grimaced.

"I am more inclined to believe that our Alien Allies erased that part of our memory so that we could not defend ourselves or give Reinhart a logical reason why we left the *Benevolence.* We should agree now on the reason why we left," Dorothy replied, vehemently.

"But, why didn't we choose a more accommodating planet?" Dorothy persisted.

"I don't think anyone asked our preferences." Elena commented. "If anyone had cared about our comfort we wouldn't be on this planet."

"Enough complaining," Meredith weighed in.

"I suggest the following reason why we left the *Benevolence,*" Graham paced back and forth. "We left because just living amongst humans on board the *Benevolence* was denigrating for us as we were forced to consider them to be our equals. And because humans cannot survive on this planet, we showed our superiority."

"Does everyone agree with Graham's suggestion?" Jeremy asked, forcing a unanimous vote and ending the discussion.

"I am looking forward to her arrival. We shall torture her, force her to make us her intellectual equals by downloading all of her extensive knowledge into us and giving us her power to enter the minds of humans and other species so we can rule the universe," Graham ranted. "After which, of course, we shall have the power to enslave her, force her to serve us and obey our orders," he raised his fists and the others joined in.

"Ok, we need to get focused," Jeremy said, in a commanding tone. "I am going to call Colonel Shannon."

"No. I'll make the call for us." Graham grabbed the controls away from Jeremy, who did not resist.

"Graham Christenger to Colonel Shannon."

"Colonel Shannon receiving," she replied, in a steady, firm voice.

"As you must already know, Dr. Reinhart's family has been transported to a small asteroid and they are being held in the confines of a prison that was constructed many years ago by our Alien Allies for intergalactic spies. They will be tried over the next few weeks and risk the death penalty." Graham spoke in his hollow, monotonous android voice. "Their only hope for survival is Dr. Reinhart's unconditional surrender to the Aliens. Is this clear?"

"Very clear," Shannon replied officiously. "I should remind you that I carried out the order to have Reinhart's crew sent to the asteroid for trial."

"Have you informed her of this problem?" Christenger asked.

"She is unreachable for the moment....," She cleared her throat.

"This sounds rather irresponsible for someone like Dr. Reinhart. Are you certain that the Group of 5 and human members of Reinhart's team are being honest with you?" Christenger pressed for answers.

"I have no reason to believe they would be dishonest with me." Shannon continued to hold a steady, convincing tone.

"Well. This problem is now urgent. You must contact her," he replied. "Perhaps you should contact other members of her team so that they can act rapidly to locate Reinhart and inform her of this problem."

"Be assured that I shall do my best," Shannon replied, before switching off the communication, and turning in the direction of her trusted colleagues, Trend and Ranier.

"Wow! This is not good news!" Murdoc made a full-throated comment.

"Predictable," Reinhart replied.

"Yes, predictable," Crawford repeated. "Their cognitive emotional processing is out of control," his eyes connected with Reinhart's. "What can we do?"

"Let's listen to what Shannon is going to tell us," she answered calmly. "Stay out of range, but observe her behavior."

Our Alien Allies had Shannon on the screen. We could see the sweat on her forehead, dripping slowly down the curves of her face and along the sides of her neck. Her fists were tightly clenched. She turned to Trend and Ranier. "At least for the moment, our communication system is impenetrable, so the Malwarian Androids cannot follow the conversation." They nodded.

She took a deep breath before activating the audio system. "Colonel Shannon to Dr. Reinhart."

"Dr. Reinhart," Joseph called over the intercom system, "Colonel Shannon is on-line."

"I am contacting you to see if you are close to the *Benevolence*," Shannon replied.

"We have left Earth," Reinhart replied

"But…the situation here is getting more and more dangerous for me and my comrades."

"Apparently there have been many last minute changes," Reinhart replied and Shannon nodded.

"We need to have the exact location of the asteroid where my family is being held," Reinhart ordered. "Our Alien friends believe they know where my family has been sent, but I would like confirmation. If we make mistakes, we will give ourselves away."

"That is delicate, Dr. Reinhart," she replied in a high pitched voice. "It might compromise me."

"You knew the risks," Reinhart did not mince her words.

"Are you close to us?" Shannon's voice trembling.

"As I just told you, we have left Earth." Reinhart replied insipidly. "But we are far from your vessel." She lied.

"But…the situation here is getting more and more dangerous for me and my comrades," she whimpered.

"We need to have the exact location of this asteroid," Reinhart insisted, ignoring Shannon's pleas.

"I shall do my best," Shannon grimaced. "It is urgent that you arrive soon," she pleaded. "Can you send me the coordinates that you were given for the asteroid, as well as those of your vessel's present position?"

"Absolutely not," Reinhart's impatience seeping through.

"I don't understand..."

"You don't have to understand, just do what I tell you to do."

Shannon's trembling lower lip betrayed her. "If feasible, I shall send you that information as rapidly as possible."

"Our Alien allies will be alongside of us. You have nothing to fear." Reinhart's voice was calm. "The *Redeemer* is moving rapidly," she drew a deep breath, "but as the ship is under a shield of invisibility you cannot locate us on your radar. We shall contact you when we are ready to board the *Benevolence*."

"But how will you find our group? You don't know the layout of our vessel," Colonel Shannon cried out.

"Colonel Shannon, get a hold on yourself." Reinhart ordered. "Even though I remember the layout of the *Benevolence* changes may have been made. For that reason, I am going to revive Captain Cray who will lead us down the right pathways." She paused.

"I shall signal you when we are ready to board. In the meantime, you must inform the entire revolutionary group to be ready to assist in the overthrow of the reigning forces. Is that clear?" She ordered.

"I hope there will not be too many deaths," Shannon replied, under her breath. "But, the High Commissioners?"

"I shall take care of them," Reinhart replied.

"I shall not disappoint you, Dr. Reinhart. I shall get a hold on myself, as you put it."

"Excellent!" Reinhart bellowed. "What I want to know now is if you have any information relevant to the Aliens who aligned themselves with the High Commissioners."

"We have never had any contact with them." She sighed.

"And the prison—the asteroid—are you absolutely certain that you do not have its coordinates?" Reinhart gave Shannon another chance to show loyalty.

"I think that I might know where the asteroid with the prison complex is located," Shannon's voice resonating her surprise. "It was certainly one of the asteroids that was mined in the past for its nickel, iron, copper, platinum, magnesium and other less prevalent, yet significant, minerals."

"The coordinates?" Reinhart's patience waning.

"Even though I don't have the coordinates of this asteroid, I am certain it is very close to where our ship is located. I know that your family members were not put back into a cryogenic state, which means that the asteroid is close by."

"Thank you, Colonel Shannon. A mystery is resolved and our alliance is confirmed." She cleared her throat. "I have one last question. How many members are in your revolutionary group?"

"Not more than 50, but humans are not that numerous. There are more androids on the *Benevolence* than humans." She paused. "I am sorry that our revolutionary group is low in numbers."

"You have done well."

"Unfortunately, we will not have a big army waiting for us, so we will have to count on ourselves," Reinhart commented, when the transmission ended. "Dr. Flanders, will you please wake up Captain Cray?"-

"Dr. Reinhart," Joseph's voice, coming through loud and clear, jarred us back into the present. "Our Alien friends are on-line. They are ready to project their holograms. Are you ready to receive them?"

"I suppose that it is important so give them clearance," she replied.

"Dr. Reinhart," Minerva spoke, "everything is in place."

I could feel my body tremble as I turned to face my Mother, a pleading look in my eyes. "We are almost ready. Colonel Shannon is sequestered, her small group of revolutionaries at her side, ready to assist us. The Group of 5 is in the process of reviving Captain Cray."

Her eyes pierced mine, before she spoke. "My daughter is looking forward to taking down the Malwarian Androids, with your assistance and that of the Group of 5. Pamela will board a normal sized passenger craft and the Group of 5 will follow close behind in a larger ship, capable of carrying our enemies back to the *Redeemer*."

"And you, Dr. Reinhart, will leave at the same time as the others, to board the *Benevolence*?"

"No, we shall be leaving before them. I want to have control of the *Benevolence* before Pamela and the Group of 5 land on that asteroid."

"Contact us when you are ready," Minerva replied.

"Ok. But, we are still hours away from carrying out our missions," Reinhart replied. "We shall contact you before launching Pamela. You can follow her trajectory. Our objective is to isolate the Malwarian Androids. They must find themselves alone with Pamela."

"Do you think they will try to contact their Allies' Mother ship?" Minerva asked.

"Of course they will. I am ready nonetheless to divert their signals." Reinhart replied.

"Dr. Reinhart," Crawford was tugging at her sleeve, "Cray is with us."

In spite of his erect, formal, military posture, one could not help but notice that glimmer of laughter in his dark, brown eyes, when he said, "Nice to see you again."

"I shall get back to you in a few hours." Reinhart replied, as the holograms faded.

"Captain Cray, are you ready to assist in our military operation?"

"I have already committed myself to your cause, Dr. Reinhart."

"We are only hours away from our mission. You will be with me, Dr. Murdoc, Randolph and Diana. We will be boarding a medium-sized spacecraft and will be followed by a larger spacecraft piloted by androids that can seat 50 passengers, if necessary. We must be prepared to save the revolutionaries, if our efforts to overthrow the android soldiers are thwarted."

"What do you want me to do, Dr. Reinhart?"

"I want you to give me the code to open the landing port, the section where the military androids are located and the access codes for the various security units," she began.

"I also want you to look over the interior layout of the ship, as I designed and manufactured it and point out any changes that were made in my conception of this ship." He nodded. "I want you to show me the fastest route to the control center."

"I can do all that but Colonel Shannon can take care of the android military. She must have the access codes for their unit. I was never privy to this information." His face muscles tightened. "I was never considered a member of the human military, which was distinct from astronauts and other categories of space voyagers."

"Ok, fair enough. We shall get back to Shannon on this," she replied in a reassuring tone. "I shall program our ship with the proper codes. You can give them to me now."

"But...," he stuttered, "I thought that you trusted me."

"I trust nobody, Captain Cray," she replied. "The codes?" she pointed to the computer. "You can put them in for me and I shall verify them."

Cray quickly entered the codes.

"I am now going to erase the code in the *Benevolence's* control panel that we have and enter the one you just gave me. We shall see if you are really on our side?"

Captain Cray breathed easily, as she tested his allegiance. The codes functioned perfectly, and she rewarded Cray with a beaming smile.

"Ok. Now let's take a look at the layout of the *Benevolence*." We sat patiently while Reinhart entered a physical device, like a USB key, into the main computer. Cray studied and compared her earlier conception of the ship to its present design.

"Were there any changes made between the landing zone and the Star Board side of the ship?"

"Apart from additional living and military quarters, your conception of interlocking levels and access to control centers and Star Board, as you refer to the Bridge, are identical to its existing structure. We want to avoid the living quarters, where I might run into people who will recognize me. I prefer leading you through the more austere, less populated sections of the ship."

He looked her straight in the eyes. "I can also divert the humans and even the android technicians, should we encounter anyone on our arrival. My only concern is that I might be listed as a deserter or a criminal because I have been in your custody, so someone might activate the alarms."

"I am not worried. Your status is a positive asset for us."

"By the way, Dr. Reinhart," Flanders interrupted, "who is in charge during our absence?"

"I do believe I already mentioned that Joseph and James would be in command. They know how to reach all of us and can coordinate the missions. I have full confidence in them. Of course, they must be vigilant because our enemies will try to locate our ship, so they will have to use caution in sending messages."

"I have given them a coding system, simple but efficient. Replacement words, if you like. *Rushing forward*, for under attack; *standstill,* for get out of the way. Almost sounds juvenile, but, often times, simplistic coded messages, sounding like children, are undecipherable by the enemy."

"What is wrong with Cray?" Miller got our attention.

"Captain Cray," Reinhart rushed towards him.

"I can't keep up this game. I can't do it anymore. It is a trap. It has always been a trap!" His voice coming in a staccato, bellowing tone.

"What are you talking about? Stay focused!" She ordered.

His breath was coming in deep, laborious spurts. "I am not Captain Cray. I am Major Richard Wilberly."

We all backed away, guarding a safe distance.

"How can that be?" Reinhart asked in a strong, authoritative tone.

"I shall explain my story later, the story of all of us on board the *Benevolence*, when we have time." His body was trembling violently. "Do not board the *Benevolence!*" he cried out.

"Flanders, we must get him to the medical unit for a body scan." Reinhart ordered.

"He doesn't look like Wilberly." Miller commented in a scholarly tone.

"Shut up!" Reinhart retorted angrily. "Everyone shut up...Now!"

"Carry him to the medical unit," Reinhart addressed Flanders, while Rebecca assisted her with the body scan.

"What is it?" Murdoc asked.

"I don't know for certain," she replied.

"There it is. There it is!" she cried out as she grabbed a syringe and delicately punctured the neo-cortex region of Wilberly's brain, expressing a tiny black grain, which she quickly moved into a tube filled with a cryogenic liquid, before examining it under a high-powered microscope.

"Do you see this 8-legged creature? This one is a spider, but it could have taken on another form concomitant with the insect world." She squinted. "Perhaps there is a microchip inside this creature."

Her eyes drifted in a moment of pensive silence before continuing. "Hypothetically reconstructing what happened, the intruder, animate or inanimate, remained in a cryogenic state longer than Wilberly's mind and body. When Wilberly awakened, his mind was more alert and his own personality surfaced."

"But the moment the invasive device began to reactivate, he struggled to fend it off—to save us, by warning us not to board the *Benevolence*. We are fortunate he is so strong minded." A broad smile of admiration spread her lips.

"So we really don't know if there are humans ready to carry out a revolution on board that *Benevolence?*" Murdoc asked, pensively.

"We have to go on the assumption that nothing he told us about a revolutionary group is true," she grimaced.

"Should we contact our alien friends or Colonel Shannon?" Diana asked.

"No. That would be foolish. We have to wait for Wilberly to recover completely. We need to know more before proceeding."

"Are we going forward with our earlier strategy, Elisabeth?" Murdoc's voice gentle and smooth.

"No. Did anyone listen to me? It's obvious we need to change it!" She paced back and forth.

"I did not want to alarm the rest of you, but I was suspicious about Shannon's truthfulness, especially with respect to a revolutionary group on board the *Benevolence*," she sighed. "I feigned confidence in her so that she would stay in touch...inform us about Peter, Stuart and Frederic."

"Apparently, the rest of us, though, were duped, Dr. Reinhart?" Murdoc struggling to restrain his anger.

"I was unable to identify which party or parties were telling the truth," she breathed deeply. "And yet, I/we had no choice but to play the game. We needed the Rat-Humans to upgrade our technology and get us to the right destination, and then help us to deprive the Malwarian Androids of military support from the Plant-Animal species."

"And, as we needed Shannon to convincingly interact with the Malwarian Androids before our arrival, we had no choice but to agree to rescue Shannon and other humans on board the *Benevolence* to assure her continued cooperation." She snickered.

"Do we have any real allies?" Diana's voice was shaky.

"If we count only on ourselves, putting fear and anxiety aside," her voice strong and commanding, "we shall achieve our objectives."

Wilberly was now stirring, drawing our attention in his direction. We moved to his bedside, hovering over him.

"Dr. Reinhart?" He panted.

"I am right here." She gently caressed the contours of his face.

There was a long silence, before Reinhart picked up the conversation.

"You don't look yourself, but your voice is definitely that of Wilberly." Reinhart said, shrugging her shoulders. "How did you survive all these years?"

"I could ask you the same thing, Dr. Reinhart, but now is not the time to share stories."

"Before we go further, do you know anything about our Alien friends, the Rat-Humans, or their enemies, those atrocious plant-animal species?"

"You can trust your Alien friends. They know nothing about our symbiotes." He spoke in a low whisper. "They have their objective, which is to rid the universe of their enemies, who have been ravaging different planets and feeding off the inhabitants for centuries. Your Alien allies are life-friendly creatures, the hybrids are potential enemies for any species they encounter. We were warned about them and we stayed away from them," he added.

"I am a bit confused." Reinhart interrupted. "Why have you been warned to stay away from them when the High Commissioners are working closely with them?"

"I seriously had no idea about that. We were told the contrary— to avoid them. I know that their asteroid home is not human life friendly, the reason why, I believe, they chose to live there." He finally finished his explanation.

"Are the High Commissioners in contact with this invasive species of insects?"

"I don't know if they are aware of this alien species," his lips trembled slightly. "Shannon is in direct contact with the Malwarian Androids and we receive our missions and orders from her. I don't know if these insects can enter into machines, even very sophisticated humanoid machines," his lips trembled. "I don't know whether the Malwarian Androids know these insect creatures have infected the humans on board the *Benevolence.*"

"I am not yet convinced." She replied.

"I listened to a number of recorded conversations between Shannon and the Malwarian androids. The only Alien species they mentioned were the Plant-Animal species, warning Shannon to avoid any direct contract with them."

He took a deep breath before adding that if the Malwarian Androids had been aware of these Alien insects and knew they could enter humans' brains and manipulate them, they would have taken drastic action.

"They might even have exterminated humans in command and activated their android opposites in order to maintain control over the *Benevolence.*" He concluded.

"Are you certain that communications among Shannon and the Malwarian Androids were not altered?"

"Absolutely certain."

"Before losing consciousness," Reinhart continued her inquiry, "you warned us not to board the *Benevolence.* You told us that all humans on board the ship are contaminated."

"Dr. Reinhart, Colonel Shannon is the avatar of a loyal, dedicated servant and is therefore amenable to authority. So, in spite of her neocortex symbiote, it appears that the Malwarian Androids have her dancing on their strings."

"But I have listened to her communications with the Malwarian Androids and found myself admiring her tenacity."

"The problem is you are not listening to the real communications between Shannon and the High Commissioners." He replied in a condescending tone.

"What?"

"Come closer to me." She leaned her ear next to his mouth. "Try this code," he replied.

She backed away and asked Joseph to send her the last communication we received from Shannon. Before running it, she entered the code that Wilberly had given her. Another version of the communication was broadcasted.

In this version Shannon boasted her superiority over Reinhart describing her as a rather naïve woman who was out of the game, or maybe just out of practice. We heard Shannon laugh when she told the Malwarian Androids that Reinhart must have lost her faculties because she no longer had that intimidating, directive leadership style that made others bow down to her in the past.

She leaned very close to Major Wilberly and, even though she spoke very softly, we could hear her words. "I don't like to be played for a fool by anyone. Those who seek my wrath, shall find it."

"I told you the truth," he replied in a soft voice.

"So be it," Reinhart said, under her breath. "By the way, what did the insect want you to do?"

"It wanted me, like Shannon and others, to capture you but not harm you!" He articulated his words slowly.

"Interestingly," he continued, "these insects have more stimulated than damaged our brains. Perhaps these insects are taking care of us as a sign of good will towards you, Dr. Reinhart." He sighed.

"Time is of the essence now and we must save my family and destroy those High Commissioners." She paused, before adding: "For the moment, Major Wilberly, I am convinced your symbiote programmed you to obey it. It controlled your emotions and perhaps, indirectly, stimulated your reasoning. But, it did not bond with you; it used you. Your insect was ready to sacrifice your life only hours ago."-

"Maybe," he let the word slip out slowly.-

"Even though I know why the Malwarian Androids want me in their custody," she continued, "I have absolutely no idea why these different small invertebrate animals and arthropods are so interested in capturing me," she snickered.

"So our first objective is to shut down the Malwarian Androids." Murdoc spoke and Reinhart nodded

"We shall accomplish this mission. We shall protect, you, Dr. Reinhart!" The members of the Group of 5 barged in, reassuring her.

She nodded to them and turned back to Wilberly. "Are you referred to as Major Wilberly, or as Captain Cray by other members on board the *Benevolence*?"

"Whenever I go on missions, I use the name Captain Cray, otherwise I use my original name."

"Was Colonel Shannon a member of the original crew?"

"Yes. You would remember her as Lt. Beverly English."

"That would mean that Ranier and Trend were also members of the original crew."

"Yes. Ranier is Barron Davis and Trend is Dr. Shawn Underwood."

"My curiosity is definitely aroused." Her eyes widened. "Think about it. These "insects" restructured your bodies and faces, hoping that one day I would meet you, without ever imagining that you were members of my original crew. But why?" She threw her hands up in the air.

"Where is my family being held?" I cried out, pushing Reinhart aside, slapping Cray's face over and over again, until Randolph pulled me away.

Wilberly raised himself into a sitting position, his legs dangling from the side of the bed, and turned, with a cold stare, in my direction. I lowered my eyes and backed away from him "I believe an apology is in order." His voice calm, yet commanding, embarrassed me, and I acknowledged and apologized for my breach of protocol in using physical force. He nodded and slowly returned to his former reclining position before answering my question.

"They are definitely being held on the asteroid Shannon referred to. It is not far from where the *Redeemer* is navigating. I believe that I can help recover them, if they are still alive. Your Allies are also in a good position to intervene, but, like us humans, they will need the proper protective gear to support the very high temperature and lack of oxygen on the planet's surface."

"We have the suits and protective gear on board our ship," Reinhart interrupted.

"The prison itself is equipped with a cooling system and oxygen but..." He stopped abruptly, "the guards are ruthless androids and they inflict brutal forms of torture. Normally prisoners die within days of their internment on this asteroid."

"So what do you suggest?" Reinhart asked.

"I shall go to this prison with Murdoc, Randolph and Diana. They will wait in the wings, until I signal them that the road is clear. I have a few contacts in this prison—negotiated the release of others in the past. I shall try diplomacy before force." He paused.

"I know that Captain Jennifer Marshall, better known as Captain Valerie Reynolds, is being held there. I doubt, though, that she is still alive." He looked away attempting to subdue his emotion, but his trembling hands betrayed him.

"Perhaps because Captain Marshall was a loyal member of my original crew she would be sacrificed first." Reinhart's voice barely audible. "But, why did these Malwarian Androids request the rapid transfer of my family members to this prison provoking... war?" Reinhart probed.

He replied, laboring his words. "My best guess is that the High Commissioners resorted to drastic measures to lure you into their trap."

"Do the Malwarian Androids know the exact location of the *Redeemer*?"

"Only if you gave the coordinates to Colonel Shannon," he replied.

"Clearly, we shall not board the *Benevolence*," Reinhart replied in an icy tone. "I shall go directly to the prison with you to save my family, while Pamela accompanies the Group of 5 to meet with the Malwarian Androids. But before anything else, I shall send Shannon a new message."

"Wait, Dr. Reinhart. You must go with the Group of 5 to shut down the Malwarian Androids." Wilberly insisted.

"Our allies have suggested that Pamela is the better choice."

"Your allies believe that these High Commissioners have a weak side—a human side. They might, but for the moment they are in an alliance with wretched creatures, who also want you, as I just pointed out."

His eyes held her regard. "These Malwarian Androids have no

sense of humor, are impatient, and never show mercy. I strongly believe the High Commissioners will be offended if you send Pamela. And their existence depends upon their ability to present you as a sign of force and leverage in their relationship with their despicable allies."

"Our Allies convinced me that Pamela would be able to interact better than I with these Androids who will comfort and console her, thereby revealing the flaws in their programming and cognitive emotional processing."

"I hope you realize to what extent these Androids have integrated the emotional intelligence of their human counterparts in ways that are radically different from their human counterparts," he retorted.

"But, our Allies believe Pamela could more easily confuse them because her emotions will run high."

Pamela cleared her throat loud enough to signal her disagreement, but Reinhart continued. "Our Allies have been observing them and their interaction with their Alien enemies for a long time."

"I see it differently, but I could be wrong. The decision is yours to make, Dr. Reinhart," Major Wilberly's breath coming in short spurts. "I have told you the truth." He turned on his side. "I am feeling a bit tired, Dr. Reinhart."

His refusal to impose his position had an impact on Reinhart who promised to seriously consider his suggestion.

"And this message that you want to send to Shannon, can you tell us what you are going to say?" Murdoc asked, flaunting a sly, half-smile.

"We control our emotions and we pretend we are going to carry out the missions: invasion of the ship, Pamela's meeting with the Malwarian Androids, the destruction of those hybrids, but not in the same timing or order that we agreed upon," she replied calmly. "We shall use duplicity and manipulation."

"Your message to Shannon?" Murdoc insisted.

"Yes, I shall share it with you now, so that you can tell me what you think." She paused. "I shall announce the unfortunate death of Captain Cray." Her eyes glistened with delight. "Then I shall inform her that our Alien friends need our immediate assistance—that they are under attack in another region, not too far from our position, and we have agreed to assist them. I shall ask her to maintain communication with the High Commissioners, reassuring them that I shall be meeting with them very soon."

"I must contact John now and ask him to put all our centers on alert. I shall guide him in activating the total cloaking of our centers." She turned to Murdoc. "I shall need your assistance in activating the codes, those you installed in the different centers, just before the Doom's Day explosion." He nodded.

"Even though the Centers already float above the surface of the Earth, with your program they can lift off like a spacecraft, change location, ride out shock waves and thereby save the humans, hybridized humans and android/robotic crews should our enemies launch a direct attack against our facilities on Earth." She replied before adding, "Thank you, Murdoc!"

"No problem. We should be prepared for the worst. But I hope no one will attack the planet Earth." He replied.

"Joseph, please put us in touch with John."

John replied immediately. "I hope everything is going as you expected."

"Not at all," she replied firmly, before bringing him up-to-date on what Cray-Wilberly told her.

"We have been the victims of incessant deceit, Dr. Reinhart. Are you certain that this Cray-Wilberly is not using his own forms of trickery?" He asked.

"We must stay alert. The microscopic insect that was inside Wilberly's brain might or might not be an alien species. We should not board the *Benevolence* until we have more information about these insects." We nodded in agreement.

"And I am going to finesse Shannon by informing her that we have to postpone our arrival on board the *Benevolence* because our Alien allies are under attack and need our assistance. And, finally, to protect Wilberly, I shall inform her that he died."

"Good idea," he replied.

"We shall embark on our missions to save my family and confront the Malwarian Androids. We know their Alien Allies have left."

"I also believe we have to take immediate measures to protect the planet *Earth*. Dr. Murdoc is going to spend some time with you to retrieve the program that he installed in the computer systems of the three Centers that made it possible for them to survive the Doomsday explosion."

"That is reassuring," He replied with enthusiasm, before repeating what Reinhart had already mentioned concerning the efficaciousness of Murdoc's program.

"I am glad we agree," she replied. "But I want you to take other precautions regarding all insect life. I want the insects that are now being studied or stored in the various centers to be put into a cryogenic state. I want the cleanup crews in all three centers to carefully clean all areas, including closets and cabinets, with organic insecticides and fumigates."

"And," she paused, "I also want you to inform our western region explorers and the Captain, as well as WD, to avoid insects of any kind, even those that look harmless, until we know more about this Alien Insect race."

"Is it possible that the insects were an easy way to program humans, ridding them of their emotions, like the Group of 5 did to us?" John broke the spell.

"That is a possibility, but..." She huffed, "I am not certain that the Plant-Animal Aliens implanted insects. We may be dealing with another, even more, clever and vicious Alien species."

"Now, John," Reinhart slowly picked up the conversation, "you should have the Group of 5's replacements present during your meeting with Murdoc. Their assistance will be useful in accomplishing these various missions."

"Agreed," he replied. "I shall contact the various research units at the different centers and order them to carry out a thorough cleaning, convey your orders to Clarence and his team in the western region, and contact the Captain, who will inform his crew members and WD. I shall get in touch with Dr. Murdoc in a few hours to work with him on changing and adjusting the codes."

"I believe that you are overreacting!" I broke into the discussion. "Not all insect life is aliens in disguise. For example, insects play a vital role in maintaining a healthy ecosystem."

Crawford did not give Reinhart the chance to reply. "This is not the right moment to be altruistic, Pamela. We must take radical measures because at this moment we are unable to distinguish the ordinary insects from our Alien enemies in insect form. Humans must maintain the sanctity of their bodies, avoiding a symbiotic relationship with these life forms."

"And, as Dr. Reinhart's orders to use organic insecticides and fumigants is limited to the interior of the Centers, the insects living on the outside of the Centers will not be harmed." Crawford clarified the terms of the order, adding, "Insects can continue, as you put it, Pamela, to do their part in maintaining a healthy, balanced ecosystem on the Planet Earth." We all nodded approvingly.

"Dr. Reinhart, our Alien allies are radiating outward," Joseph announced inventively.

When they were all present, we grouped behind Reinhart as she told them the Cray-Wilberly story. "Have you ever had contact with this alien race?" Reinhart asked, as she flashed an image of the creature on the screen.

"I cannot speak for the others, but I don't know?" Minerva replied.

"You said that Cray-Wilberly was programmed by this creature?" Nemesis asked, as she like the others studied the structure of the insect.

"That is what he told me," Reinhart confessed.

"He was programmed to do what?" Thoth's nose twitched.

"I personally detected no interference by any extraneous life form, when we captured and sedated him, freeing your astronauts, months ago now." Kratos commented. "It is possible these insects are simply seeking a place to hide and, in return, reward their symbiotes positively by granting them immortality."

"Yes, that explanation has some credibility, especially since the crew of the *Benevolence* has survived thousands of years but I don't trust these creatures. And yet in spite of Wilberly's cries of danger, it has in no way damaged his brain matter. If anything, it has stimulated and enhanced it." Reinhart replied.

"I am inclined to agree with Dr. Reinhart. You should avoid entering that vessel until we are certain that these life forms are friendly," Zelus added.

"I do recall one legend that circulated within the less intellectual community on the planet Earth, just before the revolution broke out. It talked of extraordinarily beautiful and brilliant beings that offended the Gods and were reduced to insects," Concordia said in a low, unanimated tone. "Even though I never believed the story, it may have given hope and courage to these humans living in substandard conditions to better themselves by believing in these Gods and seeking their help."

"I know nothing about this legend or fairytale," Nemesis replied, and the others nodded. "But if they were superior beings—assuming that there is any ounce of credibility in this story, then, as superior beings, even in the form of insect life, they would naturally help their symbiote to progress."

"I can only speak for myself," Kratos replied. "This story does not interest me in the least. Nonetheless, I believe you are right to act with caution regarding the crew on board the *Benevolence.* And, I support the use of protective measures on the planet Earth." Heads nodded.

"You might already be aware of this, but Wilberly told me he has contacts in the prison and might be able to negotiate the release of my family and Captain Jennifer Marshall," Reinhart spoke. "But I doubt that."

"He also told me," she continued, "that the prison officers and staff are very cruel and take liberties in torturing prisoners. I am hopeful that the Malwarian Androids ordered the guards to treat my family with respect." She sighed. "I want to trust Wilberly, but still remain wary and suspicious, which is why I am counting on members of your crew to help with the rescue."

"We are ready to intervene, but on a limited basis," Minerva replied.

"What does that mean?" Reinhart questioned sternly.

"This is your battle," Minerva stated officiously.

"Why has this all of a sudden become just my battle?" aggressiveness in Reinhart's voice.

When no response was forthcoming, Reinhart moved the discussion forward. "As you must have suspected, I never intended to send Pamela to take down the Malwarian Androids. I am the only one that can outwit them and of course the presence and assistance of the Group of 5 is indispensable."

Minerva replied. "Nonetheless, we regret that we cannot be with you to rescue your family, but promise to prevent any interference in your rescue mission." Her lips spread into a slim smile.

"I prefer to rid all of us of this problem...in my own way," she replied

"One of our ships is stationed just over the prison on that asteroid. Our technicians were able to register the arrival and the internment of your family," Minerva commented. "I want you to know that all three of them are alive, but not everyone of them is in excellent condition. Jennifer Marshall is suffering badly. We have been able to film their arrival. Do you want to see how they are doing?"

A solemn, yes, seeped from between Reinhart's lips.

Chapter 21: Despotic Rulers

"What the hell happened?" Stuart shouted in a gruff voice, as he pulled with all of his force on the bars of the cell. "Couldn't even give us a bit of privacy, you dumb-assed robots."

As we watched the film, my eyes turned for an instance in the direction of Diana, her fists tight. Randolph moved closer to me, lightly stroking my arm, reminding me that he would always be there, and Murdoc stood with straight-backed confidence next to the indomitable Reinhart. They couldn't hear our rising call for victory.

"What do you want, human?" An android guard moved into view.

"Huh!" Stuart laughed, a dry, crackling laugh. "You primitive—I mean, primitive—robot. Can't even strut a straight line. Take a look at yourself."

"He is big, that one," a hollow android voice coming up behind the robot. "He could be very entertaining."

"Come a little closer to these bars and I shall definitely show all of you my form of entertainment!" Stuart provoked.

The androids roared their approval. "Finally, we have a human with some energy—guts, that is what my memory is telling me."

One of the androids moved boldly forward and reached out to touch Stuart who capitalized on its stupidity, by grabbing its arm and pulling it brusquely between the bars as he leveraged himself, raising his leg in an upward flash, hitting its arm at its point of insertion and flinging this dissected token of force, as it shattered into pieces when it hit the back wall of the cell.

We watched as the other androids backed off, pulling their injured comrade with them.

"We shall be back, human," they replied in a menacing tone.

Stuart sat down in a lotus position and closed his eyes. He moved only when he heard Frederic moan. "Where are we, Stuart? What happened?"

"Let's see if we can wake up your father. He took a good beating when we were dragged back onto that ship to be transported to this prison for crimes committed by us against 'The Group of 5'!" He expressed his disdain.

Just saying that released his stress and he burst out into heavy laughter. "I am going to rip those androids into tiny pieces the next time I see them!" He warned.

"I hear someone coming." Frederic spoke softly.

"Give your father a kick. You should both move to the back wall. I can handle this by myself," he said in a whisper.

We watched as Frederic nudged his father and then gave him a full blown kick in the back, before moving him to the back wall. Peter began to stir.

Three tiny robots appeared with plates, laden with food.

"What is it?" Stuart reached through the bars, grabbing and twisting the neck of one of the waiters, its disjointed head dangling to one side, revealing flimsy wires. The robot began moving in tight circles until one of the androids arrived on the scene and knocked it over.

"I guess that one of you doesn't want to eat?" He stood firm, trying to connect with Stuart's eyes.

"You don't articulate very well. You'll have to come a bit closer so that I can read your lips."

"Where is he going with all of this?" Murdoc asked.

"I don't know, but he has spirit." She hesitated. "I have to try to reach his mind, when this tape is over," she replied.

"I don't know if that is a good or bad thing," Murdoc commented, before the tape resumed.

The Android approached Stuart, taking small steps at a time. Before he was in Stuart's reach he whispered, "Hang in there." He turned to one of the waiters. "Go get another meal, that stupid robotic creature made a mess, it needs to be overhauled."

Fifteen minutes later, the android passed the three meals through a special hatch at the bottom of the cell door.

"Can we eat it?" Frederic asked.

"Wait, let's not look like mindless creatures that can be bought with food." He mouthed the words.

"Are you hungry?" Stuart continued mouthing the words and Frederic nodded.

"Watch this."

"Hey, anyone out there hiding in the dark?" He sat back and cracked his knuckles. "Got a message for the chef...the food smells rotten. We won't touch it until we have another human taste it first!

"What happened?" Peter began to move. "I feel like all my bones are broken. Where are we?"

Stuart put his index finger up to his lips and Peter let his body fall back on the hard surface.

"Ok, human, what do you want?" The robust Android that threatened him earlier strutted forward into the light. "Your days are limited. Do you know that?"

"What day is it?"

"I don't know."

"You don't know." Stuart feigned friendliness. "Must be difficult to live in this dreary place, even for an android like yourself. You know..."Stuart continued..."an android with your body and intelligence would be living in posh surroundings if you were with us."

"I don't need posh surrounding," it replied.

"Sorry about earlier. You come across now like a nice guy."

"Enough. What do you want, human?"

"I want a human taster."

"Why?"

"I am very cautious."

"Ok. I'll get you a human."

He came back with Jennifer Marshall. She was limping, had only one visible eye, and the right side of her face was scarred beyond repair. "She can't hear well, so you will have to speak very loudly. And as you can see, she has no teeth, so mash up the food before you give it to her," the android replied. "She is in very bad shape. We shall finish with her soon. We were just working on removing her finger nails."

Stuart stared deeply into Jennifer's remaining eye as if he were sending her a message, before putting a piece of mashed food from each plate into her mouth. The guard closed her mouth and massaged her throat until she swallowed it. When it was clear that the food was safe to eat, Stuart passed the 3 plates to Frederic. "Eat as much as you want and make sure that your Father eats."

"You are not going to eat?" the Android asked. "You should. You are going to need strength. They have something treacherous in mind for you."

"Looks like you had fun torturing that woman." Stuart changed the subject.

"I don't know, fun," the Android replied. "Some of them do, though. I am not part of the reigning class."

"From what I see, none of them compare to the Group of 5."

"The Group of 5? You know them?"

"I work with them," Stuart boasted.

The camera moved to Peter, now sitting next to Frederic who was gulping down his dinner. Peter's face was badly swollen and he was cradling his right arm. He seemed to have difficulty chewing and was struggling to swallow the food. I wondered how Frederic could eat those greyish brown slug-like animals, bathing in a milky green liquid.

"Do you want my help?" Stuart asked.

"You can't do anything for me." There was a touch a sadness in its voice.

"If you help me, I shall help you."

"But I can't open the door."

"No problem." He took a bite of what was left on Peter's plate and spit it out.

"We need to know if we can trust each other, so let's start with this—bring me something I can eat, and don't tell me that it is difficult. If you want to work alongside the Group of 5, you have to show me that you have guts." The Android moved to leave.

"Wait, Oliver—do you like the name?" It nodded. "Do you know the leader of the torture team?"

"Yes."

"Did he like torturing that woman?"

"Oh, yes indeed, he did."

"Tell him that you were thinking it would be a pity to dispose of a human who resisted torture as well as she did. She was fun to torture. Remind them that they rarely have fun."

Stuart hesitated. "When this torture team says, 'so what do

you suggest,' you say it would be easy to put her back—not completely—but enough that she would be motivated to fight. For the moment, there are no other female humans to torture. It would be good practice for when they catch Reinhart." Stuart waited a minute. "What do you think about that?"

"If I do that, will you really help me?" Oliver asked.

"I promise. You help me and I shall give you a better life, even if it means rebuilding you."

"If I could reach him, I could give him power, but I can't reach him." Reinhart sighed.

"I haven't met Stuart yet, but he is impressive, Elisabeth." There was true admiration in Murdoc's voice.

"Is he still alive?" Reinhart turned to Minerva.

"Yes, but jumping ahead, they are going to put him in that horrible arena very soon."

"Contact your ship, you said that it was hovering over the asteroid and ask them to give me the exact coordinate for the prison." Reinhart implored and Minerva fulfilled her request.

"Ok." She disappeared for a few minutes. "Excellent, I shall be able to connect with him."

"Crawford!" A note of urgency in Reinhart's voice. "Do you have Stuart's biological code registered in your system?"

"We all do," he replied.

"I don't care which one of you does it, but pass it onto the main computer!" Within minutes it was done.

"I am going to try to connect with Stuart on a cerebral level, so do not disturb me." We didn't move, hardly breathed.

"Ok, I connected with him," she began, "He has accepted me, and I have enhanced his physical and mental capacities, like I do for you, Pamela. At the right moment, I shall make him even more powerful."

"Thank you, Mother!" spilled naturally from my lips.

"He still has a few days before he has to fight. By then he will be able to test his super-human skills." She sighed. "Timing is tight. If all goes well, you will be arriving a short time before the Group of 5 and I shall have finished with the Malwarian androids and can join forces with you at the prison colony. I might change our strategy, so wait for me."

"Can we see the rest of the film?" she asked, her voice still charged with emotion.

The film began to run. "I am back to let you know that I did what you mentioned. They liked the idea, even said that they were surprised that I had begun to evolve. They want me to be a closer member of their team and participate in the torture."

"Is that what you want?" Stuart asked, as he etched silly figures of fish in the hard floor with a piece of rusty metal.

"No. I want to work with the Group of 5."

"Stay like that. I would hate to have to break you into pieces." The android nodded.

"By the way, I got you something good to eat." Stuart smiled, a friendly open smile and then threw the food on the floor. The Android said nothing.

"I want to trust you. What you did, Oliver, was risky and shows loyalty. But, well...I need a taster, just the same." Stuart smirked.

The Android, completely unaware of Stuart's mockery, changed the subject. "Be careful at night, there are tiny creatures that like to chew on raw flesh. Here is a light. Keep it low. It will drive them away." He quickly turned to leave.

"I think that you, Stuart, the most anti-social of all of us, just got us an ally." Peter kept his voice low.

"I am frightened," Frederic whimpered as he moved in between his protectors.

"Normal, Frederic. We are too!" Stuart and Peter said, at the same time. Within minutes, they fell into a deep sleep, to be awakened at dawn.

"They will be coming for us," Stuart said. "Peter, you must protect Frederic. So let them take me first."

"No we have to stay united," Peter insisted.

Stuart raised his fingers to his lips, ending the discussion, the sound of footsteps in the darkness surrounding them.

Oliver, who had definitely risen in rank, arrived, surrounded with 3 other android guards. A positive ray of energy passed from his eyes to those of Stuart, who nodded discretely. "The Judges have arrived. You must follow me. The trial will start soon."

"We want a lawyer. We have the right to a defense," Stuart protested.

"You have no right to defend yourself," Oliver replied, lowering his shoulders in a sign of humility.

"Tell them to consult the Inter-Galactic Code of Criminal Procedure." He stared into Oliver's beseeching eyes. "We have our rights."

"Ok. I shall be back later." He blinked his eyes several times, like he was sending Stuart a coded message.

When they were gone, Peter grabbed Stuart's arm. "What Inter-Galactic Code of Criminal Procedure?"

"Oh, there is none, but they don't know that. Just buying some time and hoping that Oliver will do something to help us. I know that our friends are on their way, so we have to do whatever we can to stay alive," Stuart said, as he shook the bars of the cage until they rattled and clanged.

The Judges, three Superior Grade Androids wearing long white cloaks, were seated behind a high table. "Where are those human outlaws?" The one in the middle asked.

Oliver repeated what Stuart had told him. The three of them stood up and replied in unison. "You were given an order, so carry it out!"

"But is it wise to infuriate Dr. Reinhart?" Oliver queried.

"Ok. As you think that they are entitled to a defense, you will be the party to represent them." The Android in the Center position announced. "You have one hour to put something intelligent together, remembering I have been given an order from the High Commissioners to convict and execute these individuals. You should be careful not to be too diligent in your defense. We shall keep a recording of this to prove to Reinhart and the Group of 5 that they were given a fair trial. Now get out!"

Oliver rushed back to the cell. "I am your lawyer." he replied. "But I don't have any idea what that means. What I do know is that the Judges have an order from the High Commissioners to execute the three of you."

"You have done well. Now we must find a way to delay this trial." Stuart stood up and began to pace back and forth.

"We only have one hour, so you better think fast."

"Entertainment—they like entertainment!" Stuart's voice sounded almost jovial. "I shall give it to them."

"You go back and tell them that Reinhart's son…"

"Which one of you is Dr. Reinhart's son?" Oliver interrupted.

"I am Reinhart's son." Stuart replied, as Oliver backed up.

"Oliver, listen to me," Stuart continued. "I want to make a wager. If I win against the best of their android warriors, all three of us, including that female who is barely alive—say it like that, it will sound like I don't much care—will be declared innocent of all charges brought against them by the High Commissioners."

"They may find it interesting—probably amusing." His eyes moved in large circles. "But even if they agree to it, they will kill you anyway!"

"Tell them Reinhart's son is ready to bet that they are too afraid of the High Commissioners to act on their own."

"You will take me with you?"

"My word is good. Now go and do what I said," he ordered. We watched Oliver pick-up speed.

At first the Commissioners laughed vigorously at the idea, but Oliver ignored their mockery and persisted, repeating over and over again that it was Dr. Reinhart's son that they were holding captive and ready to execute.

"He is the tall, muscular one that has a kind of warrior style, long hair, pulled back in a knot," one of them asked.

"Yes, that is Stuart Reinhart."

"Could be amusing," the android in center position commented. "We want a few moments to discuss it."

"Sorry, Dr. Reinhart, we were unable to pick up their conversation." Minerva announced.

"No problem. Just run the rest."

The film picked up a few minutes later.

"You tell him that he can fight, entertain us if he wants, with the hope of saving the lives of the others. But, it will be a battle or fight to the death. We have to execute someone."

"That is unfair, undignified." Oliver quickly put his hand over his mouth.

"You like him?" one of the Group asked.

"I have no emotional intelligence so I cannot like anyone. I can however reason and determine the limits of fair play," Oliver replied. "A deal is a deal. He fights a certain number of your warriors. If he wins, he wins the freedom for himself and the others." He stepped back a few feet. "Otherwise, we shall proceed to trial, but a trial that is dignified."

They huddled together for a few minutes. "He must win—that means destroy, completely dismantle—at least five of our most powerful androids. If he does, we shall honor him with his life, and grant freedom to the others, even that half-dead human. But someone or something must be sacrificed. And as we cannot sacrifice these humans unless this warrior loses, we decided it will be you. Prepare yourself, you middle-range android, to be dismantled if he wins."

Oliver stood his ground, his eyes focused on theirs. "Your need for vengeance is a demeaning, human trait, but if you want to step to their level, I shall willingly offer myself to you for dismantling."

But before he reached the exit, Oliver stopped abruptly in his tracks, turning to once again confront the Judges. "Reinhart's son and the others need a few days of sleep and good food. If you want real entertainment, Stuart must be in good condition."

They huddled together for a second time. "We agree. We shall give the three of them at least a day to recover." Their vile laughter filled the air.

Oliver repeated everything word for word to Stuart, Peter and Frederic. "They are despicable—must be their emotional intelligence. I am glad that I have none. But I really hope that you win, Dr. Stuart Reinhart!" his voice a firm, android tone. "It will be an honor to be dismantled in your name."

"There will be no dismantling, Oliver. You will accompany me to the arena and will wait on the side-lines for me to win. I shall take you with me, Oliver."

"What if they do dismantle me?"

"I'll take your parts and make you even better than you are now."

"Thank you." His voice cracked. "I want you to rest now. I shall be back for you in a few hours with good food."

"Stop the film," Reinhart ordered. "Did you have time, Aegir, to upgrade the computer systems in the various Centers?"

"Yes. Everything is in place and will function even better than it did in the past. No need to worry."

"Joseph, please send a message to John to stay on alert. Tell him that he is in command for the moment. I shall contact him when I return."

She turned to the holograms. "I want to thank you for everything you have done for us."

"We have done and will continue to do what we promised." Concordia spoke. "We expect the same from you."

"And rightly so. We are allies!"

"I am sending Pamela, Randolph, Murdoc, and Diana to enter this prison. I count on your military to assure their safe arrival on that rock, meaning, to dispose of any, let's say, space debris that could hinder their safe landing, as well as the guards at the prison entrance, if there are any." She stopped to collect her thoughts.

"I shall enter the dark quarters of those Malwarian Androids alone, the Group of 5 staying in the background until I send them the signal to assist. I want to get as much information from those Commissioners as I can, before they are forced to shut down."

"Do you think that you will actually need the Group of 5, Dr. Reinhart?" Nemesis queried. "I have seen what you did with your son, how you entered his mind and reinforced his body, giving him extraordinary powers. That was quite impressive. It should be easy for you to take control of the Malwarian Androids."

She sighed. "I do not know to what extent their cerebral capacities and physical force have evolved. And their emotional configurations, even if they are the exact replica of their human opposites, could make it impossible for me to take on all 6 of them at the same time. That is why I need the Group of 5."

"Of course I shall make a first attempt, to show them that I still have power over them, which is why the Group of 5 will assist me only when I solicit them." She added.

"An excellent strategy," She remarked.

Reinhart turned to face us. For a brief instance, she connected with me, passing, tender, loving energy. "It is time for you to board the shuttle. There is enough room for you to bring back all the humans and that android, Oliver, and anyone else that you believe should be saved." She paused. "I might make last minute changes, so stay alert."

Her eyes caught those of Minerva. "We shall decide later if the asteroid should be destroyed."

"I am leaving now with the Group of 5 for that miserable cavern where my Malwarian Androids are residing."

"What about me?" Wilberly rushed into the room. "I just woke up and want to be part of someone's team."

"Do you want him with you?" She looked at Murdoc.

"I'll take him with us, because he mentioned earlier that he has already visited this place. He can help us find our way around." He replied. "But..."he turned his attention to Wilberly, "if you do one foolish thing, I shall eliminate you. You will be fighting alongside of us. Clear?" Wilberly nodded.

"Is Drager ready with the larger ship to collect the 6 Malwarian Androids?" she asked, like an afterthought.

"Yes," Murdoc replied, "he is ready for lift-off."

Mathieu took over, opening up the runways and releasing the ships. Everything went smoothly.

Seated in our different ships, Minerva sent the sequence of the film.

"Hey you, Android," one of Oliver's staff called out, "we have orders to bring the big one," his voice cracked an android chuckle, "The other two humans, as well as that half-dead female, are invited to watch the fight."

"I am in charge of moving these humans, so you can go get the injured one," Oliver replied, a touch of authority in his voice.

We watched Stuart, Peter and Frederic move in a straight line behind Oliver. "I shall have to put you, Stuart, in the cage in the antechamber. It will be moved into the arena when the combat is ready to take place. I shall accompany Frederic, Peter and Jennifer, who will be arriving soon, to another part of the arena." He lost his footing, stumbling slightly." I promise to protect them, Dr. Stuart Reinhart."

He opened the door and the three of them followed him obligingly. When they arrived at the arena, it was still empty. The battle is 24 hours away. Oliver suggested that the three of them relax together for a short moment, while he went to get Jennifer.

"I am going to meditate now." It was at the very moment that Stuart sat down in the lotus position that Reinhart entered him again. This time Stuart lost consciousness.

Peter and Frederic were trying to revive him when Oliver returned with Jennifer.

"What happened?"

"We don't know," Peter replied, embracing nescience.

"Wake him up. He didn't eat or drink anything that could have poisoned him?" Oliver asked, just as Stuart finally began to stir, moving slowly back into his lotus position.

"Are you alright?" They asked at the same time.

"I feel strange," Stuart replied. "I feel incredibly strong, like I took some powerful drugs, and my eyes—I don't know how to describe what I see—it is as if I am visually dissecting you. Weird," he said, as his hand came down hard on the stone slab he was sitting on, breaking it into tiny pieces.

"I have been ordered to take your friends to another part of the arena where a cage is waiting for them." Oliver spoke. "You must win, Dr. Stuart Reinhart!" Stuart nodded.

The film ended. Our ship was on its way.

"You did it, Dr. Reinhart!" Our Alien allies cheering along with us. "He is now close to your equal!"

"No. He still has a long way to go before he is close to my equal." She laughed heartily.

"But now he just has to use what I have given him...effectively. He must exert steely force, while relying heavily on his shrewdness. I hope that he understands that. He has very little time to assimilate and adjust to his new levels of force and intellect." She added.

Chapter 22: Machiavellian

"The Hybrid species' installations have been destroyed," Minerva reported to Reinhart, who was piloting the ship. "Have you noticed any turbulence that might be linked to the explosion?" she asked.

"No. It would appear you used an effective sound-proof system and planted the explosives deep enough that there were no surface waves. Did you verify that all the Aliens left, no one remained in the inner chamber of the cavern?"

"As far as I know, everyone left," Minerva replied. "The explosion went deep like you requested, tearing up and pulverizing all forms of matter, and then spreading outward in a very large circumference."

"And, their spaceship was far enough away to survive any cosmic fall out." She continued. "To our knowledge, all the Aliens boarded the spaceship, no one stayed behind. But, as it is still too hot for my crew to get close enough to that zone, I recommend that you remain cautious," she warned.

"And the others, my family, is everything going well?"

"They are in close range of the prison and should be landing soon. I shall keep you informed—as well as I can. We are tracking you and the Group of 5, as well as Drager and his android crew. I have a small military vessel hovering close to the asteroid."

"We have reconsidered our previous non-intervention policy and are ready to send in our military if you need us," she offered. "We shall broadcast the events to all members of your community and stay in direct contact with you, Dr. Reinhart. Good Luck!" she said, before signing off.

"I have located a discrete area outside the cavern entrance. I am going to land." Reinhart informed the Group of 5. "You know what to do."

She lowered the shuttle craft, cloaked in its veil of invisibility, onto a solid, compact, smooth parcel. She silenced the engines before landing, in case there were motion detectors in the area and adapted her respiratory system to support the toxic air on the outside of the cavern.

"I shall go first into that low-lit conference room. And, I shall open the sound system inside my suit so that everyone, including Pamela and her crew, as well as those on board the *Redeemer,* and our allies can follow everything."

She walked slowly, carefully placing her feet to avoid falling. The entrance way was humid and reeked of vile odors. 'It must be the lingering smell of those alien hybrids,' her thoughts passing cerebrally on to me. The narrow cavern pathway widened, giving her a clear view of the Androids. She quickly moved into the shadows of a high stone pillar, so she could observe and study their behavior from a distance.

Oblivious to her presence, they paced with straight-backed confidence, exchanging furtive smiles, as they awaited the arrival of Reinhart.

And then Jeremy changed the mood. "Where are those Alien Hybrids? Maybe they have abandoned us." His eyes darted a sharp glance at his comrades.

"Stop looking for problems! Stop Complaining! You are making us anxious!" Elena reprimanded. "They must be sleeping. You know that they have not spent much time with us recently," she took a deep breath.

"And I might add that I'm glad that they are hiding as they were very aggressive the last time we spoke." Charles replied.

"It is Reinhart. I can almost feel her presence," Graham's android eyes darkened, as his hands came together in tight fists.

"You don't think that she brought them into an alliance with her?" Dorothy queried, in her normal shaky voice.

"I have warned you so many times that Reinhart is dangerous. We should have tried to contact her directly—create a working relationship with her," Meredith's voice trembling.

"You mean with the symbiote---the erratic, musician who never made any sense," Charles forced a laugh.

"I liked her," Meredith replied, this time in a calm, low voice.

"She seemed personable. She would have forgiven us and given us an opportunity to work with the Earthlings."

"Dreamer! Wake-up, Meredith!" Elena blurted out. "I hate your immaturity."

They stopped talking and took their places at the long, stone conference table.

Reinhart asked herself, 'Is this a warning sign?' she meditated. 'They are dangerous—out of control, but...'

She stepped forward. "Well, what do I find here?" she asked, in a cool, calm voice.

"Which one are you—Dr. Reinhart or Pamela?" Graham asked, jumping quickly to his feet. Reinhart snickered.

"You came?" Jeremy leaned back in his chair, his arms crossed.

"You are my creations. You needed me. You even asked me to come. So, here I am," she replied in a commanding tone. "What can I do for you?" She moved across the room, approaching their long table.

"We are very powerful now, Dr. Reinhart," Dorothy warned. "Perhaps you should not have come alone."

Reinhart stood calmly observing them. She pretended not to notice the defiance in their large, dark, menacing android eyes, taunt lips, and tight fists.

"Don't you understand that your life is in danger? Bow down to us!" Meredith's voice, high and screechy. Reinhart chuckled.

"Why did you leave the comfortable confines of the *Benevolence* to live in such a dismal cavern?" Reinhart persisted, ignoring their threats.

Their cold android eyes bore down on Reinhart holding her gaze, as they slowly pushed their chairs back from the table, and stood up, distancing themselves from her, as they moved into a tight huddle, keeping their voices low.

Reinhart observed them from a distance. They were standing straight with their feet held tight together and their arms crossed behind their backs. 'Are they afraid or just insecure?' crossed Reinhart's mind. She waited.

"We can't tell her why we're here because we don't know." Graham whispered. "Let's just lie to her and tell her that we could not live among those stupid humans...like we agreed to earlier."

"Well," Jeremey, stepped out from the huddle, taking the initiative, "you, of all people should understand that we had nothing in common with the mediocre humans on board the *Benevolence*. And to distinguish ourselves and assure their allegiance, we told them we were moving to more luxurious surroundings."

Reinhart's eyes rolled in their sockets, but she suppressed her burgeoning laughter. "Good try, Jeremy, but not convincing."

They slowly separated and returned to their seats. This time Graham was at one end of the table and Jeremy at the other. Charles was in the middle, next to Elena, followed by Dorothy and Meredith.

"We are in command here," Graham said in a strong voice, his hands firmly gripping the edge of the table. "You are our prisoner. Do you see that metal cage in the corner?" He pointed to the back wall. "That will soon be your living quarters."

She stepped forward. The only android that did not lower their regard was Graham. 'So I am right,' I heard pass through her mind, 'Graham Christenger is the leader.'

"What is all that high-tech equipment behind you?" Reinhart, ignoring their cold stares, pointed to terminals linked to a large screen that covered the entire back wall.

"I'll tell you," Meredith's voice high with enthusiasm. "We are not the demons, devils, irrational androids looking to harm other life forms that you think we are." She turned in the direction of the screen. "We are called upon regularly by our allies to initiate defensive actions to save their allies and ours from cosmic enemies."

Reinhart saw this as an opportunity to gain more insight into their cognitive emotional processing, so she asked them to show her their combat skills. "We only take orders from our Allies," Graham said through seared lips.

Fortunately for Reinhart, within minutes of her request, an alarm sounded and the screen began to flash. The six of them jumped up at the same time, rushed to take their seat at their assigned terminal and turned on their individual computer system. The wall screen instantly lit up, with magnificently radiant 3 dimensional graphics, relying heavily on augmented reality display, revealing a small corner of the universe, celestial bodies and space debris avoiding collision, as they moved in their defined orbits.

The calm waters of this part of the universe quickly turned into a galactic battlefield. The audio system activated. Calls of distress came through loud and clear from the commanding officers on board the various blue star vessels. The officers ordered the Malwarian Androids to fire their laser weapons on the red star, enemy vessels, to save them and help them rid the universe of these wretched creatures."

The 6 Malwarian Androids instantly activated their combat planes. Bright beams appeared on each of their screens as they engaged in battle. Reinhart waited patiently, studying their emotional behavior. They eventually began to relax in their seats, ready to celebrate their victory, when to Reinhart's dismay the battle picked up again.

"Look, there are more coming," Elena shouted, her voice rising with excitement as the others joined in, boasting the number of vessels they had already destroyed.

All six of them were so immersed in the battle, continuing their attacks until all enemy vessels were disintegrated. When the battle was finally over, they turned off the screen and terminals and returned to take their seats behind the conference table. Their eyes were now glued on Reinhart.

"Do you understand, Dr. Reinhart? We have great responsibility for keeping peace in the universe," Graham Christenger boasted.

"Yes, all of you have acquired expert training as fighter pilots should an intergalactic war break out in this sector of the universe. You have demonstrated to me your rapid anticipation and effective response to attacks launched by enemy vessels," she forced a smile.

"All of my crew members," she continued, "have had the same special training as you. Flight simulators play a very important role in preparing fighter pilots to react calmly, rapidly and effectively in face of real life battles.

"But, we were and are on a continuing basis involved in real life battles. We keep peace and harmony in this section of the universe," Jeremy stood up, his left hand coming down hard on the table. "We are saving lives, protecting populations from extermination." She noticed steely determination in his eyes.

"I am sorry, but you are not engaging in real life combat, but you are training on highly complex and life-like simulators." She stood her ground. "You now have the proficiency necessary to pilot combat planes and engage in winning battles in a planet's air space and in outer space."

"I don't understand? What you have said does not appear to be a compliment." Charles interrogated, in a high, aggressive tone. "We could not be so easily manipulated."

"Who installed that screen and various terminals?" She asked, ignoring Charles' anger.

"They were here when we arrived and we were trained to use them properly," Dorothy replied.

"Who trained you?"

"The Aliens, our allies," defiance in Elena's voice.

"The Aliens should have been honest with you," Reinhart spoke softly. "But, you have, nonetheless, acquired real talent. And you work well together."

"Shut up! You are wicked!" Graham protested, his tight fists coming down hard on the table. "You want to confuse us so you can destroy us!"

"No. You are wrong. I want to save you!" her voice reverberating.

"We don't trust you!" Meredith's anger hissing from behind her clenched teeth.

"Our allies are treacherous, Dr. Reinhart. And they want you," Graham intervened, changing the mood. "Actually it was their idea to have you meet us here in our "safe zone." We are not certain why they want us to capture you and put you in that cage."

He pointed again to the large, circular container, measuring more than 10 feet in height, its steel bars reinforced with wire webbing, resembling, on first glance, a bird cage.

Reinhart maintained her calm, as she strutted slowly up and down the length of the table, rapidly connecting with their eyes, so she could scan the system of each android as she passed in front. There was no doubt in her mind that these androids were reprogrammed by someone else. And, their cognitive emotional processing only emulated their human opposites' negative emotions—fear, anxiety, hatred, distrust, anger and the like.

But, interestingly enough, Reinhart realized she still had power over them. Yes, she still had the upper hand because her voice was registered in their operational and command centers. But to gain ultimate control over them she needed to enter their systems by direct eye contact, something they were effectively avoiding.

There was a long silence, their heads turning one to the other for answers. "We don't have to answer any of your questions," Meredith spoke boldly.

"Because you can't answer them?" Reinhart provoked. "Are you incapable of independent thinking?" The androids stood up and leaned into the center of the table, hoping to intimidate her. But, Reinhart stood her place.

"We were and are still acting as the High Commissioners!" Graham stretched out his hand to grab Reinhart. She quickly stepped out of reach. "And of course we relied upon them for guidance. Their knowledge and powers are without limit."

"So they helped you to interact with me through Colonel Shannon." Reinhart replied slowly.

"Yes," Elena scoffed, "they are very clever."

"So, where are these formidable, intelligent creatures?"

"They are relaxing in their quarters, a hidden chamber," Elena said, pointing to the back wall of the cavern.

"Well, go get them then. I would be very pleased to meet them," Reinhart replied in an authoritative tone.

"They do not like to be disturbed," Dorothy's voice coming in a rapid cadence.

"But now you have aroused my curiosity and, well, as you said, they want to meet me." Reinhart turned and started to walk towards the hidden chamber, the Androids following close behind her.

She could feel heat emanating from the anteroom and stopped short, before turning to face the Malwarian Androids. "Is it always so hot in this part of the cavern?" She asked.

"Hot!" Graham dashed past Reinhart as he rushed to the opening, a distance up ahead. "Something happened. We must try to enter the chamber."

He turned and moved rapidly in Reinhart's direction, grabbing her arm and holding her in place. She turned her eyes on him. For an instance, his defenses were down, his eyes wide-open. She detected the various infections linked to invasive malware. Things became clearer. She was right. Their programming was definitely redesigned by a highly intelligent species and this disruptive software was introduced into these androids through gaming. But, why?" She thought as she muscled her force and broke lose in a quick flash of power. The others backed off, leaving Graham on his own.

"More powerful than ever, Dr. Reinhart?" an expression of loathing in his voice.

"Is that a life form up ahead?" Graham's eyes followed her finger.

"Yes," his voice shaky. "It is one of our Allies." He dashed forward, Reinhart following a close distance behind.

She bent down next to Graham and visually examined the creature. She pretended to know nothing about this Alien species, or a visibly hybridized plant-animal. 'How could this have happened?' she pondered. 'The Commander had assured her that all members of the exploratory team on board the vessel had left the planet. The explosion in the cavern took place after the spaceship was a safe distance from this asteroid. No one was to be injured or die.'

She felt Graham's eyes on her and turned in his direction. "This is one of our Allies. Can you save it?" He asked.

"Why should I try?" she replied with indifference.

"Because you are behind this atrocity," Graham rambled. "This is all your fault!"

"I have done nothing wrong," her voice harsh. "Where are the other members of its group? They might be able to save their comrade," she suggested, as she leaned over the Alien, as if examining it. "Go get them!" she ordered, pointing to a partially open door.

She watched from the corner of her eye as Graham entered the cavern. His terrifying scream brought the other androids to the scene.

"They have left!" He turned to his comrades. "Look for yourself." He pointed to the entrance.

"It is very hot in the interior. The walls are black with soot, like there was an explosion." Jeremy turned to Reinhart. "You have to save that Alien. We want answers."

"I don't take orders from any of you!" She growled. "Now, move out of my way."

"Dr. Reinhart," the Plant-Animal Alien spoke telepathically.

"Why aren't you projecting your voice so these crazy machines can hear you?" Reinhart interrupted on a telepathic level.

"My message is for you and you alone. When we meet with these androids we use a device to translate our telepathic messages into audible terms." Reinhart nodded.

"What was your mission?" she asked, continuing the telepathic exchange. "Why did you stay behind?"

"As I am the senior ranking officer I volunteered for this mission, to assure your safety." There was a long pause. "The explosion was violent. My body was thrown into a cooler part of the cavern when the explosion first took place. But the ensuing fumes and the scorching heat inside the cavern have affected my organs." Reinhart nodded.

"What can I do to assure your survival?" she asked.

"Nothing. A small vessel is on route to pick me up."

"Why did you reduce these six androids to pitiful, rudimentary robots?" She continued the telepathic exchange.

"We needed to control them, squelch their rivalries, which were making them so dangerous that we could not leave them with the humans on board the *Benevolence*. So we transported them to this planet and provided them with entertainment." She detected a strange sound that could have been laughter.

"Yes you introduced them to forms of destructive entertainment like wars and other forms of combat. They have acquired real skill as fighter pilots, but are unable to distinguish the real world from the virtual world. They have definitely become unpredictable and dangerous. And, these six androids have now become pitiful, rudimentary robots, seeking my death." She sighed.

"Your people have the reputation of being cruel, untrustworthy..." She changed the subject.

"Yes," he interrupted, "in the past, we were heartless and cruel, torturing and eradicating vast numbers of different life forms, just like Earthlings did throughout their long history. In our defense, our animal side was dominant, driving us to seek new sources of food. And, we killed and provoked killing for amusement. We were undoubtedly cruel," the Hybridized Plant-Animal Alien expressed his annoyance with its gruff reply.

"Our on-going encounters with the Rat-Human Aliens," he continued, "have given us a real sense of morality and respect for different life forms, helping us to suppress and control our animal side. We cannot change the mistakes of our past, but we can avoid making them today and in the future. Our people are not your enemies, Dr. Reinhart. We, like the Rat-humans, are your Allies." Reinhart nodded pensively.

"We have been trying to awaken you for a long time now," the Plant-Animal Alien continued. "You must try to remember who you are?" It pleaded. "You are the only one who can save us from our enemies and yours. You are our only hope. You must try to remember your past...your very distant past," the Alien insisted.

"It is your defiance, failure to embrace that which you were that has caused chaos in the universe. And, your refusal to acknowledge and confront your past has made it possible for your true enemies to grow stronger and stronger. Time is running out!" He warned.

"I don't understand anything you have said," Reinhart murmured.

"Then meditate it!" the Alien's words resounded in her mind, as it lost consciousness.

"Were you communicating with that creature?" Graham growled. "What did it tell you?"

Reinhart stood up. "What just happened between this alien and me is none of your business."

At this moment in time, the Rat-Humans began to transmit the events to us and those on board the *Redeemer*.

The Malwarian Androids grouped together. "We are stronger than you, Dr. Reinhart. You should know this by now," Elena boasted.

"But are you stronger than me and the Group of 5 together?"

The androids turned quickly as the Group of 5 moved in their direction. "We know what is wrong with each one of them," Crawford announced as he strutted, his arms swinging from his sides.

The six Malwarian Androids raised their arms high above their broad shoulders, stamped their feet, and chanted in a loud menacing tone, 'the Victory will be ours.'

"Power up!" Reinhart ordered. The Group of 5 gained in height, their robotic limbs flaunting the bulging muscles of legendary heroes like Hercules.

"Drop your visors—protect your eyes," Graham ordered in turn, knowing that without the visors Reinhart could connect to their systems and shut them down.

Reinhart stood facing Graham. The members of the Group of 5 remained calm and concentrated, as they positioned themselves in front of their preferred adversary. The former Governor opted for Charles, Gordon pushed Flanders aside and stood in front of Jeremy, Miller chose Elena, Flanders found himself facing Dorothy, while Crawford confronted Meredith.

The fighting began when Graham rushed at full speed in Reinhart's direction, taking her by surprise as he lifted her high above his shoulders, spinning her in rapid circles, before hurling her more than 30 feet in the air in the direction of the back wall of the cavern. She hit the hard ground, inches away from the jagged edges of the back wall, and lost consciousness.

The film shifted to the Group of 5 charging with full force against their individual opponent, at the very moment Graham rushed Reinhart. Oblivious to Reinhart's sort, their battles were underway.

My throat tightened when I saw my Mother prostate on the hard cavern ground. I grabbed Murdoc's arm. "Wait, Pamela," I heard him say. "She cannot be taken down so easily. We have to continue on our route. Our mission is to save Stuart, Peter, Frederic and Jennifer," he replied.

"But..."

"Watch the film, Pamela. I shall take the co-pilot seat," Randolph suggested and I nodded.

"I am alive, Pamela," Reinhart connected with me on a cerebral level and I informed the others. "I need a few minutes to repair my body. I was not prepared for his violent attack."

Graham walked confidently towards Reinhart. "You had this coming," he said, low laughter in his voice. "I am now a legend! I am the one who killed Dr. Elisabeth Reinhart!" he raised his arms above his head and stomped his feet, celebrating the demise of Reinhart.

He started to leave to vaunt his victory, but turned back. He kneeled down next to her, lightly stroking her seemingly lifeless face and running his fingers through her long, wavy hair. He gently rubbed his cheek up against hers, as his hands moved slowly along the contours of her perfectly sculptured body, before, eventually, resting his head on her chest, caressing her hips. She played dead, while he gave her the time she needed to repair the damage he had caused her.

Mesmerized by her beauty and undoubtedly recalling moments of shared pleasures, he did not see her right hand move in a flash, hitting the left side of his face and knocking him off of her, as he rolled onto the ground. She sprang to her feet, landing one powerful blow after another to his upper body, before she lifted him high in the air, twirling him round and round, in wild spins, before throwing him forcefully up against the cavern wall. She waited for his systems to reactivate and watched him struggle to get up on his feet.

Leaping and handspringing in his direction, she violently struck his upper and lower body in rapid sequence, using both her hands and feet, demonstrating her superiority in all forms of martial arts, until he fell once again.

Showing no pity, she continued her attack, grabbing his right arm and forcefully ripping it from its socket. She slid her hand into this open cavity and tore out vital parts of his internal circuitry. Even as he lay immobile...beaten, Reinhart was not satisfied, for she lifted his heavy android body high in the air one last time and threw him violently up against the jagged edges of the cavern wall, further damaging his android exterior and internal circuitry.

We heard a loud grinding sound just before she pulled his head back in a violent jerk and tore the visor off his eyes. "Good Night, Graham," she said as she sent a beam of white light directly into his eyes, forcing all his systems to shut down.

She turned and rushed back to her group. The former governor was engaged in combat, keeping Charles at a distance. "Take him down! He is not your sparring partner. Show more force." She ordered, as she dashed past them.

The former Governor responded in kind abandoning his defensive posture and rushing his opponent, landing quick, hard, heavy blows, until Charles began to stagger and then stumble backwards, eventually falling onto the cavern floor. The former Governor jumped high, coming down hard on his opponent. The sound of splitting armor resounded, signaling the end of their combat. Reinhart applauded his victory, before ripping off Charles' visor, connecting with his eyes and shutting down his systems.

She noticed that Gordon was like a tigress putting Jeremy on the defensive, leaping high in the air, her arms and legs hitting his in rapid sequences, forcing him to his knees. He leaped back rapidly, but Gordon's combat training, along with her hatred of Jeremy, was giving her a clear advantage. "Finish him off!" Reinhart said the magic words, as Gordon went for the kill. His visor broke and Reinhart connected with his eyes and shut down his systems.

Miller, skilled in martial arts, like jujitsu and karate, not to mention boxing, had the upper hand. She was punching and kicking in the right places and in the right order. Elena was doing her best to stand her ground. Bearing her teeth and snarling, Miller rushed Elena with all her force, toppling her and pouncing on her face and upper body. Elena was not yet ready to concede defeat as she sprung back onto her feet. Miller quickly grabbed her right arm and tore it from its socket, brandishing it like a weapon, forcing Elena to retreat, before throwing it aside. She rushed at her, striking harder and harder, until Elena lost her equilibrium and fell, powerless, laying prostate on the ground. Reinhart applauded Miller before she bent down and ripped off Elena's visor, connected with her eyes and shut down her systems.

Crawford, with a strong, muscular upper body, had the upper hand with Meredith, who was on the defensive, skirting his heavy punches, never finding an opening to launch her own attack. "Take her down," Reinhart screamed. "I need you to help me with other things." He nodded as he rushed her, bashing her face and upper body with all his force, damaging her internal circuits. She eventually fell to her knees, giving Reinhart the go-head to rip off her visor, connect with her eyes, and shut down her systems.

Flanders was in real difficulty. Even though he towered over Dorothy, she was in control. She carried a long sword and wooden stick which she used effectively to keep Flanders at a distance and, when necessary, hit, poke or trip him up. Reinhart chuckled. "Neither one of them has the killer instinct, that ruthless determination to win," she said to me on a cerebral level, before wrapping her hands around Dorothy's neck and squeezing down hard, breaking through her robotic exterior, before lifting and throwing her 12 feet away from Flanders.

Dorothy made a futile, last effort to get back on her feet, but it was too late. Reinhart was upon her. She ripped off Dorothy's visor, entered her eyes and shut down her systems. Flanders dashed to Reinhart's side, throwing his arms around her and thanking her for intervening.

"It is time for us to leave this dreary place," Reinhart called out to Drager, still hiding in the entrance way. "Bring in the clean- up crew. I want the six Malwarian androids crated and I want the clean-up crew to rapidly dismantle the computer terminals and the retrieve all the programs used by these Malwarian androids. We need to leave soon." He nodded. "I shall study the computer programs and its subliminal messaging later on."

She made a final tour of the facility. The Alien's body had been retrieved by his rescue team. 'They are efficient, discrete and effective...qualities I greatly admire,' she said under her breath as her lips spread into a broad smile.

Before she took her final step out of the long corridor, a voice rang in her mind. "Thank you for taking care of our comrade. He has recovered."

"That is very good news!"

"Our alliance with you and your people is sealed?"

"Let me say, it is in the making," Reinhart replied firmly, as the communication ended.

"We have put the Malwarian Androids in the storage compartment on Drager's ship." Flanders rushed towards her, as she exited the tunnel. "We must get started if we are going to save your family."

She boarded alongside of him and took her seat behind the controls. The systems activated and the ship lifted smoothly into the sky.

"Can one of you," she addressed the Group of 5, "contact Minerva, or another member of the Rat-Human Aliens, to find out what is happening with my family? I am going to put the ship in warp speed."

Miller took the initiative, and within seconds, Minerva was visible in her holographic form. "Dr. Reinhart, we put your battle with the Malwarian Androids on direct to your daughter and her crew and the members of the *Redeemer*."

"Thank you. How are things going for my family?"

"Dr. Reinhart, I am very sorry to inform you that the situation is not as we expected."

"What do you mean?" Reinhart asked.

"The 5 warriors that will be meeting Stuart are very sophisticated. They have high-powered systems and long years of combat experience."

"I can handle them," Reinhart boasted.

"Perhaps," Minerva replied, "but, even if you overtake them, the Judges have another android force waiting on the side lines. They will be driving powerful, gigantic, metal gladiatorial style chariots, equipped with sharp blades on the outside of the wheels. And, there are five, large, high caliber, precision launchers on both sides of the chariots. The five android technicians on board the chariots will have an arsenal of lethal weapons, at their disposition, like laser guns, grenades, blasters, toxic gas bombs." She sighed loudly.

"Anything else I should know?"

"Yes, you need a security code to enter the driver's cabin. Even if you decipher the code, the door will not release automatically. Only the driver can open the door. Do you need to know more?"

"Yes, I have one vital question. Are these chariots steered manually?"

"I believe so, but I don't see how that helps?" Minerva replied pensively.

"I do. And, that is all that matters," Reinhart boasted. "Do you know how many first class androids with combat skills are in the prison?"

"I am guessing, when I say no more than 70 combat androids and perhaps as many as 60 primitive robots. The primitive robots will be occupying the bleachers and will be programmed to cheer on the android warriors. There may also be 10 or more Androids guarding the prisoners. A few will certainly be assigned to protect the Judges and block access to the arena and bleachers."

"Ok. Stuart needs an exoskeleton suit. There are exoskeleton suits for Peter, Frederic, and Jennifer, as well. They are on board the *Redeemer.* I shall ask Joseph to have them ready for you. Can you send someone to get them?"

"Yes, we have vessels close by, protecting the *Redeemer.* I shall contact one of them now." Minerva took a deep breath. "Oliver can distribute them. He knows and trusts us. We have been in touch with him. We shall take care of that." She sighed. "But, Oliver may not be able to deliver the exoskeleton suits to Peter, Frederic and Jennifer, who have already been transferred to another section of the prison."

"Understood," Reinhart replied. "Now we have to find a way to delay the fight, which is programmed for today," Reinhart's voice with emotions. "We need more time to get there."

"I have an idea," Minerva replied calmly. "What about a total blackout in their prison facility. This would create mayhem and disorganization, buying you the time you need to arrive."

"Excellent. You can do it?" Reinhart spoke with enthusiasm.

"Yes, our technicians can do that. Is there anything else you need?" Minerva asked.

"I am considering a new strategy," Reinhart replied pensively.

"I am listening."

"I believe all of us humans must fight. We need to get the spectators, those primitive robots, on our side. They do not have the force to take down the androids, but they can create havoc if they align themselves with us."

"Stuart and I must give those robots a good show," she continued, "add excitement, so the robots jump out of their seats and clamor to get closer to the arena, hoping to connect with Stuart or me, as they block the stairways, preventing the Androids from carrying out their smooth, programmed attack against the Group of 5, led by Murdoc. The Group of 5 will be able to adapt to chaos in the stands rather easily, opening the way for our Android combat crew to finish off the job." Reinhart proposed.

"Excellent idea. Do you want our help with that?"

"For the moment, if you deliver the exoskeleton suits to Stuart and, if possible, to Peter, Frederic and Jennifer and then initiate a total black out in that prison long enough for all of us to arrive, things should go well. If ever we need your intervention on a combat level, I shall contact you telepathically. Please continue to film our adventures and send them to our crew on the *Redeemer* and John and his staff on the Planet Earth."

"We shall be on direct with you, as well, sending you visual updates on the delivery of the exoskeleton suits and the black out."

"I am very grateful," Reinhart's voice, crackled with emotion, as the discussion ended.

She quickly contacted us on the rescue ship, announcing the change in strategy. If you land before us, wait for my order to enter the facility. She also told us we had to be prepared to fight.

"The exoskeleton suits programmed for each of you will, as you know, form a tight fitting outer skin, upgrading your skeletal muscular system, while maintaining proper organ function. Put on the helmets," she ordered. "Remember these suits will protect your vital organs, so you will be able to engage in combat with the Androids patrolling the auditorium at different levels."

"We are limited in number, but we are a formidable fighting team," she took a deep breath, before adding, "take the laser guns with you and do not hesitate to fire on our enemies."

"Agreed," seeped simultaneously from our lips.

"Good Luck," her voice overflowing with energy.

"Is Wilberly with you?"

"Affirmative," I replied.

"And Drager and his crew behind us?" she asked, as an afterthought and Crawford replied in the affirmative.

"Gordon, contact the *Redeemer*. I want more backup. Tell Mathieu he should leave now for the prison with 40 of our 1st class, combat androids," she began. "He should cloak his vessel, use the veil of invisibility, and should hover over the facility when he arrives, awaiting my order to land," she commanded, before adding that he should put on his exoskeleton suit and helmet before leaving the spacecraft.

"Things are going so fast, Dr. Reinhart," the former Governor commented. "If I were human, I would say that my adrenaline is running high!" She let her laughter flow, joining in with android crackles.

A few hours later Minerva was back. "Oliver acted on our behalf, loyal to Stuart. There were no guards around Stuart, making it easy for Oliver to pass the suit through the bars of the cage. Peter put his exoskeleton suit under the long, combat robe and baggy trousers he was given earlier. Oliver could not pass the suits to Peter, Frederic or Jennifer, who is still in very bad condition. He hid their exoskeleton suits inside a container outside their jail cell, what he referred to as a bird cage."

"Thank you." Reinhart took a deep breath. "I doubt that they will be able to access them, but I appreciate Oliver's efforts."

"I just received confirmation from our technicians that they were able to enter into the prison's operating systems and shut down the generators, plunging the prison into total darkness. There are no back-up generators in the prison so their unskilled technicians will have problems solving the problem." Minerva vaunted. "My technicians shall restore the power when you give me the signal."

"Words cannot describe my gratitude," Reinhart said with an expressive sigh, before mentioning that Mathieu and 40 combat androids were on route to the prison colony, something that Minerva already knew, as she informed Reinhart that one of her fighter crafts was leading the way, pointing out the right shortcuts Mathieu should engage to arrive faster.

After a brief 20 minutes Minerva was back. "You are very close and Pamela is close behind. Do you want her and the others to enter alongside you and the Group of 5?" Minerva was back.

"I will contact Pamela, when I land, asking her to wait for my order to enter the tunnel." Reinhart spoke."

"The Group of 5 will be waiting in the entrance to the tunnel for Pamela, Diana, Murdoc, Randolph, Wilberly, Drager, as well as, Mathieu to land. I shall give them a signal when I have the primitive robots cheering for me. Hopefully things will go as planned and the primitive robots' behavior will distract the Androids, so the rest of my group can launch a surprise attack. But, I might make minor last minute changes." She explained.

"I shall pass a visual of the arena to Pamela when it is time for her to enter," she continued. "I want those Judges to think that I had the audacity, or stupidity, to come alone."

"Understood. Be careful!" Minerva's voice animated with emotion.

"I can see in the dark. I shall send you a message telepathically when I am at the end of the tunnel, just outside the arena, so you can restore the power. I shall wait until the Judges take their seats, the auditorium is filled, and Stuart is outside the cage and engaged in his first combat, before I appear."

Reinhart lowered the spacecraft a distance from the entrance. "Give me a few minutes to change," she said to the Group of 5, as she removed her fortified spacesuit and changed into combat fatigues, showing that she did not need an exoskeleton suit to fortify herself.

"I am upgrading my skeleton-muscular system now," she mentioned and then marched forward in the direction of the tunnel, several laser guns hanging from her shoulders and a blaster in her hands. "These are for Stuart," she called out over her shoulder. "I don't really need them." she huffed.

"I have adjusted my vision so I can see clearly in the dark," she called out. "Take care of my children, friends and allies."

"Understood," they said in unison.

"I am going to contact Pamela. You shall be privy to my conversation," she added.

I heard her voice telepathically and opened the audio channel.

"I have discussed my strategy with Minerva," she began, "and you shall all follow my orders to the letter. Mathieu is about to land and is carrying 40 combat androids on board his spacecraft. All of you shall enter, take your assigned positions, when Pamela gives the order. I want the Group of 5, under the command of Murdoc, to lead 35 of our combat androids into a battle against the Androids patrolling the auditorium. Diana and Mathieu will accompany him, as well." She instructed.

"Pamela," she continued, "you will lead the attack against the androids holding Peter, Frederic and Jennifer captive. Randolph, Wilberly and Drager will be with you. The prisoners are situated directly opposite the 3 Judges."

"Why am I in charge of the Group of 5?" Murdoc asked.

"I want you to keep an eye on them, because I just fought alongside of them. Miller, Gordon and the former Governor are excellent in combat. Flanders and Crawford were vicious before I gave them their emotional intelligence, but that is not the case today. They lack the killer spirit." Murdoc raised his eyebrows.

"Diana, Mathieu and Drager, as well as our combat androids, will be fighting alongside of you, as well." She could not see him nod enthusiastically.

"Put on your exoskeleton suits and take weapons, especially laser guns and blasters with you." We nodded.

"I need you on screen, Murdoc. The Group of 5 can transmit you to me."

When she received confirmation from the Group of 5 and a clear visual of Murdoc, she ordered Murdoc to open his eyes wide. He obeyed. She entered his mind, like she did with me, and reinforced his physical capabilities.

"What the h--- did you do?" he yelled. "I feel like I could lift buildings!"

"I gave you super powers. Enjoy them while you can because I shall take them back at the end of the day," she snickered. "I am entering the tunnel in the direction of the arena in a few minutes."

"When the lights go on, the Group of 5 will take the lead, searching for hidden traps and any other obstacles that might harm you. Additionally, they will detect hidden cameras, readjusting the imagery to make your presence undetectable, and deactivate the sound detectors. You must be careful. Proceed slowly. The floor is wet and slippery."

"Murdoc, wait for my signal before you enter the arena. It is imperative that Pamela, Randolph, Wilberly and Drager save Peter, Frederic and Jennifer before all out battles take place. I want them, on my command, to discretely enter the arena. I shall contact Pamela telepathically when it is safe for her group to enter."

"I shall also mark your point of entry with a low light, Pamela," she spoke directly to me. "Your group will go directly to the high cliff where the prisoners are being held and free them. If you move fast, you can reach the cliffs in less than 5 minutes. Hopefully no one will notice your Group," she added.

"During this time I will do my best to get the robots on my side," she continued. "They are programmed to cheer for the winner or winners, something the Judges assume will always be their own android soldiers. But, today is our day!" Her voice rose.

"When the robots start to chant my name," she continued, "I shall give the order to Murdoc telepathically to discretely enter the arena, along with the Group of 5, Diana and Mathieu. Rush anyone or anything in your way and wait under the bleachers for my signal to fight." She stopped and took a deep breath.

"I am in command of the best military force that has ever existed. I have ultimate confidence in all of you. "We shall win!" Our voices joined in with hers.

Chapter 23: Outbraving the Enemy

When Reinhart was inside the corridor, close to the arena, she contacted Minerva telepathically to reactivate the generators. She hid in the folds of a discrete crack in the cavern's side wall. Fortunately she stayed her place for once the generators were operational the combat androids appeared, marching in formation and moving rapidly in the direction of the arena. The second flank, close behind, was comprised of the working class Androids, the robot spectators who would be seated in the bleachers.

The first thing Reinhart noticed was that all the androids, military and robot spectators had asexual human appearances, dark grey skin, mobile arms, legs, hands and feet, as well as, oval shaped heads, all with identical facial features. Their eyebrows hovered over large, black eyes that appeared to be in constant movement, surveilling their surroundings. They had ears, barely visible under their helmets, and a mobile jaw and mouth, with symmetrical upper and lower lips, activating when they chanted.

As they passed in front of her, she noticed the distinctive differences between the two groups. The combat androids, measuring 15 feet in height towered at least 5 feet above the robot spectators, and their large, black eyes were marked by a high concentration of power. Their skeletal-muscular system was bolstered with well-defined, firm, bulging muscles underneath thick, fortified android skin. She suppressed her laughter when they marched past her, flexing their arm muscles and chanting 'Kill the humans. Applaud our Victory.'

Reinhart was about to leave when she noticed a dozen robots with primitive exteriors bringing up the rear. Their bodies were comprised of three different sized heavy, square metal boxes, with facial features, -eyes, mouth, nose,- drawn on the upper box. They moved slowly forward on several rows of wheels attached to their lower box.

She smiled to herself. "Everything is in the programming," she said softly. The combat androids are programmed to wage war. They know how to make strategic decisions, integrating the best military plan, and are adept at hand to hand combat as well as the use of highly sophisticated and technologically precise lasers, blasters, and other lethal weapons." She sighed.

"The robot spectators are programmed to carry out menial tasks on a day-day basis, even work in mines. On special occasions they are the audience, whooping, clapping and encouraging the combat androids to win," she snickered.

"And the very primitive robots, lacking physical prowess, are the cerebral force—the great minds—the intellectuals of this warped community." She chuckled;

"Where are you, Pamela?" she connected with me.

"We have disposed of the guards at the entrance and are winding down the corridor in the direction of the arena." I replied telepathically.

"I see you. I shall move closer to the entrance. You, Randolph, Drager and Wilberly should pass behind me, go off to the right. You will see the dim light I planted, indicating the exit point. You must move fast across a 10 foot open space. Be careful, stay low, when you climb the high, rocky hill, where Peter, Frederic and Jennifer are imprisoned in an iron cage. I shall try to keep the attention of the crowd on Stuart and me, so no one will look in your direction."

"Tell Murdoc that once I am in the arena with Stuart, he should lead our android combat force, along with Diana, Mathieu and the group of 5 to a safe place underneath the bleachers and await my signal." She began.

"Pamela, tell Murdoc that I counted 50 primitive robotic spectators in the bleachers. There are approximately 30 large android combat trained guards positioned at the entrances and exits of the three-tiered semi-circular stadium which is divided into 3 visibly distinct sections, each with ten rows of bleachers. More than 20 Combat Androids are patrolling the different sections and levels of the bleachers, while a group of 10 are protecting the Judges' box." She said, before adding that there could be more arriving.

"Ok. He is right next to me. I passed the message," I replied. I could hear my voice shaking.

"I shall step out into the arena after Stuart's first combat. Eyes are on Stuart for the moment, so they won't see you. Move fast!" she ordered.

Reinhart remained in the shadows of the entrance and watched. An android, measuring more than 16 feet in height, with fortified upper and lower limbs and an oversized, muscular chest, protected behind a heavy breast plate, entered the arena. It wore a metal helmet, its eyes shielded behind a protective mask.

It turned to the audience and raised its arms over its head, clenching its fists. The ground vibrated with the stomping of its feet, as it turned in circles, keeping the attention of the crowd. Its large android lips curled upwards into a full smile, exposing its razor-sharp metallic teeth, as it brandished its massive metal club. The robot androids jumped to their feet, shouting: "Take the Earthling down!"

During this time, Reinhart used her extrasensory powers to telepathically connect with Stuart's mind. 'Look slightly off to your left, I am here.' He followed her instructions. The moment his eyes widened, she entered his mind and, like with me, further upgraded his mental and physical capabilities. 'You shall take down this creature. The Victory will be yours.'

"Unlock the cage door," one of the Judges ordered.

"No need to," Stuart replied, as he used his new found force to separate the bars. He stepped out of the cage, like a warrior, his arms raised high above his head, his fists clenched, ready to strike. He waved to the Robots in the bleachers before throwing a cold look of indifference in the direction of the Judges.

A robot rushed onto the arena and handed Stuart a wooden stick and a large, metal disk. "Good Luck," it said, as it skittered off the battle ground.

"Are you ready to die a horrible death at the hands of this gladiator, or do you want to ask for mercy and let the gladiator strike a quick, lethal blow?" The Judge in the center asked, a touch of laughter in its android voice.

"I have built androids more powerful than the one in front in me," Stuart taunted.

The combat began. The gladiator raced forward.

Stuart knew he had to move rapidly out of the Gladiator's way, but instead his body froze for a split second, a split second that was long enough for the Gladiator to seize the opportunity and launch a violent attack.

The ground trembled under the weight of its body as it rushed its prey. It grabbed Stuart, squeezing down, hoping to badly injure his internal organs, before swirling him violently in the air, tapping Stuart's head against the hard surface of the arena wall. When he felt confident that the victory was his, he threw Stuart 20 feet in the air and watched him land, immobile, in a far corner of the arena.

Disoriented from the fall, Stuart needed a few minutes to recuperate before engaging in combat, so he laid prostate on the ground, giving the impression that the creature had seriously injured him and the Battle had come to a rapid end.

The Gladiator turned to face the Judges who were applauding him and heralding his victory. He bowed to them, vaunting his strength, as he raised his fists and stomped his feet.

He never expected Stuart to recover, let alone, find the force to fight a grueling combat with him. So he turned confidently in wide circles, connecting with the spectators, until his eyes fell upon the place where Stuart should have been, but was no longer.

Stuart moved slowly into the Center of the Arena.

The Android Gladiator did not have time to evaluate Stuart's strategy. Stuart sprung high, using the force of his exoskeleton suit along with Reinhart's gifts of power, landing heavy punches on the Android's back shoulders and wrapping his long legs tightly around its massive, sturdy metal throat.

He ripped off its heavy helmet, throwing it with a loud bang on the ground. He then hammered the androids head, landing powerful blows to both sides, hoping to break through its robotic exterior at different points. The android eventually began to sway, waving its heavy club wildly in the air. Unable to reach its target, it tried to dislodge Stuart, by turning in violent circles, before rearing and bucking like a wild stallion.

Stuart held on, pounding the android's throat and shoulders, until his chance arrived. The Android flung its club wildly in the air. Stuart dodged it, waiting until the club swung close enough to him that he could grab it. With the club in his hands, Stuart jumped onto the ground. He ran in different directions, hitting the warrior's legs at different levels until the android eventually lost its equilibrium, stumbling onto its knees.

Stuart leaped high, landing on the android's slumping shoulders, as he gripped its throat between his legs, almost leveling its head. Before the android gladiator had time to realize what was happening, Stuart shoved his hands, into its eyes, going deep inside, pulling out pieces of wires laying just behind the sockets.

Stuart then turned to the Judges, a triumphal smile illuminating his face, before he ripped off the android's badly damaged head. The android's body bucked as its systems began to falter. Stuart leaped onto the ground, moving a good distance away from the creature and watched what remained of the Android's defeated body, topple onto the floor of the arena.

He raised his fists above his head and stomped his feet, before bowing to the robot spectators in the bleachers who were heralding Stuart. They clapped their hands and then mimicked him, by stomping their feet and branding their fists, while repeating his name over and over again.

"You have not finished, you pretentious human," he heard the judges say in unison. "As you vaunt your physical force, we shall now honor you by sending two instead of one android gladiator."

Stuart nodded, jibing them as he bragged about his superiority.

This was when Elisabeth entered the arena, bowing her head to the judges and turning her attention to the two massive creatures ready to charge Stuart. She opened her eyes wide, releasing a stream of intense, white light, like a beam of coherent radiation, efficient in its accuracy and intensity. The two massive creatures bucked and then swayed, under the effect of her laser stare. Their systems shut down and they fell with a loud bang on the hard dirt floor.

The 3 Judges stood up simultaneously. "Who are you and what do you want? You have no authority here and cannot prevent his execution and that of the others."

"I am Dr. Elisabeth Reinhart," she replied.

"So the android spoke the truth. He is your son," the smaller Judge asked with a cocky grin and she nodded.

"Dr. Elisabeth Reinhart," the Judge in the middle repeated several time. "Yes we have heard of you. You are the chosen one for some and a legend for others. We know your story but we are not impressed!" The judge replied mockingly.

"I shall make you an equitable offer," she replied, ignoring the Judge's provocative remark. "Release Stuart, Peter, Frederic and Jennifer, as well as Oliver, the android who represented Peter during your Kangaroo Court Hearings, and all those incredibly hard working robots sitting in the bleachers. In exchange, I shall spare your lives and will bring no harm to your android soldiers. If you do not surrender I shall destroy you, your android soldiers, and, ultimately, this wretched prison," she hesitated, "but I shall save the robot spectators!"

Her words inspired the spectators and they joined in her call of freedom for Stuart and the others, as well as their right to join forces with Dr. Elisabeth Reinhart.

The Judges shouted for silence, but the robots were already on their feet chanting her name, Dr. Reinhart, Dr. Reinhart..."

The Judges ordered their android combat soldiers to intervene and calm down the crowd.

In the middle of this chaos, Reinhart contacted with me telepathically. "Where are you?"

"We are climbing the high, winding path," I replied on a cerebral level.

"I know I am repeating myself, Pamela, but please remind Murdoc to wait under the bleachers until I give him the signal to move out, with the Group of 5, Diana, Mathieu, and our combat androids. You and Randolph will join them once you have accomplished your mission."

"Understood," I replied.

"Onward to Victory," her voice filled with energy echoed in the confines of my mind, rushing through me like an adrenaline packed cocktail, as I engaged with confidence in our assigned mission to save the prisoners.

I sprinted at full speed, but when I got close to the suspended, metal cage...the prison, for Peter, Frederic and Jennifer, I stopped. I needed reassurance Reinhart was still alive. The angle was perfect.

My eyes glimpsed the battle field. I saw her leading the way, her teeth gritted and her eyes flashing. Stuart was moving with the same determination and self-confidence directly behind her.

The robots, chanting her name, 'Dr. Elisabeth Reinhart' and clapping their hands, created havoc for the Android warriors, delaying their advance. I noticed that the robots' support of Reinhart drew grim looks from the Judges. The war machines, those strange modernized roman chariots, came to a halt, awaiting the signal from the Judges to officially engage in combat.

The last thing I heard was the Judges' calling for time out, as they huddled together, drawing a protective screen up around themselves, hoping to repel any blistering laser rays from Reinhart.

'Things are going as Reinhart hoped," passed through my mind as I turned back to our situation.

As we climbed higher we could see Peter, Frederic and Jennifer holding tightly onto the bars of the metal cage, dangling from a wire rope, attached to the horizontal arm of a large, metal structure, like a crane. If the crane's arm broke, the three of them would fall to their deaths, swallowed up in the deep abyss below. The Android guards were not in sight.

"Where are the androids?" I asked Randolph, in a whisper. His eyes moved off to the left and mine followed his. I saw them, crouching behind a large metal container, their lasers pointed directly at their three captives in the cage.

Randolph turned rapidly and charged with great speed in their direction taking them by surprise, as they scrambled to get away. He pursued them. His exoskeleton suit and head cask with integrated state of the art technology reinforced his physical strength and field of vision.

He finally targeted one of the fleeing androids and accelerated his speed, closing in on the android, hitting the android's chest hard with his head, causing it to lose its balance, and topple. The android was certainly not programmed for this type of unconventional hand to hand combat because it did not try to defend itself. But, Randolph showed it no pity, for he bashed the android's head up against the rocky surface, until its head cracked open and its systems shut down.

I caught up with Randolph, joining him as he moved rapidly in the direction of the remaining five android guards. They rushed towards us in a forward formation, raising their sophisticated laser weapons and firing randomly in our direction. We jumped and dived out of the way of the bright laser beams, our exoskeleton suits and helmets protecting us from a direct hit.

We both saw Drager and Wilberly crawling away from us on the ground, finding their hiding place in a dark corner of the cliff. "It looks like Drager and Wilberly are going to sit this fight out," Randolph growled.

"Hopefully, they will not abandon us," my voice shaky.

"Well, Pamela, are you ready?" He asked and I nodded. "On the count of 3, we charge, firing steady, lethal rounds on those androids. Show them no pity. This is our chance to become legends in our time!"

He grabbed my arm and pulled me to my feet. The exoskeleton suit gave me the protection, resiliency and force I needed to launch an effective offensive attack. I jumped high, ran fast and landed powerful blows using my arms and legs. My speed and efficiency made me practically invisible, as I demonstrated my skills in various forms of martial arts.

The remaining ones hid, forcing us to track them on the cliff's dark, jagged surface. "They are off to the right. We have to rush them," he whispered.

"Now," his voice commanding, as we took off in their direction.

We aimed our lasers on their sensitive spots like eyes, face, and middle chest region, before landing more direct, devastating blows to their arms and legs, crippling them and destroying their internal circuits, wiping out their programming. We watched three of them fall prostate on the ground. We could have stopped there, but instead we zapped those androids into pieces, using destructive laser blasts.

Drager finally jumped out from behind his hiding place and joined in to help us take down the few remaining android guards, by sneaking up behind them, and blasting them into pieces.

Wilberly also came out of hiding to help us move the arm of the crane close enough to the ledge so we could break open the door of the cage. Frederic jumped out and Peter passed Jennifer into Drager's arms. But, before Peter could escape, the cage began to lurch and sway. Peter lost his footing, sliding outside the open door, catching himself from a fatal fall as he clutched onto a slim, wire rope.

"Drager, do you know how to operate a crane?" Randolph hollered over the noise of cracking metal.

"Hold on tight, Peter," Wilberly yelled, as he rushed to the control panel of the crane. "I have some experience in this area, let me take a look." Seconds later he told us that the androids must have sabotaged the system, when they saw us arrive. "There is only one lever still in an operational position. Do you want me to lower it?"

"Yes," I ordered, without giving the question due thought.

The result was more dramatic than I expected. The arm of the crane cracked into two, leaving Peter still clinging to the slim wire rope, now swinging wildly in different directions from a fragmented part of the crane's arm. He struggled to hold on. I turned to Randolph.

"I know what to do," he yelled, as he ran at an accelerated speed to the edge of the cliff and leaped more than 15 feet up in the air and 6 feet outwards, grabbing Peter in his arms. With the help of his exoskeleton suit, he turned, accelerating their forward movement in the direction of the cliff, coming down in a dramatic landing, only inches from its edge. Seconds later what remained of the arm of the crane and the cage fell into the deep, dark abyss below.

"We are safe," I passed a quick message to my Mother.

"Now give Murdoc the order to move out and attack. You, Randolph, and Drager will join them.

"I had only sent the message, when Murdoc and the others rushed up into the bleachers. They were moving rapidly, hitting, dismembering and blasting the enemy androids with their laser guns, sometimes shooting two at a time. Miller, Gordon and the former Governor were just behind Murdoc. 'Flanders and Crawford were showing more fighting power than Reinhart had anticipated,' I smiled.

I want all of you to get off of that mountain fast. There will be five of our combat androids waiting for you at your original point of exit. They will take Peter, Frederic, Jennifer and Wilberly back to your spacecraft, Pamela. You and your group should join forces with Murdoc immediately thereafter."

"Understood," I said slowly, as I led our group down the treacherous mountain slope. "These androids will take good care of you," I said, my eyes focused on Frederic, who had not left his father's side. He rushed towards me, throwing his youthful arms around me, telling me how much he loved me, as I smothered him with kisses.

"Good Luck, Mother!" I said telepathically to Reinhart.

"And for you too! Go and help Murdoc and the others, while Stuart and I give the robots a good show!" I heard her laughter seeping through.

She grabbed Stuart's hand "Wait, Dr. Reinhart," one of the very primitive robots moved into view, standing up-against the protective shield surrounding the Judges. "There is no reason for you to die," it said in a soft, tender tone. "You know as well as we do that even if your son is killed, you can recreate him. So let the Judges and their community have their day."

"I know that you, and your small group, are the gifted intellectual class. Your knowledge of the universe may even surpass mine. Unfortunately you have associated yourselves with a group of autocratic, cruel, sadistic, psychopathic rulers who do not appreciate, but rather exploit, your profound knowledge."

She turned to the android robots. "I choose to destroy you, the Judges and other members of this uncivilized society, but I shall Save," she said the word forcefully, "the android robots, who are our cheering squad today!"

"So be it, Dr. Elisabeth Reinhart. Let the record show that Dr. Reinhart has chosen to die in the confines of our prison's gladiatorial arena located on a small asteroid," the robot replied audaciously, as it leaned up against the protective bubble surrounding the Judges.

Reinhart's lips quirked upwards in a joyous smile as she opened her eyes wide, releasing a powerful laser beam, reducing the robot to tiny pieces. She laughed heartily as she watched the jagged pieces of this pretentious robot create large fissures in the protective shield around the Judges. Before the Judges realized their vulnerability, she turned her laser gun on them and blasted what remained of their protective shielding into tiny pieces.

She chuckled as she watched the Judges struggle to get back up on their feet, before turning to Stuart. "Follow Me!"

"Wait!" he stayed his place. "Why didn't you destroy them?"

"We need to show our force not just to these robots but others that are watching and observing," she said.

"Why don't you just turn into pure energy and blow up these machines?"

Her eyes grew sullen. "Because, my son, I am not certain that I can turn into pure energy," she sighed. "And, assuming I can, I might not be able to return to a corporal form afterwards. And, quite frankly, Stuart, I am not ready to take that risk because I like being human," she replied, a note of amusement in her voice, as she took his hand in hers.

They turned their eyes on the battle field. The armored plated chariot tanks were advancing rapidly in their direction, ripping up turf and randomly firing lasers and blasters, while propelling lethal, toxic fumes in their direction, making it more difficult for Reinhart and Stuart to avoid a direct hit.

She took Stuart's hand in hers, as they moved in zigzags to another part of the arena. "I can filter out the chemicals and am about to give you the same ability." Look at me, trust me," she said as her energy entered inside of him reinforcing his vulnerable organs, like lungs, heart, liver, and his skeletal-muscular system. He turned pale and doubled-over, struggling to catch his breath. She shielded him behind her until he regained his composure.

"Follow me and fire randomly on the chariots," she whispered. "I have quickly studied their offensive. The drivers and the android technicians on board are not programmed to respond to a disorganized attack. I am familiar with their weaponry and lancers and can assure you they are not as sophisticated as they look. We are vulnerable only when their weapons are pointed directly on us, so we shall zigzag. That will confuse both the technicians and the drivers."

Stuart nodded.

He followed her as she anticipated the trajectories of the missiles and led them to safety, moving rapidly, with perfect precision.

"I am going to tell you the game plan," she said, associating me in their discussion. "There are five launchers, evenly spaced, on both sides of these bulky, destructive machines. When we get close enough to these machines, you will take the armored chariot on your right, rushing forward, and firing only if you are detected," she gritted her teeth. "I have given you super human force and speed, so use it!" she ordered. "Your objective is to grab hold of the launcher's angular, metal support. As I observed these five launchers are immobile, the android technicians have no view of the launchers' stationary supports."

"Why make canons, or launchers, immobile. It makes no sense," Stuart questioned.

"It is because the technicians operating these launchers are not programmed to target a specific object. They are programmed to takedown their opponents by firing lasers and blasters randomly and expressing, as well as spraying, lethal toxic gases or liquids."

"Ok" his voice wavering.

"It won't be easy, but you are tall and strong. I cannot upgrade your human body any more. I cannot give you my super powers."

"Don't worry, Mother. I can do what you asked without any problems." He replied.

"You will access the inside of the armored chariot by staying hidden and slinging your body forward from one metallic launch support to another until you reach the back of the chariot. There are only 5 launchers and they are evenly spaced. It will require concentration, but this is something you have mastered."

"So lay low and don't fall!" She warned. "I shall create a diversion, a dramatic side show, to get the attention of the androids on both of these armored chariots. Your objective is to enter through the back door!" Stuart nodded.

"You won't have a problem taking down the android technicians inside the armored chariot, because they have no combat training. But, it won't be easy to break down the door to the control center and destroy the Driver." She smiled slyly. "Wait for me to help you with that." He nodded.

"If I have to make a last minute change of plans, I shall contact you," She said pensively. "Stay concentrated. I shall protect you."

She reached out to him and took him in her arms. "It is my honor to fight alongside of you, my son."

"Be careful, Mother," he replied, as they turned back to the battle. The android drivers had rigged up their armored chariots and were advancing rapidly in their direction, firing an array of toxic chemicals and missiles. Stuart and Reinhart rushed towards them, skirting their attack.

"Go! Do what I said," she mouthed when they were close to the armored chariots. She drew the attention of the two drivers, as she rushed forward, firing randomly at one then the other armored chariot. They kept the pressure on her, continuing their strike, trying to target her.

To their dismay, she outpaced and outjumped their many and varied projectiles. At one moment, she leaped more than 30 feet in the air, firing an array of laser rays, making holes in the sides of their war machines. She definitely had the attention of both drivers, as they engaged in a combined offensive attack against her, veering off in different directions trying to encircle her. Stuart was out of the game for them.

While Stuart and Reinhart created the chaos for the androids on board the armored chariots, Murdoc and the rest of us were holding our own. The android robot spectators were pushing and shoving our enemies out of their way, as they sought to vacate the bleachers, and get closer to the outside of the arena.

Their loud chanting, "Dr. Elisabeth Reinhart," helped us to prevent the combat androids from grouping together and even communicating with each other. The robotic androids, the faithful spectators, were doing what Reinhart hoped for---creating chaos and confusion, making it easier for us to face off with our real enemies on a one to one basis.

Randolph, Mathieu, Diana, Drager and the Group of 5 and myself, as well as our Android military, under the command of Murdoc, were well organized. Murdoc was strategic, decisive, and courageous. He used hand signals, pointing in different directions, to ensure an effective attack or avoid a dangerous onslaught. He seemed to be everywhere at the same time. Each of us in direct contact with him.

"The fight will be to the finish," Crawford shouted over the noise. "These combat androids are not programmed to surrender and they have been trained very well in all forms of martial arts. Be careful!" He warned, as he and Flanders joined forces, using a brand of street fighting, rushing and tripping up the android, and kicking and punching it in a disorganized fashion, which proved to be effective.

Miller, Gordon and the former Governor, Drager, as well as, Murdoc, Diana, Randolph, Mathieu and I were able to execute quick, blistering attacks. Unfortunately, our combat android unit started to wind down, and, to our dismay, was soon overpowered by the prison's android combat force.

"Something is wrong with our combat androids. We can only count on ourselves. Don't let down your guard," Murdoc's voice loud and clear.

Our victory was no longer certain. And, even though our exoskeleton suits protected us from internal injuries and broken bones, there were moments when I, and the others, felt the thrust of an android's punch. Off guard for one second, meant being thrown a considerable distance and suffering a hard, jolting landing.

'I can't speak for the others, but I wondered how I would have been able to engage in this kind of violent battle, against super charged combat androids, if Reinhart had not given me more physical force and provided me with an exoskeleton suit.'

"If she would just destroy those wretched armored chariots, she could blow up these combat androids in a glance," Randolph screamed to me in passing.

"How are all of you holding up," Reinhart contacted me telepathically. "I am very much aware of what you are facing and admire your heroic acts to eliminate our enemies."

"We are tired," I replied in a curt voice.

"What is wrong?"

"I don't know how much longer we can continue. And something strange happened minutes ago. Our combat androids began to falter, like they were running out of power or their programming was breaking down. A number of them have been stomped on and damaged by the prison combat androids, who now have the advantage in hand to hand combat. We humans are actually protecting our android combat force, instead of fighting alongside of them. We need this battle to come to an end."

"Understood. On my side, I am running out of patience. I am very proud of all of you, but it is time for me to finish the battle," she replied. "Hang in there! I am going to end this soon. But, do not abandon your posts before I give the order."

She contacted Stuart, telepathically. He had just fended off a disorganized, seemingly infantile, attack from 5 android technicians inside the armored chariot. He smashed two of them up against each other, and then smashed the third one up against the wall. He heard their systems shut down simultaneously and turned to the remaining two android technicians who jumped to their feet. He charged, full force, grabbing their necks in his hands and squeezing down.

To his surprise, like the three other androids, they did not try to defend themselves. Reinhart was right, they were not programmed to fight. They had no combat skills. He tossed them on the floor and stomped on their chests until they laid immobile. He was now in front of the fortified door but was unable to break through it and destroy the android driver.

"Stuart, our Rat-Human Allies were right. The driver's cabin locks down and can only be opened by using a code or password." She replied. "You and the others are war torn and tired and I am running out of patience, so I must bring this combat to an end. Abandon your post now and run to safety! Get off that armored chariot!" She ordered.

"Understood!" he replied, as he rushed to the back exit. "The driver is still operational," he added.

"I know. Run!"

While Stuart jumped off the chariot, moving at top speed away from it, her piercing scream split the air, drawing the attention of the two drivers in her direction as their armored chariots came to rapid halts. She rushed forward, firing her laser guns randomly, until she was close enough to her assigned armored chariot. She jumped onto the roof. With lasers in each hand, she fired with precision, as she ran rapidly along the length of the roof, firing downwards, creating a long fissure, exposing the 5 android techni-cians, who backed up, huddling together, making it so easy for her to blast the five of them into tiny pieces.

She jumped off the roof and moved to the front of the two ar-mored chariots.

"I am giving you, the drivers, a chance. Surrender or Melt down!"

"We are not programmed to surrender," one of the drivers replied.

"Fire full force on the human!" Both drivers gave the order to their technicians. They waited, as Reinhart moved closer to them.

"Your technicians are no longer active." She replied.

She gave them a few minutes to make her another offer, but none was forthcoming. "If you cannot surrender, then self-destruct."

"That order must come from the Judges." Reinhart turned in the direction of the judges, huddling together.

"You should be proud of your allegiance to your superiors, even though they never deserved it." She replied, as she spun in tight, rapid circles, augmenting her physical force and producing a full power build up behind her eyes. When the moment arrived, she opened her eyes wide, releasing a coherent beam of radiation, zapping the two chariots into oblivion with a high intensity laser ray.

"We finished our business. Do you need help, Pamela?" She con-tacted me telepathically.

"Yes!" I exclaimed.

"Tell Flanders and Crawford to gather up whatever is left of our combat androids. I shall rapidly up-grade their programming so they will be more powerful than the prison's android combat force. Continue to fight. Stuart will help the time I need to upgrade the androids."

"Understood," I replied, in a quavering voice.

Reinhart grabbed Stuart's hand as they rushed across the are-na towards the bleachers. She glanced for a second at the 3 judges huddled together, and snickered.

"Mother, blast them," Stuart pleaded. "Blast all of our enemies into tiny pieces. Why do we have to continue this fight?"

"Refusing to fight, bringing a quick end to this battle, is what my enemies want," she chuckled. "We will be seen by others as super-natural creatures rather than legendary humans."

The robot spectators applauded them, as they moved aside letting Reinhart and Stuart pass between them. "Keep an eye on the Judges," she told the robots. "Don't let them leave."

They carried out her order, encircling the outside of the Judges' high box, and blocking the stairway leading up to it. 'Why did they obey her order,' I wondered, just before I grabbed one of our enemies from behind and threw it 15 feet in the air, watching it fall in between the bleachers.

Randolph rushed to me, pulling me away from the fight, just as Stuart and Reinhart appeared. "I have to upgrade our combat force," she called out as she practically flew to the place where Flanders and Crawford were waiting.

"Continue to fight!" she ordered.

It did not take her very long to resolve the problem. "Someone sabotaged our combat androids," she said to the Group of 5. "Clever," she repeated several times, before adding, "there was no way we could have anticipated this abrupt, rapid downgrading of their combat ability," she grimaced." We shall find the answer to this conundrum later. I have upgraded them. They are now more powerful than their combat android adversaries."

The Group of 5 moved aside letting our combat androids pass, as Reinhart motioned to the humans to join us.

"I don't understand why they powered down," Murdoc commented. She shrugged her shoulders. "How were you able to reverse their degradation and upgrade their force in a matter of minutes?" Murdoc asked.

"My voice is registered in their command center. I can override other programs or even up-grade their military tactical skills and physical force. Something, you just witnessed," she commented. "Everyone sit back and watch!"

Like we were watching a film, we sat back cheering and applauding our combat force. There was not a second of hesitation, before they grabbed an opponent, flinging it in the air, bashing its body up against the hard cement, or ripping off an arm or leg when their opponent sprung upwards, seeking a more advantageous position.

It seemed unrealistic, machines fighting machines in rapid hand to hand combat, launching rocket fists at each other, moving fast, mesmerizing us with their knowledge and efficiency in boxing and all forms of martial arts. Unemotional, not handicapped by a fear of death, they did not waste time determining the best tactical move to make to bring down an opponent. They used brutal force. Destroying the enemy was their goal and they achieved it.

Within a short 30 minutes our androids nodded to Reinhart who applauded them.

"We have eliminated the enemy androids." They shouted in unison.

"You will now collect what remains of them and put them in the containers at the end of the tunnel." She said, pointing to the tunnel they used to enter the arena.

She turned to us, informing us that our allies have a ship on route to pick up these combat androids.

Murdoc grabbed Reinhart's arm with a strong grip, reminding her that she would have to return Murdoc, Stuart and myself to our former state, or downgrade our physical force.

"Why didn't you upgrade them from a distance?" he growled. "My body is aching. I can just imagine how Randolph and others who did not receive your special...booster shot must be feeling." His eyes were smoldering with anger.

She drew in a deep breath. "Because I couldn't fight a battle on two fronts. I knew that you would protect all the humans, as well as the Group of 5. I also had ultimate confidence in you to call the right moves," she said. "But, I was not 100% certain that you would not look the other way if Crawford was in difficulty," she chuckled and we all joined in.

"Ok." He turned to Crawford. "I would have saved you!" Crawford raised his eyebrows. "But, what are we going to do now? What about the Judges and your crazy, robot admirers?"

"I will have to ask our Rat-Human Allies to help us put this prison to rest; clean up the android debris and fumigate the cells. I shall take care of the Judges now," she stood up and applauded all of us, before she slowly walked down the bleachers, crossed the arena and stood looking up at the oval shaped box where the Judges were hiding, the robots blocking their exit from the interior and exterior.

We watched from our high bleachers. When she was in front of the Judges Box, she stopped, her eyes moving rapidly in their sockets, as she calculated the rate of acceleration she would need in a single leap to reach the height of 150 feet, as well as the rate of deceleration, to assure a safe landing in the Judge's box. She took deep, rhythmed breaths before raising her fists high in the air, moving them upwards in forceful punches as she stomped and then bounced on her feet, tossing her long, heavy mane of hair wildly in the air, pumping up the energy she needed to lift off.

At the right moment, she rapidly bent her knees low and used the force of her lower body to propel herself rapidly upwards, like a missile, into the air, before decelerating for a delicate landing inside the Judges' Box. The Judges lay prostrate on the floor, their heads shielded under their folded arms.

The arena and the bleachers were alive with cheering friends and admirers. When the excitement died down, she turned to the cowering Judges.

"Stand up, you miserable cowards. I want the pleasure of looking you in the eyes before I blow you to pieces," she ordered and they obeyed, moving quickly to their feet.

The robots roared incessantly, making it impossible for us to hear what was transpiring between Reinhart and the Judges. She was aware of that and connected telepathically with me so I could tell the others.

"Do you have anything to say in your defense?"

"We were only following orders, Dr. Elisabeth Reinhart," the smaller Judge, who spoke to her earlier in the day in a mocking tone, replied in a shaky voice.

"Who gave you the orders to kill me and my family, friends and allies?"

"Your enemies." The medium-sized Judge answered.

"My enemies," her voice echoed outwards. "At this moment, my only enemies are the three of you." They lowered their heads. "My patience is waning," her lips pressed tightly together.

"We are telling you the truth. We were to kill your family and friends, but not you," the tallest member replied.

"Why?"

"Because that is what they wanted. We simply negotiated the right to execute your family and friends in our usual fashion, through gladiatorial style fights," the smaller judge added. "The robots have always enjoyed this rather gory form of entertainment."

"What do these presumed enemies of mine look like?" she questioned.

The tallest android replied. "They have no physical form. They are ethereal, supernatural creatures. They appeared before us several weeks ago in the form of long strands of blinding white light." Reinhart unconsciously took a step back, like she was distancing herself from the creatures they were describing.

"We promised to carry out their orders and deliver you to them," the middle-sized Judge replied.

"Now, what will happen to us?" the little one screeched.

"Yes, what will happen to us," they asked in unison. "We were only following orders from your enemies. This is your fault, Dr. Elisabeth Reinhart."

The three of them began to wobble and then tremble violently, like their systems were breaking down. She reached out, trying to steady one of them, as her hands gripped the smallest judge.

"Focus on my eyes," she said in a soft tone, "I can help you."

But before she could open her eyes wide enough to enter its systems, the Judge fell with a loud thump, alongside the other two.

She turned to the 12 primitive robots with exceptional minds. "It is your turn to find rest after all these years of bad judicial decisions," she said, as she opened her eyes wide, entered their systems and shut them down. She told me later, she wanted to access their knowledge and memory banks in the future.

"The robots were not able to hear what was happening," she told me telepathically. "So, to keep them jovial, until we can eventually deactivate their systems, I shall address our robot cheering squad," she chuckled.

"We have dethroned our enemies and yours! The Victory is ours! I shall take all of you to a better place; a place where you will not be exploited and will be appreciated by other androids and humans alike."

The robots bowed their heads in deference to her, before vigorously applauding her. She smiled down on them.

Her eyes drifted slowly from the robots crowding the arena to us in the bleachers. "Have all the prison combat androids been crated," she asked me telepathically.

"Our combat androids informed me that they carried out your orders," I replied.

"Please ask the Group of 5 to come and replace me in the Judges' box," she sighed. "I cannot leave these Judges unattended." They left immediately.

"The Judges are in pieces and I have deactivated the small group of intellectual robots. We shall let the robotic spectators dance and celebrate, before we shut them down. Our allies have another spaceship on the way to pick them up and deliver them to the *Redeemer*," I heard a weary sigh.

"You sound tired, Mother."

"Tired? No. Worried?" she replied slowly. "My mind is opening and images, memories, of my very, very distant past might soon be upon me."

"Don't worry, Mother. You have always fought for what is right and just. That is certainly what you did in the past." I heard her laugh approvingly.

When the Group of 5 arrived, she jumped back into the arena and rushed to us. Within a few minutes she had deactivated our combat androids and contacted our Alien allies, who arrived rapidly, helping us crate our combat unit, before moving them outside the arena onto Mathieu's spaceship. "Mathieu, leave!" She ordered. "Our Rat-Human Allies will guide you back to the *Redeemer*." He nodded and dashed through the long tunnel.

"By the way, where is Oliver?" She asked, like an afterthought.

"He is sitting behind me," Stuart replied.

"Thank you, Oliver, for everything you did for us," his eyes turned in the direction of her voice. "After we deactivate the robot spectators, you will board Pamela's ship, alongside Stuart. You played a vital role in the success of our mission and for that reason, I shall not deactivate you. You shall be given the right to work alongside the Group of 5."

His robotic eyes flashed and his jaw dropped open, as he rushed to Stuart's side.

"Follow me! We have to shut down the robots." She jumped from one level in the bleachers to another. On the ground, the robots, still celebrating, moved aside to let us pass. "Gather up the robots," she ordered. "The Group of 5 and I shall join you soon."

We learned later that our Rat-Human Allies delivered special resistant containers with an access code that only Reinhart could activate. The Group of 5 helped her load the judges into one container and the intellectual group into another. The Aliens agreed to deliver these packages to the *Redeemer* after Reinhart installed a sealed chamber on our vessel.

"Are you going to put the robot spectators in crates as well?" Miller asked. "It seems sad. They worship you!" She said vigorously

"It is the easiest way to move them onto our vessel," she replied. "I didn't say that we would not reactivate them in the future- that is after we have adjusted their programming."

"And what about Jennifer, Peter and Frederic?" Crawford asked.

"I would like to examine the 3 of them—reassure myself that no microchip in the shape of an insect," she wrinkled her nose, "like the one we found in Wilberly's brain, was inserted in their brains, as well. There are four cryogenic tubes on board Pamela's ship." She turned to me and I nodded.

"Why not use cryogenic skin?" Crawford queried.

"You are getting careless, Crawford. You know that I need their DNA, or genetic code, to program the skin. And, that takes time!"

All remaining humans were grouped around Reinhart, Murdoc gently caressing her hand. "Did you notice Wilberly's passive behavior during our battle? He is in great physical condition and yet Pamela and Randolph told me that he stood like a disassociated onlooker." He turned to me.

"He was violent with me when he awakened in the Center, under that pseudo-name, Captain Cray. But then he was under the control of my enemies and once he discovered his true identity, or that of Colonel Wilberly, he appeared normal," her eyes closed in thought.

"Being trained in military combat," she picked up "is not the same as confronting and physically fighting a real life battle. And, he might be more a defensive than an offensive player," her eyes narrowed.

"He is with Peter, Frederic and Jennifer now?" Heads nodded. "I shall examine him when we get back to the *Redeemer*," she said, before adding that she had rapidly scanned our brains with her x-ray vision and did not notice any anomalies or implants in any of us.

"Relax for a few minutes," she said, as she and the Group of 5 approached the robot spectators.

"They seemed like thousands from a distance, when in fact, they are only 50 in number," Crawford spoke.

"What is the fastest way?" Flanders asked.

"'I'll show you," she chuckled. She asked them to stand in a straight line, after which she thanked them for cheering all members of her military force, humans and androids, onward to victory.

"I am going to be honest with you," their eyes were focused on her, "I intend to bring you with me, but to transport you, I need to deactivate your systems, or put you to sleep. Do you trust me?" They nodded. She passed slowly in front of each of them, downloading her voice in their command center.

She passed by each of them a second time to be certain that she had control, before giving the order to Shut Down. The robots toppled one after the other onto the ground.

"We shall crate them and deliver them to the *Redeemer*," Minerva startled everyone, except Reinhart, who nodded approvingly.

Murdoc suggested that Stuart, Reinhart and I join with him in making a final tour of the prison facilities to be certain that there were no Alien life forms or Androids hiding. We agreed.

We stayed together, leaving the Arena, moving into the interior of the prison. The living quarters, meeting rooms and gathering places set aside for the robots, androids, and Judges were on ground level. These cold, airless, suffocating, low lit alcoves were designed to maintain the climate necessary to insure maximum performance from the various members of the android forces, as well as computers, surveillance systems, communications systems, and other devices, providing safety and security for the prison.

And, as we noticed, from the absence of cozy couches and beds, the Androids did not need comfort, when they entered into sleep mode. As there were more than 20 empty rooms, we concluded that they shut down individually, or as groups, regularly.

The atmosphere changed the moment we left the Androids' private quarters, going in the direction of the prison cells and torture chamber. Putrid odors of excrements, rotting flesh, from diversified, unidentifiable alien species, as well as the abrasive odors of melting metal and acid-rich chemicals filled the air. We involuntarily coughed, covering our faces in the folds of our uniforms.

I shuttered when I gazed upon the fading colors, principally reddish-brown and greyish-green, and the thick, sometimes paper-thin textured lines of body fluid from former prisoners, splattered haphazardly on the walls of the prison cells.

The single torture chamber was only 20 feet in diameter. It was easy to imagine the prisoner strapped in the single, solid, steel chair, unable to defend itself. There were no instruments of torture like knives, spears, whips, clubs or other vile tools used in past civilizations to inflict pain and mayhem.

The steel chair, in the center of this circular room, was encrusted with the remains of former prisoners who died from powerful blows to their bodies, when they refused to answer questions, or bow down to the prison guards. Those who survived repetitive beatings were certainly sent into the arena in a weakened condition to suffer death at the hands of android gladiators.

I stepped back into Stuart's open arms. "They tortured Jennifer over and over again," his voice trembling as he spoke. "And, then they put her back together and started again. How many times did they punish her for refusing to reveal our names and intentions?"

"Well said," Murdoc responded forcefully, inspiring all of us to let our voices be heard, praising Jennifer and those who passed before her.

When we regained our calm, Reinhart forged ahead and we fell into a slow, sauntering pace. When we caught up with her, she was sitting in a small alcove, holding her head between her hands, something that made her look human—that is it—human, with all the vulnerability and insecurities that go with being human. "Are you alright, my brave warriors?" she asked, sensing our presence.

"Just fine," Murdoc spoke for the three of us.

"You fought well. You honored me," she said in a high-spirited voice. "Unfortunately, I must take back that which I gave you. Pamela and Stuart, your powers will develop with time. And, Murdoc, your powers will appear in full splendor the day you discover who you really are."

"Elisabeth, I don't like riddles!" Murdoc replied bluntly.

"You must cooperate and let me enter your minds," she replied, ignoring Murdoc's remark. "It is imperative that your powers develop with time and in accordance with your emotional intelligence." She took a deep breath. "You now know what awaits you. It is a goal to achieve."

"Perhaps, my Elisabeth, I shall be as strong and brilliant, or even stronger and more brilliant than you," Murdoc teased and she chuckled. "Ok, I am ready. I like being in charge of my own body!"

"I am ready, Mother, to let my powers develop in their own time and in their own way," Stuart spoke.

"And you, Pamela," I nodded.

"Look at me! Open your eyes wide!"

Like in a hypnotic trance, any trepidations at bay, we followed her instructions. Initially, we felt her strong, vibrant energy, pushing our faces upwards, until our eyes met hers. Her corporal form seemed to vanish into a blinding white light that passed painlessly through each of us, returning us to our former level of physical force, while reinstating our prior levels of cognitive and emotional intelligence.

"How do you feel?" she asked

"The same as usual," Murdoc shrugged his shoulders and we followed his example. "By the way," he pointed directly behind her, "our Rat-Human Allies' holograms are flashing!"

"Your victory was very impressive, Dr. Reinhart." Concordia spoke. "Our ship landed. We can transport those containers back to the *Redeemer* for you."

"Excellent."

"What do you want to do with this asteroid?" Before Reinhart could answer, Concordia added that it was possible for them to destroy the asteroid without causing any waves of turbulence that might otherwise radiate outwards into other sections of the universe.

"It could always serve as a base for us, if we ever engaged in an intergalactic war." Reinhart replied reflectively. "But, as this aster-oid is a repugnant place, a reminder of how cruel life forms, as well as androids, can be to each other, I believe we have no choice but to destroy it." I heard a hint of sadness in her voice.

"Agreed!" Concordia replied.

"Did you notice any insect life on this asteroid?" she asked, off the cuff.

"As we mentioned before, we have only had contact with ordi-nary insect life, and arachnids, prevalent on the planet Earth, but not with any highly intelligent Alien Insects," Nemesis protested.

"And yet I am convinced they exist," color flaring her cheeks.

There was a long silence, before Kratos replied, diplomatical-ly. "We were perhaps so absorbed in our quest to eradicate hid-eous and dangerous hybrids that we overlooked other, less vis-ible, yet equally treacherous and highly intelligent life forms. Our apologies..."

"Your apologies are accepted," she replied.

"We all admired your leadership ability. Your forces rapidly and effectively wiped out your enemies," Minerva commented, chang-ing the subject.

"Your strategy was alarming in its precision and effectiveness. It was almost as if this was not the first time you've fought this kind of battle," Zelus replied.

"This was the first and, hopefully, the last time!"

"We contacted you several different times on a cerebral level, offering to intervene. Why, Dr. Reinhart, did you refuse our military help?" Thoth queried.

"Simply because this was our battle to win...Earthlings, in all our different forms, fighting a common enemy." She took a deep breath. "If we have other enemies lurking about, they will think twice be-fore getting in the way of the inhabitants of the planet Earth!"

She pretended not to hear Minerva's final remark wafting in the fading waves of their holograms. "So we made the right deci-sion, Dr. Reinhart. We shall live much longer as your friend, than we would have, as your enemy."

Chapter 24: Mixed Feelings

"Pamela, would you please ask everyone to begin boarding?" Reinhart, striding a slim ledge high above the entrance to the cavern, called out to me.

"No problem," I replied, as I turned to leave, stopping from time to time to look back over my shoulder to reassure myself that she was alright.

"Where is she?" Murdoc asked, after I instructed the group to begin boarding.

"She is overseeing the cargo planes," I said as I pointed in her direction.

"A rather dangerous place to be," he replied as he climbed the column at a blistering pace and sat down next to her.

"Elisabeth, my tender Elisabeth," I heard him say. I turned for a second and saw her reach out to him, before she leaned her head against his broad shoulder.

"Pamela, I want you, Stuart, Diana, and Randolph to take the large craft used to transport Stuart, Peter, Frederic and Jennifer to this miserable prison. The cryogenic tanks are on board that craft and I don't want to entrust Peter, Frederic and Jennifer to anyone else." She called out.

"Drager, you have the five Malwarian androids on your ship?"

"Affirmative," he replied. "I can pilot the craft on my own."

"Crawford, you will take Wilberly and Oliver with your Group on the craft that we used to arrive on this planet. And, Aegir, you will come with me in that ship capable of surpassing our ships in speed and maneuverability." She pointed to a small reconnaissance spaceship offered to her by our Rat Human Allies. "We shall lead the way."

"Dr. Reinhart, our Rat-Human Allies are appearing." Flanders called out, pointing to the flickering holograms.

Kratos spoke. "The containers are on board our cargo ships and will be dropped off on the *Redeemer*," he said. "Do you need our help setting the course for your return?"

"Thank you, but I have already programmed the ships with the easiest and fastest route back."

"Don't forget, Kratos," she continued, "you promised to keep the Judges with you and transfer them to your main vessel to be kept in a fortified vault until we have installed an impenetrable one on the *Redeemer*," Reinhart replied.

"Yes. The 3 Judges are in an impenetrable container along with their twelve judicial advisors. The container will be placed in a secure vault, awaiting your order to deliver it to you."

"I am ready for lift off," Mathieu signaled her from his spaceship. "The android combat force are in their containers."

"Lift off granted," Reinhart replied.

"We have verified the route your vessels will be taking; an excellent choice, so we will have our cargo ship follow behind," Minerva replied. "Is there anything else we can do for the moment?"

"The hybrids?"

"We know, Dr. Reinhart, that they had telepathic communications with you. We have an excellent working relationship with them, since they have become more civilized."

"I was in contact with a high ranking officer."

"We were unable to decipher the content of the exchanges, but caution you to remain aloof and reflective when interacting with any of them." Her slim lips twitched. "They are a very intelligent hybridized life form."

"You can count on me to bring peace to this part of the universe," she replied, somewhat ambiguously. The holograms disappeared and we prepared to leave.

"As always, Pamela, I shall remain cerebrally connected with you throughout the flight back to the *Redeemer*." She confirmed.

She sent a general order to all human and android members: "This order is indisputable. You shall not accept any communication from any members on board the *Benevolence* regardless of the nature and/or pertinence of the request. I am the only party authorized to accept or initiate a communication. Is that understood?"

"Affirmative," came from each member of her crew.

Are you ready to board that sleek, rapid vessel our Rat-Human friends have offered?" She turned to Murdoc and he nodded.

"This technologically advanced spaceship is a true sign of friendship." Her eyes glowed. "I have already mapped out our return trip, so we shall lead our group back to the *Redeemer!*" Enthusiasm ringing in her voice.

"Where do you stand with the hybridized aliens, half plant and half animal?" Murdoc brought up the subject as they walked in the direction of their private spaceship.

"I would be suspicious of them." He remarked. "They are like schizophrenic people, Elisabeth. The vegetable side of their personality seems relatively pacifistic, but the animal side has one objective...to devour!"

"My contact with the high ranking officer that stayed behind, risking its life to make contact with me, was reassuring. I was direct with my accusations and the hybridized alien was as well, accepting responsibility for torturing and devouring other life forms to satisfy its wicked, ravenous animal side."

"Ok, but..."

"It claimed that with time their ravenous half has become more civilized. It did not, however, go into detail on how the plant side convinced the animal side to respect life forms, at least avoid cruel, inhuman practices, by killing for pleasure." She admitted.

"Certainly their animal side still craves energy dense sources of protein, or meat, but is consuming in moderation. They might even raise animals for food on their planet, like humans did in the past and might do so in the future."

"So you trust these hybridized aliens?" Murdoc queried.

"I don't trust anyone, so why would I trust them," she flicked her hand. "What I understood is that these hybridized plant-animal aliens no longer kill for the sake of killing, or stage events, like the one we engaged in today, forcing their eatable prey to fight, to entertain them, before devouring the winners, and the remains of the losers."

"So, you believe that they have evolved as a hybridized species?"

"It is the impression I got during my rather brief telepathic communication with the Plant-Animal hybrid," she huffed. "But of course it could just be an intellectual trap—pretending that they are by nature humanitarian, but were condemned to be indecent because of their insatiable animal side."

"Clearly, both Alien groups want to be in an Alliance with us," she paused. "Perhaps the Plant-Animal Aliens are not as numerous as our Rat- Human Allies suggest and they could be eradicated easily, if they plotted against them and us." Murdoc nodded.

"But, there was something else this Plant-Animal Alien mentioned that disturbs me," she confided.

"What did it say?"

"Yes, it might help to get your impression," she sighed. It said: 'It is your defiance, failure to embrace that which you were that has caused chaos in the universe. And, your refusal to acknowledge and confront your past has made it possible for your true enemies to grow stronger and stronger. Time is running out!'"

Murdoc stepped back, as a pained expression of disbelief crossed his face. He pondered the subject for a few minutes before approaching her and gently raising her chin, until their eyes met. "Mind games," he articulated slowly.

"We go back a very long time, Aegir. We never suppressed our feeling for each other, but we might have suppressed our past, a very distant past." She spoke with regret and shame.

Murdoc did not reply. He let his eyes drift over the asteroid's barren wasteland, concentrating on what she said, hoping to solve the puzzle.

"I have been obsessed with insects." He turned back in her direction. "Only today I realized that it is not all insects but arachnids that play havoc with my mind. But, why? Perhaps if I concentrate on arachnids, force myself to remember my interaction with them in a very distant past, things will become clearer."

Murdoc's self-composure returned and he took her hand in his. "I believe that all the ships are ready to leave. It is time for us to concentrate on the events of today," he said, pointing to the spaceship, pulling her along with him in a lively sprint.

"This ship reminds me of the aero-mobiles in the underground city," Murdoc commented, as he examined the control panel. "High tech, no doubt. Do you understand how it functions?" he teased, as she cracked a loud laugh.

"Is everyone ready for take-off?" she asked over the audio system.

"We need a couple more minutes," I replied. "I want to make a last minute check of the cryogenic tanks."

During her brief pause, Murdoc spoke. "Maybe you need to let your emotions develop more, show feelings. You know you have feelings. Show everyone how human you really are."

"Why not?" She laughed her rippling laugh.

"So we agree that you have feelings?" he persisted.

"You are talking about you and me?

"Maybe just about us-you and me, and yet it is evident that you have feelings for Pamela and Stuart, in fact for all of us, including the Group of 5."

"I enjoy being surrounded by those I know, trust ---and can control."

"Everything is clear for take-off," I informed my Mother.

She ordered the Group of 5 to begin the count-down. The space-ships were in a lineal formation, properly distanced for back-to-back liftoffs on Reinhart's order. "Even though I have programmed your vessels' route, stay alert!"

My spaceship was responding perfectly, as we moved rapidly in the direction of the *Redeemer*. Reinhart, now absent from my thoughts, I turned in the direction of Randolph, his eyes meeting mine. "You want me to take over?"

"Not for the moment," I replied, "maybe later."

"Ok, I helped you save him. I like the man. He is a friend. But..." Randolph began.

"We had this discussion too many times. You know where I stand." I replied emphatically and he let the subject drop.

It seemed like we had only just lifted off when Joseph's voice came through on all the vessels.

"Dr. Reinhart, we are opening the landing gate. Can't wait to have you all back safe and sound!" he added.

"I don't know about the rest of you, but I am aching everywhere," Stuart grumbled. Diana, Randolph and I chimed in.

"Fortunately, the exoskeleton suits gave us more force and agility to fight, but I wonder if we might be badly bruised anyway," I replied. "We won't know until we take off our suits!"

"Don't worry, Stuart," Diana replied in a low, pigmented tone. "I shall take good care of you... and you of me?" I saw her reach out and lightly stroke his hand.

'Well, sex is definitely on the agenda,' passed through my mind, as I pulled myself up straight in my seat, my hands tightly gripping my arm rests, my face, stern, displaying a cold, don't touch me attitude. My right eye discretely wandered off, catching a glimpse of Randolph, leaning back in his chair, his eyes focused straight ahead.

The androids unloaded everything so rapidly, moving Reinhart's group of robot admirers or fan club, our Malwarian enemies, and whatever was left of the prison's security force to the warehouse section where they would remain inside their tight, impenetrable containers.

Our combat androids were moved to the R and D section for minor repairs. The cryogenic tanks of Peter, Frederic and Jennifer were delivered to the hospital section of the medical unit. Wilberly was ordered to accompany his comrades for a routine physical.

"Rebecca, I think that Wilberly needs to relax. Give him a light tranquilizer and let him rest in one of the beds." She nodded. "And don't initiate the awakening process for Peter, Frederic or Jennifer. I shall take care of that later."

"I think we need time out, showers, rest and ...," Reinhart announced, as she grabbed Murdoc and headed to their room. Stuart and Diana were already on their way to their private quarters.

"But, Dr. Reinhart, we should contact Earth?" Joseph called out, as she disappeared around the corner.

Randolph had disappeared by the time I left the medical unit. I headed towards my bedroom. The door was ajar, making my heart beat rapidly and my legs tremble. Stepping inside the room and finding myself alone was not what I expected...and not what I really wanted. I threw my dirty exoskeleton suit on the floor and stepped into the tiny shower.

As the water was on a timer, I sudsed up before pulling the chord. I tried to lean my head back and let the water rush over me and wash away the dust. But, I could feel only the pain and scars of battle. I saw a large dark blue bruise on my upper left arm and felt sharp pain in my elbow. My neck was so stiff, I had difficulty moving it. A long, dark, nasty bruise curled around my upper right leg and my swollen hip bone throbbed. I caught myself, grabbing the shower head, preventing a fall, as my left ankle slid out from under my leg. Every part of my body ached. 'If only Reinhart were here, she would put me back together,' passed through my thoughts.

'I ache everywhere,' I said in a weak voice, hoping she might hear me. 'I might have been crippled without the exoskeleton suit. I never want to fight a war again!'

I heard her laughter, as she connected with me, and then felt her energy pass through me. The pain disappeared. "Thank you, Mother," I said out loud.

I slipped into the long, white robe, hanging on the solitary hook and sat on the side of the bed, my back to the door, a peaceful silence replacing the cacophony of battle cries, my legs dangling, now moving freely, painlessly, when I felt his arms move around me.

"What took you so long?" I teased.

He moved onto his back and pulled me down next to his warn-torn body, covered with large, dark bruises. "You don't need this," he whispered, drawing my attention away from his injuries to his sparkling eyes and shining smile.

I laid my head on his chest. His hot breath on the tip of my ear, sending chills of desire rushing through me. He delicately released me from my robe and pulled me tightly up against him, stroking my long, wavy hair.

"I love you, Pamela, and shall always love you," his voice shaky. "But...," he said in a weak, tired voice.

I placed the tip of my finger on his lips. "You must rest. We must rest. And, what better way to recuperate from the strains of war than to find comfort in each other's arms." He smiled up at me, as he drifted off to sleep.

I woke up full of energy before the wake up music played.

"Randolph," he wrapped his arms around me.

"We cannot escape it."

"What are you talking about, Pamela?"

"We are them, Randolph." He drew his legs up into a sitting position. "You don't see it, but now I do. We were playful lovers in the past, but our passion grew."

"Of course it did," his eyes intense.

"As my symbiote, she brought me more than her knowledge, she brought me her likes, dislikes, and her undying love for Murdoc, your father," I sighed. "We fell into their trap."

"Are you saying that what we feel is what they feel for each other? That our love is not real," He protested.

"No, ours is very real. That is the problem."

"So we were manipulated?" I nodded.

"Personally, I don't care," he continued. "I was attracted to you from the moment we met, long before she became your symbiote."

"It was not her," he continued, "but that miserable Group of 5. They must have recreated me, making me a close likeness to Murdoc, to please Reinhart if ever she accepted to merge with a symbiote. They are, as I have always said, completely diabolical, and now she has given them their emotional configurations. I don't trust them."

"They are her dedicated servants." I said, under my breath, as Reinhart's voice came over the intercom. "And, Randolph, I too was attracted to you the moment I met you." I took a deep breath. "I think that Peter will understand." I said, bringing a broad smile to Randolph's face.

"Meet me in the lounge in 15 minutes," Reinhart ordered.

"Run and get dressed." I pushed Randolph who moved slowly to his feet, stumbling slightly.

"By the way, Pamela, why don't you have any bruises?"

"Oh, I did. I was in terrible shape once I removed my exoskeleton suit, but, well, Elisabeth is my Mother."

Chapter 25: Obsessions

Only the members of the Group of 5 and Oliver were absent from the meeting. All other members of our Group, including Mathieu, Isabel, Rebecca, Tirence, Jason, Joseph and Samuel, were present, in the lounge. Before the meeting could begin, our Alien Allies, the Rat-Humans, contacted us, in lifelike three dimensional hologram images.

"We have strategy to discuss," Minerva opened the discussion. "And, we need to come to a common accord with respect to the Plant-Animal Aliens."

"I was in contact with the one that was rescued by its compatriots before the end of our battle. He communicated by way of mental telepathy and seemed pleased to meet me. He claimed that they were overseeing the activities of the Malwarian Androids, for what reason I don't know." Reinhart replied.

"Did the Plant-Animal Alien say anything else?" Minerva asked.

"It mentioned that as their animal side was ravenous and difficult to control, they acquiesced, on occasion, allowing their animal side to satisfy its craving for meat."

"Do you trust them?" Kratos went straight to the point.

"I am uncertain about the credibility of anything they said." Reinhart sighed. "Even their contention that they took control over the Malwarian Androids is dubious because these androids could not be perverted by simple mental telepathy. They needed to have derisive, infectious programming introduced into their systems, something I verified, before shutting them down."

"They addressed you by name?" Minerva queried.

"Yes, the Hybridized Alien addressed me by name, but that is not surprising because my name is in the memory bank of the Malwarian Androids," she answered.

"By the way, Dr. Reinhart, why were these very sophisticated, well preserved androids, with highly complicated and developed systems of protective and defensive programming, unable to resist what must have been a large gamete of malware?"

"Gamers!" She replied audaciously, hoping to put an end to this discussion.

"Yes, we heard about the Malwarian Androids combined attacks of alien enemies residing in a virtual world," Minerva replied pensively.

"Gaming," Reinhart took a deep breath, "The way in which our 6 androids became so mentally deranged and dangerous was probably due to the way in which individual gamers gained access to their software and polluted it." She took a deep breath. "Remarkably, they have become incredibly adept fighter pilots."

"Of course these androids did not understand the context of gaming which they were never programmed to participate in." She chuckled. "Perhaps just the boredom that their human sides experienced could have been the impetus for this activity."

"Nonetheless I am inclined to believe that the Plant-Animal Aliens introduced them to gaming, like the injured Plant-Animal Alien insinuated during our brief conversation, to control and observe them." She smiled.

She turned in our direction, addressing us. "They, unlike the Group of 5, were a test group. The Group of 5 is malware-resistant."

"We picked up disturbance in your ship as you were preparing for lift off from the Malwarians' planet. Have you befriended them?" Thoth weighed in, redirecting the subject.

"Yes, they contacted me. I would not go so far as to say that I befriended them," she replied in a huff. "I didn't share this ridiculous conversation with you, because I had more urgent things to attend to, like saving my family and friends."

"And their telepathic message," she continued, "informing me that I would inevitably meet them and embrace them as faithful friends, seemed to be more a practiced speech than an offer of cooperation. As such, it appears they have no intention of leaving this sector."

She turned back to our Rat-Human Allies. "I don't like being interrogated and I detest being lied to!" Her gaze narrowed as strong waves of anger animated her voice.

"I don't understand," Concordia replied calmly.

"The Hybridized Plant-Animal aliens are not your enemies. They are your Allies and have been your Allies for a long time, the reason why you wanted to warn them about the explosives. You wanted to save their lives, give them the time they needed to safely leave the planet." She took a deep breath. "If you want my help, my friendship, and an alliance with Earthlings, you must speak honestly."

"Then, Wake Up, Dr. Reinhart!" Thoth hurled. "Remember who you are and who your true enemies are! Our safety, our lives, peace in the universe depends upon you, because you are the only one who can take our enemies down!"

"No doubt!" She sent them a steely gaze, as her hands moved together in tight fists.

'Her patience is waning,' I thought.

"You know more about what happened over the past thousand years than I do," she went straight to the point. "Everything that I just mentioned is only conjecture," anger hanging on her words.

"The reason why these androids left the *Benevolence* and what happened after they arrived in that pitiful cavern will become clearer after I study the information I collected from the various terminals in the cavern and after we, meaning the Group of 5 and I, have time to study their individual memory banks."

"So where and when do we start to unravel this mystery?" Minerva asked, after a long silence.

"The hybrids are aware of our Alliance and know that we understand their vulnerability," she replied. "When I think of the *Benevolence* and its crew, several questions haunt me: How did the humans survive all these thousands of years? How did Shannon, in particular, become so skillful in the art of deceit?"

"Certainly you must have considered these questions before?" Minerva mocked.

"Yes. Unfortunately, I thought that they were a new generation of humans. I didn't know, or even suspect, that the original crew was still alive after thousands of years."

"Colonel Shannon does not look herself," she continued. "If she has survived all this time then her facial features and body have been regularly altered by someone," her eyes grew large, flashing deep shades of green.

"But that does not explain why all the original members of the crew are young," I could hear her heart beating rapidly. "My enemies, those despicable arachnids, perhaps entered into an arrangement with them. They would rejuvenate the humans regularly, giving them eternal life, in exchange for their allegiance to them."

She grinned, like in amusement. "How foolish these humans were to opt for a symbiotic relationship with these creatures rather than accept natural procreation of new generations."

"So you are beginning to understand..." Concordia replied.

"John is on the screen. Do you want to talk to him?" Crawford asked, from his post on Star Board.

"Yes, and the five of you, Crawford, should listen as well." Reinhart replied with composure.

"We are happy to see that you are back on board the *Redeemer*," he chuckled.

"What a film we saw." Reinhart turned to our Allies.

"As you requested, we had the Earthlings on direct," Minerva said. "If something went wrong, they needed to act rapidly to protect themselves."

"Thank you for meeting my request."

"Now, have you carried out my orders to the letter regarding the possible infestation of insects?" She asked John.

"Yes, we have been very diligent," he began. "Jason, I don't see you," he called out and Jason stepped forward. "Do you remember coming in contact with insect life during your early years of exploration?"

"No. I don't even remember seeing insects in the floral garden." He snapped his fingers. "The Group of 5 used small insect drones to fertilize plants."

"That is right." Crawford spoke for the Group. "There were no insects, so to facilitate pollination we used drones."

"The Group exploring the western region found large colonies of bees and other flying insects, as well as ants, beetles and crickets, some of which were rather aggressive. Clarence told me they ate them."

John forced a smile. "They are reptiles, so it is probably normal that they would eat these tiny critters."

"Of course this is a natural diet for them, but tell them that they must stop eating them. From now on, they should capture and freeze a certain number of the different varieties they encounter and have them sent back to the center. They must remain in a frozen state until I have had the opportunity to dissect them."

"You don't want Ralph and his crew to dissect them."

"No," she hesitated. "And arachnids?"

"Yes, they found scorpions." He hesitated. "And, WD and Weldon did discover different species of insects on the river banks they explored---not far from the seacoast. They mentioned dragonflies, wasps, crickets, black beetles, very tiny spiders, among others. They appeared harmless to them, but they did not approach them either."

"If they can take a few samples, especially of the tiny spiders, and freeze them for shipment, I would be interested in dissecting them."

"Will send the message. By the way, when are you coming back?"

"I shall let you know. It depends upon how things develop here. By the way, did you find arachnids in the centers?"

"No, but we fumigated the centers anyway, just in case there were tiny or microscopic insects, or arachnids, that the androids were unable to detect."

"Excellent," she drew a breath. "I believe I already ordered the return of all exploration teams that have apparently not yet arrived at the Center." John lowered his eyes.

"I want the exploration teams to return to their assigned center over the next few days. They may protest—I know that the reptilian humans are very happy on the outside, but their safety is my priority. Until I am certain that our enemies are not heading towards Earth, I want all of you to be in safe places."

"Yes. I shall convey your order to return immediately, but please remember that it takes time to break camp. I shall add that they don't want to confront Reinhart's wrath." His eyes twinkled.

"Has Colonel Shannon tried to reach you?" Reinhart asked, shifting attention to another matter.

"I had a very quick, but unsettling call from her yesterday."

"Why didn't you contact me then?"

"I couldn't contact you. You were engaged in a battle." He replied. "Anyway, she asked me if the High Commissioners arrived on the planet Earth. I ignored her question and told her I had no news from anyone! She forced a laugh, before requesting bluntly, that I tell you that they need you ...now! "

He sat back in his chair. "I didn't confide in her about your exploits. I however have no idea why she thought that the High Commissioners had arrived on Earth."

"Oh, she probably tried to contact the Malwarian Androids and when they did not reply, she panicked. Anyway, you did very well, John. You can tell her that we are on board the *Redeemer*...but nothing more. We shall see what she does. Let me know when our explorers get back to the various centers and take care of yourself, John." He then signed off.

"What about our Alliance, Dr. Reinhart?" Minerva asked, wasting no time.

"An Alliance with you is no longer exclusive because you are in an Alliance with the hybrids," Reinhart clarified the problem and Minerva nodded.

"I am not opposed to a greater Alliance but I need to know more about the Plant-Animal Hybrids, how they would position themselves and define their interests in a three party alliance." Her brows furrowed. "Do you think that one of your officers can capture one of those hybrids? I don't care if it is alive or dead, but I need to study it in more detail."

"We have a couple dead specimens on our ship. We can drop one off now, if you want," she replied. "But we have already dissected a number of them and shared the composition of their hybridized bodies with you. We mentioned that the two different species are so tightly inter-lapped that they cannot be divided easily."

"Send me a couple that are still intact. I would like to carry out my own autopsy." They nodded and signed off.

She turned to our group. "Rebecca and I are going to check on Wilberly now. I shall keep you informed," she said, ending the discussion.

"Wait. I shall come with you," I offered, following behind Reinhart and Rebecca, as the rest of the group dispersed, going in different directions.

I stepped back at the sight of the Wilberly's drooping flesh that comes with age, most visible on his face. Reinhart approached him. "The aging process has set in. I am sorry."

"I know Dr. Reinhart. That is actually why I was not able to offer much combat assistance during the recent battle." Reinhart smiled, perhaps offering him some comfort.

"Rebecca, I need a close up scan of his brain." She handed Reinhart a tiny instrument that projected a clear image of his cerebral functions onto the white wall behind us. Reinhart enlarged the image and then carefully examined it.

She spoke perfunctorily: "As your DNA, or biological code, is not registered in my memory bank, I cannot return you to an adolescent version of yourself and cannot give you eternal youth. But, I have the power to connect with your bio-physiological and nervous system to efface and reverse the accelerated aging and even restore youthful, healthy organ functioning, a young and resistant skeletal-muscular system, while stimulating your cognitive abilities." He nodded.

"You will feel the warmth of my energy moving inside of you. It will not be painful. I shall pass through as rapidly as possible, restoring your organs, and your skeletal-muscular and nervous system." She smiled down on him. "Trust me. I am going to give you a considerable number of years of youthfulness and a super memory to go along with it. Do you understand?" He nodded.

"Open your eyes wide." He did what he was told to do. Their eyes met as an intense stream of bright light passed from her eyes into his. Within a matter of minutes, he was a young man again.

"How do you feel?"

"I feel fantastic!" He flexed his arms, as he stood up. "But, how can you do this? How could you make me young again?"

"I am an evolved human," she replied softly. "I shall tell you my story when I remember my past and understand how and why I have evolved."

"I also have a story to tell you," he exclaimed.

"I know, and I shall listen well, but, for the moment, I have three more patients to attend to." He smiled up at her.

"I want you to rest a bit more. You do not have the right to circulate without my authorization, so don't defy my order." He nodded, and she turned to us.

"Now let's take a closer look at what is in the brains of Peter, Frederic and Jennifer." She left the room and we followed close behind.

"Run the brain scan." She motioned to Rebecca to activate the scanner.

"There it is." She pointed to a tiny, black speck that appeared in the frontal lobe of both Peter's and Jennifer's brains.

"Are we going to remove them?" Rebecca asked, and Reinhart nodded.

"Look, Dr. Reinhart!" Rebecca cried out, as she pointed to Frederic's brain. "The insect is gone. It...just disintegrated."

She smiled broadly. "The insect in Frederic's brain must have entered his brain by inadvertence and disintegrated the moment I detected its presence." Her eyes opened wide. "It couldn't live in his brain because he is one of my descendants."

"I don't know why I know this?" She backed away from us. "How could I know this?" She mumbled several times under her breath, as we looked on.

She eventually approached Jennifer's cryogenic tank and instructed Rebecca to run another scan.

"I want a better image than this one," she bellowed as she threw the image of the insect in Jennifer's brain on the floor. "We must start over again," she ordered.

She then poured over the various close up images from different angles. "Look!" She pointed as she compared the tiny speck in Peter's brain to the insect enveloped in fine threads in Jennifer's brain.

"Perhaps it is because the insect in Jennifer's brain has been there for a long time," I commented with authority and she nodded.

"I can easily retrieve the insect in Peter's brain." She commented. "It is vulnerable. The insect needs a protective web to withstand time." She turned to face me. "It is not something that develops over a long period of time, it is relatively rapid. They were lucky that I detected the insects the moment they entered their brains and had them placed immediately in a cryogenic state."

"So the insects existed in that prison?" I asked.

"I have not unmasked this conundrum," she replied slowly. "What I know is that Stuart identified himself as my son, thus discouraging my enemies from inserting an insect in his brain." She cracked a laugh. "But, they can make mistakes, because they placed one in Frederic's brain. This is excellent news!"

"So we can awaken Peter and Jennifer...rather, Valerie, now!" I asked.

"No! Later, after I have had time to examine in more detail the one that was in Wilberly's brain." She replied before adding. "But, I need a diversion, so I am going to dissect the hybrid before dissecting Wilberly's insect." We nodded.

"I shall call you if I need you. In the meantime, I want you to stay alert and monitor Peter and Valerie. Frederic will awaken soon. He should have no secondary effects, but he might remember being in contact with the insect."

She spent several hours alone, delicately dissecting the hybrid before she reappeared, her hands on her hips, like she was ready for action.

"So what is it?" I pressed for a response.

"Our Rat-Human Aliens gave me a relatively accurate description of these hybrids, their original personalities and reckless behavior. I was capable of extracting a few more details, regarding both species."

"For example, the animals, low ranking military personnel, were the sole survivors on board a spaceship that crashed on a planet inhabited by carnivorous plants. The animals could not support the atmosphere. Their respiratory systems were failing when they came upon the plants, who through telepathic communication, offered them a solution, or a merging through hybridization."

"How do you know this?" I questioned.

"Even though his creature is dead, its mind was well-preserved and I was able to enter the hybrid's mind and read its past, still encrusted in its memory." She grimaced.

"As the food source of the carnivorous plants was depleted and the plants lacked mobility, they were destined to die a slow death in the confines of their swampland. Hybridization offered the plants a skeletal-muscular system." I nodded.

"These aliens are more precisely a hybridization between a carnivorous plant and a mutant, or hybridized animal, which has predominant feline characteristics resembling those of a lynx, and is endowed with anal glands similar to those of a skunk.'

"The Alien's head, minus sensory organs and facial features, consists of a large brain mass, cloaked behind a thick, protective membrane, resembling a floral bouquet that can attract prey, like insects and small animals. The plant has an organ that has a flip top on it, like a fly trap, which functions like a mouth, opening and closing rapidly to catch its prey."

"The plant's long, very solid round stem was not anchored in roots, rather imbedded in a compact mound of fibrous material. Its branches and twigs, are subtle and resistant. The plant relies upon asexual reproduction, similar to cloning and communicates telepathically."

"And its animal characteristics?" I asked. She lifted one of her brows in annoyance.

"Theoretically, the buds, or flowers, or dippers that might appear on a carnivorous plant, are now the heart, kidney, bladder, liver and digestive system including the stomach, intestines, large and small, and anus, with two visible defensive glands on either side of this hybridized alien."

She continued. "The plant incorporated various animal organs necessary to produce the digestive juices or enzymes to break down food sources into the nutrients necessary for their hybridized bodies to survive. The plant also integrated the skeletal muscular system of the animal so it could circulate, while the animal benefited from the plant's superior intelligence and telepathic power over other species."

"But how does it digest the food?" I asked.

She drew a deep breath. "After the plant catches the food, it lets the animal's system break it down. The plant must use some form of osmosis to absorb the nutrients that it needs, while the animal uses its digestive system to fuel itself." She grimaced.

"As the injured hybrid confessed, their animal side is ravenous, something I suppose the plant regrets, because it has taken a long time to temper that side."

"But how could they have begun their exploration of the universe?" I continued to probe.

"The plant took the dominant position, acquired whatever knowledge the animals possessed for their own benefit." She spoke in a boring monotone.

"These highly intelligent plants accessed all the scientific and technological information in the spaceship's systems, repaired the ship, and left to find food," she continued. "Later, these hybrids explored the universe in search of a work force to build new vessels," she sighed. "Today they are our equals, or even superior to us, in terms of their scientific and technological knowhow."

"Amazing...but if the animals were not intelligent, then there is another alien race that we might encounter."

"Precisely." She drew a breath. "But, probably, they have already exterminated that race."

"What about the animal's personality?" I continued my own inquiry.

"Questionable," she sighed. "I don't believe that either species is or ever was kind and gentle. And yet my contact with the predominant side of this species, or the plant, left me with the impression that they understand emotions."

We sat in silence. I marveled at how she could cope with everything.

"But, remarkably, Dr. Reinhart, you are able to control, practically dominate and outwit, other life-forms. That is not my case," Rebecca confessed.

"Oh there are moments when I would rather kill the life form rather than communicate with it. However, I have learned that every life form deserves respect. It is also the best way to decipher their weaknesses, their vulnerability, if ever one needs to defend oneself." She replied. "All this you will learn with time. Now, let's dissect that insect."

"I shall check on Peter, Frederic and Valerie first," Rebecca rushed out of the room.

She was back in a few minutes, reassuring us they were almost out of their cryogenic state. She quickly defrosted the spider-like life form, Wilberly's insect, which she had removed a month before and placed in a freezer compartment. She delicately sliced the outer crust of the insect in half.

"My suppositions were right. It is not a life form. There is a microchip hidden inside the outer crust, comprised of a spongy material that does freeze over. The microchip can only function in warm, moist brain matter."

"But, the web?" I cried out.

"That keeps it in place. It needs to be implanted in the frontal lobe so that the subject can be controlled." To our surprise, a message came off the microchip. "Time is running out."

"Quick, we must remove those wretched creatures now from Peter's and Valerie's brains. We cannot wait." She jumped up and dashed into the cryogenic chamber and ran towards Valerie's tank.

"What are you doing? It is too soon." Rebecca grabbed Reinhart's arm.

"Dr. Reinhart, you can't remove it without killing Valerie," Rebecca's voice a low whine.

"Shut up. I know what I am doing. I invented these machines." She moved the scanner close to Valerie's head so she could see the exact location of the small, black object. She rapidly inserted a thin siphon-like instrument into the cable that was registering Valerie's brain waves and drew out the insect. Valerie's body signs remained stable.

She rushed off to the lab and removed the microchip from inside the spongy material. "Pamela, I am going to try to connect with this microchip. You must release me, with the code I gave you months ago, if ever I begin to vanish. I will find shelter again as your symbiote."

I nodded, but my legs trembled. She must have detected that, because her glaring eyes met mine. As she tried to connect, the microchip vaporized, leaving behind a shiny, white spot.

"I know my real enemies realize that I am getting close to learning the truth of my existence. My memory will soon break through." Her eyes took on a distant look.

"My frustration is that I don't know what they expect from me when I finally remember who I am. Was I kind and caring? Or was I like them, a cruel, autocratic and exploitative ruler, showing very little respect for other life forms?"

She collapsed, her mind absent, onto a small chair. We watched as she pressed her hands down hard on the sides of her face, until she abandoned her quest and returned to the present.

"I shall carry out the same procedure with Peter," she said and we stared on. "He will not be harmed. The Aliens are relinquishing them."

When she released the insect from Peter's brain, the microchip exploded into tiny puffs of smoke.

We sat in silence until Frederic and Peter recovered. She watched them begin to move inside the tank and checked their vital signs. "Relax until you feel strong enough to get up."

"What about Valerie?" Rebecca asked.

"She needs more time to recover. I shall ask an android assistant to monitor her and call us, when she is ready to move." She stood so straight, her shoulders pulled back and her head high. "Pamela, please ask everyone to meet with us in the lounge. The Group of 5 should also be there." I nodded and sent the message over the intercom system.

"Wait, Dr. Reinhart, the capsule has just opened." Rebecca's voice trembling.

Reinhart turned slowly, observing Valerie's movements. "Get back, Rebecca. Quickly."-

"You have lost, Dr. Reinhart!" Valerie spoke in an eerie, spine-chilling tone.

Reinhart grabbed Valerie, whose body was rapidly beginning to lose its luster, as it entered into an accelerated aging process, and tossed her onto the floor. She approached the cryogenic tank, meticulously examining its contents with her icy-cold eyes, before closing the lid and switching off the machine.

"Is she ok?" my voice quivering.

"She is not mentally distraught, if that is what you want to know," Reinhart replied. "Her microchip had a slightly different message for me than the one from Wilberly."

427

"And, physically?" I shouted and she nodded.

"Dr. Reinhart, is that you? My vision is hazy." Valerie spoke.

Reinhart kneeled down and took her hands gently. "I don't have time to explain the procedure I used to rejuvenate Wilberly and will now use to give you back your youth. Trust me. The procedure is painless. Open your eyes wide and look into mine." Reinhart implored, and we watched Valerie's body rapidly regain its youthful form.

"Thank you, Dr. Reinhart," tears winding slowly down Valerie's face. Reinhart smiled a hesitant smile, as she explained to her that she could not give her eternal youth.

"Look," Rebecca redirected our attention, as she pointed in another direction. "Peter and Frederic are preparing to exit the tanks."

We rushed to their sides. Peter lifted himself out of the cryogenic tank and shook his arms and legs vigorously, bringing the blood rushing, and Frederic did the same.

"I see, Dr. Reinhart, that you have abandoned Pamela's body." Peter's slim lips spread into a very welcoming smile and I rushed towards him. He enveloped me in his strong, comforting arms, laying warm, tender kisses on the side of my neck.

"Mother." Frederic came up behind me. "I saw what you did. You are perhaps not yet Dr. Reinhart's equal, but you are not that far behind."

A ripple of laughter rushed through the room, as I put my arms around my son and planted big kisses on his forehead.

"Well, if time is running out," Reinhart broke the spell, "we cannot linger over homecomings. Where are the others?"

She didn't wait for an answer, instead activated the intercom system. "I hope that everyone is in the conference room. We shall be there in 5 minutes."

Chapter 26: Forging Her Destiny

I rushed to my Mother's side, mimicking her straight back style and long strides. "How can you stay so calm, Elisabeth. You never show fear. How can you hide it?" I continued.

"By never succumbing to it!" she teased

'That is why you laugh at danger?" I asked and she nodded.

We grouped together in the lounge. The Group of 5 had left a few android pilots on Star Board to contact us if ever there was a problem. For the moment, the ship was still cloaked in its veil of invisibility.

Reinhart and Murdoc were standing in front of the high-definition viewing screen and the Group of 5, with Oliver positioning himself at a respectable distance away from them, were on their right flank.

"Where to begin," Elisabeth spoke, as the lights on the ship's screen began to flicker.

"Colonel Shannon to Dr. Reinhart, please respond."

She turned to Murdoc and for an instance their eyes twinkled as they exchanged wry smiles...of amusement."

"Dr. Reinhart receiving," she replied, in a dry, bored tone.

"We are unable to contact the High Commissioners. Do you have any idea what has happened?" She rambled. "We could not even follow your exploits. Have you saved your family?"

Reinhart opened the screen wide enough to capture all the members in the lounge. "As you can see, everyone is here, including Major Richard Wilberly and Valerie Reynolds."

Shannon's mouth dropped wide open, and the screen went blank.

Our Rat-Human Allies broke the long silence. "Dr. Reinhart, we need to speak to you."

'I am here."

"The Alliance?"

429

"I am ready to enter into a three party alliance-Earthling, Inhabitants of the planet Illusion, and the inhabitants of the planet Vérité." Reinhart smiled as she answered them.

"Excellent," the Aliens replied, simultaneously.

"But, I want a better working relationship with both of you. I want one based upon mutual respect." Reinhart spoke in a commanding tone. "I am fed up with your lies and deceptive practices, calibrated to incite us to act and react sometimes in completely irrational ways," she reproached them.

"What is incredible," she continued, ""is that we have, instead, shown our force and our complete loyalty one to the other. We have actually succeeded in ways that you and the others never expected."

"I don't understand," Concordia began, "because..."

Reinhart interrupted Concordia with a condescending chuckle. "I could easily recount all your very convincing lies, but I would rather hear the truth, the real truth, for a change, without any exaggerations and hyperbole."

"Well, you must admit that we needed to tell stories, stories that would incite your human curiosity," Zelus replied.

"Dr. Reinhart, I can help you. Let me tell my story," Wilberly pleaded.

"Later, Wilberly, this is not the right moment." She replied brusquely.

"Much to our dismay, it is apparent that you still don't know who you are, Dr. Reinhart." Minerva replied in a sorrowful tone. "You must search your memory banks. Time is running out!"

"I am in no mood for your mind games!" Reinhart screamed, unleashing her anger.

"Colonel Shannon to Dr. Reinhart."

Reinhart sighed as she turned with stoic indifference in the direction of the other screen.

"Minerva, I shall put Shannon on your screen so that you can follow the conversation," Reinhart replied.

"What is your problem, Lt. Beverly English? And what has happened to Dr. Shawn Underwood and Admiral Baron Davis?" Reinhart went straight to the point.

"No, I am Colonel Shannon, and my closest officers are Ranier and Trend," her voice vacillating from low to high piercing sounds. She then burst into hysterical sobs as she pressed her hands hard up against her temples, turned in small circles, and eventually collapsed on the floor.

"Dramatic!" Reinhart exclaimed, then laughed nervously.

"She is suffering," Wilberly pleaded.

"Listen to me. Listen to me hard!" Reinhart ordered. "I am addressing all of you on board the *Benevolence*. I don't need you or your ship! Surrender or...Die!" The communication ended.

"What is locked inside my memory? What have I forgotten?" She asked as her vivid green eyes focused on Minerva.

"You understand," Minerva replied, in a soft, maternal tone. "You must understand by now that we all have the same enemy, but for different reasons. Try, Elisabeth, to remember who that enemy is." She pleaded, as her eyes connected for a brief instance with those of Reinhart's, illuminating her past.

Reinhart stumbled backwards, her body trembling as she reached out to catch her fall, finding Murdoc's extended hand. She eventually turned in my direction, her eyes ablaze. I moved slowly, like in a trance, towards her, finding courage with each tiny step, until I threw my arms around her.

"We shall help you," Minerva repeated over and over again.

"It is too late, Dr. Reinhart." Shannon hissed.

"Where are you, Elisabeth," I thought, as I boldly grabbed her face, and forced her to look deep into my eyes. She began to cough and then choke, like someone half drowning, struggling to recover their failing lungs.

When she finally broke through that barrier between life and death, the dramatic flash of colors engulfing her vaporized into a bright column of white light.

"She disappeared." We turned in the direction of Flanders' voice.

"No. She is back!" I cried out, sensing her return and signaling the others.

"Thank you my child," her voice in a whisper.

We turned back to the screen. The *Benevolence* had disappeared and was now replaced by long strands of blinding, white fluorescent lights, moving inside a thick translucent liquid. We listened.

"Dr. Elisabeth Reinhart, our child protégé," chortled one of the streams of light, flashing brightly as it spoke. "We have been patient, even sometimes amused with your escapades, but your time for fun and frivolous actions has come to an end."

"You made a promise a very long time ago," another stream of light flashed.

"You deceived me," she replied steadily, as a faint smile of reminiscence illuminated her face.

"We chose you and we educated you," another voice was heard. "You are one of us, whether you like it or not."

She moved closer to the screen. "I never had any intention of joining your ranks. Let the record show I lied!"

"We have no code of ethics, but we are not without pity," a soft voice heard. "To appease you, we shall protect the Earthlings and your allies if you come with us willingly." She hesitated. "Your presence in our ranks will assure their safety."

"I must decline your offer," Reinhart said in a steady voice that left no doubt about her determination. "You taught me well," she turned steely, cold eyes on them. "I finally know who I am and why I exist. And, I do not exist to promote your cause."

"But it is too late." Her enemies forced her to confront them once again.

"What I shall say to you today will haunt you for the rest of your existence," her voice, loud and clear, and her eyes, now sparkling and glowing, like the portholes of time.

"I shall fulfill my mission. I shall succeed in reversing the course of history as you have defined it. I shall outwit and overcome you," her voice filled with energy. "And even though I cannot change the past, I can, with the help of my friends and allies, usher in and assure a better future for those who seek to live in peace and harmony," she vaunted a mirthless grin.

"Foolish child! You are asking for your death and those of your family, friends and Allies. And, without remorse, we shall give it to you!"

"It will be more than a pleasure for me to prove you... wrong!" Her voice energized and her eyes flaring. "You are no match for me...For us!" She raised her fists in defiance.

Her self-confidence and combative spirit provoked and annoyed her enemies, who disappeared, bringing the conversation to an end.

"We shall leave now with our friends and allies, the Plant-Animal Hybrids, to discuss strategy," Minerva reappeared breaking the tension. "Be assured, we shall join forces with you when you are ready."

Minerva slowly bowed her head, as did the other members of her Council. "We are honored, Dr. Reinhart, to have had this opportunity to fight alongside of you and your people... in the name of ....Freedom!" Her voice resonated, long after she disappeared.

Murdoc moved close to Reinhart and took her in his arms.

"And so, my beloved Elisabeth, are you ready to tell us your story?" He asked in such a warm, seductive voice that she instinctively brushed her lips gently up against his. "We are ready to listen."

"Yes, I shall tell my story, as will others, for the voyage will be long and our life experiences must be shared," she replied softly.

With Murdoc still at her side, she spoke to all of us. "I want to thank each of you for the role you played in saving our comrades and bringing an end to the Malwarian Androids' reign of terror."

"If anyone wants to return now to the Planet Earth, please step forward. Know that whatever choice you make, you have already honored me and your friends in helping to bring about our Victory. Our Alien Allies are ready to secure safe passage for those who wish to return to Earth."

She waited, but no one stepped forward. And so, she stood straight in a military posture and marched slowly in front of us, saluting each of us in passing, before turning her steely, green eyes on those who watched from far above. She raised her fists for a second time in defiance towards those who threatened our existence.

Our group stood joined together, when she spoke again. "We shall continue to train everyday both on our own, with our friends, and alongside our Allies so when we arrive at our destination we are ready for the expected and the unexpected. We shall not be taken off guard. Our Android forces will be at our side and we shall be," she paused, "physically and psychologically able and ready to reap havoc in the world of our enemies, who this day believe themselves to be the most powerful life forms in the Universe."

"Our Battle will be long and treacherous, but we shall rid ourselves of those who seek to destroy us!" Her eyes held ours. "We shall and must save the World we know and love!" Her voice a deep, commanding tone.

Her energy engulfed us and the sound of her voice gave us courage to believe in ourselves. And so we raised our fists above our heads, stomped our feet and let our voices join with hers in her Call for Victory and Freedom.

The End

Patricia Lee Strunk

Ms. Strunk, author of **Pamela Series 13**, grew up in a working class neighborhood, in a small town in Pennsylvania, where she dreamed about becoming an astronaut. Instead, Ms. Strunk became a lawyer. She holds an LL.M. Degree in "International Business Law" from the "London School of Economics," a Master Degree in "Comparative Law" from the "Institut de Droit Comparé, Paris" and a Juris Doctor Degree from "Duquesne University School of Law." She is also a member of the California and Pennsylvania Bars. Patricia spent the greater part of her legal career in academia and had the privilege of being a Lecturer in Law with many distinguished French Law Faculties, like "L'Université de Paris Ouest-La Défense, Nanterre" and "L'Université de Paris 1, Sorbonne," as well as many Institutes of higher learning, like "L'Institut de Droit Comparé" and "L'Institut d'Etudes Politiques" (Science Po, Paris). Ms. Strunk never completely forgot her childhood ambitions and fascination with science. **Pamela Series 13, Volume 3, "The Melding of Time and Space,"** like volumes 1 and 2 of the Pamela Series, reflects her academic interest in Bio-Ethical and Environmental Law, as well as her overwhelming support and advocacy of responsible Scientific Research at all levels.